# CLUBWHORE

A novel by Kim Jones

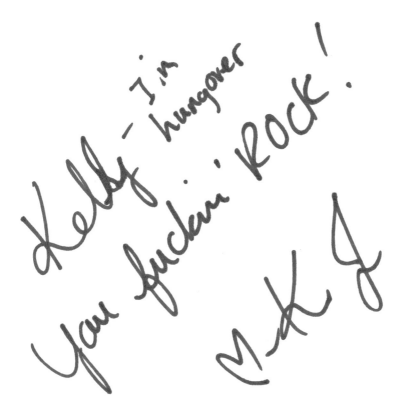

Kelly - I'm
hungover!
Your fuckin' ROCK!

MKJ

Cover Model: Jeff Morawski

Cover designer: Hang Le

Clubwhore Playlist:
Fever—Peggy Lee
Only—Nicki Minaj feat Drake, Chris Brown and Lil Wayne
The Hills—The Weekend
Sail-Awolnation
Sweet Dreams—Marilyn Manson
Leather and Lace—Stevie Nicks feat Don Henley
Only—James Young, Phoebe Ryan
Ride--Somo

This book is dedicated to:
Whores.
Truth is, you're smarter than most women. You get paid for sex, while the rest of us have been giving it away for years. So hats off to you, promiscuous women—you've figured it out.

# PROLOGUE

I've never been the type of girl to settle down. Life is too short to make sacrifices--like marrying a man you think you're in love with only to find out later that just the sight of him repulses you. Feeling guilty, you spend the next twenty years of your life suffering in silence because you think you owe him a lifelong marriage. You're miserable, he's miserable and you're sure you don't love him anymore--that is, until you catch him banging some bitch ten years your junior. Suddenly, he's the bad guy and you're the poor, innocent, devoted wife who's given him your best years.

Well, that's just fucking stupid.

Me? I'm a realist. I see shit for what it is. I don't want a commitment, I want a life. I want to call the shots. I want to see who I want, do what I want and be who I want. Keep your property patches. I don't mind being your dirty little secret.

I know what the ol' ladies say about me. I know the horrible names they call me behind my back—pass-around…white trash…skank…slut…clubwhore. They look down their noses at me. They think they're better. They have zero respect for someone like me. A weaker person might be offended or hurt—not this bitch.

So don't feel sorry for me.

I don't need your pity.

Because, at the end of the day, I'm the one who wins. I have the one thing they're most afraid of losing—their man.

I'm that girl.

The girl every woman loves to hate.

The one your man dreams about.

I live up to the name I've been given…

*CLUBWHORE*

And this is my story.

# Chapter 1

"That's right…you know how I like it, baby." *For fuck's sake…come already.* "You're so big." *Good thing I practiced my Kegel exercise this morning.* "I love how you dominate that pussy." *Blah blah blah.*

The great thing about being on your knees while getting pounded from behind by a drunken biker who closes his eyes in hopes that it will lessen the guilt he feels in his chest because you aren't his wife? You don't have to look at the bastard. For example, right now I'm studying the shitty job my manicurist did on my nails.

As if he can sense my boredom, I finally feel him pull out moments before warmth spreads across my ass. I throw in a few grunts and groan for the hell of it, while he pumps his cock with one hand and kneads my ass with the other—like I actually enjoy that shit.

My name is Delilah Scott. I used to be referred to as Scotty D —weird, I know. But around here I'm known as just plain old Delilah. I guess it's easier to bang a chick named Delilah rather than one named Scotty. By the way, "around here" is the Devil's Renegades' clubhouse in Hattiesburg, Mississippi—my place of employment.

I call myself an entrepreneur. I use my skills, body and brains to make my way in this world. Sure, I do it in a manner that some would consider unethical, but who gives a shit what they think? And the "they" I speak of are the ones who call me a whore. In reality, I'm not.

Whores get paid for sex. That's not what I do. I get paid for providing company to lonely men. If that entails having sex, fine. I consider it an extent of my gratitude to the men who I enjoy being around.

"That was great, babe. Always is."

I look over my shoulder, offering a wink and a sultry smile to the man who's just come all over my back. "Pleasure was all mine." And really, it was.

Even though this man isn't a Devil's Renegade, he's a friend to the club. Therefore, he's a friend to me. I don't generally get pleasure out of fucking married men and this was no different. I was assured that he's in the middle of a divorce. I'm not so sure it's true. But, looking at the bigger picture, I'm glad I could be of service. In turn, I've been of service to the Renegades. And that always pleases me.

I stay on my knees while he dresses--not wanting it to be awkward when I cringe at the way his dried come pulls at the tiny hairs on my back. With his pants zipped and his cut back on, he slaps my ass and leaves the room. Hell of an exit. I mean, nobody has *ever* done that before.

One of the great things about living at the clubhouse is the en-suite bathroom I have all to myself. Okay...so maybe it's not that great. But it is an added bonus. I have two hundred square feet designated especially for me. A nice, spacious bedroom with a view of the backyard, equipped with a king-sized bed, a vanity, dresser, closet and a bathroom with a whirlpool tub. The Renegades know how to take care of their own.

Luke Carmical, president of the Hattiesburg chapter, has always made me feel comfortable, safe and appreciated. Not once has he ever looked at me like I was beneath him. In addition to his hospitality and my room and board, he pays me three hundred dollars a week. In return, I provide around-the-clock pleasure for anyone who walks through the clubhouse door, keep the place clean, and make sure there's always hot coffee and cold beer.

Not a bad gig for a *whore,* huh?

Even though the men are great, the same can't be said for some of their ol' ladies. I know a lot of people say "They're just jealous" to make themselves feel better, but really, they're just jealous. They don't like the fact that I'm here with their men. They don't like that I'm loved by the guys. I'm easy to get along with, outgoing, fun and I'm not too hard on the eyes either. That alone is enough for them to hate me.

I've never slept with any of the chapter members who have wives—contrary to popular belief. I've been with a few from other chapters, but they've all been in open relationships. Most of those men like to share me with their wives too—something I'm definitely not opposed to. I don't consider myself a lesbian due to the fact that I would never have a relationship other than sex with a woman. It's just business, really. And speaking of business, I have shit to do.

Showering off the scent of the man whose name I can never remember, I let the steaming, hot water cleanse me before switching it to cold. I'm always sleepy after sex—the reprieve I feel from my internal damaged, twisted need is mentally exhausting. But the frigid water never fails to revive my senses and wake me completely. By the time I step out of the shower, I have a renewed passion to get the night started.

I guess I can be considered sexy. I'm tall, falsely tanned with jet black hair and brown eyes. I've been called Pocahontas more than once and I've always taken it as a compliment. To keep the interest of the men around here, I have to stay in shape. I do so by eating Doritos by the bag, getting extra pepperonis on my pizza and drinking plenty of carbonated beverages. I'm sure it'll catch up with me one day, but right now, I plan to take full advantage of my high metabolism.

"Delilah? You in here?" The infamous Red, property of Devil's Renegades VP, Regg. *I've always hated he was married...*

Red falls under the category of "ol' ladies that don't really like me." Although she's never been rude or forthcoming with her thoughts of me, she always makes it a point to remind me that Regg belongs to her—expressing an extreme amount of PDA when it's really not necessary.

"I'm in here." My bathroom door is opened without warning and Red takes a minute to size me up. There must be a stamp on my forehead that reads "If you're bi-curious, I'm your girl." Or at least that's the vibe I'm getting from the appreciative way Red is looking at me right now.

"Are those real?" she asks, glaring at my breasts unashamedly.

"Yes." My deadpan answer is meant to draw her attention away from my chest and to my facial expression that clearly says, "Are you fucking kidding me? Of course they're real." But she can't be distracted. Humored, I ask, "Wanna touch 'em?"

"What?" *That got her attention.* "No. I mean. No." She pulls her eyes to mine and I can't help but smile at her embarrassment. It's a first for her. "The Eagles have a Prospect that's getting his patch tonight. Luke wants to know if you're interested in giving him a...show."

My heart warms a little at her words. This is why I like Luke. He always asks, never demands. *Why did he have to be married?* All the fucking good ones were gone. "What's his name?"

"Drake." *Drake...sexy ...*

Pulling a brush through my hair, I turn and watch Red's eyes follow mine to the mirror, fighting like hell to stay focused on my face and not drop to my tits. *I wonder what she's like in bed...* "Of course I will. I'll be out in thirty." My words are dismissive and Red leaves, reluctantly, while I continue getting ready for Mr. Drake.

The Eagles are a riding club that supports the Renegades. This means that if the Renegades call, they come. A lot of the patch holders from the Renegades came from the Eagles. It's like a starter club. To get to a three patch MC, you have to start somewhere. And the Eagles are a pretty damn good place to start.

As promised, thirty minutes later I emerge from the confines of my room and walk the long hallway that leads to the main area of the clubhouse. The place is built on Luke's property, sitting right behind his house. It's a massive building consisting of ten bedrooms, a large open area with a bar, pool tables, tons of seating and a kitchen that sits off to the side. On special occasions, a makeshift stage equipped with a stripper pole is assembled where the other girls and I can dance for the men's— and sometimes the women's—entertainment.

I don't know shit about this Drake, so I didn't dress according to his preference or fetish. Instead, I chose a generic outfit of leather. I have yet to find one man who didn't approve of it. Black leather boots, corset and matching panties.

Yes…leather panties.

No…they're not comfortable.

An ensemble like that can't be complete without a leather riding crop. So I have one of those too.

Not to be conceited, but I'm a showstopper. And when I saunter into the main room, all eyes are on me. I hear the catcalls and whistles that come from the familiar voices of the Renegades. But tonight I have a mission, and I only have eyes for one man—Eagles' Prospect, Drake.

I can't help the disappointment I feel when I see him. He's tall, lanky and ugly as hell. *Why can't he be married?* Like I said, the good ones are gone. His brothers grab him and he looks like he might shit his pants. Even when they force him to take a seat in the center of the room, he still has no idea what's going on.

Grabbing the iPod from the docking station, I find the playlist I've made specifically for dancing. Finding it more than appropriate, I select Nicki Minaj's "Only." The song crackles through the room. Immediately, the electricity swims through me. Boasting from every speaker in the building, the hypnotic tempo reverberates off the walls.

I walk around Drake's seat, teasing him with the crop before smacking it lightly against his crotch. He flinches, but hardens. Then I do the second thing I do best—dance. My focus is solely on him. No one else exists in the room. I don't imagine he's someone clsc or I'm somewhere else. I just let that feeling of power course through me. If I don't already, soon I'll own this motherfucker.

He'll dream of me.

He'll fantasize about me.

He'll think of only me.

In the real world, a guy like him could never get a girl like me. He knows it. I know it. But right now, he could be the sexiest man alive, because I'm making him feel like it. And to me, he is. He's important to someone who's important to me. So I'll show him the same courtesy I would them. I'll give him everything I've got because the club deems him worthy. Therefore, I do too.

This is my job.

This is what I do.

For years I lived in a world where I didn't matter. I was a nobody. I was weak. I'm still all of those things, just not in this moment. Right now, I'm the most powerful bitch in the room. And I don't feel sorry for embracing the rare moments where I shine in my own glory. If that makes me a whore, then I'll wear the title proudly.

So keep your morals. Stay at your nine to five. Judge me through your rose-colored glasses. View my lifestyle choices however you want. But if being classified as a whore is the only penance I have to pay to feel this good, then stitch an A on my chest. Carve a W on my forehead. Put a label on me to make yourself feel better. Because the reality is, I just don't give a damn what you think.

# CHAPTER 2

Even though it's the Eagles' newest patch holder, Drake, who should be occupying my room tonight, it's the president of his chapter instead. Cape. Why does he go by Cape? I don't know, but my best guess is because that motherfucker is like Superman. He's in his early forties with graying hair, a warm smile, a stocky build and a dick like a Coke can. If he's married, I don't want to know it.

"Can you keep a secret?" Cape asks, standing just inside my doorway.

"For you I can do anything."

He shoots me a sexy smile. "The only reason I come here is to see you."

"You're lying," I say, closing the distance between us—crossing one leg in front of the other in that sexy way men love. I call it the Carrie Underwood walk. *If I only had her legs...*

"I don't lie, ba—" The word catches in his throat at the sight of me hitting my knees, grabbing his ass and pressing his crotch into my face.

Dragging my teeth over the rough denim of his jeans, I feel his cock harden beneath them. I lift my eyes and smile. "You talk too much."

In my experience, men like to feel like they're a god in bed. They want you to moan, scream, gag and whimper like their cock is the biggest you've ever had. Like it's almost too much to handle, but feels too damn good to stop. Not all dicks are as big around as a Coke can, so mostly I fake it. With Cape, it's almost not necessary. Though I do oversell it just a little.

He's in my mouth and I'm gagging. My eyes are watering. My throat is screaming no, but I'm pushing through and burying him deeper.

His hands are in my hair. His grunts are loud. Then he looks down at me and speaks, and ruins the whole fucking show. "You like that cock, don't you, you dirty little slut."

If I were his girlfriend, his wife or even his friend with benefits, I would probably want to hear something like that. But I'm none of those things. I am how he views me—how they all see me. I am a dirty little slut. I have to live with that knowledge. But I don't need him or any other motherfucker to remind me of it.

Because I'm not a whiny, sensitive, emotional little girl, I don't let his words stop me. But I can't prevent them from drying me up in a place that only seconds ago was wet and ready for him. He'll be getting no pussy from me tonight. My mouth is just going to have to do.

Like the trooper I am, I pump his cock with my fist while I work it deep inside my mouth. I suck hard, moan loud and milk his balls with my free hand, until his eyes are rolling back in his head. I don't give him the option to take me any other way, because I'm making this just too damn good. And like I predicted, a couple minutes later, I feel him stiffen just before the thick vein running the length of his dick pulses with his release. Pulling him from my mouth, I continue to pump him in my fist and give myself a pearl necklace.

He takes a couple moments to recover, and by the time he does, I'm standing in front of him forcing a smile.

"That looks good on you," he says, pointing to his sticky come that covers my neck, while he zips up his pants.

"Mmm." It's all I can manage.

Bowing like a fool, he grins at me. "Until next time."

I close the door behind him, before quickly making my way to the bathroom to wash the remnants of Cape off me. *Superman. Hmph.* From now on, I'll refer to him as Superdick.

*Shit.*

I reckon that's a compliment too.

There's really no reason for me to hate him for saying what he said. But I do. At the Devil's Renegades' clubhouse, I've always had the power to decide who I choose to sleep with. As of ten minutes ago, Superman Cape the Superdick became the first man on my "Do Not Fuck Roster."


"Lookin' good this morning, sugartits." I glare over at Regg who's in mid yawn. When his eyes close, I flip him the finger. The moment he opens them, I'm smiling.

"Now, how do you know my tits taste like sugar? You've never even tried them."

Giving me his full megawatt, all-teeth-baring smile, he wiggles his eyebrows. "It's not too late."

Looking over my shoulder at the clock on the coffee pot, I find my own self yawning. "It is late. It's after six in the morning.

Red probably has your face on the back of a milk carton by now. Why are you still here?"

He shrugs. "Drank too much to drive home."

Regg and Red live in Collins, a good forty-five-minute ride from here. I'm surprised that Regg is staying—with her consent nonetheless. She's not a big fan of him hanging around loose women. The two of them try to pretend they don't have jealousy issues, but when circumstances arise, they can't deny their insane possession of each other.

Once, I saw a man just look at Red and wink. It's like Regg could read the dirty thoughts going through the man's head. Red, in her flirty nature, smiled back. The man had only taken a couple steps toward her before Regg intervened, telling him he'd kill him if he ever looked at her again. Regg, who is almost always fun, relaxed and laid back, wore a look in his eyes that made me, the man and everyone else in the place believe him. To my knowledge, that man has never returned to the Devil's Renegades' clubhouse.

Then one time I saw Red go bat-shit crazy when she overheard two of the girls here discussing what Regg would be like in bed. She made such a big spectacle of herself, Regg had to carry her out of the bar over his shoulder. I heard she got her property patch taken from her for a few weeks as punishment— not for being a jealous wife, but for busting several beer bottles, numerous glasses and Luke's favorite barstool. Needless to say, I stay the hell away from Regg.

"I'm going to bed, sugartits. Or barbequetits. Or buttertits... whatever the fuck they taste like," he says, standing and stretching. "But"—he points his finger at me, his look becoming serious—"if I ever find out they taste like sour gummy worms, I'm cutting them off your chest and taking them home with me."

"Goodnight, Regg," I call to his retreating back. He throws up his hand on a wave as a chorus of "Goodnight, Regg" sounds around the room from the other women.

Shoving my hands in the hot, soapy water, I wash the glasses in the sink and look around to see who is still standing. It's only Friday night, meaning tomorrow will be just as busy as today. The club parties hard on the weekends, no matter if they have something to celebrate or not. I love my job. I enjoy being here. But I also look forward to the weekends the men are out of town and we get some time off.

Time off consists of different things for different people. Most of the ladies return to their homes, and their normal lives. Since I don't have one of those, I use my time to sleep mostly. Every once in a while I'll go shopping, hit a random club or catch a movie—none of which I really enjoy.

Drying the last glass, I feel a smile forming as two of my favorite guys approach—Scratch and Crash. They're like night and day, but both of them have qualities that I love.

Scratch is tall with a bigger build, a shyness about him I find charming and hair that reaches halfway down his back. He's a cautious lover, always allowing me to take control and trusts that I'll bring him and myself the most pleasure possible. I don't really have to spice things up with him. He's content with my same old boring moves, which are never really that boring.

Crash is the youngest of the group, but in my opinion, one of the most skilled with his tongue. At only twenty-two, the boy knows how to eat pussy like an old pro. His mother was a lesbian, and taught him at an early age how to make a woman feel worshipped. He's shorter and smaller in size than Scratch, but way more confident. Actually, he's a little cocky. But he has every right to be.

Together, the two of them are sure to show a girl a good time. By the way they're looking at me, I'm guessing tonight I'm gonna be that girl.

Before you start counting on your fingers, I'll remind you of what you already believe to be true. Yes, these two will bring the total of men I've been with in a twenty-four-hour period to four. Yes, by definition that does make me a slut. No, I still don't forgive Cape for verbally reminding me of that.

In my defense, the first lay was lame. It was just one of those "have to do" things that...well, I just had to do. It wasn't even pleasurable to me, so it doesn't count. Cape was a joke, as you know, but even if he wouldn't have uttered the s word, *out loud,* I still don't consider me giving him head actually being with him. But that's all history.

Right now, standing in front of me are two young men with stamina, desire and promise. I plan to take full advantage of those three qualities. Remember when I told you I enjoyed my job? When I said I wouldn't trade it for a property patch or an ol' lady title? Well, now you're fixing to find out why.


My body is in orgasm overload. Between my thighs is the mouth of Crash, licking and sucking my clit—refusing to stop until he drags me back to that euphoric place that is spine-tingling, toe-curling, sheet-gripping good.

On my chest is the mouth of Scratch, nipping then smoothing my nipples—sucking harder when my body stiffens in preparation of release as Crash's mouth finds that perfect spot that finally pushes me over the edge.

I'm still coming down from what could be my millionth orgasm of the night when I'm gently flipped on my knees and Crash enters me slowly. Being skilled with his mouth makes up for his quick release. It only takes a few minutes for him to fill the rubber surrounding his cock before he pulls out and falls down next to me in the bed.

The moment he's beside me, Scratch is behind me—replacing his brother's cock with his own. He's thick and hard, making me moan into the pillow when he drives deep inside me. My muscles involuntarily clench around him and he groans, squeezing my ass a little harder.

Usually I'm on top, but being the gentlemen he is, he's treating me like a queen because I've been working all night. The change is fresh, new, exciting and makes me proud that he's stepping out of his comfort zone. I'm impressed. He's pretty fucking good.

Rubbing his thumb over my ass, I wiggle against him—allowing him permission inside. Dragging his cock up the length of my ass, he dampens the area with my own juices before easily sliding inside me. Not wanting to be left out, Crash reaches his hand beneath me and circles my clit with his finger. The combination is deliciously satisfying, and before I know it, I'm coming again.

Following suit, Scratch slams hard one last time before stilling inside me. Falling down opposite of Crash, the two of them make a Delilah sandwich—raining soft kisses across my neck and chest in thanks. Soon we're a tangled web of naked arms and legs.

This is living—no rules, no worries and no clothes. But as I start to drift, fully sated and surrounded by two men who respect me, desire me and take care of me, I realize that the moment is not perfect. I can't put my finger on it exactly, but something is missing.

One night.

Three orifices.

Four men.

Yet there's an emptiness inside me. No matter how hard I try, no matter how many men I fuck, no matter how long I've done this, I just can't seem to fill that void. But I don't want to dwell on that. Some people would love to be me. I need to stop overthinking shit and be more appreciative of the life I have. Besides, how much better can it get?

# CHAPTER 3

"Holy shit! Are you fucking kidding me?"

I crack one eye open to see Red standing in my door, unsure if she wants to hide her face or look. Once again, her hand moves over her eyes, then drops, takes the scene in, gasps, then covers her eyes again.

"Good morning, Red. Nice of you to knock," I mutter, not bothering to cover myself or the two men on either side of me who are still fast asleep. "Why do you act all shocked and shaken around me? Didn't you once live a very provocative lifestyle?"

"I've grown up since then," she shoots at me, clearly offended by me bringing up her past.

"Well, maybe when I get as old as you are, I'll grow up too."

"I'm not that old."

"No...you're just a prude."

Crossing her arms over her chest, she fights to find a comeback. Deciding to add to her discomfort—payment for barging into my room unannounced and uninvited—I drag my eyes down her body.

In a tight leather jacket, low-cut shirt, jeans and heels, Red looks like the poster child for an ol' lady. Her long thick legs, big tits and auburn hair don't just make her good-looking. The bitch is downright sexy.

"You know," I start, dragging my finger up my bare chest between my tits. "There's always room for you in my bed." For a moment, I think she's considering it. But, quicker than I'd hoped, the battle between the new-and-improved Red and the demons of her past is over—leaving the present, boring Red as the victor.

"Thanks, but no thanks." She gives me a tight smile, and I beam back at her. "I'm on my way out for breakfast. I was just gonna see if you wanted to join me." My face falls.

"Why would you ask me that?"

"Because..." She looks at me like I'm supposed to know the reason behind her offer.

"Because...what?"

"Because it's ten in the morning and I'm hungry. I thought you might be too." Shrugging, she drops her eyes. There's more. She wants something.

"What?" I ask, already bored with whatever the hell it is she wants to talk about.

"Huh?"

"Don't play stupid, Red. I can count on one hand the number of times you've darkened my door. You've never asked me to breakfast. So what do you want?"

Her eyes move to Scratch, then to Crash before settling back on me. She mouths the word "please" and even gives me a big doe-eyed, pleading look. Who can say no to that face?

Me.

That's who.

"No."

"D..."

"It's Delilah. And I said no."

"We'll go to IHOP. My treat. They have pumpkin pancakes." She sings the last word as if it will help her case. It does. Who can say no to pumpkin pancakes?

Definitely not me.

"You fuckin' owe me," I mumble, climbing over Scratch who's still snoring lightly. Stumbling to the bathroom, I start to yell for her to give me ten, but when I turn she's standing right behind me.

She's so close, I take a step back and she enters the bathroom with me, closing the door behind her. "I can't stay in there with them. What if Regg wakes up?"

"Then stay your ass in the front." Pointing in the direction of the hall, I manage to speak in a calm voice, despite my normally shitty mood that her presence alone has made even more shitty. "Get out."

"Okay, okay."

During my quick shower, I come to hate Red a little more when I start to question the worth of the goodness that is pumpkin pancakes. In an effort to embarrass her in public, I make sure to look as homely as possible when I dress. Wearing leggings, a sweatshirt that's about four sizes too big and a pair of knock-off Uggs, I join her out front.

She doesn't give my outfit a second glance as she offers me coffee in a Styrofoam cup and a cigarette. "I heard you only smoked in the morning and you make your coffee so strong you can float a fifty-cent piece on it." Taking the cup and smoke, I lean in and let her light it before narrowing my eyes on her.

"Who told you that?"

"Luke." She shrugs, like it's no big deal. "What's the story between you two, anyway? For some reason, he has a soft spot when it comes to *Delilah*." She says my name as if he has some kind of crush on me. I don't like it. The last thing I need is for her to make Dallas think I'm into her man or that he's into me.

"Luke is my employer...the club is my employer. You are an extent to the club. Part of my job description entails that I be nice to you. We're not friends. You want something, and you're bribing me with pancakes after a sixteen-hour shift, a great lay and three hours of sleep. I'm vulnerable right now. And I'm hungry. So are you driving or am I?" I glare at her, hoping like hell she picks up on the warning in my voice. She doesn't. She laughs.

"What's so funny?" My voice is deadpan, but on the inside I'm amused and curious as hell to what's making her laugh.

"You, Delilah. You're funny. This." She motions with her finger between the two of us. "This is funny. Sometimes, I swear looking at you is like looking in the mirror ten years ago."

Placing her hand on my shoulder, I stiffen but either she doesn't notice or doesn't care. "Take it from someone who knows, life gets a helluva lot better when you stop living inside your own little world and embrace what real life is all about."

Who the fuck is she to talk to me about real life? I'm as real as they come. Maybe I do live in a bubble, but it's a wonderful bubble filled with sex, alcohol and excitement. It's safe, controlled and keeps my demons at bay.

I don't classify living as being married to the same dick for the rest of your life and sporting a "Property Of" patch. If she wants to live like that, then that's her choice. I'll continue to be who I am and she can do whatever the hell she wants. But first, the bitch is buying me pancakes.


I didn't realize how much I was starving until I had the IHOP menu in my hand. There's always so many choices. Since it's on Red's dime, I decide to order everything that appeals to me—including orange juice and chocolate milk, neither of which have free refills.

Red didn't bore me with small talk on the way here. I was forced to listen to classic country music, which I found more enjoyable than I expected. But now that we've ordered, and there's nothing more to distract us, I'm ready for her to get down to the real reason she barged into my room this morning.

"What do you want, Red?" I ask, for the fifth time today.

"I want you to give the guys a warning."

My brows draw together in confusion. "A warning about what?"

"There's a girl running with the Eagles...Carmen. She's working her way up the MC hierarchy and her next stop is the Renegades. She's a patchwhore." At the irony, I can't help but laugh.

A patchwhore is best described as a woman who will do just about anything for a property patch. But her obsession doesn't stop there. She won't settle to be just anybody's property. She'll continue to work her way up the ladder until she holds the highest position—property of a president.

"I'm serious," she says, leaning in closer to me. "There are several single guys in the club who might fall for her shit. Think of Scratch and Crash." I roll my eyes. Scratch and Crash have plenty of sense. Plus, I'm not their mother.

"You do realize that I have a lot more in common with her than I do with you."

"Why?" She's genuinely confused, or either she's really good at faking it.

"Because the world we live in has two sides. There are people like me and Carmen on one side, and on the other are people like you and Dallas. Y'all consider us beneath y'all and label us as someone who's not nearly as respected or appreciated as an ol' lady. Hence the words clubwhore and patchwhore that you so commonly use as if we don't have names and aren't real people."

Her frown deepens and her brow creases. "You think that's how I feel?"

"You called her a patchwhore, Red. To my fucking face. Am I supposed to believe you think any higher of me? Come *on.*" I shake my head in disbelief. "What do you think I do at the clubhouse? Really? Be honest."

She thinks a minute before answering. "I think the clubs pays you to make yourself available to anyone wanting their dick sucked, or an easy lay. I think you fuck because you enjoy it, but mostly because it's the way you choose to make your living." Her honesty surprises me. *At least I know she's not afraid to speak her mind.*

"I'm not judging you, Delilah. I could care less how you live your life. I once had a label too. I was a cokewhore. I'd fuck for an eight ball because at the time, it was worth it to me. I stripped for dirty old men, role played for drug dealers and never hesitated to fall to my knees and suck a cock for a single snort."

Grabbing her glass, she tosses back the remainder of her orange juice before digging into her purse. "So," she starts, letting out a long sigh. "If you're that insecure about yourself to believe that I would ever think you beneath me, then you're a fucking fool." Her voice is loud, drawing the attention of the people around us.

"Red," I snap, trying to warn her to keep her voice down. My anger is fueled by the fact that this bitch just turned the tables on me.

"Shut up, Delilah," she says on a breath. "Because honestly, you exhaust me." She goes to stand, but remembers something else to chew my ass about and stops. "Do you know why I, along with every other ol' lady, refer to you as a clubwhore?"

I widen my eyes and turn my head slightly, silently demanding she chill the fuck out with the whole "whore" reference. "Why don't you enlighten me?"

Leaning in, she drops her voice. I should be thankful, but there's something more chilling in the way she says it just above a whisper. "Because you fuck club members for money."

I give her my best poker face. Her eyes search desperately for a reaction from me. She can search all day long. She's not going to find anything. When she finally realizes that, a look of pity crosses her face. I fight the urge to slap it off her.

"What you're feeling right now? That's reality, babe. Welcome to the real world." She thinks she's finally gotten through to me. The relief on her face tells me she's thinking by explaining the definition of a clubwhore to me that she's repaid her debt to the one who made her realize what she was all those years ago—the one who called her out on being a "cokewhore." Well, fuck her.

I don't feel ashamed at her admission. I'm not embarrassed, sad or hurt either. What she said is the truth. And sometimes, you just have to hear it.

Standing, I look down at her, wondering if this is how she feels every time she looks at me. "You're wrong, Red," I say. Leaning down, I brace my hands on the table—distracting her with the empty look in my eyes while my hand fists around her keys. Poor thing...she doesn't even realize she's about to get carjacked.

"I'm wrong?" She breathes out an amused laugh. "How am I wrong?"

With a tone as cold as my heart is in this moment, I tell her the true effect her words have on me.

"I don't feel a fucking thing."

If my conversation with Red wasn't enough to put me in a shit mood, the fact that tomorrow is Sunday was. Aside from knowing what's coming, I've had to be on all night and I've not been my chipper self—and it shows. I've been getting curious stares, narrowed glances and concerned looks since the sun went down hours ago. But the world didn't stop just because I was having a bad day. Not that I expected it to.

It's after four in the morning and the party is still going strong. The music is blaring, women are naked and the place is littered with patches from several different chapters. The environment is usually a high to me. But tonight, I feel that monster inside me shake the shit out of his cage—threatening to break loose.

"Luke?" With a smile that, I shit you not, could dampen a nun's panties, he turns to face me.

Luke Carmical, aka, Devil's Renegades President, LLC. He's just too fucking gorgeous. I mean, really. It's not fair to every other male on the planet. He's six foot tall and two hundred pounds of pure perfection. Short blond hair, sparkling blue eyes and an aura of power that surrounds him and follows him everywhere he goes. Just looking at him lifts my spirits. It sucks that he's married. I could really use some presidential dick right about now.

"Let me guess," he says, replacing his warm smile with his signature smirk. He's like a super badass biker Ken Barbie doll. "You gotta split."

Even though I have no reason to be sorry, I offer him an apologetic look. I think I feel more sorry for me than I do him, though. "It's Sunday." As if I need to remind him, I hold up my wrist and point to my imaginary watch.

"Would you listen if I asked you not to go?"

"No."

He laughs at my short answer. I wonder if the worry in his eyes is because I haven't been myself tonight, or because he knows where it is I go every Sunday—even though I've never told him.

Before he has a chance to say anything in an attempt to get me to stay, I remind him of something else he should already know. "It's not your business, Luke."

At the seriousness in my tone, he sobers slightly. But concern still creases his brow. Heartwarming, really. But I like to keep as much distance between my two worlds as possible. He can respect that. Or at least he has for the past two years.

Keeping his eyes on me, he pulls his wallet from the back pocket of his ripped jeans. I feel like he's trying to read my mind, or convince me by using some telepathic communication to stay. But my walls are pretty solid and my mind is made up, so I just stare back.

"Three hundred?"

"Why do you always ask me that?" I ask, genuinely curious.

He shrugs. "You do extra shit...I don't mind paying extra money."

"We had an agreement. And I never take on more than I can handle." To lighten the weird vibe between us, I wink. Like a fog, the mood lifts.

"So I've heard, babe," he says, smiling and shaking his head. "So I've heard."

I choose to ignore whatever the hell he's talking about, which I'm sure is some perverted, private bedroom information he received from one of his many pleased brothers. Thanking him, I turn on my heel and snake my way through the crowd toward my room.

It only takes me a few minutes to throw on some sweats and a hoodie, scrub away my makeup and pile my hair on my head. Lifting my bedroom window, I grab my duffel and toss it into the yard before climbing out myself. The cold November wind hits me in the face and I breathe deep—welcoming the fresh air.

I'm not sneaking out, if that's what you're wondering. I prefer this exit opposed to walking back through the crowd and taking the chance of someone stopping me and wanting to talk... or fuck. It's just easier this way.

I decide to leave the window cracked in case I come back and the clubhouse is still booming—it's happened. Pulling the hood over my head, I sling my duffel over my shoulder and shove my hands in the front pocket of my sweater. *Fuck, it's cold.* Anxious to be out of the wind, I duck my head and jog toward my car that's parked on the other side of the building.

"Hey!" The weak attempt at a threat from the female yelling at me has me raising my eyes in search of whoever the hell I just scared the shit out of. Dallas Knox Carmical, wife of Luke Carmical, stares back at me from the shadows on the side of the building with wide, fearful eyes—until she recognizes I'm just me...not a serial killer.

"Hey," I say coolly, offering her my best shit-eating grin. I really shouldn't be smug about scaring her. The poor girl has been through hell—kidnapped, beaten, lied to...hell, she was even waterboarded. Who the fuck does that other than the CIA?

Suddenly realizing that I came out the window instead of the front door, she frowns. "What are you doing?"

"I got somewhere to be. I didn't want to walk through the mob of people like this." I lift my hands inside my pocket, drawing her attention to my unusual attire. This makes her frown deepen and I know I'm about to be questioned. She's not being a nosy bitch, she's just curious.

I like Dallas. I always have. She was a little uncertain about me at first, but when I told her she had nothing to worry about where her man and I were concerned, she listened. I don't know if she believed me or not, but she's never treated me like shit. Much like a lot of the other women, she just keeps her distance. I tend to like the ones who leave me alone best. *Red was once in that category...*

"Oh, okay," she says, narrowing her eyes at me. I do look like a thief in the night, but what the hell could I steal of hers anyway? It's not like Luke can fit in my pocket.

"Well, see ya." I step around her, and am seated inside my car before the question hits me. *What was she doing?* She was wearing pajamas, in the cold, alone in the dark. *Is something wrong?*

As much as I try to remain detached, I can't ignore that pit of worry that's building in my gut. If I do nothing and something is wrong, I'll have to live with the guilt. I couldn't do that to Luke. Hell, I couldn't do that to her.

Stepping back into the cold, I lower my hood so I don't scare her again and jog to where I last saw her. "Hey," I whisper, making her nearly jump out of her skin. So much for not frightening her. "You okay?"

Hand over her heart, she closes her eyes and pulls in a deep breath. Then I smell it. I thought it was coming from inside, but the scent is too strong and we're standing too far away from anyone else for it to be coming from anyone but her. Unable to hide my smile, I lift my hands up in apology.

"My bad."

Taking a much needed drag from the blunt between her fingers, she stares at me while she holds it in. Just when I think she's gonna pass out, she releases it on a cough.

"It helps me sleep," she explains, not that she needed to. What do I care if she smokes pot? I nod and turn to leave but she reaches out and grabs my arm. The move is so surprising that I freeze. I think this is the first time she's ever touched me. It's... weird. Especially considering this is the second time today I've been touched by an ol' lady.

"Please don't tell Luke. He'll kill me."

Relaxing, I let out a small laugh. "After the hell you two have been through, I doubt he'll kill you."

"You know about us?" *Shit.* Now she has the wrong idea. *I wonder if Red said something…*

Playing it off, I shrug. "Word gets around. Living here, I hear a lot." The relief in her face is a little insulting. "Don't worry, your secret is safe with me." For emphasis, I even pretend to zip my lips, lock them and throw away the key.

With a warm smile and a small squeeze to my arm before she releases it, she thanks me. The entire scene is so unnerving, I just walk away without even a good-bye. We're not friends. We don't talk. We don't hang out or shop or go to IHOP or do any other girly shit together.

I'm a clubwhore.

She's an ol' lady.

I'm on one level and she's on another.

That's how it is. That's how I like it, and that's how the fuck it's going to stay.

# CHAPTER 4

I know it's killing you—wondering what in the hell I'm doing. But before I discuss what's happening right now, let's go back to my breakfast date with Red.

Like I told her, I feel absolutely nothing about being called out as a whore. It is what it is. I don't even hold any ill will toward Red. I dislike her as much now as I did yesterday. So don't go getting any ideas about me having this sudden revelation about my life and deciding to change my ways. If I didn't like what I do, I wouldn't do it.

Some things you can't control. For me, it's Sundays. We'll get to that in a minute. But right now, I just want to remind you my lifestyle is one I've chosen. One I enjoy. One I want. One I need. I'm sure I could get a nine to five if that was an ambition of mine. But I'd rather take it up the ass than work in some office behind some desk answering some phone, and delivering some boring-ass spiel that involves "How may I help you?"

One more thing: yes, I stole Red's car. Is she pissed? I don't know. I haven't seen her. But I did see Scratch later at the clubhouse who told me she called him to come get her. Considering she didn't bother calling her husband, I'm thinking she wanted to keep our meeting a secret. Which leads me to believe that either he would be pissed if he found out we went for pancakes and didn't invite him, or he wouldn't have approved of our conversation. I'm betting on the latter.

Now back to the present. I know you're wondering what the hell's going on. I'm sure there's all sorts of shit running through your head.

*Is she a mom?*

*A drug dealer?*

*Is she sick?*

Well, I hate to disappoint you, but it's none of those things. I'm definitely not a mother—I can't handle all that baby slobber. *Ugh.* I'm not a drug dealer either—if I were, I'd be driving a Mercedes instead of a Toyota. Sick? Maybe...but if there's a treatment for me, I've yet to find it.

Sundays are not just my only day off, but it's my day to repent. Most people go to church. I go to my mother's. It's my hell on earth. It's the penalty I pay for all my wrongdoings.

Punishment is a means to an end for all the anxiety, pressure and self-loathing a person feels about their transgressions. If a child misbehaves, they're reprimanded. If you're convicted of a crime, you're sentenced to jail. I'm not a child or a felon, but I have a monster living inside me who has to be tamed. And my family has a way of doing that.

Right now, an incessant need is crawling through me—dominating every thought and feeling I have. Slowly it eats through me until I have no control over my own thoughts and feelings. Everything starts to blur, then begins to fade to darkness. I hate the darkness. I refuse to allow myself to go back there. So I do what I have to do. If that entails visiting the hell that is my mother's home to find that relief I so desperately need, then that's exactly what I'm going to do.

The nearly three-hour ride to Baton Rouge seems to get shorter and shorter each time I come here. Every time I think to look at the mile markers I'm always closer to my destination than I hoped I'd be. Before I know it, I'm pulling into Wilson's Mobile Home Village. Six gravel driveways down on the left sits the trashiest trailer in all of Baton Rouge.

I park behind the mini-van, grab my duffel and kick my way through the shit that litters the small walkway leading to the front door. With a deep breath, I knock twice and wait for my mother's invitation—granting me access to her palace that's a hell of a lot nicer than she is.

"Come in!" Her loud, scratchy voice can be heard all over the neighborhood through the thin walls. Pushing open the door, I walk inside the all-too-familiar hell I'm just shy of hating too much to keep me away. "Why the fuck do you always knock? I know it's you."

"Hello to you too, Mama," I mutter, looking around to see that nothing has changed since last week—not that I expected it to. The linoleum is still curling next to the walls, exposing the cheap particle board beneath it. The table is freshly covered in a week's worth of dishes and trash. The garbage is overflowing onto the floor. You can't see the sink or the stove, and I'm just talking about the kitchen.

Swinging my eyes to the living room, they land on my mother first. As usual, she's in a nightgown, in her recliner, focused on whatever cheesy sitcom just so happens to be airing at eight in the morning. She looks older, meaner and slightly heavier than her usual two hundred pounds. Beside her is a TV stand with a few half-empty Coke bottles, some coffee cups and an overflowing ashtray. Lying on the couch directly facing me is my older brother who's still asleep.

"Put on a pot of coffee." Like the obedient idiot I am, I don't hesitate to do what she asks.

The coffee pot is the only damn thing available for immediate use. Shit is cluttered around everything else, preventing me from getting to it, much less using it. While the coffee brews, I perform my Sunday morning ritual by unloading the sink. Having nowhere else to set the dishes, I start piling everything on the floor.

In between delivering countless cups of coffee to my mother, I clean her house. I wash her dishes, change her sheets, do her laundry, clean her bathroom, sweep and mop her floors and during commercial breaks, she allows me to vacuum. By the time I'm finished, I'm confident the health department won't condemn the place.

Despite the noise I've been making, my brother doesn't wake until the work is done and I take a seat for the first time since I got here—four hours ago. "Delilah...my dear little sister." His quote from *Gone with the Wind* is always funny to him—never to me.

"Craig," I offer in the most bored tone I can manage.

"Delilah, fix your brother something to eat."

"Mama, he's a grown man. He can fix himself something to eat." Even as I say the words, my muscles tense in anticipation to pull my ass off the loveseat and do as I'm told.

"Don't you sass me." Her warning has me on my feet, moving toward the kitchen.

I know what you're thinking. *How could she let her mother treat her like that?* Trust me, if I had an answer, I'd tell you. Remember earlier when I said I might be sick? This is part of my sickness. I'm fucked up. I'm a glutton for punishment. Deep down I know why, but I refuse to let it surface.

I often try to find a different reason for my being here in an attempt to avoid the truth. I like to think it's because I've had to fight so hard for my mother's love. Cliché. I know. But the chosen one—the lazy fucker whose breakfast I'm cooking—has always seemed to need all of my mother's attention. Or maybe she just likes him better. That shit don't matter. What matters is that however crappy she was and is as a mother, she's still my mother. She could have killed me with a coat hanger, but she didn't. She gave me life. I feel like the least I can do is what she asks. *Damn.* That sounds stupid even to my own ears.

"So you got a job yet?" I ask, handing my *dear older brother* his plate of eggs and bacon.

"No toast?" He looks up at me as if I've just committed some unforgivable sin.

"No bread. Answer my question."

"Do I look like I have a job to you, Delilah?" And there's the snap I've been waiting for. "Why the fuck you always gotta be in my business? Don't worry about what I'm doing."

"You're twenty-five, broke and live at home with your mom. *Our* mom. I think it's about time you started pulling your weight around here."

I'm taunting him—provoking him. I'm putting myself in a man's position in hopes he'll treat me like one. I guess you can say I get off on this shit. I have no fear of what I know is coming. I yearn for it—crave it. To survive, I need it as much as I need to breathe.

The loud sound of shattering glass when his plate collides with the wall beside me doesn't even make me flinch. When he's on his feet, so close to me I can smell the stench of his breath, I don't bat an eyelash. I don't stiffen in anticipation of the backhanded blow so powerful it throws me to the floor. Even when the corner of my eye begins to swell and I taste the tangy, metallic flavor of blood on my tongue, I look up at him...daring him...begging him...demanding him to give me more.

My brother is a beautiful creature. He's tall, with dark wavy hair, bright hazel eyes and a brooding look that's permanently etched on his face. His body is athletic. His teeth are near perfection. His skin is flawless. But my brother has an ugly soul. Besides our looks, it's the only thing we have in common. I may be damaged, but I'm not hateful—although a part of me is glad that he is.

When the shrill, evil voice of my mother pierces through my thoughts, I know all the terrible traits we both suffer from, we inherited from her.

"You're good for nothin'... you dirty whore...always provoking him...that's what you get." And so it goes.

Maybe what I'm silently asking of my brother isn't so ridiculous. At least if he put me out of my misery, I wouldn't have to hear her. But like the cold-hearted bastard he is, he doesn't grant me my wish. I'm like a wounded horse that needs to be shot. And he's a man with a rifle and no mercy. I guess he likes to see me suffer. Or maybe that sparkle of humor in his eyes is for something else entirely.

Eventually my mother shuts up and in her silence I manage to find the strength to stand and prepare to leave. My beast is caged. I've been punished for my sins. I feel almost...human. Considering this, I decide I've had enough hell for one day, and yes, I'm well aware that it was self-inflicted.

I grab my duffel from where I'd left it by the door before walking back to the living room. I don't have to look at them to know they're salivating at the mouth for my weekly gifts. A prey can always sense when a predator is on the hunt.

Unzipping the bag, I hand my mother the two cartons of cigarettes she's come to expect. Then I reach back inside and pull out her favorite weekly trashy gossip magazines. I also have a roll of tobacco for my brother, but considering I'm not unconscious and he barely brought blood, I decide to keep it.

"Here, Mama." I pull the small wad of cash from my pocket. "I'll be back next week." Snatching the ten twenties from my fingers, she mumbles something about me having a better attitude next time I come. Leaning over, I kiss her cheek that's way too wrinkled for a woman of her age. "Take care of yourself."

Then I'm out the door, in my car and driving back to a place that's the closest thing to a home I've ever had. But even there I'm an outsider. When I think about how sad my life is and how twisted the fuck up I am, it makes me want to cry.

That lasts for all of about two seconds. I've never been one to feel sorry for myself. I'm not gonna start now. Especially not today. Pity is work.

It's Sunday.

The Sabbath Day.

A day of rest.

God's not working today, so I ain't either...

# CHAPTER 5

"Who'd you piss off?" is the greeting I get when I'm halfway through my bedroom window. I was hoping to spend the rest of my day doing absolutely nothing and avoiding everyone. I guess that's shot to shit.

"Why are you in my room?" I ask Linda, another one of the women who work for the club. She's searching through my closet —tossing shit she doesn't want over her shoulder and on the floor. It's not the first time I've caught her going through my clothes, and just like every other time, it pisses me off.

"Answering a question with a question is my biggest pet peeve."

"People invading my privacy is mine." After shutting the window, I turn and glare at her—giving her my best "get the fuck out" look. She's unaffected. I really need to start working on my angry facial expressions. And locking my door.

Linda is a little older than me, and by a little I mean she's in her late thirties. She's one of the best dancers I've ever seen. I heard through the grapevine that Red is the greatest. I've yet to see it, but I damn sure want to. Our little spat, if that's even what you want to call it, doesn't take away the fact that I find her attractive. And anyways, we're even. She admitted to calling me a name I don't particularly like, forced me to endure the definition of said name and I stole her car.

Boom.

Even.

"You know," Linda says, crossing her arms over her chest and cocking her hip out. She's got really, really nice legs. "None of the girls know a whole lot about you. Why is that? You've been here long enough. You know everything about us. It's a little unfair, don't you think?"

"Life's unfair. And the knowledge I have about everyone wasn't because I asked. It's because I was forced to listen." By the way, that seems to be another title I have around here. Out of all the women that work here, I'm the only one who lives here full-time. Therefore, they think I know everything—which usually I do. So whether it's gossip or advice, the women and often the men always come to me--like there's a fucking sign above my door that reads "free therapist."

"I don't get you, Delilah. When the lights go down and the men want attention, you're a totally different person. You're fun, energetic and a pleasure to be around. Other times..." She wrinkles her face and gives me a disapproving look. "You're, for lack of a better word, a bitch."

"I'm sure I can find a better word." Ready to get rid of her, I try to force my face into some semblance of an apology. "I don't mean to be a bitch to you, or anyone. I just like my space."

She nods. "I can respect that." *Good. Now get the fuck out.* "But your life would probably be a lot easier if you weren't so uptight." Uptight? Me? Now I'm offended.

"Thanks for the pep talk." Stepping around her, I hold the door open for her to leave. With a heavy sigh and a frown, like she pities me for not accepting her help that I don't need, she leaves. Closing the door, I lock it and tell myself to make damn sure I install a deadbolt ASAP.

What is it with people who always try to save someone? And the damaged ones are the worst. How do I know Linda is damaged? Because anyone who is a part of this life has to be. The MC isn't for normal people. It's for rejects, fuck-ups and the disturbed.

It's for people like Luke whose grandfather was one of the founding members. He never had a fighting chance of a different life. Even when his father tried to protect him from it, Luke's always been a biker at heart—it's in his blood.

It's for people like Dallas who grew up privileged, but without parents—parents murdered by an ex-member of the very MC her husband is president of. From the day she turned eighteen, she became the club's property and she didn't even know it. When she found out, she realized it's what she'd been missing in her life all along.

It's for Red—a struggling drug addict who needs around-the-clock support and reassurance. She was traded from one shitty foster home to another. The MC is the only real family she's ever had.

It's for all of them. In some way or another, they're damaged and the only thing that can fix them is this club. The same can be said for me too. After all, being fucked up is how I got here in the first place.

Time flies when you're having fun. Before I know it, Saturday is here once again. It's a little after midnight and the clubhouse is packed. There are over twenty patches here. They rank from Hangarounds—men who are being considered for prospecting—to president and everywhere in between. The problem with this many men is there are not near enough women to go around.

Most of the men here are Renegades, but there are several Eagles and a few members from other neighboring clubs. To me, they're all the same. My job is to treat them all as if they were Renegades. It doesn't matter what patch they wear or what title they hold. They're here for a good time. And I aim to show them one.

"Prettiest fuckin' titties I've ever seen," the man whose lap I'm occupying says. He cups one of my breasts in his large hand. At the touch, my already hard nipple puckers further. Beneath my ass, I feel him harden. "I bet they taste good too."

I give him a sexy half smile, daring him to try. Since I suck at names, I've been calling him and the rest of his buddies seated around us "honey" and "baby." They don't care what I call them. When you're surrounded by a group of men and you're wearing nothing but a pair of shorts so short your ass cheeks hang out the bottom and a pair of killer heels—you can get away with just about anything.

Hot, wet mouths surround my nipples. The man on my left sucks softly while the one on my right nibbles across the sensitive flesh. I giggle, because they like that shit, and allow their hands to roam my body and indulge themselves. I'm beyond ready to take this party to my room, but they seem to be enjoying the public show that's drawing a crowd. *Perfect. The more the merrier.*

Leaning my head against the back of the couch, I close my eyes and get lost in the feeling of everything around me—the wandering hands, pleasing mouths, hardening cocks and lustful looks I'm drawing from the circle of men. This is my sweet spot... my happy place...my empowering moment.

A hand reaches between my thighs—squeezing me through my jeans. Back arched, head pressed further into the soft leather, my eyes open into tiny slits. My constant fluttering lids and small window of vision limits the amount of focus I have on anything. But something in the distance—something separate from the crowd—pulls at me.

Sparkling emerald green eyes shine through the cloud of smoke and muted lighting. It seems nearly impossible for me to notice them from here, and the only thing I can figure out is that they must glow in the dark. Intrigued, I lift my lids in search of this mysterious creature that silently appraises the show from his seat at the bar.

He's massive, even sitting down. I guess he's every bit of six foot four. His shoulders are wide--the muscles in his arms evident even through his black hoodie that is partially hidden beneath the heavy leather he wears. His neck is strong—powerful, thick and the only thing exposed to me other than his face...that *face.*

It's dusted in dark hair as if he hasn't shaved for a few days. But it's not enough to hide how smooth, square and perfectly sculpted the curve of his jaw is. His hat is turned backwards and sits low on his head, stopping just above his green eyes that are intense, dark and brooding. They're fucking paralyzing—pulling me in and making me forget everything that's still happening around me.

I'm completely drawn to him—this force. He's not beautiful like Luke, or handsome like Crash, or cute like Regg, but raw and dangerous—captivating and all consuming. He's the sexiest thing I've ever seen.

I'm acutely aware of voices around me—hands on me and mouths devouring me. But all I can focus on is the pull of his eyes...the tick in his jaw...the unyielding power he seems to have over me as if I've submitted complete control to this man—this Devil's Renegade I don't even know.

He stands smoothly, my eyes following his every move. At full height, he's even more dominating and threatening than I could have imagined. Worn, faded jeans hang loosely on his thighs, but seem to tighten at his crotch. Or maybe that's just my imagination convincing me what's hidden beneath his pants is just as large and powerful as the rest of him.

Like a predator, he silently prowls toward me—his movements fluid, confident and precise. The crowd parts when he nears. Talking ceases. Hands desert me. Mouths abandon me —leaving my heavy, swollen breasts exposed. My nipples stiffen without the warmth of lips and tongues surrounding them.

He doesn't stop until he's directly in front of me—leveling me with a look of desire and want. Wordlessly, he extends his hand in offering. With shaky fingers, I reach out and accept it— allowing him to pull me from the throng of men. My legs are wobbly from the sudden movement, but a strong arm encircles my waist to hold me steady.

"Your room. Where is it?" His deep, husky voice is thick with a Cajun accent that's so damn sexy, I nearly swoon.

"Down the hall," I manage, in a barely audible tone. His eyes seem to smile at me, but his lips remain soft and slightly parted —casting cool, whiskey-scented air across my face.

Breaking his gaze from mine, his eyes roam the crowd of men around us. He offers them a slight chin tip, then fixes his eyes on me again. I feel as if he's giving me the opportunity to say no. I won't. It's not that I can't, I just don't want to.

He waits a bit, and when he's satisfied this is what I want, his eyes become hooded and darken with promise. The arm around my waist falls, and my entire body shivers without his heat. With my hand still securely in his, he turns and leads us toward the hallway.

I'm thankful for the short walk, which gives me a break from his penetrating stare. By the time we reach my bedroom door, the fog I've been in since I first laid eyes on him lifts and I feel more in control. I keep my head down and avoid his gaze as he releases my hand and steps back—allowing me to enter my room first.

"I'm Delilah, by the way," I say, keeping my back to him as I mindlessly straighten things on my dresser.

The door clicks shut, and then I hear his voice. "I know." His deep tone powers through me—shaking me in places that are quickly becoming wetter. He doesn't offer his name, and I don't mind. It really doesn't matter anyway.

"Are you married?" *Please don't be married...please don't be married.*

"No." I detect humor in his answer and find myself smiling. It quickly fades when I hear the sound of the chains on his vest rattling as he unsnaps them.

"You want some music?" I ask, already powering up my iPod that's linked to the portable speaker next to my bed.

"Whatever you want, Love." *Love...*It sounds so foreign with his Cajun accent—making it that much sexier.

Selecting my playlist titled "Sexy," I put it on shuffle. I turn to face him just as the introduction to "The Hills" by The Weekend reverberates off the walls of my tiny room that just got smaller with his presence. His large body stands casually at the end of my bed—still fully clothed except for his cut that hangs from my doorknob. He's just as mighty and forcible without it as he is wearing it.

My breathing is harsh and erratic, but thankfully the music is loud enough to drown it out. Damn, I want him. I don't think

I've ever been so worked up over a man. I want to taste him…
touch him…*feel* him in places that are swollen, needy and ready
—for him.

The aura of confidence that surrounds him is infectious. I
feed off it—allowing it to fuel my courage. This is my expertise.
This is my strong suit. This is where I thrive. I'm here for his
pleasure, but I already know the pleasure will be all mine.

My hands move to unbutton my shorts and his eyes follow.
Teasingly slow, I lower the zipper. Silently, I gauge his reaction—
noticing the tick of his jaw when my smooth, bare mound
becomes visible. Pushing my shorts over my hips, they fall to my
feet. He drinks me in wearing nothing but a pair of red heels that
bring my height to nearly six foot.

"Come here," he growls, and the low demand has me
stepping out of my shorts and in his direction. The appreciation
in his eyes has my confidence soaring, and I feel sexier in his
presence that I've ever felt in my life.

The moment I'm within his reach, his large hands surround
my waist and pull me roughly against him. His head dips low,
bringing his lips dangerously close to mine. The look on his face
is smoldering--from the flash of heat in his eyes and the flare of
his nostrils to his parted lips and intoxicating breath that leaves
me feeling drunk.

His hands slide to my hips then around to my ass.
Tightening his grip, his fingers dig into my flesh as he lifts me.
My legs lock around his waist. My hands travel up his arms and
across his shoulders—gliding over the muscular plains before
coming to a stop on either side of his neck. His pulse races
beneath my palm as my thumbs trail across his scruffy jaw—
urging his head back and making his mouth available to me.

My tongue sweeps across his bottom lip, soothing it before
pulling it between my teeth. He groans, and it's the only
invitation I need. Covering my mouth with his, I start to ravage
him. But he slows the kiss—claiming my mouth as his tongue
leisurely strokes mine. The control he yields makes the kiss even
more erotic.

I'm not sure if it's the sultry, permeating tempo of the song
or if the battle to take his time is lost, but when he pulls his lips
from mine, raw, primal need dances in his eyes. His animalistic
stare is centered on me as he holds me to him with one hand,
and uses the other to pull a condom from his back pocket. He
holds it between his lips, while he loosens his jeans.

I force them down his legs with my heels, and my mouth
forms an O when I feel him against me. The corner of his lip lifts

in a sexy smirk as he presses my back against the door. Pinning me with his hips, he tears open the condom with his teeth, then spits the remaining wrapper from between his lips as he sheaths himself.

His fingers find my swollen clit. Rubbing slow, teasing circles around it, he kisses his way across my jaw until I feel his warm mouth at my ear. "Are you ready for me, Love?"

*Yes.*

*Hell, yes.*

But I can't find my voice, so I nod. Sliding one long, skilled finger deliciously slow inside me, he takes my earlobe between his teeth. "Almost." He adds another finger—stretching me... widening me...preparing me for him.

"Your pussy feels like satin," he whispers, leaning back to look at me as he withdraws his fingers. He drags them up my body, leaving a damp trail of my arousal all the way to my chin. He pushes one finger between my lips—letting me taste myself. I suck it greedily. His nostrils flare and I hear a low simmering growl from deep in his chest.

I quiver in anticipation. I've never wanted or needed something so bad. My body is on fire. My heart is hammering. Every muscle in my body tightens as he presses the tip of his cock against my entrance. Ever so slowly, he pushes inside. My walls stretch to accommodate him. The deeper he goes, the more intense the pressure becomes. It's almost uncomfortable, but it quickly fades—overpowered by a wave of pleasure that has me throwing my head back against the door.

His movements are timed and perfectly measured. The roll of his hips is slow and becomes almost lazy, then vehement and greedy as he powers the last inch inside me. He continues the torturous movement making my head roll and my nails dig deeper into his flesh. Then suddenly, he begins an unrelenting drive—savagely claiming me...not asking, but taking what he wants...forcing his cock to slide over that velvety sweet spot deep inside me over and over.

My hands use his shoulders as leverage—lifting myself before matching each powerful thrust he delivers. There's no slow build or gradual climb to my orgasm. It hits me instantly—ridding my thoughts of anything that isn't centered on this euphoric high. I'm screaming—shattering to pieces around him. When the walls of my pussy constrict and grip his cock, I feel it thicken as his thrusts become more intense with the pressing need to find his own release.

I open my eyes just as he starts to pulse inside me. He bites his lip to stifle his growl, but his eyes are unsheltered—hooded green emeralds focused directly on me and burning with a feral possession that's as gripping as the orgasm still wracking through me.

He stills inside me—burying his face in my neck. His breaths are heavy against my hair. My limbs feel flaccid as they surround him. I beg the life to return, and silently pray he's not ready to release me just yet. Loosening his grip on the back of my thighs, his hands tenderly rub the flesh that is indented with his fingers.

The moment is soothing. It's almost intimate, making me grow uncomfortable. As if he can sense my tension, he pulls back. His expression is cocky, but a little guarded. My legs untangle from around him, and his hands slide to my waist to steady me. His cock slowly pulls out of me. I want to whimper, but I bite it back and offer him a cocky smile of my own.

"Impressive," I pant, shooting him a wink.

He grins. "I try." His voice is a low husky rumble that has me wanting him to take me up against the door once again. "Mind if I use your shower?"

"No. Of course not." I'm shaking my head—a part of me hoping he asks me to join him. Instead, he gives me a smirk as he pulls up his jeans, grabs his cut from the doorknob and walks away.

I let out a long breath when he's behind the door, and walk stiffly across the room to turn off my iPod that is now blaring the lyrics of yet another song by The Weekend. The room fills with silence moments before I hear the shower start.

A light rap sounds at the door. Pulling a silk robe over my shoulders, I don't bother to tie it as I crack the door open. A Prospect stands on the other side—silent as his eyes rake up my exposed body. By the time he makes it to my face, I'm smiling warmly.

"Yes?"

He clears his throat and looks over the top of my head. "I was told to drop this off with you." He all but thrusts a leather bag in my hands, before leaving quickly. *Okay...*

"Um..." *Damn... I don't even know his name.* "Hey, sweetie, someone dropped this off," I say, inching the bathroom door open.

"Thanks." The word sounds strangled, and if I didn't know any better, I'd swear whoever this patch-holder is in my shower is beating off. It makes me feel...*inadequate? Is that the word I'm looking for?*

Dropping the bag on the counter, I pull the door closed behind me and cinch my robe a little tighter. *Inadequate...hmph.* I dig my duffel from the bottom of my closet and pack it with my upcoming trip's necessities. I'm finished and sitting on the edge of my bed when the bathroom door opens and he walks out.

Shirtless.

My tongue involuntarily runs across my bottom lip as my eyes travel up his legs shielded by a pair of sweats to his bare stomach. *Have mercy.* It's thick, strong and flat, but not rippled in muscles. That's reserved for his chest and arms. I've never seen a man so wide, or so tall. His skin is flawless, tattooed perfection. His arms are as big around as my waist, and his head is shaved nearly bald. He's like a magical unicorn—unreal and only possible in my dreams.

"I'm gonna crash here tonight, if that's good with you."

*Good with me? Damn right it's good with me.*

"Sure," I shrug, knotting my fidgety hands in my lap. Something about his presence has that incessant need inside me building. But when he draws closer to me, it seems to dissipate. *Weird.*

"I'm just gonna head back up front." I start to stand, but his eyes hold me in place.

"You're with me tonight." It's not a suggestion or a threat, it's just a matter of fact. His chin juts toward me. "Lose the robe. I want you naked." Even though the demand should make me feel as if I'm some kind of fucking call girl he's paying by the hour, it doesn't. He says it in a way that's soft and almost reverent—like he genuinely appreciates the way I look. Or maybe I'm just overthinking it.

"I need a shower," I say, but he's already shaking his head.

"I like my scent on you." *Son of a bitch...* He's like an animal —marking his territory with his smell, his mouth, his body and his cock. I feel a tingle deep in my belly. *Shit... Who knew that would be such a turn-on?*

I guess I'm moving too slow for him. Probably because I'm still sitting here, gaping open-mouthed at his caveman demands. Pulling me to my feet, his big hands unknot the delicate fabric before pushing it from my shoulders. "Much better," he mumbles, drinking in the sight of me.

Reaching above him, he pulls the string on my ceiling fan— flooding the room with darkness. The distant sounds of the ongoing party happening in the front of the clubhouse seem miles away, but I can still hear the steady thump of the music, though I can't make out the lyrics.

His brows rise as his head nods in the direction of the bed behind me. I all but fall into it and scramble under the covers. My heart is beating a little heavier than it should. There's something about this guy—something foreign, but yet distinctly familiar. *I can't quite put my finger on it...*

My breath is shaky when his massive body climbs beneath the covers of my king-sized bed. With no warning, his arm circles my waist and he pulls me to him. I'm engulfed by the scent of my soap that smells a hell of a lot more delicious on him than it ever has on me. His minty breath is cool across my face. *I wonder if he uses Crest or Colgate?*

"Goodnight, Delilah."

"Goodnight..." I start to ask his name, but his breathing is heavy and even—telling me he's already near sleep. And something about the way I'm cradled to his chest has me edging closer to sleep too.

*Fuck it.*

Chances are, by tomorrow, I'll forget not only his name, but like everyone else, he'll just be another face, another John, another Renegade—another reminder of who and what I am.

# CHAPTER 6

My internal alarm clock sounds with an ear-splitting squeal —jolting me awake just as the sun starts its ascent. The first thing I notice is the big arm that has a death grip on my waist. A heavy leg is thrown over both mine, and there's a warm, soft chest pressed into my back.

*...What's his name...*

Somehow, I manage to untangle myself from the throng of limbs. I hold my breath as I ease out of the bed, praying like hell I don't wake him. Once I'm safely in the bathroom, I become a little panicked at the loss of time. I should have been on the road hours ago. Instead, I allowed myself to fall asleep in a set of arms that made me feel safe enough to abandon the monster that is now pulling against his restraints.

I quickly brush my teeth, pull my hair back and scrub the makeup from my face. I don't have time for a shower, so I attempt to mask the scent of the man in my bed using lotion and a fruity-smelling body spray. When I look less like a clubwhore and more like a homely stepchild, I ease open the door and watch his large frame rise and fall in measured breaths.

Tiptoeing across the room, I keep my eyes on him until I'm at my dresser. I pull on some cotton panties, a sports bra, a hoodie and some sweats. My tennis shoes are on, my duffel over my shoulder and I'm at the window when a deep, very amused male voice jolts me.

"What are you doing?"

I swallow hard as I turn to look at him. He's devilishly sexy, with somber green eyes and a lazy smile. "I have somewhere to be. Make yourself at home." I can tell by his expression he's not satisfied with my evasive response. I feel my anger simmer even before he presses me for more information.

"Where the hell you gotta be at seven in the morning?" *Seven? Shit!*

"None of your business," I bite out before I can catch myself. I take a calming breath and add, "That came out wrong. I'm sorry, but I have to go. I'm already very late."

Without waiting for a response, I lift the window and clamber through. The crunch of ice sounds under my feet and I nearly lose my balance, but recover. Slamming the window, I don't bother to look back as I break into a run toward my car.

My monster is mad. My demons are dancing. The darkness is near. I allowed myself to get distracted. I deserve to be punished. I'm three hours away from relief. I just hope it's delivered to me in the same brutal fashion my body craves. And I pray like hell I'm shown no mercy.

I look down at the swirling pattern of the cheap linoleum that's stained in my blood. It seeps from my mouth and nose—the puddle growing with each passing minute. My mother isn't home today, so instead of hearing the constant babble of Dr. Phil, I'm forced to endure the sounds of VH1's tribute to eighties rock bands.

I wasn't even fully through the door when my feet were taken out from under me. I'm still not entirely sure what my brother was so pissed about, but there was something about Mama having to borrow money to go see her sister in Slidell, because I wasn't here on time. I remember telling him she could've waited a little longer, but a swift kick to my stomach rendered me speechless.

The good news is that my monster is sleeping. The bad news? I hate myself more than I have in a long time. I can't figure out if it's guilt for not being here when my mother needed me, or for being a sick fuck who needs her brother to torture the hell out of her just to feel at all. I'm leaning more toward the latter.

Pulling myself to my knees, I wipe my nose and mouth with the sleeve of my hoodie. I still have all my teeth and my nose isn't broken, so that's a plus. But my stomach aches with every breath I pull. I must have put my wrist out to break my fall, because it's stiff and swollen. I'm sure it's just badly sprained.

"You got any more cash?" My brother's voice sends chills down my spine. *Creepy fucker...*

"I got some in my bag."

"Done took that. You got any more?"

Using the kitchen table to brace myself, I slowly stand. Turning to look at him, I can see spatters of blood on his gray shirt—my blood. "You went through my shit?"

"My house, my shit." He glares at me—daring me to say something. Like an idiot, I do.

"Mama's house," I correct. Fury blazes in his eyes and his muscles tighten.

"Want me to break your jaw? Huh? Cause I fuckin' can." He sounds just as stupid as he looks—greasy hair falling in his face and a week's worth of dirt under his nails. "I don't know why Mama even lets you come over here. You need to be in a mental hospital or some shit."

I grab my empty duffel from the floor and sling it over my shoulder. I refuse to wince at the movement, even though my muscles scream in agony. My feet shuffle slowly to the door. I'm halfway out when he speaks.

"You better bring more next week to make up for what she had to borrow."

Yeah, yeah, yeah... I get it. I frown at the thought of not getting to see my mother. It's not that she's pleasant, or the least bit interested in seeing me, but I get some odd satisfaction out of not only making a valiant effort to visit her, but helping her financially too. Chances are, my brother will keep what money I had on me to himself and convince her I didn't bring anything.

I survey the damage to my face in my rearview mirror. Busted lip, nose and a knot already bruising around the edges seems to be the brunt of it. It'll be easy to hide too. A little makeup and some dark lighting will keep the questions at the clubhouse to a minimum. Just like it always has.

I'm drowsy the entire ride back to Hattiesburg. Somehow I manage to keep it between the ditches, arrive safely and crawl back through my window without having to face a single soul. My room is empty—definitely a welcome relief, and an unexpected surprise.

*Maybe God decided to shed a little mercy on me after all.*


It's been weeks since I last saw the mysterious Renegade who I left alone in my bed. I thought I would've forgotten him by now, but every time I'm with someone, I think of him. I think of how savagely he claimed me...how rough his hands were, yet soft.

I hadn't asked about him. I'm not sure why, maybe fear of gossip that I might be interested in someone. I didn't need that attention. I didn't need anyone thinking that I, like many others before me, had become infatuated with a brother they couldn't have.

Several of the women who worked at the clubhouse longed to be more. They wanted patches, titles and to be claimed. I didn't want any of that. But that wouldn't keep people from assuming I was just like everyone else. So I'd kept my questions to myself, and choose to forget it ever happened. Problem is, I simply can't forget.

It's New Year's. The party at the clubhouse is one of the biggest of the year. Naked women, leather-clad men and endless amounts of alcohol fill the room. After the bar the club owns downtown closes, the crowd grows larger.

I'm working the crowd. My smile is plastered on my face—a genuine one that comes easily at the happy men that surround me. I'm wearing a T-shirt that's cut so short the bottom of my breasts are visible beneath it. The tiny black skirt is short, tight and inviting. My body is on display—offered and available to anyone who desires it.

The looks I receive are of pure lust and want. It heightens my mood. I want the men to look at me. I want them to touch me, fuck me and use me. There's something about the humiliation of knowing who I am and what my purpose is that has my body pulsing with sexual need. But these men are not greedy. They won't request me privately—not while there are so many wanting men and not enough women to go around.

Lyrics to Awolnation's "Sail" fills the room. The booming, heavy bass vibrates the walls, and although the music isn't so loud it drowns out the sound of chatter, it does diminish conversations to nothing more than background noise. But I still hear the sound of the heavy wooden door as it swings open. Naturally all eyes turn to who's walking in. Mine included.

From across the room, I can feel the effects the man's presence has on me. My whole body comes to life. My sex tightens. My breasts become heavier. The sexual need I was feeling intensifies, and becomes almost desperate. It's *him*—the Devil's Renegade whose name I still don't know. In a way, it makes him more mysterious and that much more desirable.

A line forms. Men of different patches and ranks wait patiently—respectfully—to greet him. Whoever he is, he's someone of importance. I watch as he nods to most, takes the hands of several and hugs only a few. He towers over everyone, making even the largest men seem small. At five foot ten, he makes me feel small—miniscule even.

My view of him is blocked by the crowd. I want to edge closer, but remain where I stand—at least twenty feet from him. Still, his presence is overwhelming and I feel my body heat with the knowledge that he is here. When the crowd breaks slightly, I find him looking directly at me. It's as if he knew I was here—watching, wanting and desiring him. He stands tall and patient until the last man greets, before lifting his chin to Linda behind the bar.

With a smile, she passes him a tall glass of whiskey— straight up. A flicker of anger I can't comprehend sparks inside me at the exchange. I don't like the way she looks at him. I don't like the way she tucks her hair behind her ear or averts her gaze, as if she were shy—which she's anything but. I have no right to be possessive over this man whose name I don't even know, but I am.

He drains the glass of whiskey—still standing just inside the door. Handing the empty glass back to her, I see his lips move and watch her blush crimson at whatever he said. My anger deepens and as much as I want to feel ridiculous or stupid about my reaction, I don't.

Inquisitive, sparkling green eyes find me. Lazily, they rake the length of my body before coming back to meet my own. The very corners of his lips quirk as he walks slowly but purposefully toward me. I'm aware of the women who watch him. Their eyes sweep from him to me—noticing my obvious attraction. I don't care. They can think what they want. And if I look as desperate for him as I feel, then I don't care about that either.

Despite my effort to force a cocky grin, I remain as I am— mouth slightly parted, eyes hooded and breathing ragged. The closer he gets, the more wanton I become. Desire doesn't just reflect in my eyes and my reaction—it pools between my thighs and floods my naked sex. As he nears, I'm afraid he'll smell my arousal. Another part of me hopes like hell he does.

His gaze never faltering, his stride never slowing, he clasps my hand in his as he passes—forcing me to turn and follow him down the long hall. This is a man who doesn't ask for others' permission. He doesn't care that he's being greedy or that my company is meant to be shared among all the brothers. He wants me for himself, and he's taking me—silently claiming me even if it is just for a little while.

Just as before, he steps back and allows me to lead him inside my room … my sanctuary—the one place that I call mine, yet it feels like it belongs to him now. Hell, I feel like I belong to him. The scary thing is, I *want* to be his. At least for right now, in this moment.

I turn to face him. My intentions are to ask him if he wants music, even though we can still clearly hear the song playing in the front. But when I look at him, my words catch in my throat. His chest is a hairsbreadth away from mine. The scent of leather and whiskey wafts into my nostrils. I'm so close, I have to crane my neck to meet his eyes—those eyes—compelling and masterful.

"Hello, Love." *Son of a bitch.* His deep tone is low—hungry.

"Hello," I squeak out—sounding, feeling and probably looking like an amateur instead of the clubwhore veteran I am.

The back of his fingertips slide slowly up my arm. Goosebumps break out everywhere he touches, despite the heat I feel. He continues to drag them softly to my neck—his eyes never leaving mine. With the slightest amount of pressure, he grips my throat in his calloused hand.

I feel trapped—captured by not only his embrace but his promising glare. But I can't decide what it is exactly that he's promising. It doesn't matter. I'll take whatever he gives me. He walks, forcing me backwards until the back of my knees hit the bed.

He guides me down—his body covering mine as his hand moves from my throat to my waist. He lifts me further on the bed —climbing on top of me as his hands slide up my sides and push my shirt over my head. Dipping his mouth to my breast, he takes my nipple between his teeth. I moan when he tugs slightly— feeling a jolt of electricity shoot straight to my core.

My hands cup his face—forcing him to release my nipple and look at me. I don't want the foreplay. I don't need his mouth to tease me until I'm primed and ready for him. My pussy has ached for him since he walked through the door. My core is trembling in anticipation of his cock. I'm ready. The question is, is he?

"Fuck me," I demand, leaning up to run my tongue across his lips. He crashes his mouth to mine—his kiss hard as his tongue sweeps into my mouth. I can taste the whiskey, the leather, the strong male scent of him...a concoction that screams danger.

This man is dangerous. I can see it in the eyes of his brothers when they look at him. I can feel the thickening of tension whenever he's present. I can smell the fear of men who surround him. It's the danger that draws me to this man—this nameless man who doesn't ask, but takes what is his. In this moment I am his.

Hard, rough hands push my skirt up my thighs before sliding back down my naked legs and spreading my knees. He leans back, greedily drinking in the sight of my bare pussy that's open for him. "I can smell you," he growls, his green eyes darkening with lust.

My hands move to my breasts. They feel heavy, my nipples sensitive to their touch. His eyes follow the movement, his jaw clenching further at the sight. "Play with your pussy." His words are deep and throaty—dirty and erotic.

I do as he says, finding my lips damp and hot with arousal. He watches me slide my finger between my folds—rubbing the length of my pussy before circling my clit that throbs for his touch.

Reaching behind him, he fists his hoodie in his hand before pulling it over his head. His movements are hurried, but precise. He pulls a condom from his pocket, ripping the wrapper with his teeth before opening his pants and releasing his massive cock. Sheathing it, his eyes drag up my stomach, stopping momentarily on my breasts before meeting mine.

"I wanna fuck you hard." His accent thickens with the words. He's asking my permission, without really asking at all. Regardless, I nod my head in agreement. I'm still nodding when he grips my hips and pulls me to him—lining his cock up with my slick entrance.

In one deep thrust, he impales me. My breath catches in my throat, but he doesn't stop before pulling out and thrusting hard into me again. It's almost painful—his onslaught brutal, unforgiving and the best fucking thing I've ever felt.

Pain quickly morphs into indescribable pleasure as he pumps in and out of me—pulling almost completely out before driving in again. My back arches. My moans become louder as I feel my climax building. I feel him everywhere when he's inside me. His large cock reaches places I've never had the pleasure of feeling one before—deep inside me past the barrier that no man has ever touched.

I'm nearing my orgasm. My walls tighten around him. I'm ready to let myself go, but his voice momentarily paralyzes me. "Don't come, Love. Don't you dare fuckin' come."

But he's too late. I'm too close and the need for release is too powerful. With a scream, my pussy contracts around him—squeezing him tightly. I hear a muffled "fuck" as his pace quickens. Moments later, he's pulsating inside me. Deep, guttural moans fill the room and I'm not sure if they're coming from me or him.

I clench my muscles tight—milking everything from him. It earns me a look I can't quite decipher. His hips jerk, the tiny movement enough to send another wave of pleasure lapping at my core.

"You don't listen very well, do you?"

I give him a lazy smile, my body sleepy and sated. "I tried. You're just too good," I whisper, unable to form a more audible tone.

His eyes roam appreciatively over my body, then his brow furrows with concern. "You look tired," he says, pulling out of me. I wince, unsure if it's at the emptiness or the tinge of pain I feel now that my body isn't in orgasm overload.

"Long day. Long night." As if to confirm it, I yawn.

He walks to the bathroom, and my eyes fight to stay open as I watch him. When he disappears behind the door, I promise to rest my eyes for only a moment. Then I'll demand his name. But first, I just need a few minutes...

# CHAPTER 7

I don't wake until the sun is well above the horizon. I glance at my clock to find it's after eight in the morning. I'm naked, tangled under the covers that I don't remember climbing beneath. Thoughts of last night flood through me, and I clench my sex—still feeling where he was...how deep he was inside me. Sitting up, I take a moment to stretch before pulling a T-shirt over my head and padding quietly down the hall.

No one around here is crazy enough to be up at this hour after a party like last night, so I'm not expecting company when I walk into the main room. The first thing that gets my attention is the music. It's classical, and not the dark, creepy kind. It's soothing and peaceful. Almost like sleep music.

*Who the hell played this?*

Which brings me to the second thing that gets my attention —a huge man wearing a Devil's Renegades' cut, occupying a barstool. The difference between him and the guys from this chapter is his bottom rocker that reads Lake Charles. It's...*him*.

*Shit. I haven't even brushed my hair. Or my teeth...*

"Good mornin'." The deep Cajun accent freezes me in my tracks. *How the fuck did he know I was behind him? And why the hell do I feel hot all of a sudden just at the sound of his voice?* "I heard your door open." I take a minute to collect myself before going any closer. It doesn't take long for my desperate need of coffee to have me moving forward. And the desire to finally put a name to his face is becoming desperate too.

I round the bar to find coffee already made. I pour a cup, keeping my back to him and hoping like hell there's enough light for me to check out his features and his finger. He'd said he wasn't married, but you can never be sure. Not that it mattered now...he'd had me twice already.

Slowly, I turn and come face to face with him. I thought I knew all the guys from Lake Charles. I've met every one of them, fucked most of them and half of their ol' ladies. But suddenly I wonder if he's the ghost I'd heard rumors about. *No fucking way...*

"Devil's Renegades Sergeant at Arms Bryce, Lake Charles." *Yes fucking way.* Extending his large hand in my direction, I drop my eyes to his other one before taking it. *No ring.* "We haven't officially met." His playful tone is mirrored in his warm green eyes.

"Delilah." Did I just *breathe* my name? I did. But shit...his lips are full and curved into a small smile. He's so sexy... dangerously sexy. Actually, I'd heard he was dangerous. The silent kind of dangerous that sneaks up on you and takes you out before you even realize what's happening. The kind that can cut you and you won't even feel it until you're bleeding. *The Ruthless Gentle Giant.* That's what they call him. It never made sense before, but now I get it. He's soft spoken and kind on the outside, but pure evil on the inside. How do I know this? I swear I can see it in his eyes.

"Will you excuse me just one minute?" I offer him an apologetic smile before releasing his hand that's still warm around mine. His smile widens slightly in amusement as I hurriedly head through the side door to the kitchen.

Turning on the tap, I splash my face with the freezing cold water that nearly takes my breath. I continue to cup my hands under the faucet and douse my face until I feel more like myself and less like whoever in the hell that girl was that walked in here.

Once I'm fully awake, my face is dry, and I've rinsed some of the disgusting from my mouth, I head back to where Bryce is still sitting.

I feel marginally more in control, but not as much as I wish. This guy's doing something to me and I don't like it. Needing him to prove to me he's an asshole or say something that will make me like him less, I decide to strike up a conversation with Mr. Fuckingwithmyhead.

"I thought you were a ghost. Or a figment of everyone's imagination," I say, topping off my coffee and his. "I've been here two years and I've only seen you twice." *Fucked you twice...*

"I can assure you I'm real." No shit he's real... My belly flips when I remember how thick and filling his cock felt inside me.

"So where've you been hiding?" I'm trying like hell not to flirt, and failing miserably.

"Around."

"Evasive much?" I ask with a smile, which he returns.

"I like to keep to myself." I nod in understanding. I know all too well about that. "And you?"

"And me what?"

"Why are you hiding?"

I let out a laugh, then remember I'd yet to brush my teeth. Taking a step back, I lean against the counter behind me—making sure there are at least a foot and the bar between us. "I'm not hiding. You see me, don't you?"

"I see you." There's some underlying meaning to his answer that I refuse to overthink this early in the morning. "But why are you here?"

"Because this is my job."

"Don't you live here?"

"Yes."

"Then wouldn't this be your home? Not just your job?" The way his eyes narrow when they appraise me makes me feel like he's trying to figure out the answer before I say it. And the soft, smooth sound of his voice seems to match perfectly with the music playing in the room. It makes me want to tell him everything.

"I don't like the word home, and this isn't a house. It's a place which happens to be where I'm employed, therefore it's just my job. I'm all work, all the time."

"So do my brothers offer workman's comp? Or did you sign a waiver?" At my confusion, his thick finger points in the direction of my face. Without makeup, the fading bruise near my hairline from last Sunday is still visible.

"This was personal." He gives me an expectant look and it's the first step in the direction of me liking him a little less. "Personal as in nobody's business but mine."

I see a flash of anger in his eyes before he dips them to his cup. I also notice the way his body stiffens and the veins in his neck seem to thicken. But when he meets my gaze again he's relaxed and any trace of anger is gone—replaced with determination.

Threading his fingers together, he lays his arms on top of the bar and leans closer. "I'm making it my business." The cold in his voice is seriously chilling. Like, I have goosebumps. I've never felt afraid or uncomfortable around any of these men. But this guy is starting to scare the shit out of me.

"I need to go," I whisper, dropping my eyes and wrapping my other hand around my cup in an attempt to keep them from visibly shaking.

"Do I scare you, Delilah?" His tone is strong, rich and confident, but I can hear the hint of regret. Suddenly, the desire to reassure him that I'm okay and I'm now aware that he didn't intend to scare me outweighs my desire to turn and run. *What the fuck?*

"No. I mean. Yes, but it's okay." *Damn. I can't even lie. This is bad...really, really bad.*

"Why is that okay?" Regret gone. Control back. Did he do that intentionally?

"It's not okay. I just..." I just what? Nothing because I feel stupid and I sound stupid and I don't understand what in the hell is going on with me right now.

"Look at me, Delilah." On their own accord, my eyes meet his. I think he put something in my coffee. I feel hypnotized. "It's not okay to feel afraid in your own home. And this is your home, no matter what you choose to call it."

I'm nodding, repeating his words in my head like a mantra. *This is my home. This is my home.* Why? Because he says it is and for some reason, I feel like he has that much control over me right now. I liked him better when he was fucking me and I didn't have to think or feel anything but what he was doing to me.

"It's not okay for a man to put their hands on a woman either. Not like that. I don't care who they are." The walls inside me shake a little. It's like he's an earthquake, and as long as I'm in his presence, he has the power to crumble something inside of me I thought was indestructible. But I can't break away. I can't run from him. Some magnetic force is emanating from him and holding me here. A part of me hates it, but a part of me wants to give in.

He's so...different than the others. He seems educated, worldly and although his appearance suggests he's the epitome of a bad-ass biker, the way he speaks and acts suggests something totally different—like Luke. He belongs, but in an unconventional kind of way.

"Nobody told me you were still around." The sound of Linda's voice has never been so welcome. Giving me a wink, Bryce turns on his barstool to face the woman whose arm is around his shoulders. The instant his back is to me, the trance breaks and I pull in a deep breath.

"Please tell me you haven't staked your claim, Delilah."

Now fully in control of myself, I set my cup down on the bar with a little more force than necessary—pissed at myself for letting someone else control me in the first place.

*That's not who you are anymore.*

*You don't need to be controlled.*

*You have Sunday.*

*You have your brother.*

At the reminder, my hand moves to my head, softly caressing the bruise there.

Linda clears her throat and shoots me a look, wanting an answer. But thankfully, Bryce keeps his back to me.

"No, ma'am. He's all yours."

She beams as I pass. I want to slap her. He's not mine. What we had was sex. Hot, dirty, mind-blowing sex. Nothing more and nothing less. But even though I know these things, something sparks inside me—something infuriatingly unwelcome and completely maddening.

*Jealousy.*

# CHAPTER 8

"Knock, knock."

I look past my reflection in the mirror on my vanity to see Red and Dallas walk inside my room—like they fucking own the place. After my morning with Mr. Drivesmecrazy, and my afternoon of shitty TV, I'm not really in the mood for trespassers.

"You know," I say, spinning in my chair to face them as they take a seat on my bed and get comfortable. "Saying 'knock knock' isn't really considered asking for permission to come in. Especially when you don't bother waiting for an invite."

"You stole my car."

"That doesn't justify you being in here. Uninvited. And besides, that was weeks ago."

"Well, your door was open."

The more Red talks, the less I like her. But she's like a fungus that won't go away unless you treat it. In this case, the quickest way for her to leave is for me to listen to whatever it is she has to say. This time, it's gonna cost her more than pumpkin pancakes I never got to eat.

"What do you want?" I ask, turning back to face myself in the mirror. This war paint isn't gonna apply itself.

"We were hoping you could help us get something." I raise my eyes to Dallas' in the mirror. To be such a confident multi-millionaire who is the CEO of her own company, she sure does look uneasy from where I'm sitting.

"How much you want?" They glance at each other in question. Shaking my head, I grab my mascara and opt for the bathroom mirror. Climbing on the counter, I sit cross-legged and lean in close. I was hoping for a break from their watchful eyes, but of course they followed me.

"You don't even know what we want."

"Yes I do. You want pot." No sooner are the words out of my mouth than they're shhhing me and running to close the door. *Idiots.* I'm thankful every day that I'm not an ol' lady—asking favors from *clubwhores* and keeping secrets from my husband. But I'm especially thankful right now. *Damn, I hope I never look that desperate.*

"We just need a couple blunts." I can't tell you who said it, both of them sound the same when they whisper.

"It's cheaper if you buy it by the pound." I nearly snort at my own words. I know what Dallas is going to say even before she says it.

"Money isn't an issue." Of course it isn't. *Must be nice...*

I make them wait until I've finished coating my lashes in bat crap before I turn to face them. Swinging my legs over the side of the counter, I just sit and enjoy the moment. No matter what they think now, at one time they didn't like me. Hell, they probably still don't.

Even though it's been confirmed that, in their eyes, I'm just the girl the club pays to suck cock, there's no telling what other kind of shit they say about me behind my back. Yet, here they are, looking like a bunch of underage girls hiding from their parents and at my mercy. It makes me smile.

"You know it's gonna cost you, right?" This isn't the first time I've made some extra money off the very women that despise me—well, maybe not me in particular, but definitely what I'm about.

"Name your price." There's that confident CEO, I-own-the-fucking-world Dallas I know.

"I'll buy enough weed to keep you girls happy for a couple months, and I'll stash it out here. When you want it, you can get it from me and that will prevent me from having to go out every time y'all have a birthday, or party, or anniversary or whatever the fuck it is y'all are always celebrating."

"I like it." Red smiles, jerking her head on a nod and turning to Dallas—the one with the fat check book.

"Fine. How much?"

I grin at Dallas who narrows her eyes on me. She knows when she's getting taken advantage of. But turnabout is fair play. I'm getting taken advantage of too. And she knows that as well.

"Five hundred for the pot, and you pay me whatever you think my silence is worth."

"So if it's not enough you'll rat us out." Red's words make my blood heat and I glare at her.

"I'm not a rat. This is a 'you scratch my back I scratch yours' kinda deal. If you think my silence is worth a nickel and I think it's worth a dime, then next time you come asking for a favor, I'll tell you I can't. That's it. I'll never talk. The two of you get yourself in enough shit. You don't need my help."

Like the baller she is, Dallas pulls a wad of cash from her designer purse. "Five hundred for the pot," she says, flipping bills like it's George Washington's face she's looking at and not Benjamin Franklin's. "And a G for your silence."

"A G?" I ask, raising my brows in amusement. "You do realize you don't have to speak thug around me? I mean, this is a drug deal, but saying 'a thousand' doesn't make you any less of a criminal. Money sounds the same in all accents and languages."

"I'm in the moment, okay? Red has me feeling all gangsta and shit."

"Yeah, dog." Throwing her hand in what I can only guess is a gang sign, Red lifts her chin to me. I can only stare back at her with a look I hope makes her feel as stupid as she sounds.

Snatching the money from Dallas' fingers, I shake my head at both of them. "Just...get out. I'll text you in a little while."

Forty-seven thank yous and an almost hug later, they leave. Placing my hands on the counter, I pull in a deep breath. Just their presence is enough to exhaust me.

"And they think your life is pathetic..." Maybe it's time they find a mirror of their own.

Knowing better than to use one of the brothers for the amount of weed I plan on purchasing, I make a call to a guy who's frequented the clubhouse a few times. He hooks up some of the members with stuff when they want to party.

After catching him eyeing several of the men a little too appreciatively, I pulled him to the side and warned him that being so obvious about his homosexuality might interfere with business in a place like this. But heeding my warning wasn't necessary. The club, or at least Luke, was aware of his lifestyle. They didn't care. I guess when you have access to the best weed in Mississippi, it really doesn't matter who you share your bed with.

I haven't seen him in several months, but he seems excited enough to hear from me and assures me he has what I need. Texting me his address, he tells me what I want will be ready when I get there. Once again, I use my bedroom window as an exit to avoid questions. This time, I lock my door before I leave.

Since I'll be gone a couple hours and there are a few brothers around needing company tonight, I make sure to wear something sexy beneath my hoodie and sweats. When Dallas sees me creeping around the side of the building, she gives me a thumbs-up instead of an inquisitive glare. From her position under her carport she can't see me, but I flip her off.

Willy Hux lives in The Avenues—a neighborhood consisting of homes built in the twenties and thirties that housed the wealthiest part of Hattiesburg at one time. The east end of the neighborhood is still filled with old money and considered a good part of the town to live in. But the west end butts up against the part of downtown Hattiesburg you don't want to be caught in after dark. Living on the street that divides the two worlds, Willy is able to stay off the radar and still be within walking distance of his best clients.

Growing up in a neighborhood with a bad name, filled with bad people, I've never been scared or felt out of place in areas where crime is more common than not. So there's no fear when I park on the street across from the apartment building I'm sure more than one criminal calls home. Wrapping my hands around the cash in the pocket of my hoodie, I don't even bother looking over my shoulder as I walk up the path in complete darkness.

"There's a face that ain't easy to forget." I return Willie's smile as he holds the door open wider and gestures for me to come in. The place smells like incense and is filled with antiques. Several people sit scattered on the vintage furniture that surrounds an original fireplace that still burns wood. Feeling something warm against my cold hand, I look down to find Willie's pale, almost translucent hand clasped in mine.

"I want to show you something."

"Another time? I have to be getting back. I have some entertaining to do tonight." Flashing him my best smile, I give him a wink. He laughs knowingly, but ignores me and continues to lead me through the living room and into the kitchen.

Despite how much I need to get back, I can't help but admire the beauty that is his home. The original hardwood floors are lined with rugs that have me feeling guilty for walking across them in my shoes. Nearly every space on the wall is covered in portraits and paintings that each have to be at least fifty years old.

"This was my grandmother's house. She left it to my mother when she passed, who left it to me. Everything here once belonged to my family. My great aunt, who is now deceased, was also a collector. I inherited everything she had too. But this," he says, waving his hand around the small kitchen, "is a modern renovation that I'm very proud of." As he should be.

The electric blue cabinetry is so loud and absurd, it's perfect. The under-cabinet lighting illuminates the white granite countertops and stainless steel appliances. It's a completely different style compared to every other part of the house, but I can't imagine it being any more perfect.

"I copied the idea from a home makeover show. It's gonna be featured in the *South Mississippi Magazine* next spring. I'm bringing class back to The Avenues."

"It's beautiful," I say, smiling proudly up at him. There's something admirable about a guy like him rising above the challenges he's faced with every day and making something great of himself. To me, it doesn't matter how in the hell he makes his living. I'd be just as proud if he worked at Wal-Mart.

"Help yourself to a drink." He points to the endless bottles of liquor and wine covering the island. "I'll be back shortly with your stuff."

I nod, even though I hate the word "shortly." That's a little longer than "a few" but not as long as "a while." Really, it means, "I don't fucking know when I'll have your shit ready, but you'll get it when you get it."

Twisting off the cap on a bottle of Jack, I pour a decent amount in a glass before opening the refrigerator in search of ice. Filling it up, I top it off with a splash of Sprite, and shut the door. I don't react, but my heart pounds a little heavier when I come face to face with a guy whose pupils are the size of quarters.

"You're new." He licks his lips and I start to smile, but then I remember I'm not at work. And I don't have to do any fucking thing.

"Not interested," I say, leveling him with a look before stepping around his tall frame to lean against the counter—on the other side of the kitchen from him.

Laughing, he shakes his head and walks toward me, dragging his finger along the counter. I just stare in amusement. I wonder if he realizes that's only sexy when girls do it. "You don't even know what I'm offering."

"I guess it's a damn good thing I'm not in the market for anything, isn't it?" Taking a much needed pull from my glass, I close my eyes and savor the taste as it slides down my throat. When I open them again, he's standing right in front of me.

"That was sexy."

"I can assure you I wasn't intending it to be that way. And no, I'm not some girl who's playing hard to get, then doing sexy shit for attention. When I said I wasn't interested, I meant it. So run along and find someone else to annoy."

He continues to look at me with the same expression he wore the entire time I was speaking, as if it's taking the words a little longer than necessary to sink in. I know the moment it hits him because he looks slightly offended, but undeterred.

"I think attention is exactly what you need." I'm guessing he's a pretty college boy who's not used to being told no. He has the whole Zack-Morris-from-*Saved-by-the-Bell* vibe going for him, and judging by his expensive polo and designer jeans, I'm almost positive he's had a privileged upbringing. *Ugh. These are always the worst.*

"This will make the fourth time I've told you to get the hell away from me. That's three more than I'd have told anyone else. Leave, or I'll make you leave."

He smiles, then noticing the look on my face, turns the corners of his lips down. "Hey," he snaps, narrowing his eyes and taking a step closer. "Don't threaten me, bitch."

"I wouldn't."

I'm so caught up in my own thoughts on how to bring this very deserving man as much pain as possible that it takes me a moment to realize the voice I hear doesn't belong to me. Or to the man in front of me.

It belongs to *him*. I don't want to look.

But I do.

And when I do, I'm glad I did.

Familiar green eyes stare back at me.

This man is a force to be reckoned with.

He's like a god—a mythical one, but he's the best one. The big one. Zeus. The god of the sky and ruler of all the other gods who are insignificant in his presence. Far-fetched? I think not. He's just that fucking powerful.

He's six foot four, three hundred pounds of pure muscle. His forearms are bigger than my thighs. And he's just standing there, his thick hands shoved in the pockets of his jeans that had to be custom made to accommodate them. His head is tilted back just slightly, his chin pointing in the direction of the man he's speaking too--making his appearance even that much more intimidating. Not only that, but his big lungs must require all the oxygen in the room, because I can't breathe.

"Huh?" The man in front of me is less than a foot away, but his voice sounds far off. It's like I'm in a tunnel, and Bryce is the light at the other end.

"I said, I wouldn't." The accent is thick, but the guy must understand.

"I won't." And he didn't.

I have no fucking clue what the demand entailed. I don't know what might have become if he had--whatever. But the guy leaves the room—maybe even the entire country. Bryce didn't threaten him. But he didn't have to. There's an underlying meaning in everything he says, and people just get it.

"You shouldn't be here." *Shit.* Now he's talking to me. He's looking at me. And I can feel that control I had only moments ago slipping away quickly.

"I'm leaving," I promise, avoiding his eyes at all costs. I even find something appealing about the ice cubes in my glass—anything to keep me from looking at him. I'm searching for a reason to my sudden change in behavior. I only come up with one answer, but it doesn't explain shit. I'm this way because of him—this man I don't even know.

"Everything okay?" Willie asks, looking between me and Bryce whose eyes I can still feel on me.

Without a second thought, I nearly trip over my own feet to grab the paper sack from Willie's fingers. With so much shit happening all at once inside me, I simply forget to pay the man and turn to leave. Reaching out, he grabs my arm and stops me. I look down at his hand at the same moment I feel the floor shake beneath my feet. Immediately he lets go.

"My bad, man. I just need my money," Willie says, holding his hands up in surrender.

Shoving my hands in my pocket, I pull out the wad of cash and thrust it in his palm. Not bothering to thank him, I speed walk through the house then break into a run toward my car. I don't allow myself to breathe until I'm safely behind the wheel.

Tossing the bag on the passenger seat, I fumble for the keys in the ignition, but they're not here. Frantically I search the floorboard, my breathing coming in short gasps as I become more panicked with every second that passes and I don't find them. *What the fuck is wrong with me? I'm never like this.* This—whatever this is—feels foreign and familiar to me all at the same time.

With no warning, my door is jerked open and I'm so on edge, I let out a scream and scramble backwards across the seat away from my intruder.

"Hey." Bryce's soothing voice fills the dark car and instinctively I look up at him. His brows are drawn together in confusion and worry is etched all over his face. It's too much. His presence is too much. I feel those walls crumbling again and I finally put a name to what I'm feeling in this moment. *Fear.*

I'm afraid.

I'm terrified.

I have to get away from him.

Rationally I know he'd never hurt me. But terror overpowers any lucid thought and uses it as a trigger to memories. Bad memories. Things I thought I'd forgotten, but are now at the forefront of my mind. So I do what I have to do. What I never got a chance to do before.

I run.

# CHAPTER 9

## Two Years Ago

"Can I help you?" My eyes scan the room, searching for Lucas Carmical, owner of Carmical Construction. They fall to the nameplate on the desk the man speaking is sitting behind.

"Ma'am? Can I help you?" *No fucking way. Surely he's sitting in his boss' chair.* Guys like him don't work on Sunday. Hell, men as pretty as him shouldn't have to work at all. If he was mine, all he'd have to do is just wake up every morning.

"I'm looking for Lucas Carmical?"

He smiles, and it's so magnificently charming, it's nearly surreal. Actually, the whole fucking scene is surreal. This guy is beautiful. Stop-and-stare, take-a-picture, must-be-a-movie-star beautiful. Too beautiful to steal from. Which is exactly what I'm here to do.

"Call me Luke." Standing, he extends his hand out to me. He's tall, I'm guessing around six two or six three. The sleeves of his white dress shirt are rolled to his elbows, giving me a nice view of the tattoos that crawl up his arms. The top three buttons of his shirt are undone, exposing a chest that's hard and flawless and the start to what I'm sure is a perfect physique.

"Delilah." *Shit. Did I really just use my real name?* I'm nervous for all of two seconds. Then my hand touches his and I'm calm. *Weird...*

"How can I help you?" He's amused at my reaction. I'm sure he gets this a lot. That's probably why he didn't say my name. I'm glad he didn't. I might've died.

At the thought of death, I'm snapped out of fairytale land and back to the present. *Die...* That's what's going to happen to me if I don't get my shit together. I'm going to die.

Straightening my spine, I lift my chin and find a voice that isn't all breathy and stupid. "I'm looking for a job."

"What kinda work you do?" My mind fills with dirty thoughts of the work I could do to him. I'm getting sucked right back into the land of never-gonna-fucking-happen. Even thoughts of Mario killing me isn't enough to prevent me from daydreaming. But noticing the golden ring on Luke's left hand is.

"Well, fuck," I mutter, not realizing I've said the words out loud until Luke asks me to repeat myself. "I'm sorry. It's been a long day." He offers me a sympathetic, understanding look. *If he only knew the real reason behind my dismay.* Fucking marriage... Who came up with that shit anyway? And why do I have to have morals?

"Here." He hands me a piece of paper and I nearly laugh at the bold words centered on the top line. "Application for Employment." *Haven't seen one of these in a while.* "Take this home and fill it out. You can drop it off later this week."

"Thank you." Letting my hair hide my eyes, I pretend to look at the application while I search his desk for the keys to his truck. I find them tossed carelessly to the side. "I hate to bother you, but do you have something to drink?"

He pauses a moment. His eyes narrow slightly, but there's still a hint of a smile on his face. *Maybe he's thinking of stepping outside his marriage...* Doesn't matter. I couldn't do it if I tried. Well, with him, maybe I could.

"Of course. It's in the back. Just give me a minute." He walks away, leaving me alone and his keys only inches from my sticky fingers.

I always trust my gut. Right now, that bastard is telling me something is wrong. But my mind sees everything in black and white. Either I take the keys and live, or I don't and die. That's my choice. To hell with my instincts. This is about survival.

Quickly and quietly, I snatch the keys from his desk and shove them in the back pocket of my jeans. When he returns with a bottle of water, I graciously accept it.

"I'll get this back to you tomorrow," I promise. Then frown—feeling guilty for lying. "Thank you."

"My pleasure."

I allow myself one more glance at the beauty that is him before leaving. When my feet hit the concrete, my pace quickens. I look down the street for the black Mercedes parked a few houses down and nod. Even if he can't see me, he'll know in just a moment that it worked.

Without thinking twice about it, I hit the unlock button on the truck just as I'm rounding the hood. Climbing inside, I turn the ignition, slam it in drive, and tear out—not bothering to look and see if Luke walked outside or not. Truth is, I couldn't look.

There was something about his presence that made me feel different than I've ever felt before. I felt safe and protected. I had the sense he cared about me—a complete stranger to him.

"You're a fucking idiot," I tell myself. Out loud. I need to hear it, so I tell myself again and again until I make it to Mario's. By the time I get there, I finally believe it. And if I forget again, I can rest assured that Mario will remind me. After all, that's what I've been trained to believe. Not that I'm an idiot, particularly. But that I'm whatever he says I am.


"Get the fuck out of the truck." My heartbeat quickens at the tone of his voice as he jerks open the door.

Climbing out, I keep my eyes down and try to keep as much distance from him as possible. But it doesn't work. I'm still within arm's reach. My skull shakes and white light flashes behind my eyelids when his opened palm connects hard with the back of my head.

"What did I tell you, huh?" Now in front of me, his hand comes up again. This time, it slams against my ear causing it to ring and hurt in places deep inside my brain I never knew existed. "What the fuck did I say, D?"

"I'm sorry." I don't even know what I'm apologizing for. I'm just hoping the words are enough to keep me from getting hit again. *Nope... That didn't work.* A sharp pain shoots down my neck. I'm not sure where the blow actually landed, because the ringing still happening in my ear is enough to take my mind off it

"I told you three minutes. You took twice the time. What the fuck were you doing, D?" Grabbing my chin, he jerks my head back until I'm staring up at him. "Don't you lie either. You know I'll know if you are."

He's telling the truth. He can read me like a book. Even if he couldn't, I'd never lie. It's not possible. Not to him.

"He wasn't what I was expecting. I thought he was old, but he's young. And attractive." My voice falls slightly at my admission. *The truth.* Ha. *I really am an idiot.* The truth is fixing to get me killed.

I look up into Mario's big, dark eyes and see nothing but hate and evil. He's a massive man. He reminds me of that wrestler...The Bigshow...I think. But even if he were small, he'd still have the same power over me he holds at nearly six foot five. I've never feared a man so much in my life. Craig, my piece-of-shit brother, is a saint compared to this man.

I wish I could leave him. I want to walk away. But I can't. He owns me. If I stay, I live. If I leave, I die. My life is like a quarter—a quarter I can't flip because I'm scared of the answer no matter the outcome. Life as I know it is just as bad as the idea of death. Maybe even worse.

"You're a fuckin' whore. You know that?" I try to answer, but the hold he has on me makes it impossible to open my mouth or nod my head. "You're sick. You gotta itch that can only be scratched if you're on your back. You're a damaged bitch with some nasty fuckin' issues goin' on. You were used early and you fuckin' liked it."

While he stares down at me in disgust, I let the hate I feel toward myself cripple me further. He's right. I do have issues. As much as I despise him, I thank him for reminding me of how fucked up I really am. I was introduced to sex at an early age. It doesn't matter what kind of creature preyed on a young girl starved for attention. All that matters is it ruined me.

Now I'm addicted to sex. It's all I want. All I think about. I crave it like a drug. The release I get from it helps to distract my mind from a bigger issue—the monster inside my head that eats away at my feelings. Every time I have sex, it's like I'm chipping away at the memory that reminds me why I am the way I am. Maybe if I do it enough the memory will eventually fade and the monster will stay caged.

"Don't ever forget, D. Don't you *ever* forget who you belong to." He releases me, and instead of feeling relief, I feel rejection. I want his hands on me. I need him to punish me. To remind me. It's what I deserve. It's the only thing that makes me feel better.

He doesn't give me what I need, he just walks away. But I know he'll come back. He always does. He's not stupid enough to leave behind the one person who is his personal servant. His property. His submissive.

You see, Mario isn't my husband. He's not my boyfriend or my lover either. Hell, he's not even my friend.

He's my dominant.

Well, kinda.


Sunday is considered a day of repent. With repent comes forgiveness. But forgiveness is earned. In the eyes of Mario, the only way to earn something is to pay the price for my sins. I actually look forward to the physical punishment. It offers me a break from the mental abuse I have to endure the other six days of the week.

Today, I'm serving out my punishment in the cage, which is actually a dog crate just large enough for me to be on my hands and knees—mirroring the position of a dog. A rubber ball gag is strapped tightly around my face, preventing me from speaking and making it nearly impossible to swallow. This causes me to drool—like a dog.

I'm naked, cold and afraid of the unexpected. I long for Mario's return, even though I know with him comes pain. But with him also comes company. My fear of being alone outweighs my fear of pain which is something I enjoy. Something I yearn for.

Judging by my previous experiences, I have until my elbows nearly collapse from holding me up before he comes back. On his last trip in here, which could have been hours ago, he shoved a plug into my ass that was much larger than I could accommodate. He made it work, though--but only after he got pissed when he had to spit on it. It seems the greater my pain, the greater his pleasure. Even with my limited knowledge of BDSM relationships, I'm pretty sure that isn't how this is supposed to work. I mean, don't I get some aftercare? Some reassurance? Some special prize if I do well?

I might be sick in the head, but I'm not stupid. I know this isn't right. Truth is, I need this. I need to be told what to do. I need control in my life. I need to feel the physical pain. It's the only thing that keeps the darkness at bay. Before Mario, I never had that. And something was always missing. Now that I have it, I feel...almost human.

The worst part? I see this as a cure. He sees it as a turn-on. He's one sadistic, fucked-up monster who gets off on this shit. On controlling me. On hurting me both physically and emotionally. There's no aftercare or reassurance or prize. So he might be dominant and I might be submissive, but it's not in a traditional BDSM-lifestyle kind of way—if one even really exists.


I'm no longer in the "caged animal" position. My arms have given out on me. My legs would fail me, but they have nowhere else to fall. He's been gone entirely too long. So long that even though I'm in a windowless room, I'm pretty sure dawn is breaking.

My throat is dry. My skin is clammy. My heart seems to be beating a lot slower than it should. My ass is numb, as are my limbs. The skin around my mouth is cracked and sore. And I'm praying I'm near death. I'm ready for the darkness to take me, but as always, the universe cheats me out of an early death once again.

The sound of a door being opened is far off, but I'm conscious enough to know that it's the one leading to the storm cellar in Mario's backyard. Heavy footsteps descend the stairs— too hurriedly and too light to belong to Mario.

"Motherfucker..." The whispered word is like a song to my ears. If I die, I would at least like to do it in a more comfortable position. I can't see anything but the jeans and boots of a man standing merely feet from me. But I know that voice.

*Luke Carmical.*

I mumble a hello, but I don't think he hears it. *I wonder if he'll be willing to untie this ball gag from my mouth...* If so, I can properly greet him. And maybe even ask him WHERE THE FUCK IS MARIO?

"Just hold on, babe." He sounds so concerned. *How sweet.* I think he thinks I'm out of my mind. Or unconscious. I try again to speak—just to reassure him I'm alive and well...well, kinda. But the words are jumbled and incoherent.

He's mumbling a string of "motherfuckers", using the word in every form imaginable, while searching for something to open the locked cage with. I'm impressed at his ability to use such profane language in so many ways, but I'm even more impressed when he finds a way to break the lock.

"I got you," he says, reaching in and pulling me out. Carrying me in his arms, he takes me to a wooden chair on the other side of the room—the chair Mario often sits in to tell me how pathetic I am. *Where the hell is he?*

I scream my protest when he tries to sit me down. He whispers the famous heroic words, "Nobody is gonna hurt you," and "I got you now," in my ear. I could give a shit less about that. My problem lies in the plug still occupying my asshole.

"Ugh! Ugh! Ugh!" I scream, like an idiot. When he lowers those powerful baby-blue eyes on me, I motion with mine toward my ass—hoping like hell he can read between the lines. He can't. He just looks at me in confusion. His whole face wrinkles with worry. Finally, he puts my feet on the floor and holds my weight with one arm while he undoes the gag from around my head.

The moment it's pulled from my mouth, I flex my jaw— cringing from the pain and relief I feel all at the same time. I let out another string of incoherent mumbles, but he still doesn't understand. So he just bears my weight and looks down at me. While I look up at him.

There's a fire in his eyes. He's angry, but sympathetic. I'm assuming his anger isn't directed toward me. I have a feeling Mario will soon meet his wrath--if the fucker ever decides to show up.

After I manage a couple dry swallows and have control over my mouth, somewhat, I try again. "I can't sit down."

"Why?" This part should be embarrassing. But I've felt a lot of things in my life, most of which were a lot worse than embarrassment. This is nothing.

"Butt pug." I guess he gets what I'm trying to say, because his face darkens and he closes his eyes a minute. I find it amusing. "Untie me." He quickly unties my hands, and spends the next few minutes rubbing the life back into my wrists.

"You need me to..."

My eyebrows raise at his words. Or at least I think they do. I'm still kinda numb. And I'm kinda dizzy. And for some reason, everything around me is blurring. And then, there's nothing.

Over the next day, I drifted in and out of consciousness. The first time I woke up, I was in a tub filled with warm, soapy water. I recognized the bathroom as Mario's. The second time, I was on a couch that wasn't Mario's with an IV in my arm. I tried to pull it out, but was too weak. The third time, someone was holding my head while I drank water.

Now I'm fully awake, my whole body aches and the clock on the wall says it's after eight. The lack of sunlight filtering through the windows says it's night time. And the man propped on the desk across from me just told me it was Tuesday. Last time I was conscious, it was Monday. By the way, the man is Luke Carmical.

"Do you have any pretzels?" I ask, hoping like hell he does. Giving me a smirk, he crosses his arms over his chest and shakes his head.

"That's your first question?"

"Is that your answer?" His smirk turns into a warm smile.

"No."

"No that's not your answer, or no you don't have any pretzels? 'Cause I really want some."

"I'll get you whatever you want to eat, but first you have to answer some questions." He's still smiling, but his tone is more serious.

"Ask away," I mumble, coming to a sitting position on the couch. The IV is gone and in its place is a cotton ball covered by a Band-Aid. A Ninja Turtle Band-Aid. *Impressive.*

"What were you doing in that cage?"

"Mario put me there."

"Were you willing to go?"

"Yes."

"Why?"

"Because it was Sunday."

My rapid-fire responses seem to annoy him. I guess he wants more. He ain't getting more.

"You seem like a no-bullshit kinda girl. Is that right?"

"That's right."'

"Then I'm going to give it to you straight."

"Please do." I won't lie to this man. I have no reason to. I presumed Mario was coming back. He didn't. Therefore, this man saved my life. Either I hate him, or thank him. He seems too nice to hate. So I'll have to go with the alternative.

"You stole my truck." *Shit.* I did steal his truck. I'm assuming he's waiting for confirmation.

"Yeah...sorry about that."

He shrugs. "It's the twenty-first century, babe. I tracked it with GPS. Clearly, you're an amateur."

"And here I was thinking I'd impressed you." I'm flirting. I know that. But it's innocent, I swear.

"I tracked it to an address that belongs to Mario Hernandez. He told me where I could find you."

"How thoughtful of him," I grit through my teeth. Luke's jaw tightens, mirroring my anger.

"It wasn't in that fucking storm cellar either." Now I'm confused. "I was leaving when I saw him walking in the backyard. He looked suspicious. I got curious, went to see what he was up to, and he ran. I started to chase him, but I saw the door to the cellar. Something told me to look. So I looked. That's when I found you."

"Wow. That's really...such an amazing story." I have more sarcastic shit to say, but he cuts me off.

"You were caged like an animal," he growls, his eyes darkening further with every word he speaks. "Dehydrated, cold and abused. Your hands and feet were purple from lack of blood circulation. Your lips were cracked and bleeding from being pried open so wide. Not to mention the plug in your ass fit for an elephant. So don't sit there and try to play this off like it's nothing."

I sit and study him a minute. This brooding man. This Luke Carmical—heroic savior slash butt plug remover of mine, and wonder just how much of my life I should actually tell him.

There's something demanding about him. The same thing I found in Mario, only he's more sympathetic and soft. *I wonder if he's...*

"I took care of you. Brought you here and haven't left your side. Nobody knows your secret but me. I need to keep it that way."

Wait... What? "Why?"

I was betting on him insisting I go to the police. But by the look in his eyes, I'm pretty sure going to the police is out of the question.

"Because I found Mario."

"And?" I ask, feeling a sense of uneasiness at his hesitation.

"And...I killed him."

*Well...that changes things.*

# CHAPTER 10

## PRESENT

My Nikes pound the concrete at a pace I never knew I was capable of. After I'd managed to escape out the passenger door, I'd tripped and now Bryce was only several feet behind me. Still, if he's gonna catch me, he's gonna have to work for it.

I know Mario is dead. I know this man isn't him. But there are some striking familiarities that I just can't shake. I can't believe I didn't see it when we had sex. Maybe it was the intimacy I felt with Bryce that shielded the similarities between him and Mario. But now they're all I see. They're so frightening, I'm running harder and faster despite the protests of my lungs. And he's gaining on me.

Figuring fuck it—he'll just have to catch and kill me—I slow down to a steady jog. Surprisingly, he slows too. Either he's just as winded as I am, or he's respectfully keeping his distance. I'm calling bullshit on the latter. If he were willing to give me some space, then why the hell is he chasing me?

"Please," I call over my shoulder. Or rather pant. "Just…" I struggle to find the wind to finish my sentence. "Leave me alone."

"Can't do that, Love," he says, the endearment just as spine-tingling in this moment as it was when he whispered it in my room. *Hey! You're running for your life, dumbass! Stop finding shit sexy about your potential abductor.*

"Why?" I ask, thinking of how absurd it is to keep running if I'm still going to carry on a conversation with him.

"'Cause you're not in the best part of town." Noticing my surroundings, I find myself in the deepest part of the projects Hattiesburg has to offer. *Shit.* Only I would run in the wrong direction.

Considering my chances of being killed by a stray bullet, he suddenly doesn't seem that damn scary. Plus I'm on the verge of dying from exhaustion anyway. So I stop. My hands rest on my knees as I lean over and greedily fill my lungs with the cold night air. I've noticed he's stopped too, but is still several feet behind me. And the bastard ain't even winded. Good thing. I need all the oxygen for myself.

"Didn't mean to scare you." The low voice I once found threatening is now soothing in the quiet night.

"Well, you did," I snap, turning around to face him. *So much for all that work...I'm winded again just at the sight of him.* In the glow of the streetlight, he appears larger than I remember. But there's something soft and welcoming about his eyes. He's wearing his cut, and I mean *wearing* it.

The thick black leather seems to mold to his shoulders and chest. Chains cover his stomach, connecting the two sides. The black hood from his sweater is pulled over his head, and stops just above his green eyes that seem to sparkle even in the darkness. He looks like a beast. *A very sexy beast. A beast that fucks me hard and makes me come even harder.*

"I said I didn't mean to scare you. I meant it. If I did, I apologize. I won't apologize again." Clearly, he's telling me to fucking drop it. And for some reason, I fucking want to.

"Sorry I ran." I don't know why I'm apologizing, but I hold my breath in anticipation of him accepting my apology.

"It's okay." And just like that, I feel like a weight has been lifted off my shoulders.

Yes, I know I was running from this big scary man only moments ago. No, I don't want to discuss the level of fucked up this brings me to. We've already established I have issues. Moving forward.

"You remind me of someone from my past. Old memories were triggered. Memories Luke helped me to forget and fears he helped me to overcome. You awakened them. I haven't felt that way in a really long time. It was...scary and foreign to me."

Curiosity sparks in his eyes at my admission. "You're not afraid when I'm fucking you." My body sizzles at the reminder.

"That was...different."

"Different?" Boy, he just doesn't want to let this go.

"Well, when we're fucking you're...I don't know..." I throw my hands up in confusion. "Nothing you did reminded me of him. But tonight I saw some of him in you."

His face darkens, and I instantly feel guilty. "You'll tell me about him one day. But right now, we need to get back."

I'll *tell* him? Can he not ask? I start to come back with some snarky remark, but his demand awakens something inside me. Something I don't fear. Something I long for. Something I hadn't realized I'd been missing until this moment.

*Control.*

We walk in comfortable silence back to my car. Once we're there, he opens the door for me, puts the keys in the ignition and even buckles my seatbelt. I don't particularly enjoy the over-show of affection, but I refrain from saying anything.

"Go straight home," he says, his face so close to mine I can smell the cool whiskey scent of his breath. "I'll be a few minutes behind you." He doesn't wait for my response. He just closes the door and walks away.

I really want some chocolate. I would give my left tit for a Skor bar. I'm determined to stop and get one. Not just to defy him, but because, dammit, I'm a grown woman. I can do what I want. I want to fight against that urge to let him control me. But even my determination isn't enough to persuade that submissive girl I thought was buried deep inside me. Before I realize it, I'm already home.

Not just the clubhouse.

Not just my place of employment.

*Home.*


Sneaking back through my bedroom window like a teenage girl, I barely have it shut before I feel eyes on me. Turning, I find Red and Dallas sitting on my bed.

"We need to establish some ground rules," I say, knowing good and damn well they won't work. "Don't come in my room unless you're invited. By me." Glancing at the locked door, I frown. "How the hell did y'all get in anyway?"

"The window." Red shrugs, reaching for the duffel in my hands. Jerking it out of her reach, I give her a look of warning. She just rolls her eyes.

"Don't come into my room again without my permission. Understood?" They both nod in agreement. "Good. Do you need this shit right now?"

"Yes," they say, a little too urgently. *Idiots.*

The next ten minutes of my life are wasted rolling them three perfect fat blunts with Hattiesburg's finest weed, while they sit in silence and watch. Until Red speaks. "I can roll a blunt, ya know."

I give her an incredulous look. "You tell me that now?"

"Well, it's been a while. I figured you could do it better."

"Well..." I start, mocking her annoying voice that really isn't very annoying. "You can bet your ass I won't be doing it again."

Handing them the cigars, I offer my best fake smile before lifting my window. "Get out." Too excited about their soon high to be bothered with my curt dismissal, they exit the same way they entered.

I lock the window behind them, then strip down to my evening attire—cutoff shorts and a "Support Your Local Renegades" tank. Taking one final look in the mirror, I darken my red lips and fluff my hair before walking into the main room, ready to get the night started, but not as anxious as I am for it to end.


I find myself looking for him all night. Every time the door opens, I wait in anticipation for his face. When I don't see it, a feeling of disappointment I'm not comfortable with courses through my body. By two a.m., I decide I hate him. I hate him for not being here. I hate that my body craves him. I hate I feel this way when I really want to feel nothing. But mostly, I hate that I don't hate him at all.

It's been a slow night. I've spent most of my time on my phone, playing a stupid game that's highly addictive and makes me borderline crazy. Tonight I've been nothing more than a pretty face to look at. And that's pushing it. The guys here have been more interested in their endless pool games than they have with me. But I give them beer when they need it, and I even pop popcorn. So I'm doing my job.

"Go to bed, Delilah." I look up from my phone to find Scratch in front of me smiling. "We're good here."

"I don't mind, really." As I say it, I can feel a yawn forming. I fight like hell against it, but there's no stopping those damn things.

"Goodnight, babe." He leans over the counter and grabs a beer, placing a sloppy, wet kiss on my cheek.

"As long as y'all are up, I'm up." He shakes his head and shrugs. As bad as I want to go to bed, the desire to do my job and do it well is greater. All the other women have abandoned me. This isn't the first time I've been the last girl standing, and I'm sure it won't be the last.

"You really don't listen, do you?" Something warm spreads through me at the sound of Bryce's voice. My heart even stutters a little. *Weird.*

"What's the fun in that?" I ask, smiling up at him. He looks tired, like he hasn't had sleep in some time. I'm reminded that he's been up longer than I have. Still, he looks incredible.

"Come on." Snatching my phone from my fingers, he tucks it inside his cut. "We're going to bed."

"I'm good."

"Delilah." The way he says my name…that underlying meaning and evident warning in his voice…it does something to me. Scratch could tell me to go to bed all day, hell, he could even scream it. But it doesn't have near the effect Bryce's one-word demand has. And all he said was my name.

I join him on the other side of the bar, and look up into his bloodshot eyes that look like they'll close just any moment. He gestures with his hand toward the hall and my feet immediately start moving in that direction.

I fidget with the hem of my shirt the entire walk to my room. I'm nervous, anxious and overwhelmed by his presence. I like it, and I don't. A part of me wants to turn and run again, the other wants to know what this night has in store.

*Will he want to fuck me again?*

*Do I want him to fuck me again?*

Well, hell yeah. My thighs clench together at just the thought.

"Are we going to fuck?" I blurt out, turning to face him just outside my closed door.

"No." His one-word answer is a blow to my pride. I'm a little disappointed, and can't help but frown.

"Then you can't come in." He studies me a minute with a blank expression. The longer he stares at me, the more nervous I become.

"Open the door, Delilah."

"This is my room. I have the right to say no. And I don't want you here." *Liar.*

Shoving his hands in his pocket, he looks down at me. He looks a little perturbed for a moment, but quickly conceals it. "I've had a long night. I'm tired. I'm cold and I stink." *I don't think he stinks… I think he smells quite delicious—like fuel and leather and cigarette smoke.* "I want a hot shower and to sleep in a warm bed with a pretty girl under sheets that don't smell like another man's ass."

*He thinks I'm pretty? He said it. He thinks I'm pretty. But I know I'm pretty. So why does hearing him tell me make me blush?*

"Is that too much to ask, Delilah?"

"Um…no?"

"Don't answer my question with a question. Tell me the truth." He drops his voice and quirks an eyebrow at me, leaning in a little closer. "Is that too much to ask?"

"That's not too much to ask," I say, honestly. I mean, my job is to entertain. This can be considered entertainment. Intimate, but entertaining nonetheless.

"Thank you. Can I use your shower?" I nod, noticing for the first time the bag he has slung over his shoulder.

While he showers, I sit on my bed and pout. Never have I been turned down by a man. Here I am, all but throwing myself at him, and he doesn't want me. I've never doubted myself more than I do in this moment. I thought the last time was great. And on top of that, he's a man. So why the hell doesn't he want to fuck?

Kicking off my shoes, I pull the band from my hair and shake out the long locks. Keeping my clothes on, I curl under the covers in a ball—making sure to put as much distance between me and the other side of the bed as possible. I feel insecure and unwanted. My body is the only thing I have going for me—I'm not smart, I'm not very funny and I'm beyond damaged. Besides sex, there's nothing else desirable about me.

The bed dips and I freeze. I'd been so deep in my own thoughts I must have missed the sound of the shower cutting off or the door opening. But the clean, fresh aroma of his skin fills my senses. Without realizing it, I close my eyes and inhale deep.

"Is something wrong, babe?" *Babe? Shit... Why does that suck so bad too?*

"I'm just tired."

"You're just lying." I roll my eyes at his words, even though he can't see them.

"I'm not used to men sleeping in my bed. Usually, there's a reason for them to be in my room. You confuse me...You make me feel unwanted." I don't know where I got the courage to admit that, and I damn sure don't know why in the hell I would. It makes me sound pathetic.

"There are six empty beds here. I could've chosen any, but I'd rather stay here...with you. How does that make you feel unwanted?"

Rolling to my back, I look up at him. His face is stoic. "I'm the only woman here. You don't want to sleep on sheets that smell like a man's ass. You didn't have a choice. I was your only option."

He offers me a smile with a hint of sadness. *Great... Now he feels sorry for me. If he offers me a pity fuck...* "If there were a hundred beds, filled with a hundred of the hottest women, I'd still want to spend the night in here with you."

I roll my eyes. "Really? I'm not an insecure little girl who needs to be reassured that she's pretty and desirable."

His eyebrow quirks. "Then stop acting like one." Not very many people have ever put me in my place. But he just did. With a smooth, cat-like movement, he crawls over me. My breath hitches at his nearness.

"You know you're gorgeous," he says, his green eyes sparkling with amusement and mischief. "There's not a man here who doesn't want to fuck you." Sliding his hands up my sides, he pushes my shirt over my head. "I *want* to fuck you." Fisting the waistband of my shorts, he leans back on his haunches and jerks them down my legs along with my panties.

"But tonight, I wanted to prove to you you're more than just a lay. You're a woman I find desirable despite how good it feels to be inside you." His hands slide up my legs as he once again covers my body with his own. "Or how sexy you look when your tits bounce up and down."

His mouth surrounds my nipple and my back bows. The sensation shoots straight to my core, and I grind my hips against him. "Or how good you smell." He buries his face between my breasts and inhales. "But," he starts, kissing a path down my stomach, "maybe if I tasted you"—his mouth moves lower, planting a soft kiss on my bare mound before he stops and looks up at me through his lashes—"I could find the most desirable thing of all."

Pushing my knees apart with his hands, his mouth closes over my exposed pussy—nearly devouring its entirety. My fingers fist at his head—searching for hair that's not quite long enough to grab. My back arches further and I press my head into the pillow. A low, guttural moan builds inside me at the feel of his mouth kissing me...licking me...sucking me...feasting on me as if I'm the most delicious thing he's ever tasted.

Two thick fingers press against my entrance and I buck my hips against them. With one last long, slow stroke of his tongue, he pulls back and thrusts his fingers deep inside me. "You feel like satin." His voice is low, dirty and erotic. "You taste like sweet rain." I moan louder, feeling my orgasm building around his fingers and heightened by his vulgar words. "And you have the prettiest, wettest, most *perfect* fuckin' pussy I've ever seen."

His confession is my undoing. It's mind numbing...all I can do is feel—the coolness of his breath across my oversensitive flesh...the steady rhythm of his fingers...the feather-light kisses on my thighs...the electricity flowing through my veins with every beat of my heavy heart. It's riveting.

The next few moments are lost in a blur. I'm vaguely aware of his voice, but I can't make out his words. My rubbery limbs are folded and my body turned until my back is against his chest. Lips are at my ear—softly demanding I do something. I hope like hell it's sleep. Because that's exactly where I'm headed.

# CHAPTER 11

A warm, manly scent invades my nostrils—waking me from slumber. I stretch, smile and roll to my side to face the one who is occupying my bed. But he ain't here. There's not even a note on the pillow. My mood takes a nosedive. *Bastard...I knew he was too good to be true.*

I search my bedside table for my phone to check the time, fumbling with the random shit cluttering it and knocking nearly everything to the floor. Then I realize Bryce took my phone, and never gave it back. *Maybe he left it on the bar...*

I have bed head, morning breath and am wearing nothing but an oversized, rumpled-up T-shirt. I look like a throwaway from trash city. And he's sitting at the bar—just like yesterday. I hate I look like shit, but glad I caught him before he left.

"Good morning, Delilah," he purrs. When I face him, I abandon thoughts of my phone when I find him looking well rested, happy and something else...

Wait.

I know that look. That's a just-fucked look if I've ever seen one. But he didn't just fuck me, so who in the hell is the culprit? And why am I so angry and possessive over him?

*Fucking Linda...*

"Are you not speaking to me today?" I can feel him smiling behind me. I don't like it. And he sounds amused. I don't like that either.

"I'm not a morning person," I mumble, pouring my first cup of java of the day. When the hot, delicious liquid slides down my throat, I can't help but let out an audible sigh. My eyes are even closed. When I open them, they're magnetically pulled to his. And he very much likes what he sees.

Who knew drinking coffee could be so sexy? Especially mixed with morning hair, breath and disgusting eye crust. By the way, nobody wakes up looking flawless. We all look like shit. Except for him, of course. He looks perfect. Or maybe my standards just aren't very high.

Grabbing my smokes from under the bar, I pull one of the thin cigarettes from the pack. The damn things are super tiny, but incredibly satisfying, and a perfect way to start my day.

"You smoke?" he asks, reaching his huge arm across the bar to light my cigarette before I can do it myself.

"Only one. Only in the morning. Only with coffee." I take a few puffs, making sure it's well lit, then pull in a deep drag, letting the nicotine calm my nerves and the smoke coat my lungs.

"That's...unusual."

"Is it?" I ask, fighting like hell to keep my attention on anything that isn't him. I opt for the neon beer sign behind him.

"Why do you only smoke one? Only in the morning?"

I shrug. "A metaphor, I guess. I stole it from a movie, but my reason is different." Bracing my arms on the bar, I lift myself up and turn toward him, dangling my legs over the other side. "This guy in the movie walked around with an unlit cigarette in his mouth. He said by not lighting it, he was taking away its power to kill him."

"So what's your reason?" He's intrigued. Nobody has ever found me interesting before. I kinda like that he does.

"I light it for the opposite effect. I'm *giving* it the power to kill me. That way, I'm taking the power away from anyone else."

"I don't follow."

I hold up the cigarette between us like it's some sort of magical object. "If someone were to kill me today, whether it be by accident or intentional, they would be doing me a favor. Statistics say if I smoke, I have a sixty percent chance of dying from complications related to smoking. So if someone accidentally kills me, they should view it as doing me a favor. If someone intentionally kills me, I refuse to give them the glory. Because chances are, I'd have suffered a much more horrible death."

Taking another drag, I patiently wait for him to reflect on his recent knowledge of me. Just when I think he isn't going to say anything, he speaks.

"That's the craziest fuckin' thing I've ever heard." The humor in his voice is a first for me, and I can't help but look at him. He seems playful, fun and very similar to the other guys. He's nothing like the brooding, demanding man he usually is. It's... refreshing. And maybe just a little disappointing.

"What in the hell have you been doing with your time to find the opportunity to even think about this shit?" He lets out a laugh--standing and grabbing my cup before walking around the bar and refilling both our mugs with fresh coffee.

"I do a lot of deep thinking," I say in my defense. He laughs harder. The sound is deep, throaty and way too foreign on his lips. But I like this softer, more normal side of him.

"You need a hobby." He hands me my coffee, still shaking his head at my ridiculous way of thinking.

"I have plenty to do around here, trust me." I take a gulp of the hot coffee, cringing when it burns my tongue. I feel his eyes on me and turn to find them narrowed. He looks like he wants to chastise me, or some shit, but he says nothing.

"And I have a hobby," I say in hopes of lightening the mood. It works. He smirks up at me, a twinkle of mischief in his eyes.

"I'm dying to hear it." Taking the cigarette from my fingers, he puts it between his lips and winks. It looks even smaller on his lips and I find it funny. So funny, I snort. Like an idiot.

"I'm practicing to be a trampoline gymnast." He looks at me like I've grown an extra nose.

"A what?"

"You know, one of those people who do tricks on a trampoline."

"Show me." There's a dare in his eyes. He doesn't believe me.

"Well, I don't have a trampoline or I would."

Rolling his eyes, another move that doesn't match his personality at all, he stubs out the cigarette. "You can't be a trampoline gymnast and not have a trampoline, babe."

"Shit," he mutters, suddenly standing and pulling his phone from his cut. He checks it, then mumbles something about being late. "Gotta run. I'll see you next week."

A sudden wave of sadness crashes over me. A whole week without him? I mean, I'm not attached or anything, but I kinda like having him around. "K, bye." I give him a small wave, but he pushes my hand aside and grabs my chin in his massive fingers.

"Be good." Two words. One demand. And a set of lips that's merely centimeters from mine. *He's going to kiss me.* And he does. On my fucking forehead. Then he's gone.

And he still has my phone...

*Great.*


"Morning, girl." I look up from my now cold coffee to see Linda sauntering in the room. From the hall. *She didn't go home...*

"Did you fuck Bryce?" I ask, knowing good and damn well I don't have the right to. She stops in her tracks and wrinkles her face up at me.

"Um, no. I tried, but he wasn't having it." She dismisses the issue with a wave of her hand. "To hell with him," she says, walking behind the bar. I spin on the counter to face her. "Any man who doesn't want pussy or head first thing in the morning is gay in my book."

On the outside, my face is impassive as I give a bored nod. On the inside, I'm fist punching the air and grinning ear to ear.

"Maddie's coming home tomorrow." Linda rolls her eyes at the news and I groan.

"I don't like her," I mumble, poking my lip out on a pout. "I feel like we have to walk on eggshells when she's here."

"Yeah, I don't like her either. But she's family." Linda uses her best Luke impersonation which always makes me laugh.

Maddie is like an ol' lady, but she doesn't have a man. Her and one of the guys had a thing for a while, but that shit ended soon after he got his patch. But Maddie is like Luke's little sister. She's been raised by the club and is held to the same high standard as all the other ol' ladies. But for some reason, she's worse than the others. The best way to get along with her is to just keep my distance. Which isn't a difficult task.

"They're going out of town to get her." Linda raises her eyebrows suggestively at me. "I say we take the night off and do something fun."

"Work is fun," I remind her. It's a party here all day and all night. Who the hell wants to do that shit on their day off?

"I mean real fun. The kind that involves us being catered to, not the other way around." Thinking harder, I could use some strange cock. And maybe even a strange woman--if she appeals to me. I wouldn't mind being wined and dined for a night.

"Okay. What time we leaving?"

"As soon as you get your cute little ass dressed."

I like it.


Normally I wouldn't be dressing to go out at eight o'clock in the morning. But when we go out, we go away—meaning if we're hitting a club, it damn sure won't be in Hattiesburg. Linda scored us a free night at The Roosevelt in New Orleans, thanks to her cousin's friend's dog walker's some shit, who works there. Bottomless Hurricanes, jazz music and hundreds of weird people are just what I need.

Jealous yet? Well, you should be. Keep in mind that it's Tuesday—some claim it's the most productive work day of the week. I'll be partying in The Big Easy...eating beignets at the world-renowned Café Du Monde...shopping for art in The French Quarter...listening to small children make music with random shit like beer cans and buckets.

My bag is packed. I'm dressed—not in my going-out clothes, but still stylishly sexy. You never know who you'll meet on the journey. I lock my bedroom door, not that it'll do any damn good, and slip out the window. Linda is ready and waiting by my car when I round the corner.

"Tonight is gonna be epic!" She's way too damn excited.

"You sound like an ol' lady." At my words, she frowns then shudders.

"Ugh."

We don't hate the ol' ladies. Sure we talk shit behind their backs, but it's nothing we wouldn't say to their annoying little faces.

Tonight their heads will be held high while they sit around some bar, drink cheap beer and force themselves to behave so they don't bring any unwanted attention to their man. They'll wear their patches proudly, and walk with a little more confidence to the bathroom knowing they're untouchable.

Me? Tonight I'll be sitting in some bar, drinking expensive wine and not giving two shits about my behavior. I'll do what I want and who I want without feeling guilty or ashamed. Nobody will be claiming any territory on me tonight, because I belong to nobody. Hell, without my cell phone, they won't even be able to contact me.

Maybe Linda is right about our epic night. Maybe she doesn't sound like an ol' lady at all. Maybe she sounds like who she is—who I am. Who everyone should want to be.

A clubwhore.

\*\*\*\*

"Where have you been?" Linda yells over the music. At this point, the two hours she spent on her hair and makeup seems like a waste. Her mascara is running, her lipstick is smeared and her hair is sweaty, and sticking to the side of her head. She looks like she's having a blast. "I've been calling and texting you all night!"

Once we left the room, we went our separate ways—neither of us needing the company of the other. Or the competition. "I've been in Hustler. I forgot my phone at home," I yell back, leaving out the details about Bryce having it. But she doesn't care. She's pointing to the ass on the man next to her and giving me a thumbs up. I return it. "I'm going to Esther's."

"Where?"

"Esther's!" She nods and I turn to leave, anxious to get the hell out of this place before I become sweaty and gross and mess my two-hour face up.

I stumble onto the crowded, cracked sidewalk filled with people celebrating the fact that it's Tuesday. Some are dressed like me—super high heels that are uncomfortable as hell and a mini dress that looks more like a tube top. Some are dressed more casual—jeans and T-shirts. Some are in costume. So far, I've seen about a gazillion *Day of the Dead* faces, a few pirates, a silver man, gold man, blue man and green man, a couple brides and even Barney—the big purple dinosaur.

This is what I love about this city. You can be anybody you want. I just spent the last three hours of my life thinking I wanted to be a stripper. They just make it look so fun. But they soon showed me the real truth about stripping. The routines get repetitive, the strippers get lazy and the men become more obnoxious as the night progresses. In other words, they crushed my dreams.

Esther's is the most upscale club on Bourbon. They even have a velvet rope and a big bouncer like you see on TV. And, just like on TV, if you're hot enough, you don't have to wait in line—you're ushered in to one of the many tables and often seated with someone you don't know. Judging by this crowd, I'm afraid I might have some competition. So I wait patiently at the back of the line.

It's cool tonight, but not cold. Just enough to make me shiver every now and then, but not enough to have me snatching a parka off someone's back. Compared to the clubs that are hot and make you feel sticky, it's refreshing—even with the scent of piss, sewage and vomit in the air.

An overly loud group of men wearing suits makes its way down the center of the street. They're drunk, obviously rich and very good looking—like, all of them. *I wonder if they're brothers.*

"We need three girls!" one shouts, and I'm astonished at the amount of women in line ahead of me that raise their hands like a bunch of desperate losers. I guess the pickings are pretty slim tonight. But I'd take Barney home before I raised my hand. I'm not that hopeless.

"You." He's looking at me. The girl in front of me, who I'm woman enough to say is better looking than I am, points to herself. "Not you. You." This time, there's no denying who he's talking to. And all eyes in line are on me.

"Wanna party with me and my boys tonight?" *Ugh.* I hate when they refer to their friends as *boys*. But what the hell? They look good. My feet hurt, and my hair is starting to frizz. And...I didn't have to raise my hand to get their attention.

I flash him my best smile. "Only if you can keep up."

"Oh, baby," he says, giving me a devilish grin. "I can keep up. Question is, can you?"

Stepping out of line, I loop my arm through his. "I guess we'll find out," I whisper seductively, nipping his earlobe with my teeth. He growls a promise of taking me places I've never been, or some shit, as we move to the front of the line and follow the group inside the club.

The place is very dimly lit and lined wall to wall with large booths that surround the dance floor. Red chandeliers illuminate the center of the room, and one single red bulb hangs over each booth. There's no bar, only waiters who come to your table. If you don't have a table, you don't get in—hence the long line outside.

Some techno beat is pumping out through the speakers while people dance wildly. This is the type of place you can order ecstasy. Or if you hang around long enough, someone will slip PCP in your drink. Thankfully I'm buzzed to the point of not giving a shit. But I do make a mental note to keep an eye on my drink at all times. Until I forget, of course.

The guys I'm with must be "somebody" because we're ushered to the VIP section reserved on the back wall, centering the dance floor. It's quieter here, considering the speakers are pointed away from us—I guess important people need to be heard when they have shit to say.

The booth can accommodate at least eight people, but twelve of us manage to squeeze in. Somehow I end up in the center with a girl on my right and the "You" guy on my left.

I'm handed a champagne flute already filled to the rim. The guy on my left leans up and gives a toast. "Congratulations, Mark. You fuckin' deserve it." I don't know who Mark is. I don't know what he deserves. But I smile and clink my glass to everyone else's.

Turning to the girl on my right, I find her smiling at me, before holding her glass up and taking a sip. "I think you're so hot..." Her eyes fall to my cleavage, then lower to my exposed thighs. Leaning closer, I put my mouth at her ear—noticing how she holds her breath in anticipation. I smile.

Tonight will be epic indeed.

# CHAPTER 12

Lucy is her name. She doesn't bore me with small talk about her shitty little life. She only wants one thing—for me to keep doing what I'm doing to her.

We've been making out, dancing, drinking and having the ultimate girl-on-girl experience for hours. I like to leave a little to the imagination, so I haven't been too forward with her—yet. But my hands and mouth have been on every part of her exposed skin. I slipped my hand between her thighs once, but had to pull back when she all but dry humped my fingers. I like a more intimate setting for the good stuff, and these guys have gotten a free show for long enough.

Mark, the man of the night, has joined in, making this a threesome. The man I walked in here with is still around, but he wants me to give him attention. Tonight I want to be the one receiving it. So far, it's worked in my favor. For everything I don't do to Lucy, she attempts to do to me. Mark is the ultimate giver too—never asking me to touch him, but anxious to put his hands on me.

I'm in the middle of telling Mark and Lucy about my fabulous job as an offshore scuba diver when a tray of shots arrives. The waiter passes them around, then waits patiently for us to finish.

I quickly throw mine back, replacing the glass on the tray before leaning back in my seat and pulling Lucy's leg into my lap. Throwing my own legs over Mark, he scoots closer and somehow we manage to make our own little private nest in the booth.

But suddenly it doesn't feel very private.

It's been invaded.

By green eyes.

*He's here.*

Standing front and center.

Looking across the table.

Staring blankly...at me.

He's not angry. But he ain't happy either. He's just...well, like I said—blank. Expressionless. Emotionless. Oh, and intimidating as fuck. The whole booth just shut up, and there's now space between me and Mark. Lucy could give a shit less.

Reaching inside his cut, he pulls out my phone. "Having fun?" he whispers. Or shouts. Or maybe he says nothing. Hell, I don't know. I'm hammered, I'm horny, he's here and suddenly I don't want Mark or Lucy or Barney anymore.

I. Want. Him.

"Who is that?" Lucy asks, raking her fingers up my naked thigh. The movement is a turn-on. Not because it's her hand, but because she's doing it and *he's* watching.

"This is Bryce. Bryce, this," I say, turning Lucy's face to mine and giving her a slow, sexy kiss before turning back to him, "is Lucy." I'm expecting a flicker of excitement...a flash of heat... that tongue of his to run across his bottom lip...something. Instead, his eyes darken. And not in that sultry bedroom kind of way either. The other way.

Instantly he owns me. Nobody else exists in this room but me and him. We could be the only two people on the planet, that's how I feel right now. Before, there were no butterflies, nor was there shortness of breath. I blame that on the alcohol. But right now, there's not enough liquor in New Orleans to make me ignore the power he has over me.

"I told you to be good, Delilah. I meant it." I feel his voice everywhere. It seems to reverberate through me—shaking parts of my body I want to feel his mouth on. My head is swimming. I'm weak...vulnerable...submissive...

He sets my phone on the table, making the move seem monumental. Or maybe he's just monumental. "Nice to meet you, Lucy." He doesn't look at her. Hell, he's not even looking at me. He's looking right through me. I can feel the intense heat of those emerald greens, scorching my lungs and melting my heart. It's hard to breathe—hard to just...be.

I watch every step he takes toward the door. My soul seems to ache as he walks away. But the fog lifts when he's out of sight. My head is clear. I'm no longer burning on the inside. I'm free to go back to doing whatever the hell I want. His absence has broken the spell he put me under only moments ago. Problem is, that's not the only thing that's broken.

My desire to be here is broken. My hungry appetite for the delicious Lucy is broken. My selfish want I felt for Mark is broken. I hate this place. I feel alone and abandoned. Every part of me aches. I know who for, I just don't understand why. Reality is, I barely know the guy.

Instead of telling the gang bye, exchanging numbers, or hugs, or promising to accept their MyFace friend requests, I leave without a word. Crawling over the bodies in the booth, I fight my way to freedom, grab my phone and throw back one of the shots still left on the tray.

I'm stumbling through the club, drunk and attention deprived. Outside, I feel even more alone in the near vacant streets of the city. It's nearing six, and the streets are beginning to shut down for cleaning. With every dark alley I pass, I pray he'll grab me and pull me into it.

I keep looking over my shoulder in hopes that he's near. I even force my face to look frightened, thinking maybe he's watching and will come to my rescue just to reassure me the bogey monster ain't got shit on him.

Nothing.

It's just me, the homeless and a few other drunks who pay me no attention. Soon I'm at the revolving doors of my hotel. In one final desperate effort, I scream my room number to the streets—cupping my hand around my mouth. Pathetic? Yes. Do I care? No.

No matter the crazy events that transpired tonight, I'm still not embarrassed, ashamed or regretful. I've come to terms with accepting that my life can sometimes suck. I mean, everyone can't have it all. At least not all the time. But right now, I just feel like I have nothing. It's a first in a long time for me. Good thing I'm a look-at-the-glass-half-full kinda girl.

I guess the upside to having nothing is having nothing to lose.

I don't know where the hell Linda is. But she can take care of herself. I hope. Meanwhile, I'm gonna take advantage of having this nice room all to myself. I'm gonna shower, not brush my hair and sleep naked. I may even try to find some cartoons to watch until I pass out from exhaustion. Or alcohol overload.

I did those things—all of them. I'm lying in bed, naked, freshly showered, with unbrushed hair watching cartoons. Linda still hasn't showed up, and I'm starting to worry just a little. Chances are she's having awesome sex with some not-so-awesome dude. *I envy her...*

Shit...I have my phone. Kicking at the covers excitedly, I scramble out of bed in search of the bastard I dropped somewhere on the floor along with my room key. I feel guilty saying this, but I'm gonna say it anyway. I'm more amped about collecting my free money for my pretend slot game app on my phone than I am about having a way to contact Linda.

I find my phone on the bathroom floor, with the LED indicator rapidly flashing. Fourteen new text messages, three calls and the face of George Washington telling me my bonus is ready to collect. The messages are all from Linda, basically asking where I am. The missed calls on my call log are all from her too. But there's an outgoing call to Linda that I couldn't have possibly made.

That bastard.

That's how he found me. He got to Linda.

That bitch.

She ratted me out. *To hell with her...*

Reckon what the chances are that Bryce put his number in my phone? I go to my contacts, scroll to the Bs and hold my breath. And there he is.

*Bryce 867-5309*

Do I call? Do I not call? Too late. I'm already dialing. It rings twice before I hear his deep, throaty voice.

"Delilah." OMG. *Love those letters...*

"Was it stupid for me to hope you'd be waiting for me in an alley when I left the club?" I ask, not fully knowing why.

"No."

"Was it stupid for me to attempt to look scared in hopes you were watching?"

"No."

"Was it stupid for me to shout my room number to the heavens in hopes you'd hear me and pay me a visit?"

"Yes." I frown.

"Don't call me stupid," I huff. I get like this. After a good drunk, when I'm alone, I act like a petulant child. Add it to your growing list of "Weird shit about Delilah."

"I didn't call you stupid, Love. I said you acted stupid." *Love. He called me Love.*

"Why did you come tonight?" It's the million-dollar question —one he should take time to prepare the right answer for. But he doesn't. His response is immediate.

"Because I can."

"Well, what if I didn't want you to come?" Seconds tick by and I hear nothing. Hell, maybe this is the million-dollar question.

"Tell me what you really wanted tonight." His voice is confident, dark and low. Even through the phone, I can't deny him of the truth. He's just so...demanding.

"I wanted to have a great time. I wanted to party. I wanted someone to feed me alcohol, drown me with their undivided attention, then *fuck* me into oblivion." My tone is angry. My face is hot and my breathing ragged. Not only did this man spoil my night, he denied me of the only thing that could have made it better—him. Him kissing me...eating me...fucking me...

"Delilah..." It's a warning. One I should heed. But I want to push his buttons. I want to make him mad at me. I want to know his limits, then I want to push them too. I'm sexually frustrated. I'm angry with him. I'm angry with myself. I hate myself for being angry at him. I hate myself for being angry at me. *Why am I so stupid? I'm damaged. I'm fucked up. I'm...*

"Lay down, Delilah." His tone is harsh, demanding and powerful enough to cut through my thoughts.

"I don't want to lie down." There's not a lot of fight in my voice, as I curl my toes into the carpet and force myself to defy him.

"I didn't ask." My feet are moving. I didn't tell the damn things to, but they are. When I'm under the covers, I feel safer—like he's here somehow, tucking me in.

Two minutes ago, I was on the verge of losing it. I felt the anxiety growing just like it does at the end of every week. It's still there, but I feel much better. It's not the same rejuvenating feeling I get after enduring the pain on Sunday, but it's enough to stop me from falling off the edge.

"How did you..."

"That's the difference between me and you, Love." His soothing voice dips almost to a whisper. "You may know what you want, but I know what you need."

# CHAPTER 13

Linda came crawling into the room just after the sun rose the next morning. After the cleaning lady banged on our door for over an hour, we finally got up and checked out. The ride home was silent—Linda too hungover to speak and me too deep in my own thoughts.

Bryce's dominant nature and demands were what I needed to get through that night. I don't know how he did it, but he did. I hadn't heard from him in two days. My heart seemed to grow heavier with each passing hour that he didn't call...didn't text... didn't show. Now it's Friday, and my confused feelings about him mixed with his absence and the anticipation of Sunday has my mind racing and my monster roaring.

What I'm feeling is like a toothache. You can't do a damn thing for it. If cat shit were numbing cream, you'd coat your mouth in it if you thought it would ease the pain just a fraction.

Then you find that if you apply pressure, you get a painful relief. It hurts so good. So you keep doing that—inflicting pain on yourself until the day finally comes for extraction. Now there's no pain. Only a hole in your mouth to serve as a reminder.

That's my life in a nutshell. My temporary relief is sex. My extraction is Sundays with my brother. And that hole isn't in my mouth, it's in my soul. I guess it's a good thing I have more soul than I do teeth. Because my need for extraction happens every week.

The later in the week, the worse I become. My emotions seem to fade away—all but one that is a constant trigger.

Anger.

I have forty-eight hours until I visit the family, and I don't think I'm gonna make it. I've tried everything. I've fucked Scratch and Crash nearly to death. I've gotten shit-faced drunk every night, and most days. I'm becoming detached—even from myself.

"Hey, you okay?" Linda asks, resting her hand on my shoulder.

"I'm good. Just got a lot on my mind." I try a reassuring smile, but she's not buying it. "I think I'm gonna take a walk."

I don't wait for her response as I walk quickly to my room, locking the door behind me. I've never been a hardcore cutter.

The few times I've tried it, I bled like a stuck pig and still felt the ache. But I'm desperate. I'm willing to pull my fucking toenails off at this point.

Sitting on the toilet, blade in hand, I try to find the best location to slice through my skin. I need it to be somewhere that's not very noticeable, but that'll still deliver a significant amount of pain. I'm not educated enough about my body to know where the worse places to cut are. So I opt for the last place I used that didn't kill me. Obviously.

"Knock, knock!" *No. This cannot be happening.* "Delilah, you in here?"

"I'm busy, Red." I'm fighting to stay calm, keeping my focus on the door handle. I've decided if she turns it, I'm going to kill her. Even if I don't really want to, I'm afraid I might.

"I need..."

She trails off and I hear a door closing just as the handle begins to turn. *I locked the door. She had to have used the window. Did she let someone else in? Am I gonna be forced to kill Dallas too? Luke's not gonna be very happy about that...*

The door opens and instinctively I clutch the blade in my palm. My brow furrows when I feel my skin split from fisting it too hard. It hurts like a bitch, but it doesn't hurt good. Just like I figured it wouldn't.

I watch in the mirror for Red's face to appear. I want to read her reaction before I kill her. If she didn't see anything and leaves as quickly as she appeared, then maybe I can spare her life. *Why the hell am I so obsessed with killing?*

The pain in my hand becomes unbearable and I loosen my grip as Bryce's face comes into view. Red is gone. It's only him. For some reason, I whimper. Pushing the door open further, he takes in the scene. At first he doesn't notice anything. But I know the moment he does. If his eyes on my hand aren't a dead giveaway, the flare of his nostrils and the shock on his face is.

In one step, he's close enough to grab my wrist in his large hand. My mouth parts in anticipation of the pain I should feel by his touch, but there is none. He's so gentle, I barely notice his grasp.

Uncurling my fingers, he removes the blade from my hand. Anger and desperation are a poisonous mixture. And I'm both. "Don't touch me!" I scream, jerking my hand out of his hold. He seems taken aback by my outburst, but recovers quickly. His eyes darken as he narrows them on me.

"Calm down."

"No! You don't know me. You don't know what I need." I spit the words, seething as I feel the blood from my palm drip onto my thigh. "Get out!"

"Delilah, you're bleeding." His fight to stay calm is a struggle. Fuck him and his struggle. This is all his fault anyway.

"I said, get out!" I scream, squeezing my eyes shut and fisting my hands at my head. My nails dig into the cut and the pain is there, but so is the turmoil I'm feeling inside. It hasn't numbed at all.

Before I can fully process what's happening, I'm jerked from my sitting position and pushed roughly against the vanity. I'm confused about what's happening. This isn't like him. He's never put his hands on me like this. Even though he hasn't hurt me, the possibility that he might seems to weaken that beastly monster inside me. That alone is enough to have me throw caution and concern about his behavior to the wind.

I feel my shorts being pulled up by my belt loops, causing them to tighten over my ass and give me the mother of all wedgies. I'm on my toes, my face pressed against the mirror when his hand that must be made of steel collides with the cheeks of my ass. I let out a yelp that catches in my throat as he quickly follows up with another blow.

His hand is so large it seems to touch every inch of my backside. The impact is so loud, I'm sure it can be heard in the front of the clubhouse. But I don't care. With every spank he delivers, a part of the mayhem inside my head seems to die. It hurts so bad...and so fucking good.

I'm crying. I'm begging him to stop. I'm pleading with him to let me go. But really, I don't want him to. Either he knows this, or he's just a sick fuck who gets off on spanking women. I don't give a shit one way or another. I need this—to hell with why he's willing to give it to me.

When my cries become whimpers and I quit struggling completely, he stops—just as quickly as he started. Then I'm pulled in his arms, lifted to his chest and carried to my bed. I wish I could tell you how good he smells, but all I smell is snot. I wish I could tell you how wonderful his arms feel, but I'm too distracted with the burning ache in my ass. What I can tell you is how good I feel—mentally.

Aside from the pain in my behind and my palm, I'm like a new woman. My slate has been wiped clean. The anxiety I've been feeling has completely vanished. So has the pressure in my chest that made me feel like I was suffocating. That demon I have inside me has been put to rest. For now.

Laying me on my stomach, Bryce kneels beside me and takes my hand in his. Pulling a bandana from his back pocket, he uses it as a tourniquet. I turn away from him—unable to look in his eyes. I'm not one to get embarrassed, but this is more than that. I hate I forced him to do this to me. I hate he's now aware of the sickness inside me. And I hate how good I feel in this moment.

Bryce doesn't speak the entire time he wraps my hand. I know the cut can't be too bad if he's managing to treat it without as much as a first aid kit.

The bed dips and I hold my breath. Now that I'm not in need of any physical pain, I'm hoping like hell he doesn't give it to me. But if he does then I'll take it like a champ. He doesn't seem like that type of guy, but I can't keep the fear from creeping inside me. I guess I'm a little too scarred.

His hand touches my shoulder. He leaves it there a second, and when I see he has no intention of breaking it or anything, I decide it's okay to breathe. The moment I take a breath, he slides it down my back then across my bruised ass. I pinch my eyes shut and bite my lip, trying to prepare myself just in case. But his hand curls around my hip as he eases me to my side.

I avoid looking at him by keeping my eyes closed. His fingers make quick work of the button on my shorts, and I'm trying to talk myself into asking him to just let me sleep a little while. But I can't find the will.

The bed dips again as he stands, before rolling me back to my stomach. I hate not being able to see what's happening. I wish I wasn't too chicken shit to open my eyes.

I'm more than surprised and beyond relieved when he finally speaks. "I want you to stay in here for the rest of the night. Can you do that?" His voice is velvety smooth, without the least bit of anger. I nod into my pillow. "An answer, Love." *Love.*

"Yes."

"Good girl." Okay...why does that make me all tingly and shit? I'm not so sure I like it.

Gripping the waistband of my shorts, he pulls them gently over my ass that has got to be black and blue. I listen hard for his reaction in hopes that he'll give me some idea of what it looks like. He doesn't. His breath doesn't even hitch. *Maybe it's not that bad... It really doesn't even hurt—especially considering I've had much, much worse.*

After covering me with a quilt, his fingers run through my hair with a touch so light I almost wonder if it was real. I feel him lie down next to me, softly stroking my head. This is something new for me. And the feeling is so comforting, I start to drift. Minutes later, I feel his lips press against my scalp before whispering, "Sleep."

He didn't have to tell me--hell, I'm already there.

You ever just wake up feeling amazing? Like you slept on air and cuddled with rainbows? Yeah, me neither. My hand is sore, my ass is kinda sore and I have this big ball of shame lodged in my throat.

Bryce now knows my secret. He may not know all the details, but he's got the gist of it. There's a part of me that's disappointed in myself for allowing him to give me what I needed. Having the secret wasn't a burden to me. Now that someone knows it, it suddenly is.

I don't like the idea of involving people in my own problems. I don't like that someone knows the real me. Luke, of course, is very aware of my situation, but he's never treated me any different. I'm not so sure I can say the same about Bryce. He seems too...connected.

The truth is, I'm embarrassed.

There it is.

I'm so ashamed, I want to bury my head in a pillow, stay in the room and starve to death. Okay...maybe that's a little extreme. But if I never saw Bryce again, that would be okay with me. Would I miss him? Sure. He's somehow claimed a role in my life without me even realizing it. I've spoken less than a hundred words to the man, yet he's one of the closest people to me.

Damn. That sounds really, really pathetic.

The spray of hot water feels good on my face. There's nothing like a scalding shower to clear your head—that is, until it runs down your back and scorches your battered-and-bruised ass. I bite my lip and force myself to feel the pain as I gently wash the tender flesh. When I'm finished, I stand naked in the tub, contemplating whether or not I should even attempt to dry off.

*You're the one that needs the pain, Delilah.*

Wiping the steam from the mirror, I turn and glance back over my shoulder. I'm surprised at what I find. My ass is bright red, with only a few purple bruises in the areas that got the most attention. I look down at the vanity, remembering how it felt when he shoved me against it. It was better than any orgasm I'd had. The feeling of reprieve was instant.

I grab a bottle of lotion and lather my entire body, rubbing an extra amount on the one place that needs it the most. I find an oversized T-shirt in my dresser and slip it over my head—deciding against any underwear.

I spend the next ten minutes tidying my room, and wishing like hell for a cigarette and a cup of coffee. No matter the time, this is still considered morning to me. Afraid I might see Bryce's face, I text Linda and ask if he's here. She doesn't replies.

Easing open my bedroom door, I lean out into the hall and listen hard for any sign of life up front. It's eerily quiet—almost too quiet. I tiptoe down the hall, and into the main room. There's not a soul in sight. *Weird...*

I put on a pot of coffee, constantly surveying the room and keeping my ears open in case someone walks in. If they do, I'll fake a smile, then a cough and excuse myself to my room. Luckily, I don't have to do any of that. My mountain of a coffee cup, my entire pack of smokes and my naked, bruised ass make it back to the safe confines of my room without one human encounter.

I'm standing by my window, taking my first sip of morning goodness when my door opens. By the way, nobody fills out a doorway quite like Devil's Renegades SA Bryce. His shoulders are so wide, I'm surprised he doesn't have to turn sideways to enter.

"I'd have gotten that," he says in greeting, pointing to my coffee and unlit cigarette as he closes the door.

I shrug. "It's fine. Nobody's here anyway." I avoid looking at him, but I don't drop my eyes. I read once that submissives do that. I don't want him getting the wrong idea. Just because he spanked me doesn't make him my master.

"I brought you something." *Well, shit.* How am I supposed to avoid him if he brings me presents?

He pulls what looks like a tube of lotion out of his pocket. It takes me a second, but I finally catch on to what he's suggesting. "Oh," I say, letting out an embarrassed snort of laughter. I shake my head. "I already took care of it. Thanks, though." To show that my thanks is genuine, I meet his eyes. His brow is furrowed and he looks a little...put off. But in true Mr. Igotmyshittogether fashion, he recovers quickly.

"You feeling all right?"

"I'm good." It's the honest truth. But I'd be great if he left.

"You wanna talk about it?"

"No." My rapid response is so amusing to him, he smiles. I look away once again. I can feel sadness forming in my gut and behind my eyes. I don't need him to poke fun at me or find me amusing. What I need is to get angry. But I guess I used all that up earlier.

"Hey," he soothes, taking a step toward me then stopping. I'm thankful for the distance. I bite my lip, trying like hell not to focus on the burning behind my eyes. *Don't you cry. You do not fucking cry!* "Talk to me, Delilah."

I turn my back completely to him—struggling to light my cigarette with my shaky fingers. Pulling in a couple deep drags, I try to relax, but it's impossible with him in the room. *I can smell him...*

"I need to know what you're feeling." He sounds pained. For some reason, hearing the distress in his voice saddens me further.

"It's not funny," I say, losing the battle with my tears. They've yet to spill over, but they're teetering on the edge. "I may be fucked up, but I'm still human." I don't have to look to know he's right behind me. I can feel him. He's so warm. So inviting. I don't know if I want to hide in my closet, or curl myself in his arms.

"You're right." He's so close, his breath tickles my hair when he speaks. "There's nothing funny about what happened. I apologize if I hurt your feelings. I just wasn't expecting you to be so distant. I thought you'd want to talk."

"Well, I don't." I stand taller, finding a little courage with his apology. "I just want you to go. I want to forget anything happened. And I want you to forget it too."

"Can't do that, babe." We're back to babe, which tells me we've moved past the dominant and submissive role play shit. It's reassuring enough for me to turn and face him. His face is impassive, his eyes still sparkling green, but giving nothing away.

"Look," I say, pulling in a deep breath as I drop my half-smoked cigarette into my full cup of coffee. I don't know the source of my bravery, but I'm thankful for it. "I'm not your submissive. What happened, happened. But it's over. We're over." I motion between the two of us with my finger.

"I'm not a dominant." His deadpan admission nearly floors me. My eyebrows rise in disbelief, as I stare back at his emotionless face. "I don't get off on controlling women. There's no pleasure for me in hurting women, either. Like I told you before, I know what you need. Just because I give it to you doesn't mean I expect you to kneel at my feet."

Somewhere in my mind I have a response. I just can't find it. Instead, I keep opening and closing my mouth like an idiot. What do I say to that anyway? He's not offended, but I can tell something about my words bother him—I don't give a damn how well he tries to conceal it.

"I put my hands on you earlier. I hurt you. I'm the type of man who follows through on my actions. That means, it's my responsibility to make sure you're okay both physically and emotionally. Does that make sense to you?"

I nod, dumbfounded, because I have no clue what else to do.

"An answer, Delilah."

"Yes."

"Good. Now turn around, pull up your shirt and let me look at you." Blood rushes to my cheeks at his demand. A fucking hurricane of emotions is happening inside me right now. I'm shocked, nervous, embarrassed and so turned on, I'm tempted to dry hump his leg. But the one thing I don't want to do is exactly what he asked. It seems almost too intimate and I don't like it.

"I want to talk," I blurt out—willing to say anything to distract him, even if it's a lie.

"No, you don't. You're just embarrassed." He's calling me out on my bullshit, and I can sense some energy crackling around him. He looks calm and collected, almost bored. But I can tell it's just a front. His face is relaxed, but his body is tight and fighting to keep his control. I don't think he wants to hurt me, but I believe I've pinched a nerve.

In the midst of our stare down, I decide I can't hide anything from him. Even if I try, he'll see right through me. My voice, body language and eyes can't cooperate with the deceitful part of me—instead they give away the truth.

"What do you want from me, Bryce?" Anger is my best defense, and it comes easier than I anticipated. "Do you want the truth?"

"Always. But first, I want you to calm down."

"You can't tell me what to do. You're not my *dominant*. Remember?"

"Last warning, Delilah. Watch your tone."

"Or what?" I've found his limits, and I'm pushing them. I can't help it. I don't deserve for him to be nice to me. So why the fuck is he doing it? Why can't he just beat me and leave? Why does he have to be so nice?

"I don't need you to take care of me. That's not what this is. You gave me something, thank you, now get the fuck out." I'm daring him to make a move. I was betting on all that controlled rage he was holding in to finally bust loose. Problem is, I don't think there ever was any rage. And if there was, it's gone now.

It's like he's suddenly realized something. His face softens, his body relaxes and he narrows his eyes slightly as he appraises me—not in anger, but confusion. Meanwhile, I'm battling those fucking tears again because I've recently had my own realization.

He finds me worthy.

I'm worth caring for.

I'm worth his time.

I'm worth hurting to a man who doesn't enjoy hurting women.

*Me.*

A sob bubbles up my throat and out my mouth before I can stop it. Joining the pity parade are my tears that flow freely down my cheeks. All the while, I'm looking at him as he's looking at me.

"Don't," I cry, pointing my finger at him. "Don't you dare feel sorry for me." Not satisfied with just pointing, I poke my finger in his chest. Of course he doesn't budge, but he doesn't get mad either. So I ball my fist up and hit his chest. I wait in anticipation for his reaction that never comes. He just lets me beat the shit out of him.

"Hit me!" I cry, needing it now more than ever. His kindness is too foreign to me. I can't handle it. I need him to be a bad guy. I need him to be a Mario... or my brother Craig. "Hit me and go!"

Catching my wrists in his hands, he halts my punches that really weren't doing much good anyway. "Stop it!" he snaps, his tone low but so powerful that I still.

My shoulders heave with every hiccup as I fight to catch my breath. When I'm calmed to the point of only a small gasp every now and then, he relaxes his hold but doesn't let go.

I feel so lost. I haven't been like this in years. For the second time today, I find myself at his mercy. He's the only one who can help me. He's the only one that knows my secret.

"Please," I beg, though I'm not sure what for. But I bet I'd feel better if he just knocked me unconscious. "I need it to stop." At this point, my pride is nonexistent. He can shout my secret to the world, I just need to cage that beast one more time.

"I'm not going to hit you, Delilah." I whimper at his words. "Hey." His stern voice gives me hope, and when his grip tightens I let out a breath of relief. My eyes flutter closed as I anticipate the pain that never comes. Instead, I'm pulled to his chest. I start to fight, but he holds me tighter. Surprisingly, I feel better.

With one arm around my waist he lifts my feet off the ground and moves us toward the bed. My face is buried in his chest, and I inhale deep the scent of leather. I'm on top of him when he lies down, then he rolls to his side. When his hand travels down my hip and under my shirt, I let out a gasp.

The feel of his rough, calloused hands against the tender flesh on my cheeks is both soothing and painful. I'm slightly turned on, and the pressure slowly lifts from my chest. But I need more.

"Harder," I breathe, pleading with my eyes as I stare up at him. His hand kneads my ass a little firmer, and I moan. When it travels lower, barely grazing the lips of my pussy, I thrust my hips against him.

Maybe this is what's wrong with me—I'm just sexually frustrated. Even though I've been having endless sex for days, it has yet to fully satisfy me. I've been searching for the same high I get when he takes me...fucks me...*claims* me. But nobody can measure up.

There's something about his hands—the same hands that hurt me—touching me and pleasing me that's more rewarding than being touched in any way by any other man.

He hoists my leg over his hip—opening me up. The movement causes me to shiver in anticipation when the cool air tickles the inferno between my thighs. My mouth is parted, my eyes are closed and I can feel his lips closing in on mine. When they touch, something ignites inside me and I can't hold back.

I struggle to free my hand that is trapped between our bodies, but he doesn't allow it. I want to grab the back of his head and force him to kiss me harder. I want my hands free so I can roll him to his back and straddle his waist. But I can't. I'm forced to lie here, completely immobile, and move at the pace he sets.

Torturously slow, he simultaneously slides his tongue between one set of lips and his finger between the other. He kisses me with a soft, lazy passion a man as large as him shouldn't be capable of. I can taste a hint of whiskey on his breath and it's so heady, my head swims.

His long, thick finger pumps slowly inside me. On each thrust, his palm roughly massages my lower cheeks—mixing the sensation of both pleasure and pain into a delicious, orgasm-building concoction.

He's the only man that's ever brought me to orgasm by simply fingering me. But then again, he doesn't have your average-sized hands. Every time he pushes inside me, I feel him graze that sweet spot he seems to find every time he touches me. Then I get the twist of pain, all while he makes love to my mouth —kissing me as if we're intimate lovers.

The slow build is infuriating, yet I don't want to ever hit my peak. I want to continue to feel what I'm feeling for as long as I possibly can, even though the anticipation of what it will be like is killing me. I choose to not overthink the moment and just let the tsunami of emotions crash through me. I feel the full impact of them all—pleasure, pain, sadness, anger, guilt, shame, peace...

Then it happens. My whole body clenches with each wave of ecstasy that pulses through me. He doesn't move faster, or thrust harder—he keeps his pace, milking every last ounce of each sensation from me. It's euphoric, liberating and completely consuming. I can feel it in every fiber of my being.

Pulling his lips from mine, Bryce looks down at me. His green eyes are smoldering—burning with an intensity I've never experienced from him before. But as always, the fog fades and I'm no longer the weak, vulnerable girl who needs him. I'm just Delilah.

"I need a cigarette." My confession shatters the moment and his eyes soften as he gives me a lazy smile. I feel like I can breathe a little easier now that the connection isn't so powerful.

He doesn't speak as he unfolds my leg from around him and stands. Grabbing my pack of smokes from the dresser, he lights one and ambles back over—a little too cocky for a guy who didn't even get off.

"Glad to see you in a better mood," he says, all throaty and sexy like as he hands me the cigarette. I smile up at him, stretching and rolling to my back before taking my first drag. It's perfect.

"Why were you trying to cut yourself?" I cut my eyes at him, surprised by his question. He looks back at me from his seated position on the edge of the bed. He's expecting an answer, and to be honest, he's more than deserving of one—even if I don't want to give it to him.

"It was stupid." I shrug, focusing on the swirl of smoke above me.

"That's not good enough."

I take a couple more long drags, hoping the nicotine will give me the courage to say something that will pacify him. "I'm not really sure myself. I just know the pain makes me feel better."

"You do that often?"

I shake my head. "No. I've tried it before but it never works. I end up causing myself more pain, which leads to even more self-loathing."

He sits silent, waiting patiently for me to continue. I'm not ready to tell him everything. I'm not sure if I ever will be. But he wants more and talking to him isn't as uncomfortable as I thought it would be.

"I've always had this...need for something," I start, trying to understand it myself as I attempt to explain it to him. "It's like a hunger. But even though I eat, I'm never fully satisfied. I haven't lost it like this in a really long time. I think it just finally caught up to me."

"So if cutting don't work, what does?" In hopes of distracting him, I smirk.

"Having an officer of the Devil's Renegades spank me. That seems to do the trick." He's not amused. There's not even a hint of a smile on his face. Frowning, I let out a breath. "I deal with it, okay?"

He pauses for a minute, narrowing his eyes on me as if he's trying to read my mind. *Good luck with that.* "Okay." *What? Can it really be that easy?* "But I need you to make me a promise." Well, that's a loaded request. It could mean anything. *I knew this wasn't gonna be that easy.* Hoping he'll drop it, I nod my head in agreement.

"Promise me you won't hurt yourself anymore. If it gets to be too much, you'll call me."

"That's two promises," I quip, but the joke is on me. He's very serious. And he wants my word. So I give it to him. But it doesn't count. Unbeknownst to him, I'm crossing my toes. Surely that excuses me of the lie. And if it doesn't...well, he can just spank me again.

# CHAPTER 14

I wasn't sure why Bryce left in such a hurry. I was actually a little wounded that he didn't try to fuck me while I was lying there all vulnerable and half naked. I mean, he could've had it. All he had to do was ask. But he didn't. I gave him my toe-crossing promise, he gave me a smile, then left.

That was two days ago.

Now it's Sunday and I have shit to do. Just like I've done for the past two years, I head toward Baton Rouge. I'm not sure what to expect. This will be the first time I've visited without that heaviness in my chest. Well, the first time since Mario left... died...whatever. Anyway, this time I'm hoping to have a decent, normal time with my family. Test the waters and shit... Who knows? We may even hug or play Scrabble. It's possible.

When I arrive, I'm not surprised to find a yellow notice taped to the door warning that the power will be turned off tomorrow if the past due balance isn't paid. I yank it free, knock twice, announce myself and receive the usual greeting from my mother —screaming at me to come in and asking why the fuck I always knock.

"Hello, family." I'm smiling as I walk in. Even the filthiness of the kitchen and the stench of week-old garbage doesn't get me down. My optimism about today is unwavering.

"What the hell you so happy about?" my mother asks. The question sends her into a coughing fit and I wait patiently for her to die or regain her breath before speaking.

"Nothing, really." I shrug, joining her in the living room and taking a seat. "How's your week been?"

"Shitty. Same as last week," she mumbles, snatching the notice from my fingers.

"I found that on the door."

"People these days have no sympathy for the disabled."

"But you're not disabled, Mama. You could work, you just don't want to."

Ever heard of putting your foot in your mouth? Well, if you Google it you'll find my name in the description of the phrase. Even in a cheery mood, I can't seem to keep my mouth shut.

"You sassy little bitch. Why you think you better than me? What the fuck do you do for a livin', huh?"

"She's a prostitute, Mama." My brother opens his eyes to look at me. His evil smile tells me he's hoping to wound me. Unlucky for him, I don't feel like being wounded today.

"I'm not a prostitute. I'm a bartender."

"Same shit," he says with a shrug. *Dumbass.*

"Whatever." I turn to my mother, plastering a smile on my face that for once is genuine. "Hey, I was thinking of going out shopping today. I thought maybe me and you could get some lunch."

"Don't be ridiculous, Delilah." She looks over the top of her reading glasses at me. "Dr. Phil's coming on in a minute."

My smile falters a little, but I force myself to remain positive and try another tactic. "How about after Dr. Phil?"

She heaves out a breath and looks at me annoyed. "What the hell's the matter with you, huh?" My brow creases in confusion as I shake my head. "Are you on drugs?"

"No, Mama. I just thought it'd be nice to get out of the house a little while."

"Well," she says, lighting a cigarette. "That's what you get for thinkin'. Why don't you think your ass in there and make me some coffee."

Like the obedient child I am, I do as I'm told. While it's brewing, I start my routine of uncluttering the kitchen sink. By the time it's empty, the coffee is finished and I pause my cleaning to bring her a cup.

"When you mop the floors, don't put that waxy shit on them again. I nearly fell twice last week. And don't use bleach either. Your brother don't like the way it smells. Use that pine stuff." I stand beside her, next to the table filled with a week's worth of cigarette butts, glasses and empty food wrappers—feeling just as disposed of as everything else she's used and thrown to the side.

In this moment, my relationship with my mother is clear. For endless Sundays, I've come here, waited on her, cleaned for her, given her money and allowed her to use me as her personal slave. She doesn't want to be my mother. She doesn't want to do mother-daughter shit with me most classify as normal. And she sure as hell doesn't want to play Scrabble. *Why did I think this time would be different?*

The only thing that's different about this Sunday is me. I realize it doesn't matter how I mop her floors, how I wash her clothes or how many endless pots of coffee I make—it will never make her love me more. If she even loves me at all...

I want to leave. I want to turn around and walk out. But I can't. It's just not in me—this girl who, caged beast or not, needs her family in her life. So I don't mop with the cleaner that leaves a waxy film on the floor. I don't use bleach either, because my brother doesn't like the way it smells. I use the pine-scented cleaner, and make sure to do a better job this time than I ever have.

"Don't you owe Mama some more money?" Craig asks, glaring down at me. He's standing so close, I can hear him breathe.

"I don't owe Mama anything. I give her two hundred a week. Just like I did last week, and every other week I've been here."

"You didn't give me any money last week," my mother interjects, eyeing me suspiciously but not giving my brother a second glance. As I suspected, Craig took the money for himself and claimed I didn't give her anything.

"I gave the money to Craig—"

"You're a lyin' bitch too, Delilah. You didn't give me shit!"

I hold my hands up in defense. "You're right. I didn't." I level him with a look—feeling awfully brave for someone who is fighting a losing battle. "You took it from me."

White light flashes in my eyes, and I stumble back. My hand flies out in search of something to steady myself. I end up falling on the couch. The pain hurts so much more when my mind doesn't crave it.

"Stop!" I scream, holding my hands up in front of my face. Panic simmers in my veins. For the first time in years, I'm afraid of my brother. "I'll give you everything I have!"

"Damn right you will." Fisting my hair in his hand, he pulls me from the couch and drags me to the kitchen where my duffel sits by the door. He releases me with a shove and I fall hard on my knees. I have to blink a few times to uncloud my vision before I can manage to open the zipper.

I can hear my mother's shrill voice through the fog in my head. She's still pleading her case that she never received the money. Craig is telling her I never showed up last week. I'm just fighting like hell to give them what they want so I can leave. *Had it really never occurred to me until now that he could actually hurt me to the point of it being life threatening?*

"Here." I hold up the money in my hand. Snatching it from my fingers, Craig flips the bills and counts them out loud. Five hundred dollars—all I have on me. I don't know where I'll get gas money to get home, but it doesn't matter. I'll worry about that later.

Getting to my feet, I'm nearly out the door when it's pushed shut and Craig leans down to growl in my ear. "We need to talk." My blood chills. Pushing me toward Mama's room, he keeps a firm grip on my shoulder so I can't break away.

"Mama owes a thousand dollars to Gary," he says, his tone even and cold.

"Who?"

"Gary. The guy she borrowed the money from last week." I start shaking my head, already knowing where this is going.

"No, Craig. I won't. And I don't have that kind of money!" I'm pleading, begging him not to make me do what I think he's trying to make me do.

Closing the distance, he pokes his finger into my forehead as he glares down at me. "Gary don't fuck around, Delilah. You're gonna give that man his money or something else."

"I am not fucking him. Mama wouldn't allow it, and you know it. That's why you won't say it in front of her."

"You think she gives two shits about how you pay the debt?" The humor and truth in Craig's words hurt, even though the reality should be clear to me by now. "She just don't want everybody knowin' you're a whore."

"I am *not* a whore."

"Well, you are today." Pushing the duffel from my shoulder, he starts to pull my hoodie over my head. I fight back, but he quickly wrestles me to the floor and removes it. I'm left in nothing but my sports bra and sweats.

"That'll do. Take your pants off, and get in the bed. I'll call him over and distract Mama while he comes in."

"Are you out of your fucking mind? I am not doing this!" I yell. His hand comes down hard over my mouth, silencing me.

"Delilah, I swear I'll kill you." The fear in his eyes sends a series of light bulbs flashing in my head. When he moves his hand, I speak with as much malice as I can muster.

"You owe him money. Not Mama." His eyes drop, giving him away. "Get. Off. Of. Me."

Surprisingly, he stands. "Fuck you, little sister. I'll remember this shit."

"I'm looking forward to it," I bite out.

He walks out, slamming first the bedroom door, and then the front door as he leaves the trailer. I pull the hoodie back over my head, proud of myself for putting my foot down. He's a sick bastard.

The sound of a car cranking has me rushing toward the window. I find him leaving in my car just as the blinds are raised. Banging on the window, I scream at him, but he can't hear me.

I'm pissed at him. Pissed at myself for letting him get his hands on my keys, and pissed at Mama for giving birth to such an idiot. Problem is, I'm not sure if the idiot is him or me.

"Delilah?" The worry in Bryce's voice has me wishing I'd have called anyone but him. Well...technically I did. He's just the only one who answered. The other bitches I consider "friends" sent me to voicemail.

"Hey, you busy?" *Please say yes. Please say yes.*

"What's wrong?"

"I asked if you were busy."

"And I asked what's wrong. I won't ask again." *Fucking man...*

"I'm—" The sound of gravel crunching has me opening the blinds again, but it's only the neighbor.

"Dammit, Delilah..."

"I need a ride," I blurt, wishing I could endure this hell a little longer, and keep my pride. But I've been here all day. It's nearly ten at night, and Craig still hasn't showed.

"Where are you?" I can hear him already walking, and my heart comes to life for the first time today.

"Baton Rouge." His footsteps cease.

"What?"

I swallow hard. "I'm in Baton Rouge. My car got...stolen." It's not a complete lie.

"I feel like you're not telling me something."

"I'm telling you my car was taken. I'm asking you if you can get me a ride. It's simple. Yes or no." My nerves are shot. My anxiety is at an all-time high. And this sadness I'm suddenly overwhelmed by is worse than all that combined.

"Give me the address and I'll have someone there within the hour."

"Thank you," I breathe. I give him the address and hang up—avoiding any further questions. He calls me back twice, but I text him that my battery is about dead. He answers with a simple "okay."

I tell Mama bye, and leave with my empty duffel slung over my shoulder. I'd given Bryce the address to the convenience store about a half mile from the trailer park. I didn't need him knowing where my mother lived. I'd done a good job of keeping my family and my job separated, I wasn't about to combine the two worlds now.


The smell of coffee wafts into my nostrils when I open the door to the store. My mouth waters at the scent, and my anger intensifies when I realize I don't even have a dollar to buy a single cup. Scanning the room, I find several booths in the back next to the deli and take a seat. The bitter January cold has me pulling my hoodie tighter around me despite the warmth of the building.

I've been here all of ten minutes when a man I don't recognize, wearing a familiar cut of a Devil's Renegades' support club, approaches. His tall, tattooed body is slim, but muscular. He appears to be in his mid-twenties, despite the dark, scruffy beard that covers his jaw. Even though his face is hard, and his body donned in thick leather, his eyes are soft, warm pools of brown that make me feel safe. Tears threaten to fall for some reason, but I force them back.

"Delilah?" he asks, his voice surprisingly deep. I nod. "I'm Malfuctional Secretary York. DRSA Bryce wants you to come with me. "

"Are you taking me home?" *Home...*

"I'm just following orders, ma'am."

"What the hell does that mean?" I ask, wondering why in the hell he can't give me a yes or no answer.

"It means I'll be taking you where Bryce told me to take you. Would you like something before we leave?" On their own accord, my eyes sweep to the row of coffee machines behind him. The corner of his lip turns up and he nods, his face softening.

He reaches his hand out to mine and I take it. His fingers are cold but smooth and feel small compared to the massive hands of Bryce. He releases me before gesturing toward the coffee. *If he's not aware I don't have money, he will be when he realizes he has to pay.*

Not to be greedy, but I choose the largest cup available before tipping the spout on the strongest Columbian blend they have. I avoid his gaze, but follow behind him to the register—blowing over the hot liquid in an attempt to cool it. I don't know why...that shit never works.

Without question he pays, then places his hand at the small of my back, guiding me to the door. Outside, I find two bikes occupied by leather-clad men who are smoking. Next to them is a black Jeep with tinted windows.

"Can I get one of those?" I gesture to a cigarette dangling from the mouth of one of the older men.

"Sure thing, baby," he replies, pulling one of the full flavored Marlboros from his cut.

"Thank you," I breathe, already feeling relief from just the thought of the nicotine. I lean in, allowing him to light it. I close my eyes, taking a deep pull. When I open them, I notice their eyes are on me. Well, not on me, but what I assume is the swell of my eye from Craig's brutal backhanded blow.

"Let's go," York suddenly says, making me jump. The older man glares at him, but he's unaffected as he leads me to the passenger side of the Jeep. Helping me in, he shuts the door before coming around to climb in himself—folding his cut and placing it beneath the back seat.

I crack open my window, blowing the smoke out as we follow the bikes out of the parking lot. "Where are we going?"

He doesn't look at me. "To a motel a few miles away," he answers in a low tone that gives me the feeling he doesn't approve.

"Why can't you just take me home?"

"Like I said, ma'am. I'm just following orders." Knowing I won't get any more than that from him, I sip my coffee and finish my cigarette—wishing I had another. As if he could read my mind, he offers his pack to me. "Help yourself. You look like you need it." I ignore the comment, but take the smoke and lighter.

We ride in silence down the two lane highway, until he pulls into a Days Inn. The two-story building is small, but looks new and clean. We walk past the reception desk, and down the long hall all the way to the end. He pulls a key from his pocket, unlocks the door, then holds it open gesturing for me to enter.

I become nervous. I don't like that I'm here with no money, no reason and no familiar faces. The hair on the back of my neck prickles—warning me something isn't right. I'm about to throw my hot coffee in his face and bolt when he speaks.

"Would you like me to call Bryce?" I look up at him to find him fighting a smile. I narrow my eyes, attempting to snatch the phone from his fingers. He pulls it out of my reach, and dials a number before handing it back to me.

"What?" The hard, menacing tone of Bryce's voice makes me flinch.

"It's me," I say, my voice not nearly as snappy as I'd intended. Other than a few deep breaths, he's silent. I wonder if he's trying to calm his temper.

"You okay?" he asks, his voice softer now. His concern has tears brimming my eyes. *What the fuck is wrong with me?*

"Yeah," I say on a whimper. I sniff—sloshing hot coffee on my sleeve as I raise my hand to wipe my nose.

"You're safe, baby. Calm down and I'll be there soon." My heart flips at his words. In this moment, I want him more than ever. Not sexually, but just to feel his big arms around me—embracing me...rubbing my hair...whispering "shhh" in my ear, just like those damsel-in-distress moments in romance novels.

"Put York on the phone." I wordlessly hand York the phone and walk into the room. It's spacious and neat with a king-sized bed, desk and flat-screen TV. The bathroom is large too, and equipped with a whirlpool tub. Without thinking, I go to it and turn the hot tap on.

"If you need anything, I'm right outside the door. Just yell for me," York says, laying the pack of cigarettes and lighter by the sink. I mumble a thank you, and push the bathroom door closed—turning on the heat lamp in the room.

The water is scalding, but I welcome the burn in hopes it will warm the chill I feel in my bones. I turn on the jets, light a cigarette and lean back—allowing the painful memories of today to resurface in my mind.

Craig had taken my money, and my car—the one thing I owned. Now I was penniless. Aside from the hundred or so dollars I had stashed out in my room, I had nothing. Clothes. That's it. Even my bed and dresser didn't belong to me. They were property of the club.

The threatening tears finally spill down my cheeks. I cry them silently other than an occasional sob I can't prevent. Pushing myself beneath the water, I let the warmth wash away my tears. But the moment I resurface, a new wave of sadness hits me—flooding my cheeks once again.

I cry for my mother—a bitter, old bitch who hated me even more than the father who made me this way. I cry for my brother —a man willing to sell his sister's body to pay his own debts. I cry for Bryce—the man who fucked me, held me, spanked me and came to my rescue even though I'm not worthy. And I cry for me—my soul, my demons, the incessant monster who claws at my skin, and ruins not only myself, but everyone in my path.

I cry until the weight of my problems becomes too heavy of a burden. Then I give myself to sleep—my temporary reprieve. The only break from reality I have.

# CHAPTER 15

Thick, cool hands rub my head—the fine strands snagging on calluses as fingers caress me. A thumb brushes over my cheek, and I open my eyes to find Bryce's green and blazing with anger at the spot he's so gently stroking. When they meet mine, the anger diminishes and something warm and understanding replaces it.

"Hello, Love." *Love.* I'm not sure if it's that word, his tender touch or just his presence, but my eyes well with tears I wasn't aware still remained. Swiping one with the pad of his thumb, he gives my face a gentle squeeze before standing.

I watch, crying hot, heavy tears as he pulls the drain on the tub. He grabs a thick towel from the rack, shaking it open then throwing it over his shoulder. Leaning down, his hands slide beneath my arms and lift me from the tub as if I were a toddler. Once I'm steady on my feet, he starts to dry me—keeping one hand on my waist while the other wipes the droplets of water from my skin.

My tears still fall. My face burns from their salty sting, but I don't try to stop them. Other than a slight tremble in my lip, I'm otherwise unaffected. My breathing is normal and my pulse steady. My limbs feel heavy as if they're weighted in lead, but I'm pretty sure that's a result from Craig—not the crying.

I look at myself in the mirror. My naked body is visible to the tops of my thighs. I look tired, older. Dark, wide circles are beneath my red, puffy eyes. The corner of my left one partially closed from swelling. A bright crimson welt joins it and runs the length of my cheek. My hair is a wet, tangled mess. I seem smaller—more vulnerable than I've ever been.

Bryce's reflection is the complete opposite of mine. His back strong, powerful. His patches are worn and faded—dirty and used. The reaper's face centered on his back is hidden by the hood of his cape. I've never found a skeleton draped in fabric sexy, but this one...

Faded jeans sag on his hips. A black cap sits backwards on his head. The muscles in his neck are thick and visible before he covers my head with the towel—gently massaging the water from my sodden hair.

When I'm dry, my body slightly trembling from the cold and my fragile state, he wraps me in a fresh towel and finally—pulls me to his chest. He holds me...pets my hair...whispers to me.

"Shhh, Love. You're okay. I got you." He's got me. Him. Bryce. I've never felt more protected—safe and secure—than in this moment. In his arms.

"He took it all," I sob, a shiver wracking through me and shaking me to my core. I really didn't care that Craig took my money and my car, it was that sliver of dignity he stole that was my undoing.

"It's over now. You're safe." Soft kisses rain over the top of my head. "Come on." He gives my butt a light tap, and pulls away.

I walk out of the bathroom and to the window that overlooks the parking lot. Other than a few cars, it's vacant. Rolling clouds illuminated by the partially hidden moon pass quickly through the sky—warning us of an impending storm that will likely bring warmer weather.

The dark, looming shadow of his presence reflects in the glass as he stands silently behind me. The tension in the room thickens, or maybe it's just the tension I feel burning inside me. I rub my hands up my arms—searching for the part of me that itches--it seems to be located somewhere I can't scratch.

"Do you have an ol' lady?" I ask, turning to face him. I'm not sure why I asked, but I'm gonna go with me trying to make conversation.

"If I had an ol' lady, do you think I'd be here with you?" He pierces me with that intense glare of his. It's a little unnerving.

"Well, I don't know." My hands involuntarily move up my arms again before sliding over my shoulders and neck. *Dammit. I feel like something is crawling on me.*

He watches me, wordlessly appraising my every move. I know what this feeling is. It's not just my skin that's crawling, but I can feel my blood tickling my veins. I can also sense the heavy fog that's coming. I didn't anticipate feeling this so soon, but after the day's events, I'm not surprised either.

The longer he looks at me, the more fidgety I become. "Would you like to watch TV?" I ask, searching for something that will distract my mind and his stare.

"If I wanted to, don't you think I would?" *Well, shit.* "Why don't you ask me what it is you really want?" I look at him confused.

"I don't understand," I say, letting out a nervous laugh. "I was just trying to be polite." *What the fuck is wrong with me?*

*Why do I feel all shy and antsy? Say something rude, and force him to hurt you, idiot!*

"Okay." *Okay? That's it?*

I stand in shock as he moves toward me, pausing when his giant body is next to mine. Leaning down, I feel his breath tickle my ear as he speaks. "If you have something to say, say it."

After a few beats of silence, he straightens, and I watch as he turns and walks away. "I'm going to get a drink." My gut churns and my breath hitches as I realize he's fixing to leave. The moment his hand rests on the doorknob, something inside me bursts—making me forget all sense of reason and focus on the sole thing that's making me ache with need.

"Wait!" I call out, immediately clamping down on my lip as soon as I speak. His eyes meet mine. His expression is void. I'm not sure if that's because he feels nothing, or because he doesn't want me to know what it is he's feeling. *Stop overthinking everything!*

"I-I…" I'm stuttering like a fool. I'm unsure of what to say. So I close my eyes. The moment I do, I feel my mood darken. My fingers claw at my skin. My hands pull at my scalp. Finding the tender flesh on the back of my arms, I pinch the skin between my fingers looking for release.

Without seeing him, it's like the little control I had, I was channeling from him. Now that all I see is darkness, the fog in my head thickens and I'm back to that emotionally detached, aching need I crave every Sunday—despite Craig's vicious attack from earlier. It should have been enough. But it wasn't. Not anymore. I feel guilty for being so weak. And my guilt only has one cure. There's only one thing that can make it go away.

"I need you."

I hear the click of the lock, which seems to echo loudly through the silent room. I sense him closing the distance between us. I can feel his presence—the heat of his body, the scent of whiskey and leather, and the sound of his deep, controlled breathing completely surrounds me.

"Tell me what you need." He nearly growls the words and I suppress a moan. Even in my current state, I can't say the words. I've never had to. I know this man won't hit me or treat me like I'm used to. His method of pain is so much more intimate —so intimate it makes it even more impossible for me to ask.

"I can't." I shake my head, having to pinch my eyes tight to keep from opening them and looking at him.

"Do you trust me, Love?" *Love…*

"Yes." I don't have to think about it. It's a given. Even if I didn't trust him, it wouldn't matter in this moment. He can do to me what he wants. But I do trust that he couldn't do any more damage to me than what's already been done.

"Do you want to feel pain?" Before now, this has never been an option. Now that I'm hearing it out loud, I don't want to answer. But I do anyway.

"Yes," I whisper. I should be feeling a sense of shame, but my need overpowers it—so much so, I open my eyes.

His face is tilted down slightly, so his mouth is near my hair. Surprisingly, I find his eyes are closed.

"How much?"

"It doesn't matter." At my admission, a pained look crosses his face. His brows draw together, and his head turns slightly as if the impact of my answer was like a slap in the face.

I feel guilty for asking him to do this. I don't want to see him hurt. I don't want to force him to do something he's not comfortable with. *I don't enjoy hitting women.* His words play on a loop inside my head. I'm just before telling him to forget about it when his face smoothes out and his jaw tightens. Without moving his head or straightening his stance, his eyes open and he's meeting my gaze.

They're on fire—blazing with dominance and determination. It's a look that's familiar—once again so intense I feel my knees go weak. He's like a powerful force that instantly has my mind and body under complete submission. He takes several steps away from me, then stops when he reaches the foot of the bed.

I hold my breath in anticipation, while I fist another handful of my hair at the nape of my neck and pull—looking for some kind of immediate release. It doesn't work.

"Come here, Love." His soothing demand has my feet moving toward him on their own accord. When I'm so close I swear I can hear the steady rhythm of his heart, I stop. Pulling an orange bandana from his back pocket, he gives it a shake—causing the muscles in his neck to tense.

"Cover your eyes." I frown at his demand. I open my mouth to protest, but he speaks. "It wasn't a suggestion, Love. I won't tell you again." I'm not afraid of him hurting me more if I refuse, I'm afraid of him not hurting me at all. Right now, the only way this punishment could be worse is if he simply walked out and left me to deal with my demons on my own. It's not worth the risk.

I take it from him, tying it tightly around my eyes. The room is bright enough I'm not engulfed in darkness, but I can't see anything other than the orange material. My breathing becomes heavier as I stand blindfolded and completely at his mercy. My pulse quickens with every moment that passes in silence.

Finally, I hear the rattle of chains as he moves from in front of me. Then his voice fills the room. "Bend over and put your hands on the desk." He takes my elbow, guiding me a few steps before releasing me. I lean forward as my hands wander aimlessly in front of me until I feel the cool, smooth wood. Palms flat against the surface, I'm bent at the waist forcing my ass in the air.

When his hand touches the small of my back, my body jerks then immediately relaxes. After a moment, I feel his hand smooth over my hip before gripping the towel that's tied tightly around me. My flesh is on fire, and the moment his cool fingers connect with my skin I shiver. With one swift movement, the towel falls away.

"I'm going to spank you, Love. Do you know why?" His voice is stern. Even the sweet endearment doesn't soften the powerful effect his tone has on me.

"Because I deserve it," I breathe, allowing myself to feel the full impact of my self-loathing.

"Why do you deserve it?" The guilt of my sins becomes heavier. I know that's part of repenting—I just wasn't expecting to verbally admit all my wrongdoing to him. Too desperate to go through the entire list, I sum it up with the simplest answer.

"Because I'm sick."

For a minute, there's complete silence. Then I feel his hand gently caressing my ass. "No, Love." There's a hint of sadness in his voice. "I'm doing this because you hurt yourself, after you promised me you wouldn't. You lied to me."

My brow furrows in confusion. "I didn't—" His hand at my back silences me. The sound of his belt unbuckling at his waist makes my knees tremble in anticipation, and a hint of fear.

"Yes, you did. You clawed your neck, pulled your hair and pinched your arms." *How the hell does he know that? Oh yeah... he was watching.* "That's why you deserve this. Nothing more. Do you understand?"

My head is spinning, trying to process what he's saying. The hate I feel toward myself about all the horrible things I've done in my life lifts. Suddenly, I only feel guilty about the transgressions I committed today. It's a welcome relief I wasn't expecting. This is what I'm owed. It's not just a medicine to me, it's a cure.

"I'm going to make sure you remember the consequences of endangering yourself. When I'm through with your pretty little ass, you'll be reminded for days of what happens when you're careless about your own wellbeing." He's serious. His threat is real—menacing. He's angry with me. Angry I lied. Angry I hurt myself. And I have a feeling he'd have spanked me even if I didn't ask him to.

Hot, searing pain lashes across my ass. The crack of the belt sounds loud in the room. I gasp at the contact, but welcome it. Another jolt of pain shoots through me as he swings again— hitting the exact same spot. I can feel the flesh swell from the attack, but the belt strikes me in a different position— temporarily taking my mind from one sting to focus on another.

My toes curl in the carpet as blow after blow comes. Tears fall from my eyes and pool in the fabric covering my face, but I've yet to cry out. Several strokes later, I begin to lift my knees and try to wiggle away from the next lash. After a while, my slick palms begin to slide and sobs burst from behind my lips.

His hand moves between my shoulders—the small break from his whipping welcome as he changes position. He has to force me to stay still as I fight against him, but his one hand pressing against me is strong enough to make any attempt at my escape worthless.

"Stop! Please, stop! I'm sorry!" I wail, beg, sob and plead for him to quit. My demon is caged. My vision clear. The reason for my crying is evident—no longer a result of my monster, but now solely due to physical, unrelenting pain.

"Bryce! Please!" He ignores me. He continues to hit me, over and over until every inch of my ass and the very tops of my thighs have been punished multiple times.

I'm going to die. He is going to beat me to death. I'm pretty sure he's working on my third layer of skin—he has to be. I can't remember anything being as awful as this. Something in my head screams at me that this is the first time I've had a punishment I actually deserved.

I did put myself in danger by going to my mother's. I knew what would happen to me, yet I went anyway. I'd gained nothing from the trip. I'd only lost—my car and the flesh of my ass.

My hips jerk from the sting of a blow that hurt worse than the others. Two more follow before I hear the belt fall from his hands. My knees give way, but he catches me just as they're about to hit the floor.

Wrapping an arm around my waist, he supports me as he rips the bandana from my eyes. I'm sobbing with reprieve— feeling just as good as I did the last time he spanked me. Maybe even better. Pulling me to his chest, he bears my weight while he strokes my hair. When he speaks tenderly to me, I block out everything and focus on his words as he holds me tightly in his arms.

*"It's okay, Love."*

*"Shhh...it's over."*

*"I got you."*

*"Calm down."*

*"Just breathe."*

*"You're okay, Love."*

And I am. I mean, I'm okay. I'm better than okay. Sure, I'm weepy and exhausted and I feel like someone shot me in the ass with a case of Roman candles, but I'm okay. Emotionally, I don't feel paralyzed or shut off from the world anymore. Most of all, I know exactly why he did what he did.

Not because I needed it.

Not because I asked.

But because I deserved it—for reasons specified by him. Justifiable reasons that leave nothing to my imagination. My slate is clean. He's no longer angry with me. Him and I are good. In turn, I'm good. Maybe better than I've ever been.

"You're okay. Calm down, baby. Deep breaths. The spanking is over." The word "spanking" has me flushing as red as my ass. It sounds so erotic on his lips. But there was nothing erotic about what he just did. It was a punishment—a well-deserved, well-delivered, well-received one I won't soon forget.

I concentrate on the steady rhythm of his heart and hands as they caress my back. My sobs die. My tears stop. When he pulls back and cups my face in his hands, I don't meet his eyes. I've never been one to get embarrassed, but this is downright humiliating. He'd just *spanked* me. *Again.*

"Look at me, Love." When I don't, he clears his throat. When that doesn't work, he threatens me. "I have no problem tearing your ass up again. Now look at me." I do. How can I not?

*I have no problem tearing your ass up again.* I shiver.

"Better?" he asks, kinder, gentler than I expected. I nod. I know he's not talking about my tight, raw, burning cheeks. He's talking about my sickness. He gives me a warm smile, his thumb brushing over the swell of my cheek, but he keeps his eyes on mine.

"You need to rest. Take some time to relax and get yourself together. I'll call Luke and tell him your car got stolen, and you won't be in for a couple days." Panic fills me at the thought of him telling Luke what he...did to me.

"Please don't tell anybody." Shit. What if he already had? What if York was still at the door? My eyes shift behind him, and he shakes his head—aware of my thoughts.

"I won't tell anyone. I haven't told anyone. York left when I got here. I'll tell Luke your car was stolen and I'm staying with you until you hear something from the police. That's all he has to know."

Guilt has me dropping my gaze, and the subject. "I'm really tired."

He nods. "Lay down and let me look at you." My flush deepens. I don't like this aftercare shit. It doesn't feel right. Doesn't he have something to do? Somewhere to go? A liquor store to rob?

But I don't ask. I just do as I'm told—physically and mentally too tired to care anymore. He pulls back the covers and I wince as I bend my knees to lie on my belly. My skin feels too stretched—tight and burning, even throbbing in some places.

"Stay put," he demands, disappearing into the bathroom. I roll my eyes. Where the fuck am I gonna go? I can't even wear underwear...

He returns moments later, carrying a bottle of lotion from the bathroom. "This will have to do for now," he says, taking a seat on the edge of the bed beside me. I turn my face to look at him, noticing how he keeps his expression blank, but it's a struggle.

"I didn't go easy on you," he starts, his voice nearly a whisper as his hand feathers across my battered flesh. Even the light touch burns. "But only because you deserved it." His eyes move to mine—the intensity of them emphasizing the warning in his words. "Don't ever lie to me again, Delilah. When I ask you not to do something, and you promise me you won't, I expect you to keep your word. I don't tolerate liars in my club, and I won't allow you to get away with it either."

His threat was meant to scare me. And it did. He's right. The club doesn't tolerate liars. It's an unforgivable sin. Something warm swims through me at the thought of him holding me to the same standards as he does his brothers.

"Spread your legs, Love." My stomach constricts and I let out a long breath—my nostrils flaring and my eyes widening as I shake my head. His hand smoothes the hair from my face. "I'm not going to hurt you, Delilah. I'm not going to fuck you either. I just need to take care of you."

My eyes well with tears for the millionth time. This time it's not from the pain or the humiliation, but from the tenderness in his touch. The reassurance in his voice. The care of him. *Damn, I'm fucked up.*

Parting my knees, I do as he says. To some, this would be a turn-on—the pleasure/ pain mixture is often craved by submissives. But to me, they are not one and the same. As if he wants to see for himself, I notice his eyes dart to my exposed sex. His jaw tightens when he finds my folds dry without a hint of arousal. *Now he knows too.*

Squirting lotion in his hands, he warms it by rubbing his palms together. When one large palm covers a cheek, I wished he hadn't warmed it at all. His touch is like fire, causing me to hiss through my teeth. "Shhh..." is the only offer of reassurance I get.

He continues to rub the lotion into me—moisturizing the too dry, overheated flesh. His hand moves from one cheek to the next, before coming to the back of my thighs. That seems to be where the pain is worse—the skin there more tender than that of my ass. I bury my face in the pillow and bite hard on my lip.

He's finally finished, and when his hands leave me, the cool air in the room feels heavenly on my damp bottom. It's like aloe to a sunburn. "Get some sleep, Love. I promise I'll be here when you wake up."

Something about that promise unnerves me. I really don't want him here when I wake up. I want him to be gone. Why can't he just let me heal on my own, and take care of myself? As I drift, I hold tight to that hope. Maybe, just maybe, I'll wake up and realize this was all just a bad dream.

# CHAPTER 16

"Delilah..." *Go away.*

"Delilah." *Hardening your voice won't help you.*

A loud sigh. *"Delilah."* It's a warning, but I'm too tired.

A swat to my ass has my eyes flying open and tears pricking the back of them. *Motherfucker, that hurt.* "Ow!" I yelp, seconds after the contact. The pain seems to intensify as it lingers. "Why would you do that?" It's the most pitiful whimper I've ever managed.

I look up to find green eyes flash with regret. I'll have to remember that sleepy whine and use it to my advantage in the future.

"We have to go. I'm needed in Hattiesburg." *What? No apology?*

"Why?"

"Why's not important. Get up and get dressed." Glancing at the clock, I find it just a little after four in the morning. I hadn't been asleep three hours, and my body demanded more.

"Come on, babe. You can sleep in the truck."

"Truck? Where's your bike?" I ask, cringing as I slide off the bed—avoiding sitting on the side. I'm being a wimp, but I don't care.

He shoots me a look, his eyes moving to my naked pussy. "I don't think you want to ride bitch in your state." I hadn't thought about that. Just the idea of how painful it would be to feel the vibrations from his bike on the bruised cheeks of my ass has me shivering.

"Well, where did the truck come from?" *Damn, I'm nosy.* If I'm annoying to my ears, I can only imagine what I must sound like to him.

But he doesn't seem bothered by my questions. "It's the club's. Someone will bring my bike to the clubhouse later. I'll ride one of the extras from the garage until they get it to me."

I start to pull my sweats up my legs, but he calls from across the room. "Wait." He rifles through his bag on the bed that wasn't here earlier, and pulls something out of it. Turning to me, he nods toward the desk. "Bend over."

Immediately, I begin to back up, shaking my head the entire way. He rolls his eyes. "I'm not going to spank you, Love." He holds up a tube of ointment for me to see. "Trust me, you want it." I tilt my head as I appraise him. He must read the question through my eyes.

"I bought it after I spanked you the first time. I wasn't sure I would need it again, but I wanted it just in case. It was in my bag, on my bike, so I didn't have it earlier. While you were sleeping, I went outside and got it." He seems exasperated by the time he's finished. I can see the stress in his eyes from whatever is going on with the club, accompanied by his growing impatience with me.

"Tight schedule, Love. Now bend over. If I have to tell you again, I'm gonna whip your ass before I put this on you."

"Okay, sheesh." I hold my palms up and walk to the desk—tentatively bending over for him.

"Good girl." Now I'm aroused.

The scent of sandalwood hangs in the air as he spreads the thick cream over my ass and thighs. The relief is almost instant, and a moan of reprieve escapes me. "Please," I beg, once again uttering the one word that seems to be generic for everything—please fuck me, please spank me, please kiss me...

"You're killin' me, babe," he mutters, the words laced in desire. To be a jerk, I wiggle my ass against his hand. He groans. "Stop." I don't. I move against him again. This time, he rewards me by gripping my hips and pressing his thick length against my ass. The rough material of his jeans hurts despite the healing power of the cream.

"Be careful what you wish for, Love." He pulls away then, leaving me wanting him inside me. But if the pressing need to get on the road is enough to overpower his desire, then I should take it seriously.

I pull my sweats on, opting out of underwear. Tucking them in my pocket, I grab my hoodie—contemplating going braless too. I figure what the hell and shove it in my other pocket before pulling the sweater over my head. By the time Bryce has the door open for me, I've managed to pee, and put on my socks and shoes.

He makes a call on his cell, taking my hand in his as he all but pulls me down the hall. "On my way. Be there in two."

"So what exactly is it you do in the club?" I ask, climbing into the truck. I lean on the console, putting my weight on my hip to avoid the pain of sitting on my ass.

"I'm sergeant at arms. Put your seatbelt on." I start to protest, but he shoots me a look of warning. "Now, Delilah." I strap in, but not before giving him a nasty eye roll.

"If you're the SA, shouldn't you be with your chapter?"

"My chapter has two SAs. Luke is down a man, so I help out when I can." He pulls us onto the highway that leads to the interstate—the speedometer hitting eighty in the fifty-five-mile-an-hour speed zone.

"But how come I haven't seen you until recently? I mean, you don't even come when the chapters have a party. Or at least you haven't when I've been around," I add, my tone petulant.

"I worked offshore. I was only home six months out of the year, and when I was, I handled things for the club. My job is to protect my president and maintain order, but I'm somewhat of an enforcer too. When people fuck up and break the rules, they send me to handle it."

"Why you?"

He turns to me and grins—his eyes shining with an evil that's visible even in the darkness. "Because I'm good at punishing people." I swallow hard, having to break my gaze when he refuses to look away.

"My turn." He props his elbow on the console, his body angling toward the center of the truck. It's so close I can smell the lingering scent of leather on his clothes, even though he's not wearing his cut. "How did a girl like you end up working at the clubhouse?"

"I met Luke," I start, forcing myself to turn and face him. I scoot toward the door, trying for extra space knowing I'll need the distance if we continue this conversation.

"Where did you meet Luke?"

"His office. I was looking for a job. He gave me one." *Liar.*

"Really?" He's smiling at me. Challenging me—like he knows something I don't.

"Yeah, really," I snap, offended by his reaction. "You think I'm lying?"

"I know you're lying." That smile is still there. It's teasing and oh so handsome on his masculine face. The man really is good looking.

"Since you know so much, spill it." I curl my fingers around the seatbelt and lean against the window, giving him a wicked smile of my own. Let's see what Mr. Knowitall thinks he knows.

He quirks an eyebrow. "You sure?"

"Oh, I'm sure." *Sure you don't know shit...*

"You came from a broken home, were looking for a way out and found security and comfort among all us biker trash." He lifts his hands from the steering wheel a moment, like he's really done something, and shoots me a cocky grin. I shake my head and laugh. Normally I'd insert an "idiot" in my thoughts, but something tells me he's not an idiot at all.

"You're wrong. What do I win?"

"I didn't realize it was a competition."

"Everything's a competition. So what's my prize?"

Mischief dances in his eyes and plays on my lips, as he glances between me and the road—the tension from earlier still there, but masked by this refreshingly cheery mood. But all too soon, the playfulness fades slightly and the moment becomes more intense.

"Would you tell me the truth if I wanted to know?"

The story of how I got here is a very serious one for me. For years Luke's kept the truth to himself—telling everyone the exact story Bryce just told me verbatim. I've never told anybody anything about me. But he's already aware of my situation, and I want to tell him—not everything, but the reason behind my need for him to hurt me.

"Yes." My one-word whisper is a milestone for me. And the look he's giving me says it's a small triumph for him as well.

"I want to know, Delilah. I want you to tell me the truth."

There's something very comforting about his presence. The transition from dominant Bryce to understanding psychiatrist Bryce doesn't seem possible. They're two different men. One I want to spank me. The other I want to tell my story to.

"I left home at sixteen," I say, noticing the pack of cigarettes in the cup holder. Pulling one from the pack, I light it and crack the window. Hell, I've already broken my one-smoke-a-day rule anyway. "By then, I was damaged beyond repair—or so I thought. I lived a couple years on the street before I met this guy in a nightclub. I went home with him after he defended my honor by beating the shit outta these guys."

I smile at the memory of Mario and what he was like when we first met. "Like me, he was fucked up. We worked our frustrations out with sex. It didn't matter where we were or who was around...whenever the urge hit us, we just did it. For a while, that worked. But I needed more. I lost it one day, and he didn't know how to handle it. So he hit me. When he realized it made me better, he didn't stop."

I take a deep pull from the cigarette—searching for some form of encouragement from the nicotine. The headlights on the interstate fade away—Bryce fades away as I allow the dark memories to come back to life.

"I became so dependent on him. He was the only one who could fix me. And he knew it. There was no end to the shit he would do to me. I used to pray he'd just kill me … put me out of the misery that was my mind. I think he tried to a few times, but I always managed to pull through. Even after all that, I wanted him to want me. To love me and be proud of me. He never was."

I'm silent for a moment as the black fades and I'm brought back to the present. Releasing a breath, I force a smile, but refuse to look at Bryce—I'm too afraid of what I'll find.

"Then I met Luke. He helped me. What I needed in my life was control. I needed someone to make decisions for me… someone to tell me what to do. He taught me to think for myself. By letting me live and work at the clubhouse, I was able to fulfill my sexual desires and have a safe place to sleep. Soon I became what I'm known as now…a clubwhore." I swallow at the sound of the word on my lips—noting how ashamed it makes me feel to say it to him.

"It was easy to give myself to the men. Easier than I imagined. Even the first time was fun. It came like second nature to me. The brothers aren't monsters. They'd never hurt me. And I love having sex. A part of me needs it. It makes me feel powerful and wanted. It doesn't solve all my issues, but I manage to deal with the others on my own."

I'm pretty sure he thinks he knows what I'm talking about. I'll bet anything images of me cutting myself are flashing through his head right now. When I called him last night, he was clueless about the truth. He assumes I was carjacked, and attacked. He knows nothing of my family. And that small secret is one I'm happy to hold onto—it's a burden no one but me should bear.

"Anyway." I thump my cigarette out the window and roll it up—shoving my cold hands into the front pocket of my hoodie. "Even though I can think for myself, I really don't have to at the clubhouse. My job is simple. Luke did that for me. I owe him my life."

I turn my eyes to Bryce as I say the last words. I want him to feel the full impact of what I'm trying to say. His club was a godsend. Luke Carmical was a godsend. Without them I'd be dead…or worse.

He meets my gaze, his expression blank. He doesn't speak until his eyes are back on the road. "How do you deal with the need for pain?" I flinch at his question. I wasn't expecting this to be a Q&A. I was expecting an I-talk-he-listens kind of approach.

This also tells me he believed me when I told him I usually didn't cut myself when he found me all those days ago. Now he wants the source of what I really use to cope.

"I just do."

Without enough time to process my evasive answer, he fires another question. "Who do you let hurt you?" I try to ignore him, but he presses further. "I've seen the bruises, babe. I've seen the ones on your stomach, along your ribs, your face ... Is that what happened yesterday? Do you know the man that hurt you and stole your car?" He sounds patient, but I can feel the tension thickening in the truck.

"I don't want to talk about this anymore."

His hand curves around my knee. I jerk at the touch. "Look at me." Abandoning the road, his eyes are hard and narrowed on mine. "It's not okay for someone to hurt you out of anger. I don't care how much you think you deserve it." Speaking of anger, it's emanating off him. But even as the rage clearly shows on his face and flashes in his eyes, his grip on my knee never tightens. He might be mad, but he's not taking it out on me.

"This conversation is over." Slapping his hand away from my leg, I turn to lean against the window—ignoring the irritating burn in my ass. I close my eyes in search of something to occupy my mind—anything to distract me from the past twenty-four fucked-up hours.

He must understand—read my mind in that weird way of his. Instead of continuing the conversation, he turns on the radio. The same blend of classical music he'd played in the clubhouse fills the cab. And thankfully, it's enough to tame my thoughts and lull me to sleep.

\*\*\*\*

I don't remember being carried to my bed that night. But I will never forget the eerie silence that came the next morning. Everyone was gone—except for me. Luke's house that stands within a stone's throw of the clubhouse was vacant as well. There was no Dallas, no sign of Red, or the recently returned Maddie.

Something was wrong. I could feel it. The fear of the unknown hung heavy in the air. When I could stand it no more, I contacted Linda first. There was no answer, which wasn't unusual. I tried several of the other girls, but it was the same.

I knew better than to call the men. Linda made that mistake once before, and she'd been put in her place quickly—Luke told her club business wasn't her business. Besides, it wasn't like I had anyone who I should feel responsible for. I didn't belong to any of the men. I was an employee—nothing more.

After nearly twelve hours of not hearing a word from anyone, I felt my anxiety start to peak. Then finally, the phone rang. I hurried to it, scared of missing the call and desperate for some hint about what in the hell was going on.

"Hello?"

"Hello, Love." My entire body sags with relief at the two words. Sliding to the floor behind the bar, I reach for my cigarettes and shakily light one. "Delilah?"

"I'm here," I breathe, my reprieve nearly too much. I wasn't sure if it was from knowing he was okay, or the sound of another human voice.

"The club has a problem that needs handling. We'll be gone the rest of the week. I need you to stay at the clubhouse. Don't leave until one of our own shows up. Do you understand?"

"No, Bryce. I don't understand. What is going on?" There's silence for a moment, as if he's contemplating telling me the truth.

"Nothing that concerns you." I close my eyes, feeling hurt by his words, even though I shouldn't.

"Please tell me *something.* Is everyone okay?" I need to know. I *have* to know.

"Everyone is fine, Love. Just some shit that requires all of us to be where we are."

"Where is Dallas? And Red? Are they with y'all? What about Linda and the other girls? I haven't seen any of them. They—"

"Calm down, babe. Dallas and Red are fine. I'll have Luke find out about Linda and the other girls, but I'm sure they're at home. When I got to the clubhouse, Linda was there. She knew the club was going on a run." Everyone knew. Everyone but me. The hurt I shouldn't feel intensifies.

"I don't like to be alone," I admit, feeling stupid for doing so. It's not his fault, and there's nothing he can do from where he is.

His silence is deafening. I can almost feel his uneasiness through the phone. I hate myself for making him worry. "I'll be fine," I blurt. "I'll binge watch Netflix." My smile is forced, but I hope it reflects in my tone.

"If you start feeling it, you call me." I know he's referring to my need for pain—but it's the darkness that scares me most.

"Really. I'm good." What could he do anyway? He wouldn't abandon his club for a whore...would he? I shake the stupid thought from my head.

"Don't leave that clubhouse. I mean it. If you do, I'll find out. And I'll make sure you don't sit for a week. Understood?" My breath hitches at his promise, and I nod, forgetting he can't see it. "An answer, Love."

"I understand. I won't leave."

"Good girl. I'll see you when I see you." He hangs up, not even giving me a chance to say good-bye.

I stand and look around the empty room. A void slowly fills my chest as I take it in—feeling the full impact of my harsh reality.

For the first time in two years, I'm alone.

# CHAPTER 17

Four days.

It's been four days and I haven't seen a single soul. Bryce has called me at least twice a day to check in. Each time, I manage to fake my mood. I lie to him—lies so convincing even I'm starting to believe them. But if he calls today, I won't be able to lie. I'm too close to clawing my eyes out.

In four days, I've had a total of ten hours of sleep. I've been living on caffeine, French fries and cigarettes—all of which are running low.

I don't even wait for the coffee to finish before I replace the pot with my own cup—making it even more deliciously strong. I've settled on the bar, coffee in hand, one drag into my cigarette when the phone rings. I'm quick to grab it, sure that it's Bryce.

It isn't. It's a recording reminding me of the rapidly approaching Valentine's Day. Out of pure boredom, I listen to the entire message as the robotic woman urges me to go out in the cold, fight the onslaught of crazed lovers and purchase meaningless gifts for people I really don't give two shits about. I politely decline, then hit zero to participate in their survey.

By the time I hang up, cup one of coffee is down and I'm lighting cigarette number three. I think this whole smoking thing isn't working out for me like I'd planned.

I check the clock again, and only two hours have passed since I last looked. I've kept myself busy since I've been awake—playing pool, alphabetizing the liquor, practicing my trampoline gymnastics...minus the trampoline. But the inevitable is happening. I'm beginning to break down.

I haven't had sex in six days. It may not sound like a long time, but when you're addicted to it, six days might as well be six years. I crave it. Not just the company of another person, but the feeling of release.

As long as I'm having sex, my body and mind focuses on the moment—what it needs to do and think to continue the constant build until I finally peak and reach that euphoric, orgasmic state. But to me, sex has a dual purpose. Not only does it satisfy my hungry urges, but it helps keep my mind off the other thing that breaks me down—the need to feel pain.

My mind is always in constant turmoil. Every minute of every day, I feel it. When I'm distracted by work, or other people, it's not as intense, but it's still there. I can control it—monitor it and treat it when necessary. But when I'm alone, it's only me against my mind. I have to fight the losing battle with my demons solo. And it's nearly impossible.

I hate going to the darkness. It's a place that you have to feel to understand. But I'll do my best to explain it. If you close your eyes, you see nothing. The problem with nothing is that it doesn't exist. So soon, you begin to wonder what it is you're actually seeing. You get so caught up in the war with your mind that you simply forget you're even in existence.

You feel nothing.

You taste nothing.

You hear nothing.

You're like a zombie, wandering mindlessly around with no purpose other than survival. When you're hungry, you eat. When you're sleepy, you sleep. You physically function like a human being, but you're detached—completely cut off from everything that emotionally makes you human.

If you're in a deep slumber and someone throws cold water on you, instantly you awake. Well, it's like that. Only my cold water is pain. When I'm forced to feel, eventually I wake up. The process starts with anger, but it's the final thing I feel before the darkness swallows me whole.

That's where I am right now. I'm angry. I'm downright pissed. I generally use the tactic to get what I want—someone to lash out and hit me. I continue to provoke them until they beat my demons into submission and lock them in their cage. I've learned to cope with the aftermath on my own. Bryce is the first man who's ever been there to catch me when I fall. But I'm sure it was more for his guilt than it was for my wellbeing.

I have to find relief. I have to do something—today. If I don't, the darkness is going to consume me. Then I'll end up doing something I regret. I'll put myself at the mercy of my brother. Even with the knowledge that this time, he might kill me.

Chances are, he won't get the opportunity. At the rapid rate I'm declining, someone else will most likely beat him to the punch.


I make it through the next night without having sex, killing myself or having myself killed by someone else. It's Thursday morning, and I'm finally catching a break. In search of something to relieve the pounding in my head, I come across a bottle of pain relievers behind the bar. Inside, mixed with every kind of over-the-counter medication you can imagine, are several Xanax.

My fidgety hands break two glasses before I give up and uncork a bottle of bourbon. Tossing several of the pills to the back of my throat, I chase them with the slow-burning liquid until I feel the fire in the bottom of my gut. I'm acutely aware of my surroundings and the constant ringing of the phone. But I ignore it, barely managing to make my way down the hall to my room.

I'm exhausted. My mind has been spinning, my beast has been rattling the bars on his cage and I've been tempted to cut myself to find relief. But every time I started to, images of Bryce would flash in my head. I had to hold on. I promised him. It shouldn't mean a damn thing to me, but for some reason it does.

Falling face first on my bed, I close my eyes and pray for the pills and booze to take effect. I want to find the nothing I've been searching for. I want it all to just disappear. I've fought against the darkness long enough—it's time to give in.

Just before everything fades to black, I see his face one last time—those green eyes blazing with promise and dominance and everything I've always needed, but never really wanted until I met him.

*Bryce.*


I feel the darkness. It engulfs me—consumes me. Inside and out, I'm numb. My body is functioning on survival and instinct. There's a buzzing in my head, my memory is foggy, but if I feel like this, then it has to be Sunday.

I have things to do on Sunday. I have to visit my mother and my brother. First I have to have coffee and a cigarette. Then I think I'll have some oatmeal.

There are people here so I smile. Linda is talking to me, asking me what I've been up to. I tell her not much, then sit in silence while she tells me about her week. I drink my coffee, eat my oatmeal, smoke my cigarette, then politely excuse myself back to my room.

I got paid last week since Luke was out of town this week. I pull two hundred dollars from the envelope I keep hidden in my closet. I shove the money inside my duffel, along with a change of clothes. I need the extra suit in case my others get blood on them.

My car isn't here, but Linda's is outside and I know she leaves the keys in it. I'll just borrow it. I have to visit my mother and brother. It's Sunday. I have to repent.

I crawl out of my window, sling my duffel over my shoulder and pull my hood over my head. It's still dark out, so no one should see me. If they do, I'll lie and say I'm going to see a friend. I won't say I'm going to Baton Rouge—Bryce won't like that if he finds out.

It must be cold outside, but I don't feel it. I'm only aware because of the goosebumps that cover my skin and the involuntary jerk my body does every few steps. The wind is howling—whipping stray strands of hair across my face. Still I feel nothing. But what is nothing?

"Delilah?" Bryce?

My eyes follow in the direction of his voice. I have to speak. I have to smile. I have to be polite. I can't let him know where I'm going.

"Hel-lo." I'm stuttering. My teeth are chattering. He's close to me.

"Where are you going?"

"A friend's." His eyes drop to mine. Even though everything else is a blur, mostly dull and lifeless, I see the intense green of his eyes. They're blazing and hypnotic.

"Did you hear me?" *Did he say something?*

"A friend's." I've repeated my answer to his first question, but he doesn't seem to understand. He mumbles something, but I can't make out his words.

"Listen to me, Delilah." His fingers curl around my arms as he brings his face level with mine. I need to go to my mother's. It's Sunday. But for some reason, I need to listen to him more. "What did you take?"

"It's Sunday. I have somewhere to be. It's my day off. Luke says I have Sundays off."

I'm guided to a truck—Luke's truck. Bryce lifts me and puts me in the passenger seat. I'm not supposed to be in here. I need to borrow Linda's car. But he's in the driver's seat. In Luke's truck. And he's driving us away.

"Tell me what you did today." His voice is so soft, I almost don't hear it. I don't want to hear it. I don't want to talk anymore. I don't have to. I was polite. I smiled and listened and said hello. "Talk to me, Love." His voice is louder. Is he angry? Mario hits me when he's angry. It makes me feel better. But Mario is dead. My brother hits me when he's angry too. He's not dead. It's Sunday.

Something is touching my leg. I can feel it. I shouldn't but I do. I look down, and Bryce has his hand on the inside of my thigh. He squeezes, and somewhere deep inside, I feel a tiny ache. I want more of it. I close my eyes, and the tiny pain grows like it's trying to push to the surface.

"Look at me, Love." His threatening demand has me wanting to look at him. So I do. He glances between me and the road. "Can you feel that? Does it make it better?"

I shiver. Then I realize I'm cold.

*Cold...not nothing.*

"Answer me, Love."

"I'm cold." His hand leaves my thigh. The pain fades—sinking deeper back into the darkness with me. Then he puts it back. I watch as his big hand pinches my thigh again. The ache returns, but it's small and distant.

The truck stops moving. I don't know where we are. He's not touching me anymore, and something inside me yearns to feel his hands on me again. I want him to touch me. I want him to hurt me. I *need* him to hurt me.

I'm in his arms. It's cold outside. I can feel it, and my body shakes. He's carrying me inside a house. It's not cold in here. Lights come on, but everything is dull. Not like his eyes that are green, and shine bright.

He's taking off my clothes. I don't stop him. I can't. I think he told me to stand still. I don't remember. My arms are stretched out. My hands are tied. I'm lying on my stomach. He's next to my face, looking at me.

"Did it make you feel better when I pinched you?" I can't look away from him. He's all I see. His voice is paralyzing. It's all I hear.

"Yes." It made me feel cold...not nothing.

"Do you want me to make you feel better?"

"Yes."

"I'm going to spank you, Love. Twenty times. And you are going to count each one. Do you understand?"

"Yes." I hear him. His voice makes me want to listen. I want to do what he tells me to do. He's going to make me feel better.

I can't see him anymore. He's behind me. There's a buzzing in my ears, and I can't hear anything. Only his voice. "Are you ready, Love?"

"Yes."

Something strikes me. I don't know what it is, but just like in the truck, there is a distant ache. He's spanking me. I have to count.

"One."

"Good job, Love. Again."

Another strike—this one can be felt more than the last. He said twenty. He told me to count.

"Two."

He's hitting me over and over. I'm counting. I'm at fifteen and the ache is no longer distant. It's on the surface. It hurts. I want more. He continues to give me more. After twenty, he's beside me again.

"How do you feel, Love?" I don't want him to stop. When he stops, the hurt goes away. I want the hurt.

"I need more." He doesn't look sad, or angry. He looks in control. I want him to control me.

"I'm going to give you more. Thirty this time. Count."

The pain is back. It's dull.

"One."

More spanking.

"Ten."

The pain is above the surface.

"Eighteen."

It hurts. It hurts so bad.

"Twenty-five."

I'm crying. I'm sad. Not because he's hitting me, but because I'm sick.

"Twenty-eight."

There is no darkness. I can see in color. I'm crying hard—screaming, but I don't ask him to stop. I need everything he promised me. I'm no longer drowning. The reprieve is overwhelming. I'm exhausted, both physically and emotionally.

"Thirty," I manage through a sob. I don't want him to hit me anymore. I don't want to be alone either. I want him. And he's here.

"Talk to me, Love." The tone of his voice is soothing, nurturing and the most beautiful thing I've ever heard as he unties my hands.

"I'm sorry!" I wail, unsure of what I'm particularly apologizing for. I guess for it all—my weakness, vulnerability, lack of control...the list is endless. "I'm so sorry. Please forgive me." For some reason, the thought of him hating me for dragging him into the cesspool that is my life is worse than the darkness and the pain.

"You have nothing to be sorry about," he assures me, curling me in his arms. My hands fist around his T-shirt—clinging for dear life. I bury my face in his chest and sob, just letting him hold me. He's the only man that's ever done it. I can't imagine anyone's arms feeling as good as his.

"Calm down, Love. I'm not going anywhere." His words break through my panic and I loosen my grip. He's here. I'm here. It's just the two of us. There's no darkness...no pain...no *nothing.*

Time passes, and he holds me. I don't know how long it's been, but at some point my sobs die and my tears stop. I've kept my mind free of any thoughts that aren't centered around the way he smells—masculine and clean like he's freshly showered. Or the way he feels—strong, warm and protective.

"I'm not always like this," I whisper to his chest. His arms tighten around me. "For years, I've found a way to cope. I've let people take advantage of me ... hurt me. Then for days my focus was on healing. I found things to occupy my mind until I needed it again. But sometimes, I lose it. Sundays are always the worst."

"Today's not Sunday, Love." My brow furrows at his words, but I remain silent. I was sure today was Sunday. But Bryce has no reason to lie to me. I guess the past several days I've been alone, time had somehow fused with the darkness—preventing me from distinguishing the difference between reality and imagination.

"Who helps you when you get like this?" I almost find humor in his question. It helps to soften the blow of the truth. But I feel so raw and open with him. There's no point in sugarcoating the truth—not with Bryce.

"Nobody. It's just me." I feel him tense at my admission. "I try not to let it get this bad. It's harder to bounce back." *It wasn't very hard this time...*

"You're a strong woman. A helluva lot stronger than me."

"No, I'm not. I'm weak." Raising my head from his chest, I look him in the eye. "What kind of person lets people beat them? And not just allows it, but craves it. I feel like I can't breathe without the pain. Do you know how damaged I am?"

Pushing my hair back from my face, he looks at me so appreciatively. Reverently. As if I'm something special. "We all need something, Love. For you it's pain. For me it's the club. You just have to find a way to manage it so it doesn't control who you are. I can help you do that."

"How?"

"Do you trust me?" The question is genuine, and I can see the apprehension on his face. He's nervous about my answer. He shouldn't be. He's asked me twice, and both times I've given him the same response.

"Yes. More than I've ever trusted anyone."

"Then let me help you."

"You keep saying that, but how? I can't be fixed, Bryce. I've tried everything."

"Not everything." He gives me a sideways, confident smile. "You don't need to be fixed, babe. Because you're not broken. You just need someone to teach you how to embrace who you are."

I've never been good at riddles. He's jumping around the "how" and straight to the "say yes." I can't lie though--telling me I'm not broken is the nicest thing anyone has ever said to me. It's a lie, true. But that line alone is enough to have me agree to whatever he wants.

"Okay." I shrug, as if we're talking about something as simple as what's for dinner rather than my life. "But I'm not calling you master." I yawn loudly, ready to close my eyes and put an end to this nightmare that has taken a surprising turn to a wet dream.

Smirking, he plants a kiss on my forehead that warms me in places I didn't know I could feel, before giving me a wink. "Good. Like I said, I'm not a dominant."

*Sure he's not.*

# CHAPTER 18

There's this constant buzzing in my ear. It's annoying. I don't have an alarm clock, so that can't be it. But then I remember, I'm not home. I'm here—wherever in the hell "here" is —with him. Bryce.

Stretching, I hit the alarm with my hand, silencing it. I look around the small room that consists of four white walls, a bed and a dresser. It's...efficient at best. The door is open, allowing me to see into the living room that's just as boring as the bedroom. I notice a couch and a coffee table, but there is no décor, lamps, rugs or even a TV. The entire house is quiet and I wonder if Bryce is even here.

In search of a bathroom, I slide out of bed, feeling slightly sore as I do. My hands slide to my backside. The flesh is tender, warm and coated in some type of moisturizer. *The spanking cream...* I flush and my stomach flips at the thought of him taking care of me even as I slept.

I pull the sheet from the bed—wrapping it around me before slowly making my way to the living room. My ass isn't the only thing that's sore—my entire body feels sluggish. I feel like I've been drugged. *Oh yeah... I guess a handful of Xanax will do that to you...*

I find the bathroom situated right next to it. Inside, I discover every kind of toiletry item I could hope for—all brand new. What the hell is this place? *Oh shit...* What if I'm not the first woman he's brought here to "help?"

"Good morning." I nearly trip over my own feet at the sound of his voice. Then my knees turn to Jell-O when I look at him. He's standing in the door—stretching his arms over his head as he grips the frame. He's shirtless, big, sexy, barefoot...powerful.

"Morning." I grip the sheet tighter to my chest—suddenly self-conscious now that he's so close.

"I made coffee. Kitchen's that way when you're finished." He juts his thumb in the direction of the kitchen, then smirks and disappears.

By the time I've used the bathroom, brushed my teeth and splashed freezing water on my face, I've asked myself at least a hundred times what in the hell I'm even doing here.

Still wearing a sheet, I make my way to the kitchen that is just as boring and standard as the rest of the house. The only thing that makes it interesting is him standing in it—shirtless, big, sexy, barefoot...powerful. *I know, I've already said that.*

On the small wooden table is a steaming cup of coffee, and a pack of cigarettes. I don't even think about how weird it is, I just fire up and sip.

"You're going to stay here with me a few days."

I look at him over the top of my cup. "I have to work."

"You're taking a few days off." Judging by his tone, there's no point in arguing, so I don't. And anyway, I did agree to this. After the hell I went through yesterday, I'm willing to try anything.

"Where are we?" I ask, looking around the place once again. It doesn't look very lived in.

"It used to be a safe house. Back in the eighties, the club had their hands in some shit that put a lot of people at risk. Club's different now, so we just use it when we need it."

"Like when you need to tie women up and spank them?"

He gives me a wicked grin. "Sometimes."

I drop my eyes, contemplating on lighting another cigarette. "Have you done this before?"

"Yes." His immediate answer comes as a surprise to me. I wasn't expecting him to be so...honest.

"Who?"

"Doesn't matter. All you need to do is trust that I know what I'm doing. That's the key here. Trust." *Was it his wife? Girlfriend? Another clubwhore?* "Delilah? You listening to me?"

"You know...I am, but I really want to know who else you've done this for." There's no point in putting it off. My curiosity generally gets the better of me.

He shakes his head, smiling. "Will it make you feel better?"

"It would," I admit, nodding and even giving him my best puppy-dog eyes.

"When I was in college, I shared an apartment with a girl who was a lot like you." I hold my hand up to stop him.

"Wait. You went to college?" I'm dumbfounded with the knowledge, and I may have just insulted him. He raises his brows amused.

"You want me to continue or not?"

"Of course. What did you major in?" His jaw tightens as he looks at me no longer amused, but annoyed.

"Discipline." *Oh...* His eyes narrow, and suddenly I no longer want to interrupt him. After a few moments, a very pleased look crosses his face—no doubt due to my silence—and he continues. "She had a temper. She'd pick fights with me, but I always ignored her. One day, I finally had enough. So I spanked her. The rest is history."

"Um, hardly. What happened after that? Did you keep doing it? Did you do other stuff?" I'm firing off questions left and right. And he's ignoring them all.

"That's enough about me. It's time we talk about you." He grabs something from the counter then pushes it across the table at me. "Eat." I look down at the steaming oatmeal and smile. It even has the little blueberries I love.

"Is there anything you're not comfortable with?"

I shake my head. *This oatmeal is fantastic.*

"I didn't think so," he mumbles. I'm vaguely aware of him watching me eat. I didn't realize how hungry I was. He must have, though—there's enough oatmeal here to feed a small village.

"Mario."

At the mention of his name, I lose my appetite. *Damn good thing I was nearly finished.* I keep my eyes on my spoon as I swirl what's left of my breakfast around the bowl. "What about him?"

"What did he do to you?" His question pisses me off. I don't know why, but dammit...it does.

"Emotionally? Physically? What is it exactly that you're asking?" He ignores my tone, and gives me a blank look. "I couldn't please him. Nothing was ever good enough. I was never good enough. And he never let me forget it."

"So why did you stay?" I shoot him a look. I can feel the blood in my veins beginning to boil. My ears are hot. My nostrils are flaring. He's pissing me off. And he knows it.

"That's not fair and you know it," I warn. My anger isn't an act just to get him to lash out at me—it's genuine.

"Seems fair enough to me. He was a piece of shit. But you stayed. Why?"

"You know why." I'm spitting through my teeth. I'm not intimidated by his presence, or the fact that I'm wrapped in a sheet, sitting at a table, inside a house I've never been in.

I'm still seething in the silence when he smiles. "What you're feeling? We call that anger." *Well, no shit.*

"I'm very aware of what anger feels like."

"No, you're not. You force anger to get what you want. This," he motions with his hand at me, "this is the reaction of someone who is pissed because they actually have a reason to be. And I bet you have no ulterior motive either. You don't want me to reciprocate the anger and hit you. You want me to shut up and drop the subject."

On the inside, I'm a little stunned. I try not to show it, but by the cocky look in his eyes, he can see right through me. I fucking loathe reverse psychology. I never fall for it. Well, I haven't before now.

"How do you know all this? I mean, spanking your college roommate hardly qualifies you to aid in my *rehabilitation*." I hold my fingers up to quote the word.

He silently appraises me a moment. A deep sadness flashes in his eyes, but he conceals it and tightens his jaw. "I majored in physiological psychology. My roommate's condition inspired me. I wanted to learn the human mind. Understand the reasoning behind pain addiction. I dropped out after two semesters, but I continued to study it on my own."

"Why?"

He shrugs. "I was intrigued. Can we get back on topic?" I nod, fully aware that the subject is dropped and he won't be talking about it again.

"You may have it easy at the clubhouse, but in the real world, there are jerks just like Mario who will take advantage of you. I'm not gonna let that happen."

I have questions swimming through my head, but I don't let them surface. I've always been an in-the-moment kinda girl. To hell with the future. I want right now. I've never had anything good happen to me. So I'm gonna take this opportunity and run with it.

Closing the distance between us, he takes my chin in his fingers and gently forces me to meet his eyes. They're burning with raw, primal dominance. "There are other ways to cope, Love. I'm going to teach you how to find that release, and I'm not going to do it with my fist. I'm going to show you your true worth." His voice dips, as he pierces me with his striking, green-eyed stare. "As long as we're here, you belong to me. I'm your Bryce and you're my Love. No dominant. No submissive. Just us. Do you understand?"

"Yes."

There's no hesitation on my part. No second guessing. No deliberating. No other option. Not just because he said so, but because I want to be.

I *need* to be.

I am...his.

Fifteen minutes later, I'm in the shower. Why? Because he told me to shower, dry my hair then meet him in the living room. The need for control isn't foreign to me. I have freedom at the clubhouse, but I rarely use it. I function much better when I know exactly what I need to do—serve beer, be polite and provide pleasure to the club in any manner they desire.

Simple.

There's not one person in particular who yields power over me, they do it as a whole. But here, there are no patches. There's no bar or other people to entertain. It's just me and Bryce. On my own, I wouldn't last three days before I found myself wandering the streets aimlessly in search of someone to tell me what to do. I don't have that fear now, because I'm not alone. I don't have to think. I do as I'm told, and my reward is as simple as feeling alive.

As I start the tedious process of drying my long hair, I wonder what it will be like with him over the next several days.

*Will he put me in a cage?*

*Keep me tied up?*

*Force me to do grotesque things to him?*

*Make me eat from the floor?*

The list is endless, really. My previous experience with Mario has all these scenarios coming to mind. I doubt Bryce is as sadistic as Mario was, but at one time, I thought Mario was a good guy too.

You'd think after the torture he put me through, I would be scared to embark on this journey with Bryce. But as awful as it was, sometimes I find myself missing it. Some people are just naturally submissive. I guess I'm one of those people.


"I don't have any clothes," I tell Bryce, already slipping into that submissive role by dropping my eyes and speaking in a soft, pleasant voice.

"Look at me, Delilah." He's relaxed on the couch, flipping through a magazine. He's fully dressed now in jeans and a black Henley. The material clings to the large muscles on his arms, but hangs loose around his waist.

"Stop." I frown in confusion. "You're a grown woman. Stop pretending to be something you're not. Treat me like you would if we were at the clubhouse."

I feel a tinge of disappointment, and it must show. His face softens as he leans forward, resting his elbows on his knees. "I want you to be who you are. Act how you feel. Not how you think

I expect you to act. You need to learn how to function on your own. I can't teach you that if you're one way with me, and another with everyone else."

*You belong to me... Wasn't that what he said?*

"I'm not sure what you expect from me," I admit, feeling warmth spread through me when his lips twitch at the bitchiness in my tone.

"Do you want a dominant, Delilah? Do you want me to tell you when you can eat, sleep, shower and come?"

"Yes." His lip twitches again.

"I'm not a dominant."

I roll my eyes. "Then what the fuck are you? Why are we here?"

He seems to be throwing my question around in his head. When he answers, he avoids meeting my eyes. "I'm a guy interested in a girl. We're here because there are too many distractions at the clubhouse."

I can't help it. I smile at his admission. "You have a crush on me," I tease, raising my brows. But the joke is on me, 'cause my belly is swarming with butterflies. *He likes me...*

Shaking his head, he lets out a breath of laughter. I think he's slightly embarrassed. Is it possible? Nope. He's just amused. "I have you something to wear on the bed. Put it on." He's yet to meet my eyes, and I wonder if the look I see is guilt. *Probably because he's lying...he wants to be my dominant as bad as I want him to be.*

That "something to wear" is a bathrobe. It's soft, thick and black. It's so long it grazes the tops of my feet. On the floor next to the bed is a pair of matching slippers. There are no panties or bra, and I silently thank the heavens for gracing me with nice boobs that have minimal sagging.

"Okay, *master*," I taunt, looking at him through the opened door. "I'm ready for you to have your way with me."

He stands, clearly not in the mood for my jokes. He's back to that dominant Bryce he swears he's not. His face is hard, his jaw tight, his lips pressed in a thin line. And those eyes...centered on me and blistering with such intensity I nearly take a step back to break the hold they have on me.

"Follow me," he demands, as he heads toward the kitchen. *If he'd have said "come," I swear I would have.* Even as I'm walking, I can feel my desire for him moistening the inside of my thighs. *Why am I just now realizing how turned on I am?* Deep down, I know the answer to that question. *He's fixing to fuck me.*

*He hasn't said it, but I can feel the sexual tension crackling between us.*

I follow him through a door at the back of the kitchen. Three steps lead down into a small hallway that is cold and drafty. He opens another door, and we enter a room that must've been added on after the original house was built. It's dark, windowless and not nearly as boring as the rest of the house. Actually, it's like we've stepped into a whole other world.

The entire room is built out of aromatic cedar wood, except for the floor that is layered in brick. I breathe deep, allowing the intoxicating smell to fill my lungs. There's something calming about it, and I'm guessing whoever built it knew they needed that to keep people from freaking out about the rest of the place.

There aren't shelves lined with various sex toys, or an array of whips and belts hanging from the walls. But there is a slightly elevated bench in the room, a set of chains hanging from the ceiling and a single cabinet with a lock. I'm not sure if I should be excited or nervous.

"This isn't a playroom," Bryce says, watching me intently.

My eyes immediately move to the bench I know is called a "spanking bench." I've seen *Fifty Shades*. I focus on it a moment longer before moving to the chains hanging from the ceiling.

"The chains are for punching bags. And the bench is just a workout bench." He points to the corner of the room, and I notice several sets of weights and two punching bags. There's also a large sectional, a massive flat screen and huge speakers in every corner.

*How the hell did I not notice those? Oh yeah, I was too busy staring at the other shit that made this room appear to be a playroom.* Looking at it now, I feel silly for even thinking it. Clearly you can tell this room is used as a man cave—to work out and watch football.

"Love."

That's me. He's calling me. *Love.* I turn my attention back to him. The room fades away and he's all I see. Fake dominant Bryce is the sexiest thing I've ever seen. My thighs clench as I try to focus on his words and not his body.

"Earlier, I told you as long as we're *here*, you belong to me. Do you remember that?" I nod my head, a little too vigorously. "This," he lifts his hand and twirls his finger, motioning to the room, "is here. Outside of this room, you're just Delilah. In here, I'll refer to you as Love, and you'll call me Bryce. Not master. Not sir. Just Bryce.

"In here, I don't want you to think. I only want you to feel. I want you to trust that I'm going to take care of you. Just like I did last night, and the night you cut yourself and the day you put yourself in danger. You trusted me then, do you trust me now?"

I'm quivering with desire. I want him. To hell with trust. Even if I didn't trust him, I'd still let him chain me to the ceiling and fuck me half to death. But obviously this is important to him. So I nod.

"An answer, Love." The deep baritone of his voice mixed with the sweetness of his endearment is a delightful, panty-wetting mixture. *If I were wearing panties...*

"I trust you." *I also promise to nod my head more, just so he'll refer to me as Love.*

"Perfect," he breathes, wickedly sexy. His eyes darken, and he seems to grow in size, or maybe I'm just shrinking—melting into a puddle of want and need.

With every step that brings him closer to me, my heart hammers harder against my chest. My breathing is ragged, uneven and shallow. He's like a tornado, sucking up everything in his path and using it to gain momentum.

"Do you want me, Love?" he whispers, standing so close that I can feel his cool, minty breath tickle my face.

"Yes." My voice is low, breathy and nothing compared to how controlled his is. But it's not just his voice, it's his stance. He's so confident.

His finger trails down my neck to my chest—sliding beneath my bathrobe so that we're skin on skin. The burn is delicious, and I can feel it in the pit of my belly—like I've just drank from the bottle of the smoothest whiskey.

"There's a fine line between pain and pleasure. You have a weakness for both." His finger continues its path down my chest and between my breasts, parting the bathrobe as he goes. "You abuse pleasure, by forcing yourself to feel it as often as possible. I'm going to teach you how to let it build." His voice dips and his finger reaches my navel. "And build." Lower... "And build."

My bathrobe parts, exposing my naked body to him. He seems to drink in the sight of me. His big hands rest on my hips. His head is dipped, as he continues to look at me. Then his eyes lift and his hands drag slowly up my sides—feeling every curve of my body.

"When I finally let you come, Love, the relief is going to be greater than any pain you've ever felt." I let out a moan and my chest constricts—fighting hard to pull oxygen into my lungs. I hadn't realized I'd been holding my breath.

My bathrobe lays at my feet, and his hands are on my neck. I don't even know how in the hell they got there. Then he moves closer, his clothed body pressing up against my naked one as he angles his head and softly presses his lips to mine.

He controls the kiss—arching my neck to gain better access to my mouth. I open up to him, and his warm tongue slides between my lips. It's smooth, soft and I can feel it in places other than my mouth. Everything inside me tingles. My toes curl inside my slippers. My body is on fire, but goosebumps break out across my skin. Sooner than I'd hoped, he pulls back—leaving me wanting more.

"When I ask you how you feel, you're going to tell me the truth."

I nod, knowing what his next words will be.

"An answer, Love." *Motherfucker... What that does to me...*

"Yes. I'll tell you the truth."

"There are no safe words, because you don't have limits. So when I ask you how you feel, if you're in pain or if you feel like it's too much, you have to be honest. You have to trust me and I have to trust you. If you lie to me, this ends. All of it. Do you understand?"

I nod again. But this time, he catches on to what I'm doing. He gives me a look of warning, and I cave. "Yes. I won't lie."

A flicker of something flashes in his eyes. I'm gonna say it's pride, because it makes me feel good and I really don't have the time to try to figure it out. He looks away as he takes my hand and leads me to the chains. From his back pocket, he pulls out two leathers cuffs that have a clip and a buckle.

"I'm going to handcuff you to these chains so you can't touch yourself." It's not a question, but he pauses before wrapping them around my wrists—as if he's giving me the option to decline. *Fat chance of that happening.*

He checks to make sure they're not too tight by sliding them around my wrist. Even though they have enough room to move, I still won't be able to slide my hand through them.

My arms are stretched above my head and clipped to the chains. Testing them out, I move my arms but the motion is limited. My elbows are slightly bent, so it's not terribly uncomfortable, but now that I can't, I suddenly want to touch myself.

"You have a beautiful body, Love." I watch as he circles me. When he's out of view, I arch my neck trying to find him. In slow, graceful strides, he rounds me completely. I find that I breathe a little easier when I can see him.

"I'm going to touch, taste and fuck every part of you." I whimper at his promise, and the sound morphs into a moan when his finger grazes my nipple. Circling it, he watches my reaction as he continues to barely touch me. I close my eyes and let my head fall back—trying like hell to force my breast into his hand.

Then I feel his mouth on me. I let out a cry as he shows the same courtesy to my breasts as he did my mouth—kissing, licking and sucking me gently. My thighs rub together, desperately searching for some kind of friction, but finding none.

He alternates between my breasts, never leaving one unattended for too long. Then his hand joins the party as he cups my pussy, squeezing firmly but making sure to not touch my throbbing clit that will surely send me into the explosive orgasm I yearn for.

"Please!" I yell, when his fingers rub the crease of my thighs —barely grazing my lips.

"I promise, Love. It's going to be well worth the wait." I doubt that. I'm pretty fucking sure it will feel just as amazing if he will just move his hand a little to the right and apply some pressure. "Open your eyes." I do as he commands, lifting my head to find us only a hairsbreadth from each other. "Watch," he whispers.

Slowly, he lowers his body—planting a kiss just above my navel on his way down. His eyes never leave mine as he kisses his way across my hips before pressing them against the soft, bare flesh just above my pussy. Sliding his hands up my legs, he pauses when he gets to my thighs, offering me a wicked grin before he widens them.

I whimper, begging him with my eyes to let me come. With one slow, soft stroke, his tongue moves between my lips— scarcely touching the tender, exposed flesh. It's so light, it could be a feather. But since I know it's his tongue, it makes the feeling more intense. I try to thrust my hips, but his tight grip on my thighs holds me in place.

With that devilish grin on his face, he stands. I want to scream at him, but he speaks before I can. "Do you remember when I fingered you?" As if I might need a reminder, his thick finger eases past my lips and teases my entrance—completely avoiding my clit.

I nod, unsure of what else to do. When he raises his eyebrows and thrusts his finger deep inside me—pausing when it's buried completely—I suddenly remember what I'm supposed to do.

"Yes..." I moan the word as it rips through me.

"I tasted your pussy on my fingers," he drawls, slowly pulling his finger out of me before thrusting it roughly back in. The movement causes me to cry out. "Do you remember when you came on my face?" My stomach flips at the reminder. I make a mewling sound that seems to please him.

"I've craved it ever since." Leaning closer, he presses his lips against my ear and whispers, "It tastes better than I remember."

*Son of a bitch...* Just two tiny flicks of his finger against my clit... Or if I could just move my hips a little, I know he'd hit that sweet spot inside me. One stroke and I could be coming around his fingers—flooding his entire hand with my release. But I don't get the chance to try. He pulls his finger from inside me, and reaches for something else behind him.

"I've taken away your ability to touch. Now I'm going to blindfold you. Then I'm going to play music to drown out your screaming thoughts. I want you to stand here and imagine what it will feel like when I come back. And I want you to listen to the words of the song. You don't have to think, see or do anything. Just what I tell you to."

My breath hitches, and I feel a moment of panic. He mistakes my look of fear for anticipation. He gives me that cocky grin again, then I see nothing as a blindfold completely engulfs me in darkness. I rattle against the chains—my breathing heavy as my heart races.

I don't want to be left alone. What if something happens? What if he doesn't come back? The fear I'd often felt when I wondered what would have happened to me had Luke not found me that day comes crashing back full force.

I don't want this to stop. I don't want it to be over. I'm scared if I say something, he'll end the session. But if I don't, my fear will lead me to somewhere darker—even darker than where I was last night.

*Be honest.*
*Don't lie.*
*Tell the truth.*
*This isn't Mario.*
*You can trust him.*
*You said you trusted him...*

"Bryce!" I scream, shaking harder against the chains. "Bryce!" I yell so loud my throat hurts. *He's left. He's gone.*

"Bryce!..." Gripping the chains with my hand, I lift my feet off the ground and jerk against the restraints.

"I'm here!" The sound of his voice isn't enough, and I fight against the cuffs until the blindfold is ripped from my face. "I'm here, Love. I'm here." He's looks just as panicked as I am, but his voice is still controlled as he quickly uncuffs me.

"Don't leave me alone. I don't want to be alone." He's nodding as I speak. "I can't be alone. Not tied up like this."

"Okay, Love. Just calm down," he soothes, wrapping his big arms around me. I'm not crying—fear doesn't do that to me. It makes me strong—fight or flight mode, I guess.

My panic fades away as he holds me. It doesn't take long for me to recover, and I take a deep breath before pulling away from him. "I'm okay."

"You sure?" His hands frame my face as his eyes scan me from head to toe looking for any sign that I'm not.

"I'm sure. I just freaked out. I'm good now. I swear." I force a smile, trying to reassure him. He looks doubtful, but nods.

"Let's take a break." I frown. His lips curve into a warm smile. "Just a break, babe." *Babe. We're back to babe.* I guess "in here" doesn't always apply "in here."

His hand wrapped around my elbow, he guides me to where my robe still lays discarded on the floor. Sweeping it up in his hand, he slides it over my shoulders before ushering me to the couch. I'm relieved when he pulls me down into his lap. He snatches a bottle of water from beside him and hands it to me.

"Talk," he demands, but it's not in his dominant tone. Although he says it with enough force I know there's no negotiating.

"How you gonna hand me a bottle of water, suggesting I drink it, then demand I talk? Which is it?"

Smirking, he seems to relax a little more. "Drink first. Then talk." I take a few sips before handing it back to him. He tosses it aside, keeping his focus directly on me. I take a deep breath, trying to mentally prepare myself for the truth. But I soon realize it comes a lot more naturally than I thought—just as it's done before with him.

"I've been left in a cage for hours," I start, figuring at this point, there's no reason to beat around the bush. "I've been gagged, blindfolded, tied up and left unattended for so long, I prayed for death. I have a fear of being restrained and left alone. It's not that I don't trust you, I've just never dealt with the fear. It got the best of me."

His face is a whirlwind of emotions. His lips are slightly turned down, making him appear sad. His brows are drawn together in confusion. His jaw is tightened in anger. But his eyes are what have me feeling my own whirlwind of emotions. They shine with an unspoken promise—one that says I'll never have to endure pain and neglect like that again, because now I have him.

"Thank you for being honest with me," he whispers, tucking my hair behind my ear. "I trust you, Delilah. You're now one of the few."

I feel the intimacy between us. It's so strong, I know I have to do something to cripple it before I start feeling things I have no business feeling.

"So," I smirk, dragging his attention from where he's still stroking my hair to my face. "Do I get a medal or something? I mean, 'one of the few' sounds like a pretty damn big deal."

He lets out a low chuckle and shakes his head. "What is it with you and always wanting some kind of prize or award? You've got to be the most competitive woman I've ever met."

"Wait till I go to the Olympics. You haven't seen competitive."

"That's right," he says on a nod. "You're a trampoline gymnast with no trampoline." We smile back at each other, enjoying the silence and light mood—something him and I haven't spent a lot of time doing together.

Dropping my eyes, I finger the button on his shirt. "I ruined the mood, didn't I?"

"Not for me." His low admission stirs my arousal that had completely faded only moments ago.

"I hate I freaked out. It was getting pretty intense. Can we pick up where we left off?"

"No." My mood nosedives. Finger under my chin, he lifts my head to meet his gaze. Dark, dominant, powerful, controlling Bryce is back—just like that. "We can't pick up where we left off, Love." *Love.* My thighs quiver at the endearment, as his voice drops to a whisper. "We have to start all over again."

# CHAPTER 19

I'm once again chained to the ceiling of the room. I can't see shit, but I know Bryce is here. He promised me he wouldn't leave, and every so often, he walks around me—trailing his finger up my ribs or across my thighs ... always touching me, teasing me, keeping me on edge and reminding me I can trust him.

I don't know how long I've been standing here, but Marilyn Manson's "Sweet Dreams" has been playing on a loop. I've heard the song six times. I've timed Bryce's movements with the beat of the music. I've memorized every word—finding their meaning to be completely relevant to my life. *He chose this song for me.* The thought is as pleasing as it is unsettling.

My entire body is burning with need. That build he promised me is like a volcano—hot, liquid lava just waiting to explode. My breasts feel heavier. My pussy is so sensitive, even the warm breeze Bryce creates as he passes me makes me moan with pleasure.

I'm naked.

I'm exposed.

I'm at his mercy.

But it's the control he has over me that turns me on most. I can't see him. I can't hear him. I can't touch him. But he's here, making me wait until he's ready to give me what I crave. I'm completely submissive to him. By yielding my power to him, all I have to do is feel—just like he said.

The introduction of the song starts again, and his hands are on me. I whimper, begging him to take me. I feel him behind me, trailing his finger slowly down my spine. When he reaches the top of my ass, his entire palm flattens against my skin—smoothing over the flesh that is still tender from last night.

His hand slides lower to the inside of my thigh. He pats it lightly, urging my legs apart. I oblige, and his hand falls between my legs—softly stroking the outside of my pussy before pushing a finger between my lips, and thrusting it inside me.

The position has him reaching that spot inside me I beg to be touched. When I throw my head back on a gasp, he backs off. I give a low, guttural moan of protest, but he ignores me—slowly pumping his finger in and out of me. It's just enough to bring me to the edge, but not enough to push me over.

He continues until the song is over, then withdraws his finger and moves away from me. I'm on the verge of crying I'm so desperate. This orgasm denial is worse than anything I've ever felt. I'm nearing the point of mental exhaustion. But as the song starts up again, he removes the blindfold.

It takes a moment for my eyes to adjust, and the first thing they notice is his. They're hooded, dark and smoldering with the same desire and need I feel inside me. I'm so caught up in his stare, it takes a minute for me to notice he's shirtless. My head lolls and my breathing stops when I realize he's not just shirtless —he's completely naked.

His thick cock is hard, heavy and the biggest motherfucking dick I've ever seen in my life. For the first time, I get to see him in his full glory. I can't imagine how I ever took his length before. Wrapping one hand around my throat, he forces me to look at him. I'm expecting a cocky grin, but he's not the least bit smug— he's fucking hungry.

Crashing his lips to mine, he once again controls the kiss— forcing me to surrender to him. As the song starts to build, his kiss becomes more urgent. His hand leaves my throat and grips my waist. The rough texture of his palms tickle as they smooth over my hips then around to my ass—spanning its entirety.

He squeezes and a jolt of pleasure fires straight through my core. Then he's lifting me, and my legs lock around his waist. I grip the chains, hoisting myself higher—obeying his wordless demand. Centering his cock at my entrance, he slowly pushes inside of me—breaking the kiss so he can gauge my reaction as I absorb every inch of him.

The process is painstakingly slow, but oh so rewarding. There's a pinch of discomfort, but I welcome it. One hand slides between us while the other keeps a firm grip on my ass. His thumb circles my clit with just the right amount of pressure, and the discomfort fades completely.

"Don't come until I tell you to. If you do, you'll spend tomorrow tied up and begging." It's meant as a warning, but I consider it an invitation. My sex tightens—squeezing him hard. "Fight it, Love," he says, his voice authoritative—demanding. But I don't fight. I give in to the desire building inside me.

He pulls back and thrusts inside me, taking advantage of my walls opening up and swallowing him. The orgasm is never-ending—white light bursting behind my eyelids...a series of electrifying currents pulsing through my veins...my entire body convulsing with an immeasurable amount of endless, wave-crashing euphoria. The reprieve is more than I ever could have imagined. I feel him...everywhere.

My body is being deliciously ravaged by him.

My mind is consumed with thoughts of only him.

My heart is beating solely for him.

His words echo inside my head—"You belong to me."

He was right...

*I do.*


My forehead rests against his as I hang limply around him while we both fight to catch our breath. We didn't make it to the end of the song—not that I was expecting us to. He might've had it in him, but I damn sure didn't.

He recovers quicker than I do, and I wish he weren't such a fucking Superman. I would really like to enjoy this moment a little longer. My lips tremble and I whimper as he pulls out of me. The emptiness is a little overwhelming.

The music is still booming through the speakers. Now that I'm sated, tired and emotionally drained, I've decided I hate this song. It's almost depressing.

With one arm still tightly around my waist, he unclips the cuffs from the chains and drapes my lifeless arms around his neck. I'm as limp as an overcooked noodle—completely relying on him to support all my weight while I just lay my head on his shoulder. He doesn't seem to mind or struggle in the least as he walks around the room with me suctioned to his chest.

The music stops suddenly, and I'm aware of my loud breathing. Grabbing my bathrobe from the couch, he drapes it over my shoulders—repositioning his arms so they're on the outside of the robe, and I'm completely engulfed in warmth.

It's cooler inside the house, and I realize I've lost a slipper as the air swirls around my toes. He passes through the kitchen and doesn't stop until he's in the bedroom. This entire time, he's been carrying me with one arm while keeping the other one free to open doors and now pull back the covers on the bed. *Damn, he's strong.* I'm dead weight and he's not the least bit winded.

"You okay, Love?" *Hmmm... Love.*

"I'm perfect." More than perfect—if there is such a thing.

"You wanna loosen up that grip?" His tone is playful. I realize we've been standing here beside the bed and I've inadvertently been tightening my hold in fear he'll set me down.

I attempt a shrug, but my limbs feel liquefied, so I'm not sure he notices. "Not really," I admit, trying to suppress a yawn and failing. He doesn't object, he simply lies down with me on top of him. "Okay, now it's uncomfortable."

I try to roll to my side and succeed with a little help from him. He throws my robe to the floor, and he pulls the covers over both of us. I curl into his chest, hoping he doesn't ruin the moment by talking. I'm pretty sure he doesn't, but if he did, I was too close to sleep to acknowledge it.

I slept for nearly six hours. The first thought when I woke was how wonderful a hot bath would feel. Sinking down into the old claw foot tub, I let the near-scalding water soothe my achy limbs. The only thing it doesn't soothe is my ass that I'm beginning to think wasn't just spanked with a hand—a barbed-wire fence comes to mind.

Aside from the pain of my backside, I've never felt better. I honestly can't remember a time I've been so ... free. There are no dark thoughts or itches to scratch. No incessant cravings or imminent needs. It's a new kind of relief I could definitely get used to.

Other than the fact it's dark outside, I have no knowledge of time. I don't care either. I feel more at home, more at peace and more alive in this tiny little house than anywhere else I've ever been. The glory belongs to Bryce, but I'm pretty proud of myself for being willing to take a chance.

After my bath, I walk into the living room to find him on the couch. He smiles up at me as I take a seat on the other end of the sofa.

"I'm hungry," I whine, folding my arms across my chest. I could definitely get used to the liberating feeling of wearing nothing but a bathrobe.

"I don't have anything but coffee, bottled water and oatmeal here. But lucky for you, there are several Prospects in line to get a patch. Food will be here shortly."

I frown. "Well, how much longer are they gonna be? I'm starving."

Apparently, he doesn't find my petulant act amusing anymore. He shoots me a look of warning. "You're not a brat, Delilah. Stop acting like one."

He's right. I would never complain like this at the clubhouse. It's just not who I am. But somewhere deep inside me, the desire to be spanked is still alive. I want his hands on me. It's not the pain I yearn for in this moment, it's the way he holds me and makes me feel safe after the punishment that I crave. Problem is, it's not my body craving it, but my heart.

"I can't help it. I get like this when I'm hungry." I poke my lip out, but he's not looking at me.

"No, you don't." He sounds bored as he flips through the pages of the magazine in his lap.

"I'm seriously starving. If they're not here in five minutes, I'm taking Luke's truck and going to get something myself."

He lets out an exasperated sigh, and gives me a blank stare. "I know what you're doing, babe. But be careful what you ask for. Sometimes shit ain't as rewarding when you don't need it."

I hadn't thought about that. He's probably right, but I'd like to find out on my own. If it doesn't work out, I'll blame it on my mommy issues. But I have a feeling I'm going to enjoy it much more than he thinks.

I pretend to look at my wrist, knowing he's watching me out of the corner of his eye. "Four minutes."

"Last warning, Delilah. Drop the act, or I'm going to treat you with the same level of humiliation a parent would a snot-nosed brat in a grocery store." Lucky for me, humility is something I rarely feel.

There's something in the back of my mind reminding me that the last time I felt embarrassed was around him. But I ignore it—allowing my need for that sense of security I feel when he holds me to fuel my act of defiance.

I count to thirty, wait for what I presume is the most opportune moment and look at my imaginary watch once again. Even as I do it, I can feel my heart flip and my blood rush faster in anticipation of what's to come. "Three minutes."

Wordlessly, Bryce drops his magazine on the coffee table, grabs his phone and stands. I hold my breath—eager for his next move. When he doesn't return, I decide I better breathe before I pass out. My enthusiasm begins to fade as nervousness sets in.

The loud rumble of pipes echo in the distance, and the closer they get, the more fidgety I become. *Where the hell is Bryce?* Headlights flood through the windows in the living room as they rumble down the driveway. The engines die and I strain to hear any movement from Bryce who's still somewhere in the house. I'm not sure if he walked to the bedroom or the kitchen, and I'm too shaken with nerves to get up and look.

Someone knocks on the door, and I don't have time to think about what to do before I hear Bryce's footsteps as he comes from the kitchen. He's carrying two dining room chairs in his hands. He ignores me as he passes, and I watch as he calmly sets them down before he walks to the door and opens it wide, inviting the two Prospects in.

I know them both—Chuck and Bass. One got his name from the shoes he always wore and the other from his trophy fishing days. I've had sex with both of them, but it wasn't anything worth remembering.

They tip their chins at me. I smile and stand to greet them— you know, be polite like I'm supposed to be.

"Sit." I'm not sure Bryce's demand is for me until I look up to find him pointing his finger … at me. I look nervously at each of the men in the room. Bryce is stoic, while both Chuck and Bass seem to be fighting a smile.

*Oh shit. Ohshitohshitohshit… Surely this isn't about to go down like I think.*

"Take a seat, Prospects. You're in for a treat." The men take a seat and now they're facing me…

*Oh shit…*

I let out a nervous breath of laughter. "Bryce?" My voice is more like a squeak—a childish, bratty squeak.

"I warned you, babe." It's the only explanation he offers. He sits on the other side of the couch—directly opposite from where the men are seated. It's only then I notice what he holds in his hand—a wooden spoon. *Ohhhh…shit.*

He did warn me. He warned that he would punish me like a bratty child in a grocery story—humiliate me. He wins. I'm humiliated. No sense in following through. Message received.

"Come here, Delilah."

I shake my head as my eyes fill with tears. It's not intentional—they do it on their own accord. "Bryce, please. I'm sorry," I plead, but it falls on deaf ears.

"Come here, Delilah." His voice is a little sterner this time. I search his face for any sign of weakness I can play on. There's nothing. There's not even a sparkle of amusement, regret or desire in his eyes. They're dull, but determined. *Shit!*

I'm struggling. Not because I'm scared he'll hurt me, but because this is a first for me. I use my anger to get what I want. This time, that shit backfired. And I have no idea how in the hell I'm gonna crawfish my way outta this one.

Bryce seems to sense my discomfort, and hope soars through me at the possibility of him shedding some mercy on my bratty little soul. "You have two options here, babe." I'm nodding before I hear them. His lip twitches, and he tries to conceal it by continuing, but it's too late. I saw it.

"Option one, you willingly comply and afterward we forget this ever happened. All of us." His eyes swing to Chuck and Bass. Out of the corner of my eye, I see them nod. "Option two," he says turning back to me. "You force me to hold you down, and afterwards I take you home and they forget this happened, but I won't."

*That's the shittiest options I've ever heard.*

"Either way, I'm giving you exactly what you deserve. I don't take shit off nobody. Not the club, not them." He nods his head in the direction of Chuck and Bass, but keeps his eyes on me. "And not you, sweetheart. So what's it gonna be? The choice is yours." His matter-of-fact tone is almost as bad as the bored one he's been using.

*Dammit. Shit. Fuck. How did I get myself into this mess?*

I bite the corner of my lip, knowing there's really no choice for me. Something tells me he knows that too. In one final effort, I widen my tear-filled eyes at him. "Bryce, please. They'll see," I whisper, like they can't hear me anyway.

"That's the point, babe."

"What if they tell people? That's my job."

He shakes his head. "They won't." If he could maybe sound a little more convincing, it might make this a little easier for me. I'm sure that's another thing he knows. *Fucking know-it-all.*

"Come here, Delilah. I won't tell you again." He's at the end of his patience rope. I'm out of options. My lips turn town and my throat tightens as I stand. *Dammit. Why do I feel so shitty about this? Embarrassment is a horse pill to swallow.*

I stifle a sob, fighting hard to hold onto what little dignity I have. My shaky knees somehow manage to keep me upright as I walk the few steps toward him—stopping when my legs brush against his thigh. I avoid making eye contact with him. Instead, I find a spot on the wall to stare at.

"Lie down." I'm shocked at his demand. Narrowing my eyes, I meet his gaze to see if he's serious. He is. *Over the knee? Really? Boy, he's going all out.*

"Fine," I snap, but immediately regret it when he shoots me a look of warning. I try to apologize with my eyes, but I'm not sure if it worked. *Fuck it. Let's just get this shit over with.*

I lie across his lap and bury my face in the cushions—happy that I can't see the two men who have front row tickets to my spank show. Just as eager to get the ball rolling as I am, Bryce wastes no time lifting my robe and baring my ass to the world—well, not really.

At the angle I'm laying, the only thing the Prospects can see is my hip. They're sitting significantly lower than Bryce is which obstructs their view of my ass. I'm pretty sure he planned that too.

There's no warning, no counting and no warm-up. One moment my ass is getting tickled with air, the next it's getting spanked—hard. Or maybe I just feel it more this time.

The blows are relentless—as unyielding as the wooden spoon used to deliver them. The only sound is the constant crack that rings out across the room every time the wood makes contact with my flesh.

I don't scream. I don't yell. I don't beg or move a muscle. I lie perfectly still, and keep my face buried in the couch as I cry silent tears. Even though I wasn't told to, I've been counting. Fifteen whacks later, Bryce stops, covers me and says two words.

"Get out."

The sound of chairs scraping against the floor is quickly followed by footsteps and the opening and closing of the door. Then there's a loud rumble of pipes that eventually fade into the distance. The lack of noise makes my sniffles sound like an air horn.

I stay across Bryce's lap, not ready to face him just yet. He doesn't speak, but after several minutes, his hand lifts my robe. I guess he's surveying the damage. The thought that he might hit me again doesn't even cross my mind. He kept his word, did what he promised he would and now it's over. If I don't know anything else about him, I know this—he doesn't enjoy hurting me.

He slides out from under me, laying my legs across the couch before leaving the room. I figure he's going to let me suffer in silence, but he returns and I feel his hand on me again—smoothing something cool across the heat of my ass. The relief is instant, but my tears still silently flow.

When he's finished, he covers me, then plants a kiss on the back of my head. His hand pets my hair a minute before he speaks. "I'll be in the kitchen." With one final kiss to my head that lingers a little longer this time, he walks away.

Immediately, I feel more alone than all the endless hours I was in that dog cage combined. Not only was I humiliated, but I didn't get that aftercare I yearned for. A part of me believes he might have suspected that's what I was up to. Sadness fills me at the thought. But as seconds tick by, I find myself forgiving him.

Minutes later, I leave all my dignity, pride and humiliation on the couch and give in to the desire to be near him. I just miss him too damn much.

# CHAPTER 20

By the look on his face, he's surprised to see me so soon. "Hey..." he says, eyeing me cautiously as if he's not sure of what I might do.

"Are you mad at me?" I ask, not fully realizing how dependent my state of being is on his answer.

His brow creases. "Why do you ask that?"

*Honesty...the silent reminder is always there.*

"Because it's the only thing that matters to me." A sob bubbles up my throat, but I close my mouth to stifle it. Although I can't prevent the quick rise and fall of my chest or the brimming tears that give me away.

He wears a pained look as he crosses the room and frames my face in his hands. "No. I'm not mad at you." I can't stop my flow of tears even though his thumbs are working double time to stop them. *What's with all this crying? Get your shit together, girl!*

"I shouldn't have pushed you. I made you do something you didn't want to do." He gives me a sideways smile. It immediately makes me feel better.

"Trust me, babe. You deserved it. It definitely hurt you more than it hurt me."

"Well, that's a relief," I say, rolling my eyes.

His smile widens. "Go wash your face. Take a minute. I promise you'll feel better."

I slowly move toward the bathroom, each step reminding me of my transgressions. My poor ass probably has zero skin left on it. After last night and today, I'm afraid it won't ever heal. Call me stupid, but I would probably be okay if it didn't. The reminder is comforting—it confirms that he really does exist.

My face is red and splotchy, my eyes are puffy and my nose has a crease in the center from me constantly wiping it. I look—like shit. But after I've had a minute alone and washed my face, Bryce was right. I do feel better.

His back is to me when I walk in the kitchen. The spoon he spanked me with is laying on the table, and I have a fleeting thought to take it and whack him across the ass just to give him a taste of his own medicine. But he turns, shitting on my plans, and I'm thankful for the interruption.

"What makes you so sure Chuck and Bass won't say anything?" The thought of them sharing what they witnessed tonight fills me with dread. I don't need the entire club knowing my business.

"'Cause if they do, I'll beat the fuck outta them, take their Prospect rockers and make damn sure they never ride with another MC in the country again." His answer is touching, really. But...damn.

"That's a little extreme, don't you think?"

"Nope. It's all about trust, babe. Everything always comes down to trust." Well, it does make me feel better that they'll have to eat through a straw if they do rat.

"How long you been in the MC?"

"Six years."

"Oh."

"That surprise you?"

"A little. I figured you were in longer than that."

"Sometimes it feels like it." There's a distance in his voice, but he's smiling. "You like steak?" he asks, holding up a plate filled with food.

"Of course I like steak." I give him an incredulous look. "What kind of question is that?"

I start to pull a chair out from the table but he shakes his head. "Let's eat on the couch. It's a little more comfortable." He nods toward my midsection, and I look down. *Ohhh... I get it. Funny fucker, ain't he?*

After dinner, I brush my teeth and startle when I walk in the bedroom to find him sliding naked beneath the covers. Our eyes meet, and he pats his side. "In bed, Love."

I'm hesitant to join him. The act feels too intimate—something partners would do instead of lovers. He waits patiently, as if he's in no hurry for me to join him. But his eyes have a demanding, magnetic gaze that lures me to him. I force myself to put one foot in front of the other, slow and cautious at these feelings swarming in my chest. I welcome these foreign feelings—yet they scare the shit out of me.

But then I'm in bed. And his strong arm is around me. His scent engulfs me. The calm, steady rhythm of his heart drumming out a beat against my cheek.

It's warm.

It's safe.

It feels like home.

Almost instantly, I fall asleep.

Yesterday, Bryce promised me if I came without permission, that I'd spend today tied up. Well, he keeps his promises.

I've been dangling naked from the chains for what feels like hours. In reality, I'm sure it hasn't been that long, but I have no sense of time. My body begs for release—not just from the restraints but from the sexual desire pulsing through me.

The constant ache is turmoil. My skin is ravenous for his touch—so eager and sensitive that even the lightest brush of his fingertips sends a bolt of electricity sizzling all the way to my core. My clit throbs. My walls constrict. Hot, liquid arousal spreads down my thighs like warm honey.

"Please!" I cry out, pulling against the restraints—widening my eyes in hopes of seeing him through the dark material covering my face.

"Remember, Love," he says, my head jerking in the direction of his voice. "Bad girls get punished. I told you what would happen if you came when I told you not to, but you didn't care." He's near. I can feel him. I try to swing my body out to meet his, but all I hit is air.

"You didn't even try." He's behind me now, and I can feel his fingers tracing the fading welts on my ass. My entire body sings at his touch. The marks are no longer painful. They now only serve as a scarred reminder of what happens when I act like a brat. Which is exactly how I want to act right now.

"I hate you!" I scream, allowing my anger to surface. Damn him for doing this to me. It's worse than any spanking. But he only chuckles—fucking chuckles.

"No, you don't. You want me." I feel his breath across my cheek as his voice dips. "You want me to fuck your tight little cunt that's dripping wet for me." He inhales deep. "You smell scrumptious. Good enough to eat."

The sound builds deep in my belly—gaining momentum before it escapes my lips. It's deep, rich, textured—a cross between a moan and an animalistic roar. He's right. I want him. I want him to talk dirty to me while he fucks me hard. Then I want him to eat me ... devour me ... feast on my release until I'm sated and he's full.

"I want you to learn to control it, Love. I want you to come only when I tell you to. The pleasure will be much more intense. Not just because you waited, but because you'll have pleased me."

"I'm ready! I've waited so long..." I whine, begging for something—anything at this point.

"Be quiet, Love. Feel it. Take it all in. Instead of focusing on immediate release, center your thoughts on how good it will be when you do come." *I hate this game.*

"I want it now. I *need* it now, Bryce."

"I *know* what you *need*, Love." His voice is a deep rumble of warning—grim and threatening.

"Then give it to me!" I scream, twisting my body as my hands fist around the chains and lift me so I can kick at the air— hoping a flailing limb connects with his groin.

"Hush!" he snaps, his hand winding around my throat— applying just enough pressure to remind me who's in charge here. "One more word, and I'll spank you. Hard."

I bite my lip, fighting against the growing urge to tell him to fuck off. I can't see him, but I know the bastard is smiling— knowing he just uttered the magical words that will make me comply. He pulls his hand from my throat, but leaves a single digit that starts under my chin, then trails down between my breasts.

"Good girl." I clamp down hard on the inside of my cheek to trap the whimper that threatens at his whispered words. My sex dampens—my thighs growing stickier with the appreciation in his tone.

His finger lifts, leaving me feeling chilled and alone once again. The fiery trail from just the tip of his finger simmers to cold ash. I try to do as he said and let my approaching orgasm be my focal point. But I can't. My entire body is hypersensitive. I can feel my muscles tightening...my heart beating...my lungs constricting...the swarm of butterflies in my belly. The feelings are not dense, but sharp—making me even more aware.

He told me he'd spank me—hard—if I spoke. I really don't want him to spank me. I don't want to disappoint him either. But no more than a few minutes could have passed since he touched me, and I know that I won't last much longer. I can't. I want his attention. Even if it's negative. Even if it hurts. I want to feel his hands on me.

"Please..." The word is so softly spoken, I wonder if he heard it. But I don't have to wait very long to find out.

"What did I say, Love?" His voice is so close, I jump at the sound. It's as if he knew exactly what I'd do, and was standing here waiting for it.

"To be quiet."

"And what did I say would happen if you weren't?"

I swallow hard, my pulse quickening as dread swims inside me at the thought of what's to come. It embarrasses me to say the words, but I know if I don't answer, my impending doom will be much worse. "You'd spank me," I whisper, my lips trembling as cold fear engulfs me.

His warm breath invades my senses, making me dizzy. "That's right." The rich tenor of his voice drops to a harsh whisper. "If we have to do this every day, for weeks or even months, we will. How long it takes is up to you. But you will learn, Love. One way or another."

"I'm sorry!" I cry, no longer wanting him to punish me. I can hold out—I'll force my body to comply. I'm stronger than this. I can do it. Fear is my fuel. And he's scaring the shit out of me.

"Too late for apologies. Maybe after this, you'll think twice before you defy me." His voice comes from behind me, and I crane my neck to try to see him, despite the blindfold.

"No, really. I swear. I'm ready."

"That's not how this works, Love. Disobedience has repercussions."

"Please! Just talk to me! I don't understand!" My plea is desperate, and genuine. I'm so confused with all of this. I deserve a second chance.

"We will talk. After I give you exactly what I promised." He's not retreating. This is going to happen. My breathing becomes ragged—panicky. I jump at the feel of his hand at my hip, but his touch is soft. He slides it up to cup my jaw as he walks around to face me.

"Shhh..." He pulls the blindfold from my face. I calm almost the moment my eyes adjust to the dimly lit room as his thumb rubs soft circles over my cheek. "I'm not going to hurt you because I simply want to, Love. I'm doing this to teach you a lesson." His eyes are soft—patient as he continues to explain.

"Orgasm denial is very powerful, but beneficial for you. If you can learn to control it, you won't need the pain. The reprieve from sexual release will be enough."

He tips my head forward, placing a kiss at my hairline. Instead of feeling the gesture in my groin, the tender touch registers in my chest. "You didn't even attempt to try, Love. If you had, I'd have shown you mercy. You don't get pleasure from pain. That tells me you'd rather me hurt you than not touch you at all."

He gives me another kiss, this one at the corner of my lips. Green eyes bore into mine—calm and considerate. His explanation is discerning and I cling to every word. "Not everyone is like me, Love. They won't have limits. They won't stop when they know you've had enough. So you have to understand how to control the urges. You have to fight against the desire, and use it to your advantage. I will teach you, but you have to listen to me. Do you understand?" A fat tear rolls down my cheek as I nod.

"An answer, Love."

"I understand." Disappointment swells in my gut. He's going out of his way—devoting his time to helping me, and all I've done is waste it.

I close my eyes in an attempt to stop my flow of threatening tears. I'm thankful as he slides the blindfold back over my face—engulfing me in complete darkness once again.

"Now," he starts, stepping around me—his voice once again hard and demanding. "I'm going to deliver on my promise. Then I'm going to fuck you. And you will not come, unless I tell you to. Understood?"

"Yes," I manage, a sob already building in my throat. It breaks free of my lips when my body jerks with the impact of something hard. Pain—throbbing, sweltering pain envelops me. It's quickly followed by another searing ache that lands just above the last one.

The loud crack that rumbles through the room doesn't come from his hand. As promised, he's spanking me hard. The thick leather belt is unforgiving as it lashes my vulnerable skin that was already too hypersensitive—making the pain that much worse.

This spanking hurts worse than all the others combined, but it doesn't last nearly as long. After the sixth blow, my body tenses in anticipation for the next one that never comes. But I keep my guard up as I fight to control my breathing—my cries loud and broken.

*Broken.*

Exactly how I feel.

But much like my punishment, the crippling feeling in my chest doesn't last long. The blindfold is ripped from me again as Bryce's arms circle me—holding me tight to him...lifting my legs around his waist...embracing me as I sob into his neck.

"I got you, Love." His lips rain kisses over my hair, as he repeats the words. "I got you." And he does. He's got me. He's got my submission. My complete surrender.

"Look at me, Love. Let me see your pretty face." Somehow I find the strength to pull my head from his chest and meet his eyes. They're filled with adoration—praise and pride. "You are beautiful even when you cry." My stomach constricts as I fight another sob at his admission.

"Shhh, Love. I don't want you to cry anymore. Let me pleasure you. I want you to fall to pieces in my arms. And when you do, I swear I'll be here to put you back together."

His words shatter any walls I had left. The vise around my heart shatters. The most vital organ in my body thumps a steady, heavy rhythm against my chest—and in this beautiful moment, it beats solely for him.

He kisses me then—sensually, erotically and passionately. His tongue sweeps through my mouth—not leaving one inch untouched. He masks my scent with his own until he's all I taste. One hand drags slowly across the curve of my hip. My skin tingles from his gentle caress as he hoists my leg higher up his waist.

I want to touch him. My hands burn with the need to trace the planes of his muscles…feel his warm skin beneath my fingers…claw the tattooed flesh that covers his arms. But I refuse to ask—my desire to be under his command and do only as he asks more crucial than my own selfish greed.

The thick, swollen head of his cock presses against the inflamed lips of my pussy. He works his way between them—rubbing his length against the slick folds and gaining access to my entrance that quivers on contact.

Slowly, he drives into me—pushing through the satiny, narrow passage that stretches to accommodate him. A wave of bliss ripples through me as he inches further until he's seated deep inside me. His eyes disappear behind his heavy lids as a breathy sigh escapes his lips.

Unmoving, he closes his mouth and swallows—composing himself. When his lids lift slowly, striking emerald eyes stare back at me—dominant and salacious. His arm around my back tightens, as does the hand beneath my thigh—securing me to him.

Then he moves in long, stimulating strokes that awaken every nerve inside me. The thick, warm feel of his length sliding gracefully through my channel ignites the fuse of my impending orgasm. I greedily close my walls around him—my pussy tightening and pulsing involuntarily…acting out of pure instinct…trying to trap him inside me…refusing to release him without a fight.

He groans deep—the low vibrations tickling my stomach that's flush against his. "You're killing me, Love," he growls, as he flexes his hips hard and impales me with a sharp thrust.

"You're killing me," I cry, when his cock rubs against that tiny scrap of velvety flesh tucked away deep inside me. I want to hold back. I don't want to disappoint him anymore. But it's been too long. I'm too desperate. And even though my mind is strong, my body is weak—threatening to release without my permission. Without *his* permission.

"Is that it, Love?" He thrusts hard once again, and my entire body pulses with the euphoric feeling. "Is that the sweet spot?"

"Yes!" My head falls back and my hands fist around the chains for leverage as I arch my back.

"Look at me." I react instantly to his demand. My mouth parted, my eyes heavy as I meet his gaze that darkens when he speaks. "Come, Love."

As he says the words, his cock surges inside me. Not just brushing across the spot that triggers my orgasm, but completely absorbing it—fusing the hard flesh of his length with the delicate, erogenous tissue.

My climax erupts—the irrevocable feeling bringing me to the brink of unconsciousness. Heavenly sensations like I've never experienced swim through me—splashing waves of carnal, wet heat to every pore...every fiber...every cell in my body.

I never knew how beautiful coming could be. But in this moment, I fully understand. I'm reveling in the aftershocks of my own release when he floods me with his. He showers me with bursts of searing hot liquid—once again masking the scent of my own arousal with his. He's marking me—staking his claim. And I want him to.

Moments pass before he lifts my body from his. When his cock slides out of my sodden pussy, I shiver with the friction, then from the loss. Keeping me to his waist, he uncuffs me—catching my wrist in his hand before my leaden arm can fall. He folds it around his neck before doing the same with my other arm. Pain shoots from my shoulders, across my neck and down my back. I make some unintelligible noise of discomfort.

"Don't worry, Love. I'll take care of you." My heart flips again, while the pain slightly subsides at his promise. There's no doubt he'll take care of me. Ever since I've known him, that's all he's done.

A burst of cold air surrounds me as he passes between the doors that lead inside the house. Even though I shiver, the wintry weather is welcome on my damp skin. His hand moves in large circles across my back—spreading the heat from his hand across my goose-bumped flesh.

My eyes follow the dark wood paneling of the hall as he carries me through the house. We come to a room near the front of the house I'd yet to explore. For some reason, I'd thought it was a closet. But the dusty smell of unused furniture fills the pitch black air. Another door is opened and a light comes on, illuminating a small bathroom.

A long mirror runs the length of the wall behind the sink, and I'm greeted with our reflection. Like a child, I'm curled around him. I look small in his arms—vulnerable and shy compared to him, who's big, powerful and fully in control.

He leans down to turn on the shower, and our reflection disappears from my view. "You still awake, Love?" he asks, placing a kiss on my shoulder while he waits, I suspect, for the water to heat.

"I'm so tired," I whisper, my body so drained I wonder why I'm not asleep.

"I know." His lips press softly against my neck. "I'll make this quick." He steps into the tub, pulling the curtain closed behind us. "Unwrap your legs from around me, Love. I'll hold you up."

I unlock my ankles, thankful that he catches me or else I'd end up on my ass—my very sore ass that burns as the hot water sprays across it. I'm too tired to react. Instead, I hang my head and teeter on the edge of consciousness as Bryce bathes me the best he can with one hand while one arm holds me up.

My thighs are sticky with the remnants of our release. The reminder makes my belly flutter. Orgasm denial really was a powerful thing. And definitely worth the wait.

When his hand slips between my thighs, my exhaustion takes a back seat to my desire. Everything feels swollen and raw, but comes alive just the same. I grind against his hand, but the movement only causes him to let out a breath of laughter. Too soon he's rinsing the soapy foam from me, and then shutting off the water.

Instead of lifting me from the tub, he only assists me— stepping out and taking my hand in his. My legs feel like I've been running through sand, as I slowly lift them over the side of the tub. But that's nothing compared to the throbbing ache in my shoulders. Having my arms suspended for so long wasn't something I'd be looking forward to in the near future.

I half-ass dry myself before wrapping the towel around me. I frown when I realize Bryce is already dry, and I missed the show. Taking my hand, he leads me back to the bedroom. With one swift jerk, he removes my towel.

His eyes travel the length of my naked body before turning me. I can feel his gaze on my backside, and the pain I feel in my chest is ten times worse than the pain of my ass—which is saying something.

"How bad is it, Love? Honestly." He spins me to face him, and the warmth in his eyes has me spilling the truth before I can think better of it.

"It hurts." My admission causes guilt to settle in my gut, but if he feels sorry for me he isn't showing it. *Thankfully.*

"On your knees." He points to the bed, and I bite my lip to hide my frown. I want him, but I don't think my body can physically handle him right now. And the worried look on my face doesn't go unnoticed.

Lifting my chin with his finger, he places a sweet kiss on my lips. "Trust me, Love." If there were any doubt that I didn't, all traces of them are gone.

Slowly, I crawl to my knees, wincing as the skin on my ass tightens with the movement. My arms have yet to regain their strength, so I splay them at my sides and bury my face in the mattress. The position opens me to him—completely baring not only my punished bottom, but the entire length of my pussy and everything in between.

"Beautiful," he murmurs, just as I feel his lips on my bruised cheeks—tenderly raining kisses over them. Somehow I feel like it's his way of trying to tell me he's not sorry, but that he hates I'm in pain.

After he's managed to pay special attention to every exposed inch of flesh, his hands wrap around the backs of my thighs, forcing my legs further apart.

With no warning, his tongue slides between my lips and my whole body jerks in response. He alternates between licking and sucking me—completely defining what it means to eat pussy. But he's not just eating me, he's devouring me—consuming me with his mouth. I can't determine what's better...his hammer of a cock or magical tongue.

Really, you can't compare the two. They're equally as amazing and rare as a unicorn.

"Don't come, Love. Not until I tell you to."

I groan, already nearing that point of no return. My body starts to betray me even as my mind insists I do as he says. "Bryce," I whimper. "I can't. It's too good. It feels too...fucking... good..." My words are a plea, as I bite my lip and fight the urge to give in.

"You heard me, Love." His dark voice causes everything he says to sound like a demand—even if it is softly spoken. If he'd just keep talking, I might be able to hold out. It's the only break I get from the onslaught of his mouth covering me...his tongue circling my clit with the perfect amount pressure to have me...

"Come."

If he hadn't said it, I'd have done it anyway. But his demand added the pleasure of obeying him to the explosion of ecstasy already pulsing through my body. Even the flow of blood in my veins can be felt. He heightens all of my senses—making me aware of even the smallest movements...the curl of my toes, my fisted hands, the tickle of disarrayed hair on my face... everything.

This is the second hardest, most powerful orgasm I've had. And my top three all belong to him. Coming down from them is nearly as good as the climax of the moment. Somehow it means more. It can be felt in places deep inside my chest—foreign to me but welcome in times like this. The way he gathers me in his arms, tucks me to his side, splays his hands across my belly, rubs my aching shoulders, kisses my hair, whispers for me to sleep...

*Son of a bitch...*

I'm falling in love.

# CHAPTER 21

We've been in bed for hours. I've tried to sleep, but just when I near it, the thought hits me and I'm awake again.

*I'm falling in love.*

No.

It's not possible.

I'm a clubwhore.

Sex is what I do.

I don't love...

I'm not even sure what in the hell love is.

I refuse to think I'm already there. So I'm clinging to the belief that I'm merely falling and either someone is going to catch me, or I'm going to end up face first on the pavement. I'm just not sure which is worse.

"What's on your mind, babe?" Bryce's voice is laced with sleep, but I'm not surprised to hear it. Every time I shift, his breathing changes and I know he's awake. It's like he's programmed his mind and body to respond to my every movement.

"I think I'm gonna take a walk," I say, sliding out from under his arm. Grabbing my bathrobe from the back of the door, I don't even wait to clothe myself in it before I'm walking toward the front door.

Outside, there's a thick frost covering the ground and trees —illuminating everything in white. The sky is clear and painted in bright stars. Its beauty is enough to make the cold tolerable, but I cinch my robe tighter and silently wish I had some shoes. Folding my legs beneath me, I sit on the edge of the steps and try to lose myself in the night.

Love scares me.

Not because I've never felt it, but because it's never been reciprocated. I've never found someone to love me in a way I need to be loved. I'm different. I need things. With Bryce, I have the whole package. He grounds me, tames my monsters, controls me when I need controlling, but allows me to still stand on my own two feet and think for myself. He's tender, loving, passionate and most of all—he understands. But what in the hell could I ever offer him?

By being with me, he'd be forced to hurt me, even though he's already said he doesn't enjoy it. I'm a loose cannon. A bomb with a lit fuse. I'm no good for him, and still, I want him to love me back. I've never been so selfish in my life.

Sure this is all his fault. He's made it entirely too easy for me to fall for him. He should've known what he was getting into. Right? You can't take a weak-minded, vulnerable fuck-up like myself and treat her with any form of decency. It's like feeding a stray dog—you can't do it once and not expect them to come back for more. I'm the stray dog. And I'm hungry.

As bad as I want to be selfish, I can't. It's not who I am. Bryce is a really great guy—so great that I know if he doesn't share my feelings, the guilt of knowing he's crushed me will hurt him. I don't want to hurt him.

I need to distance myself from him. I need space to think. Someone important once said: "Absence makes the heart grow fonder." If that's true, then maybe distance between us will strengthen his feelings toward me. Or better yet, make me more aware of my own.

It's easy to think I love him when my world is centered on him. Maybe going back to the clubhouse will remind me of how much I'm not ready to give up my life as a clubwhore . And maybe, just maybe, I'll learn I really don't love him at all.

"I w-want to go home," I announce, or stutter. My body shakes from the cold—masking my nerves.

Bryce is still sitting on the couch, wearing the same curious expression as when I walked in a moment ago. It took me a minute to find the courage to say what I needed to say. Now that it's off my chest, I'm hoping to feel a little relief. But it's yet to come.

"Can't do that, babe."

I try to frown, but my face is numb. "But I w-want to."

"Three days. That's what you agreed to, and I'm holding you at your word." He's so matter-of-fact. I wish it would piss me off. But it doesn't. It just makes this harder for me.

"I'm going home." The strength in my voice is pretty impressive. But only to me. He's as dismissive about my tone as he is my statement.

"No..." He drawls out the word as he leans up, narrowing his eyes on me. They darken and I feel my resolve slipping. "You're not." His gaze becomes penetrating, leveling me with a force that's so demanding, I'm already preparing to nod in agreement to whatever he says. But he doesn't say anything. He stands.

I feel warmer when he's in front of me. I can feel the heat of his skin even through his shirt. He stares down at me a moment before taking my hand and leading me to the bathroom. The scent of lavender engulfs me, as the light from several different candles illuminates the room. The tub is filled to the brim with bubbles, and a glass of red wine sits next to it on a small stool. *Yeah... I'm not going anywhere tonight.*

His dominate act is gone, as if he knew he wouldn't need it after showing me this. Now his eyes are soft and full of understanding as he looks down at me. "I know this isn't easy for you. But I can't let you leave. You need this. We both made a commitment, and we're going to follow through with it. You're going to stay, and I'm going to help you."

My bottom lip quivers and I pull it between my teeth. Why do I always feel so sad around him? I'm so raw...open...exposed. He seems to pull emotions out of me I blocked years ago. Now a lifetime of tears I've managed to not shed has done nothing but spill when I'm with him.

"Just take some time to relax. I'll give you some space for a while." He doesn't touch me as he leaves and for some reason it hurts. I wanted so bad to feel his lips on my face, or my body pressed against his chest. I wanted him to hold me and tell me everything was okay. Instead, he gave me space—the one thing I wanted only minutes ago, but now hate the thought of.

*This is bad...really bad.*

If I can't stand to be away from him for a few minutes, then how in the hell will I ever make it when he leaves?

I'm crying again. Hell, that's an understatement. I'm a blubbering fucking mess. Even the hot water, bubbles and wine aren't enough to hold me together. But I keep sitting...keep drinking...keep hoping that maybe I'll find a small piece of the old Delilah that refused to shed a tear over anyone. Especially her own, pathetic self.

*Dammit, Delilah!! Stop! Grow some friggin' balls!*

Finishing off the glass of wine, I will myself to stop the tears and quit feeling sorry for myself. When I'm finished, I take a deep breath and submerge myself completely in the water—keeping my eyes squeezed shut to fight off the tears. I stay there until my lungs are near exploding before sitting up, taking another breath and sliding beneath the water again. I continue the process until most of the water is out of the tub and on the floor.

I've stopped crying, but I still feel like shit. Reaching my hand around the side of the tub, I search blindly for a towel to wipe the soapy water from my eyes. I finally locate it, pressing my face into the thick fluffy cotton. Covering my mouth, I scream into the towel—muffling the noise. It feels good, so I do it again.

A part of me is hoping he's sitting on that stool next to the bathtub when I open my eyes. But he's not. I'm alone in the bathroom—just me and my shadow that dances on the wall across from me in the reflection of the candlelight.

*Space.*

He wants to give me space. I want him to give me space. Or at least I did. But in the midst of my underwater experiment, I came to a decision. I'm going to tell him the truth. I'm going to tell him I love him.

Or that I think I love him.

Or that he's forcing me to love him.

"Bryce!" I yell at the top of my lungs. I wait a beat, and when I don't hear his footsteps, I try again. "Bryce!..." This time, I hold it for as long as I can, feeling a sense of relief as I do. *Maybe I should scream his name more often.*

What sounds like a herd of cattle comes barreling down the hall moments before the door bursts open. I'm smiling when a very panicked, very red-faced Bryce appears. His eyes sweep my entire body and then the room. Finally, he seems to notice my face and the amused look I must be wearing. He lets out a breath and runs his hand over his head.

"Don't do that shit to me, babe. You scared the fuck outta me."

"We need to talk." *Wow.* Now I sound like a dominant. *Impressive.* But he's still reeling from all the bad thoughts of what could've been wrong with me to notice.

"Okay." *I swear I hate that word. What does that even mean? Okay... Hmph.*

"Sit." I point to the stool next to the tub. *I like this version of me.*

He narrows his eyes in warning. "Watch it," he says, in his signature spanking voice—that's what I'm calling it now. But he sits. His knees touch the side of the tub and he's less than a foot from me—so close...too close. I scoot further back in the tub searching for a little distance and not finding much.

He stares at me expectantly. "Well? What is it?"

Now that he's here, I'm chickening out. I need a moment to get my shit together, so I try for a distraction. "Will you get me some more wine?"

"No. What did you want to talk about, Delilah?" *Sheesh...* So rude.

"I have a problem," I admit, squeezing my eyes shut because it's better than looking at him. I'm afraid if I do, I'll lose what little bit of courage I have left.

"What's your problem, babe?" He's exasperated. Maybe a little annoyed. But at least he isn't demanding I look at him.

*Just do it!*

"I think I'm falling in love with you."

Silence.

I might be able to get an idea of what he's thinking, but my eyes are closed. And that's how they'll stay. Unless he—

"Look at me." Warmth spreads through my belly at his gentle tone. It's almost a whisper. But he didn't call me Love like he does when we're in role play. He didn't call me babe like he does when we're not. And he didn't call me Delilah like he does when he's angry. He just said "Look at me." His demand needs to be more specific.

"Who?" I whisper, hoping like hell he calls on the one I want. Although I'm not quite sure which one that is.

"What?"

"Who do you want to look at you?" After a moment, he seems to understand, and I hear him let out a breath.

"Just...look at me."

I do. He might as well be wearing a mask—that's just how well he's hiding whatever it is he's feeling. "It's not unusual for you to feel like this," he explains, almost as if he's a teacher speaking to a student. Not quite what I was expecting, but... "For the first time, you're around someone who knows and really appreciates who you are. You're naturally attracted to me because I give you everything you want."

"Well..." I quirk an eyebrow at him and he smiles.

"If I were a dominant, and you a submissive, then you'd have some really strong, confusing feelings toward me. I knew after last night when you asked if I was mad at you that it wouldn't take you long to experience those feelings."

For a fleeting moment he looks wounded. He tries to recover with a smile, but I can see a hint of sadness in his eyes. It twists my insides. "You don't love me," he whispers. "You just love the idea of me."

Um... I disagree. I mean, everything he says makes sense, but I know my heart. That bastard has been dead for years. When I'm with him, I feel something. But there's no point in arguing. In his quiet, assured, passive way, he's dismissed the entire conversation. He's back to sweet, playful Bryce and I half ass expect him to poke my ribs or nudge my chin like a brother would. Well...not *my* brother. But you know what I mean. It's so unsettling I decide I need to get him back into dominant Bryce mode.

Lifting my glass, I lean back in the tub and dangle it at him. "I need more wine, master." Yep. That did it. His jaw tightens and his eyes flash with anger. "You know," he says, coming to his full, intimidating height as he stands. "You're not as smart as you think."

I feign innocence. "Whatever do you mean?" I'm getting pretty good at my voice alterations. I sounded like a southern belle that time.

"You think you know what buttons of mine to push to get exactly what you want, but you're forgetting something."

"Yeah?"

His lips curve into a wicked smile. "Yeah." His voice darkens, sending chills down my spine and puckering my nipples. "I know exactly what you need. Remember this, *Love*," he narrows his eyes. "There are other ways to punish you that don't involve spanking your cute little ass. That's what you want, isn't it? Me to hurt you so you can gain my affection?"

His words hurt. They wound my heart and my soul. The blow is worse than his belt. But my hurt quickly morphs to anger. Damn him for fucking with my emotions. To hell with the repercussions. I do know his buttons, and I plan to press them. Maybe if he does hit me, the force of his strike will be enough to rid me of my ridiculous idea of love, and replace it with hate.

"How about you get my wine...*master.*" His face falls and I get the feeling that in pushing his buttons, I've pressed my luck. Leaning down, he braces his hands on either side of the tub and brings his face so close to mine our noses nearly touch. "Get out. Dry your hair and go to bed." I swallow hard and nod. He straightens, shoots me one last look of warning and leaves.

Fear of the unknown has my heartbeat still racing long after he's gone. When my hair is dry, I nervously cross the hall to the bedroom and climb in bed. My hands fidget and my nerves sing as I wait. And I wait.

And wait.

Nothing.

Not knowing what's to come is scarier than the fact that I actually wanted him to hurt me not long ago. But it wasn't the pain I wanted, it was this feeling in my chest to disappear. Now the idea of me not having feelings for him sounds more preposterous than embracing my emotions. He's all I want. All I crave. All I need. Reality starts to slowly sink in as the minutes tick by.

He's not coming.

This is my punishment.

And in this moment, I realize there is a greater fear than his wrath.

*His absence.*

At some point I fell asleep. The first thing I do when I wake is notice that he isn't here. The alarm clock by the bed tells me it's after four in the morning. Meaning I've been asleep for a little over an hour. I should be exhausted enough to sleep through the night, considering my training session, love revelation and crying spell from earlier. But his absence stirs a deep part of my brain, preventing me from feeling any sense of peace.

I more than don't like this feeling. I loathe it. Physical pain I can deal with. Emotional pain, not so much. I get it. I deserved this. But I'm willing to trade my loneliness for anything. He can tie me up, keep me from coming, blindfold me and spank me until my skin blisters. Anything but this.

I crawl out from under the covers that are tucked tightly around me. *I wasn't under the covers.* He must have come in at some point, and I feel warm at the thought of him coming to check on me—taking care of me even when I don't deserve it. What I deserve is to have my teeth knocked out for being such a dick to the only guy who's ever been this nice to me.

Pulling on my robe, I tiptoe through the house in search of him. He's nowhere in sight, and I hesitate before opening the door to the man cave/playroom. The moment the door opens, I hear grunts and the sound of chains rattling. I find Bryce shirtless, sweaty and beating the shit out of a punching bag.

*Have mercy...*

His muscles roll with every punch he throws. His moves are swift, fluid and effortless—hitting the bag repeatedly in the same place every time. My mouth is dry, but it's the only part of my body that is. Sweat breaks out across my brow, under my arms and there's a small river flowing between my thighs. He's just so...*hot.*

I don't know if I sighed or moaned or hell, maybe I called his name. But his arms drop and he looks over his shoulder at me. His chest heaves for air. It's the first time I've seen him winded. But it's his eyes that floor me. They're not just dark—they're stormy.

"Didn't I tell you to go to bed?" There's grit in his tone and my guilt thickens. If I wasn't such a selfish asshole, he'd be in bed instead of in here sweating off his frustrations.

Pulling the door closed behind me, I stand just inside it, keeping my distance. "I don't like being alone."

"I know. That's the point." He takes a sip of water, keeping his eyes trained on me. Damn, they're intense. And a little scary.

"I shouldn't have been such a jerk. You were right. I was provoking you to hit me...again."

"Don't say that." My blood chills at the ice in his tone. "I've never hit you. Not like that."

I nod, trying to find a way out of this hole I just keep digging. "I mean...well, you know what I mean."

"Say it," he demands. Boy, he's not letting me off easy on this one.

I swallow again, wishing I had a sip of his water. "Spank me. I wanted you to spank me, so I said what I thought would make you angry enough to do it."

He stares at me a long time before he speaks. "I've never touched you because I was angry, Delilah. I did it because you needed it, or you deserved it."

Dropping my eyes, I toy with the belt of my robe. "I know. I was wrong, and I'm sorry."

"Don't you think your ass has been through enough? Do you have no limits to the amount of pain you want? Have I not taken care of you? Do I not give you enough attention without you forcing my hand?"

"I said I was sorry," I snap, raising my eyes to meet his.

"Are you? Really?" he presses, and I'm not sure if this is another tactic of his, or if he's actually pissed. "Why did you come in here?"

"To find you."

"And what?" His eyebrows raise expectantly. I notice whatever trouble he was dealing with must have passed. Now he's more in control. Still demanding as hell, but not in a way that makes me worry about him.

"To find you and apologize."

He shakes his head. "Try again."

I throw my hands up in confusion. "What do you want me to say?"

"The truth."

I have no idea what the fuck he's talking about. So I just shrug. Apparently that pushes his button too.

"I told you why I came in here. That's the truth."

"So if I told you there's a way to trade one form of punishment for another, that'd be the first time you thought about it?" *Oh...that's what he's talking about. What the fuck is he? A mind reader?*

"I mean, I thought about it. But that's not my intentions."

"Then go to bed." He turns away, clearly dismissing me.

"Wait," I call, stopping him mid-punch. "I wanna trade." He turns to face me again. "I'll do anything, just...don't leave me alone." Immediately his face softens. I might have overplayed it just a little. But fuck it. I think it's going to work in my favor.

Walking, well, more like strutting toward me, I keep my eyes on his face to avoid looking at his body. It arouses me too much, and I want to be fair. Tackling him to the floor and forcing him to fuck me isn't very fair.

Stopping in front of me, he looks down while I look up. I try not to, but I can't help it—I inhale. Sweaty Bryce smells better than I could've imagined. If masculine had a scent, it would be him. I literally want to lick his chest.

"You're meant to feel the full impact of your punishment. You're supposed to feel uncomfortable and ashamed. That's the entire reasoning behind it. That's the only way for it to be effective...for you to feel better afterward." He tucks a strand of hair behind my ear, and the simple touch seems to make everything okay—no, not that word. I hate that word. It makes everything better.

"But I never want you to feel like I've abandoned you. I wouldn't do that." His finger trails across my jaw to beneath my chin. He tilts my head back a little to keep my focus as he leans in. "Trust, Love. You have to trust me to help you overcome your fears."

*I'm not going to cry... Nope. I ain't doing it.*

"Now." His voice deepens, and the softness disappears. "You came in here for a trade. It's your ass on the line. So what do you have to offer? " Mischief dances in his eyes. I know if I told him to spank me, he'd make damn sure I wouldn't be requesting it again anytime soon. As appealing as that sounds—insert sarcasm—there's something else I need more.

I agreed to this because I was willing to try something to help cure this sickness inside of me. No matter how hard or how much he spanked me, it wouldn't fix the part of me that's broken. Sometimes I need it. Sometimes I deserve it. And here lately, I just want it. Not this time. I need, deserve and want something much, much worse.

I try to drop my head, but his finger under my chin holds me in place. My eyes prick with tears, but I force them back. I will not cry and make him feel guilty. It's not fair to him or to me.

"I trust you."

Without waiting for his reaction, I step out of his grasp and quietly leave the room. I won't let the beast win this time. No matter how much I hate this, I'll endure it. The moment I slide between the sheets, I welcome that feeling of loneliness and fear. But even as it settles inside me, there's a calming voice in the back of my head reminding me of what I know to be true.

I'm not alone.

Hours later, long after the sun has rose, I feel arms circle my waist as Bryce's warm body curls around mine. With his hand splayed on my stomach and his lips at my ear, I welcome his demand to go back to sleep. But what I hear is so much more rewarding.

"You're perfect."

# CHAPTER 22

It was early afternoon before I woke. I found Bryce in the man cave/playroom, sprawled on the couch watching TV. Wordlessly, he gestured with his hand for me to join him. I spent the day curled into his side watching movies on the large flat screen.

Neither of us mentioned the events of last night that bled into the early hours of this morning. Actually, we barely spoke at all. The silence was nice and never grew uncomfortable.

The sun is just setting when I catch sight of something on the bed as I come out of the bathroom.

"What's this?" I ask Bryce, who had appeared out of thin air and now stood leaning against the door frame. I hold up the plastic bag filled with clothes.

"Put it on. We're going out." I start to drill him with questions, but he disappears from my view.

The jeans, boots and long-sleeved shirt are from my own closet. As are the bra and panties. After being naked for two days, wearing clothes seems unnatural—especially the panties. My lady parts have very much enjoyed the freedom, as have I.

I don't have any makeup, but luckily my lashes are naturally dark and my skin is clear. Without my straightener, my hair is an untamed mess, but when I walk out in my skinny jeans, brown knee boots, white V-neck shirt and wild hair, Bryce says I look good. So does he.

In jeans, a black Henley and riding boots, he's the biker without the patch. But it's folded in his hand. He's wearing a hat that sits backward on his head. He looks delicious naked, but there's something even sexier about him being dressed.

Maybe it's the mystery of what's hidden beneath his clothes. Or it could be the chain that loops around his thigh. Or the way he pushes up the sleeves on his shirt exposing his forearms. Actually, I'll take him just about any way I can get him.

"So where are we going?" I ask, letting him slip my brown jacket, which matches my outfit, over my shoulders. *I wonder who packed this...*

"Out."

I roll my eyes. "I know that, but where?"

"Dinner. A movie. Maybe a trip to Wal-Mart, if you're good." He winks at me.

"Are you taking me on a date?" I tease, flashing him a broad smile.

"Yes."

What? His admission freezes me in place. A date? A real date? Had I ever been on one? Not in a long time. My spine tingles and my cheeks heat.

He smirks and I drop my gaze. *Why am I so uncomfortable with this?* Suddenly, I don't want to go. I want to stay here, detached from the outside world. I want to live in this bubble we've created with just me and him. I don't want the pressure of a date. How will I act? What if I do something stupid?

My anxiety has me fidgety. I twist the belt to my jacket in my hands. Then mindlessly, I bring one to the back of my neck. Closing it around my hair, I start to tug, but Bryce grabs my wrist. He shoots me a chastising look, but kisses my palm before closing his hand around mine.

"Calm down." He stands in front of me, giving me a playful smile as his hand curves around the side of my face. "Why are you freaking out?"

"Well, I wouldn't be if you hadn't said this was a date. Now I feel all pressured."

He breathes out a laugh. "Tell you what. Fuck all this." He looks around the room before meeting my gaze again. "Forget it all. Let's have some fun tonight. Just be ourselves."

"But I get confused when I'm with you. The whole "*babe*" and "*Love*" thing completely transforms me." I wave my hand around for dramatics, pulling another huff of laughter from him.

"If it makes you feel better, I have some business for the club I have to handle. So technically, it's not a real date." I sigh in relief.

"Yes. That does make me feel better. Why didn't you just say that?"

He shakes his head, intrigued by my reaction. "You have got to be the strangest woman I've ever met." I frown and look away, forcing my lip to quiver. "Hey." His voice is pained, and I can't follow through on my joke.

I poke his stomach and smile. "Gotcha."

His eyes narrow. "Not funny."

"Oh, that was funny."

"I'll remember that when we get back."

This time, my frown is real. "Oh, come on," I whine, mentally kicking myself in the ass for ruining my mood.

With a cocky smirk, he gives me a wink. "Don't worry. You'll like it."

Great. Now I *really* don't want to go.

The "date" isn't awkward at all. Bryce still has Luke's truck, and I sing along to every rock song that plays, while he simply listens in quiet amusement. He drives us to TGIF's, and after a few drinks at the bar, we're seated at a table. I order the biggest damn hamburger they have. Bryce on the other hand, orders grilled chicken and a salad.

"Your sexy meter just dropped."

"My what?" He looks amused.

"Your sexy meter. You were a ten. Now you're an eight."

"Because I ordered grilled chicken? That hardly constitutes for a two point decline."

I shake my head. "No. The chicken is fine. You lost a point for the salad, though. The other you lost when you ordered a Long Island Iced Tea at the bar."

"What?" he asks, shrugging in confusion. "They're good."

I shake my head. Only this man would be confident enough to order such a feminine drink. And he looks so damn sexy drinking it, I move him back to a ten on my sexy meter. But his ego doesn't need to be stroked, so I keep it to myself.

The banter is fun. It feels natural and helps me forget what we've been doing the past couple of days. Well, it did. Now that I mention it, I'm back in that tiny house in my bathrobe getting spanked, fucked and completely dominated. My thighs rub together at the thought.

"So, what movie you want to watch?"

I let out a gasp. "You're letting me choose?"

"Yep. Whatever you want."

"I think they're running an anniversary special for *Titanic*."

"Anything but that."

I laugh. "Well, what's the point in letting me choose if I can't … choose?"

His playful smile falters as he pulls his phone from his pocket. The air instantly changes and I know something is wrong. I'd ask, but I don't get the chance. Sliding out of the booth, he throws some money down on the table and reaches for my hand.

"We gotta go. Now." I take his hand, feeling a sense of uneasiness spread through me. This isn't dominant Bryce. It's not playful Bryce either. This is Devil's Renegades SA Bryce. And that motherfucker is livid.

I have to bite my tongue to keep from asking the burning question in my head, as he pulls me through the parking lot. He releases me when we near the back of Luke's truck with one simple demand. "Get in." I'm barely in the seat before he's slamming the truck in reverse and peeling out.

*Don't ask. Don't ask. Don't ask.* Fuck it. I'm asking.

"What's going on?"

"Don't ask, babe," he says, and if he hadn't had thrown "babe" in there, I might have been offended. But I know how shit works. Club business is just that—club business.

The rumble of the diesel engine is loud as Bryce moves in and out of traffic at a pace that is so exciting it's scary. I can hear my heart pumping in my ears, fueled by adrenaline. For some reason, I'm biting my cheek to keep from smiling as my knee bounces excitedly.

We're at a red light on Hardy, the busiest street in Hattiesburg, when he flips down the console between us. "Climb back there and get my cut. It's under my seat."

With more grace than I thought I had, I unclip my seatbelt and scramble over the console. I feel his hand on my thigh and freeze. Then he guns it and makes a sharp left, which would send me flying in the event he wasn't holding onto me. I giggle.

"Something funny, babe?"

Snatching his cut, I clamber back into my seat—gripping it to my chest as if my life depended on it. "Yes."

He shoots me a curious look. Damn, he's sexy. "What?"

"This!" I say, bouncing in my seat. "This is exciting."

His lips twitch, but he refrains from smiling. "Glad you think so, gorgeous." *Gorgeous...* That's a new one. *I like it.*

I hear the rumble of pipes and turn in my seat to find a pack of bikes speeding toward us. My heart hammers against my chest and my smile widens. *What I wouldn't give to be riding on one of those.* If this is exciting, I can only imagine what that would be like.

"Make me a promise," I say excitedly, turning to face him.

"What's that?" He seems to enjoy my distraction. Every time I speak, his jaw isn't so tense.

"Promise me you'll take me riding."

"This not thrilling enough for you?" There's humor in his voice. But he doesn't look at me. His focus is on something up ahead.

"Please?" He remains silent, his jaw tightening again. He presses hard on the brake, sending me flying toward the dash. I reach out to stop myself, but there's no need. His hand is fisted in my shirt, preventing me from...oh, I don't know...breaking my face.

"Stay in the truck. No matter what, you stay in the truck. You understand?"

I'd answer, but I can't speak. The small rundown bar we just pulled next to is filled with bikers. And they're all fighting. I can hear the low rumble of voices through the window as fists fly and men with several different patches give new meaning to a bar-room brawl.

"Delilah!" he yells, and I force myself to look at him. "Do you understand?"

I nod, and this time that's answer enough. Snatching his cut from my arm, he barrels out of the truck, throwing it around his shoulders. I'm in shock. I want to tell him to be careful, but my voice is caught somewhere in my throat.

I must look terrified. Really, I'm not. Bryce is a big guy. He can handle himself. But if there were any doubt he takes the moment to erase it completely.

Like someone flipped a switch, he completely transforms from badass biker back to fun, playful Bryce and gives me a cocky grin. "I promise." Winking, he slams the door just as several of the Renegades make it to the truck. Together, they rush into the crowd.

I try to keep my sights on Bryce, who is flanking Luke. He seems to not only be behind him, but beside and in front of him all at the same time. Someone rushes toward them. I see Luke slow, his hand fisting at his side prepared to fight, but he's too late. With one lick, Bryce nearly takes the guy's head off.

"Hell, yeah!" I shout, jabbing at the air in the truck. I realize my fists are drawn up like I'm prepared to fight. Dropping them, I focus my attention back on the crowd, but both Luke and Bryce have disappeared. Actually, the whole damn crowd has shifted to the back of the building out of my view.

There aren't enough spoons or belts in this world that could persuade me to stay in this truck. To hell with punishment. I've got to see what's going on. And besides, we're not the same couple we were at the little house in the middle of nowhere. We're normal people on a date. His words...not mine.

Jumping out of the truck, my feet barely hit the ground before I'm running. Then I notice everyone else is running too. And they're coming toward me. Well, in my general direction.

The sound of pipes ring out as one by one everyone scrambles to their bikes and fires up the engines. People are everywhere—running full speed as the sound of sirens can suddenly be heard in the distance.

Before I can turn and run back, I see familiar patches round the corner. Luke is first with the entire club behind him. *Shit.* I'm hoping Bryce is too preoccupied to notice me, but he does.

"Get in the truck!" Luke yells, snapping me out of my temporary moment of idiocy. He breaks off to the left toward his bike that's parked somewhere behind us, while Bryce continues to barrel straight at me. *Damn, he's fast.*

Not everyone can say they've experienced a Lois Lane moment. I may not be falling out of the sky, but my Superman grabs me around the waist—knocking my breath from my lungs as he does. It's not as graceful and rewarding as the movie makes it out to be.

Slinging open the driver's side door, Bryce hoists me inside. He gives my ass a push when I don't move fast enough and jumps in behind me. I manage to right myself just as he floors it, spinning tires in the process.

"Do you even hear me when I tell you to do something?" he asks, breathing heavy as his head whips around trying to locate his club. He sounds just as excited as I feel.

"Not really. There!" I point to a line of bikes crossing the grassy lot between the bar and a hotel. Whipping the truck to the left, he honks and I notice the pack turn and head in the same direction.

The light ahead is red, but Bryce ignores it and I brace myself as he pulls out into the street blocking traffic. Horns honk and blue lights flash only a couple hundred yards away as we sit in the middle of the road.

Pipes rumble beside me and I look out my window to find the club heading down a side street completely unnoticed by the cops that are coming from the other direction. The truck blocks the view, and I beam at the thought of being involved in something so dangerous and law breaking.

"Here." Cold leather smacks me in the chest as Bryce flings his cut at me. "Fold it inside out and shove it under your seat. These too." He tosses me several cuts I don't recognize.

I'm still folding when the last bike passes and Bryce presses hard on the gas, spinning us in the same direction as the bikes. We jerk to the left and then the right until he regains control. I look behind us but the cops are too involved with the motorcycles to pay any attention to a truck.

"You are so getting fucked tonight," I say, though I'm not sure if I'm telling him or reassuring myself.

"If we don't go to jail, I'm holding you to that."

"Why would we go to jail?" Even as I ask, I notice the blue lights that were once in the distance are directly behind us. "Oh shit."

Bryce slows, making sure to wait until the bikes are out of sight before pulling into a driveway. Putting the truck in park, he looks down at my floorboard making sure the cuts are out of sight. Then his eyes narrow on me.

"You're my girlfriend. We were having a drink, a fight broke out and we left. To avoid a wreck, I was forced out into traffic. We have no affiliation with any club."

"The truck is Luke's!" I blurt, earning me a look of warning.

"Don't talk unless they speak directly to you. If you breathe one word, Delilah, I will take you to the clubhouse, take off my belt and spank you in front of every patch holder there."

I bite my lip. Something about the way he said it makes me let out a low moan. Not from the thought of him spanking me, but his tone. Shaking his head, he rolls his eyes and lets out an exasperated breath. A giggle rips through my chest. Even though he tries to hide it, I can see a hint of a smile on his face.

A light tap sounds on the window and Bryce lets it down, already handing the officer his license. Another tap sounds on my window and I press the button, painting an upsetting look on my face as another officer shines his light in my eyes.

"You okay, ma'am?"

I nod and swallow hard. Dropping my gaze to my lap, I ignore the way Bryce's deep, heavily accented voice affects me, as he tells the rehearsed story to the cop at his window.

"Wanna tell me what happened?"

"I don't know, really. We were just sitting there drinking one minute and the next everybody was fighting. The rest is kinda a blur. We ran to the truck, some bikes almost hit us, then we were in the intersection." My eyes pool with water. "I told him we shouldn't have went with all them bikes there."

"Hey," the officer soothes, dropping the light from my eyes and placing a hand on my shoulder. "Your boyfriend did the right thing by getting y'all out of there. Those bikers are nothing but trouble." Something ignites inside me at his words. Immediately, I become defensive. *That's my fucking family, pig.*

"Baby?" Bryce's hand reaches for mine. "You okay?" Yeah, yeah, yeah, Bryce. I hear your underlying meaning. He's telling me to keep my shit together. So I nod, knowing the cops are still watching us.

"Y'all have a safe trip home," one says. Bryce thanks him and we roll the windows up, neither of us speaking until we're back on the road.

"I did good, huh?" I ask, wiggling my eyebrows at him.

He smirks. "Yeah, babe. You saved our asses on that one. The cop I was talking to didn't believe me until you started your sob story."

"So what happened back there? Why was everyone fighting?" I'm so sure he won't answer, I'm stunned when he does.

"Fist fights are more common than you think in the MC. That's how we handle our business. Problem with that is, sometimes it's hard to maintain order when there are so many men involved." He pauses a minute, glancing at me to gauge my reaction. I keep silent, but can't hide the fascination on my face. It makes him smirk.

"Tonight shouldn't have happened in a public place like that. It rarely does. But disrespect is never tolerated. The men that wear our patch should always be treated with the utmost respect. Tonight, they weren't."

"You mean all that was over disrespect? That seems a little extreme."

"Respect is earned, babe. And when you work as hard as my club has to get it, you demand to be treated with it. This town belongs to the Devil's Renegades. Nothing happens here without our approval. Some people agree, some don't. Tonight, both sides fought for what they thought was right."

"So who won?" I ask, already knowing the answer.

Pride dances in his eyes as he shoots me a wicked grin. "Who do you think?"

I pretend to contemplate my answer. "Well, that seems like a lot to accomplish in such a small amount of time. From what I saw, five minutes wasn't long enough to really do anything."

His grin widens. "You'd be surprised, babe. Not only did we win the battle"—his eyes move to the floorboard where the pile of unfamiliar cuts is hidden just out of sight—"we won the whole fuckin' war."

# CHAPTER 23

In my head, I'd planned for our evening to go a little differently. Something along the lines of us pulling up at home, him telling me to strip, dragging me to the playroom, tying me up, then fucking me until I pass out. But the moment we walk through the door, I abandon my well-thought-out plan, and go straight for the kill.

I leap in his arms without worry of whether or not he'll catch me. I know he will, and he does. With my hands holding his face, I crash my lips to his in a desperate, hungry kiss. He growls deep in his throat, and I swear it's the sexiest thing I've ever heard.

"I just want you to be that man I met the first time you fucked me. And I just want to be Delilah," I pant, while my mouth nibbles along his jaw. "When I didn't even know your name. When it was just me and you hot sex...the *best...fuckin'... sex...*"

"Tell me how you want it, baby." His fingers dig into my hips as he holds me to him. "Hard?" His tongue slides up my neck and I throw my head back to grant him better access. "Soft?" He pulls my earlobe between his teeth. "Fast?" His eyes meet mine— heavy and hooded with lust. Then he plants a sweet kiss on my lips, lingering so long my body seems to melt. "Or slow?"

"I want it all."

Wrapping one arm around my waist, he stretches his other out to catch us as we fall on the bed. I wasn't even aware he'd walked to the bedroom. But the ceiling is above me, I'm pressed firmly into the mattress below me and his lips are on fire when they collide with mine. His hand runs the length of my thigh, hoisting my knee around his waist. I can feel him hard and ready as he presses against me.

He takes his time kissing me as his hands roam my body— squeezing, touching, feeling every inch of me through my clothes. Reaching behind him, he fists his hand in his shirt, breaking the kiss just long enough to pull it over his head. Then his scorching chest is bare and against me—making me long for the feeling of skin-on-skin contact.

I'm breathless when he pulls away, and I watch him as he makes quick work of disposing me of my clothes until I'm completely naked and he's looking down at me. There's a new sense of appreciation in his stare. Like for the first time, he's actually seeing me.

"You are so fuckin' sexy." And he's just given new meaning to the term "eye fucked." If he continues too much longer, I may come at the intensity of his stare alone.

In one swift movement, his jeans disappear—leaving him completely nude and me wondering if he'd went commando tonight. Crawling across the bed, I moan the instant his skin touches mine. It's warm, inviting and smells so delicious I can't help but lift my head and drag my tongue across his chest.

"Soft," he whispers, forcing my head back to the pillow as he kisses a path across my collarbone. My legs are stretched wide to accommodate his massive body—making it easy for him to guide himself inside me. Then as promised, he softly kisses me while he slides in gently.

The feeling of him stretching me is nothing compared to the intimacy of his hands and mouth. He makes love to me like I'm the most delicate thing he's ever possessed. And he does possess me—completely.

"Slow." I moan at his word, hoping like hell he'll continue to take his time, while another part of me begs to reach that euphoric state that is just out of my grasp. But he moves with a fluidity that's just as pleasing and pleasurable soft and slow as it would be hard and fast. Seconds later, my back arches and my head falls back as I come.

He takes his time and keeps his strokes slow, steady—prolonging my climax until finally, I'm nothing more than a big pile of mush beneath him. Then his movements quicken, bringing me back to life as he pulls a nipple deep into his mouth and sucks hard—igniting the dying embers inside me once again.

"Hard," he growls, and I hold my breath as he pulls almost completely out before slamming back inside me. Fireworks burst behind my eyes on every thrust. My mouth hangs open and I let out a sharp, high-pitched wail of approval every time his hips meet mine. An intense, tingling sensation spreads through me over and over as he collides with that sweet spot inside me.

My fingers claw at his back. My toes curl into the mattress. My tits bounce hard on every drive. Opening my eyes, I look up at him as he gazes down at me in a heated passion that's just the push I need to send me spiraling over the edge again. I'm no longer moaning, I'm screaming in pleasure.

The sound rips from my chest and reverberates off the walls —completely drowning out his words. I want to hear what he says, but I can't stop my shattering wails of pleasure, fueled by his powerful thrusts that drive me into a deep pool of ecstasy.

I'm still coming down from the high of my orgasm when he flips to his back, leaving me straddling his waist and clinging to his chest in search of balance. He's deep inside me—deeper than he's ever been. And I can't focus on anything but how good it feels to swallow him completely.

I shift slightly and the movement causes his hands to tighten at my waist and his eyes become even heavier. We've covered every level except for fast, but now that I'm in control, I'm wanting to draw this out as long as possible. The sight of him beneath me—his chest heaving, his eyes glassy, his lips parted, on his back and at my mercy has a sense of power coursing through me.

"Tell me what you want, baby," I tease, earning myself a look of warning. My hips flinch and he surrenders his control once again. *I could get used to this.*

Leaning down, I brace my hands on either side of his face. Moving just my ass, I lift myself a few inches before sliding back down over his cock that is wet with my release. My pussy grips him tightly—pulling a groan from deep in his chest.

I want to tease him. I want to take my time and fuck him in the same controlled manner he's fucked me. But he has another idea. Gripping my ass in his hands, he easily lifts me up and down—raising his hips to meet mine, and making my body yearn for that final stage we never made it to.

Sitting back up, I regain control once again, and finally give us both what we want. *Fast.* Our bodies are so hot and my pace so rapid, I'm afraid we'd ignite a fire if it weren't for the flood of my desire preventing the flames. His hands are on my ass, on my breasts, on my hips, my thighs and everywhere in between—feeling me as if the urge to touch me can't be ignored.

I come hard, throwing my head back and relinquishing my power to him, as he grips my waist and thrusts roughly inside me—finding his own release just as I start to come down from mine. When his hands relax around me, I realize they're the only thing holding me up and I collapse on his chest.

My hair clings to his arms and chest—the sheen of sweat covering him acting as a glue. We both fight for breath as we slowly regain the ability to speak and move.

"I had fun on our date," he says, breaking the silence as he smoothes his hand down my spine.

"Uh-huh," I grunt, still unable to form a coherent word. I feel his body shake beneath me on a chuckle.

"Good night, Delilah."

"Uh, uh, uh…" I may not say it, but the smile on my face and the warmth in my belly proves there's truth in my mumble.

*It was a good night, indeed…even better than the first.*

\*\*\*\*

"What day is it?" I ask on a yawn as I pad into the kitchen.

Bryce hands me my coffee, lights my cigarette and lets me take a sip and a drag before answering. "Sunday." I'm aware of his eyes on me, so I force myself not to react. But on the inside, alarm starts to spread.

"Okay," I shrug, giving him a smile. "I'm going to shower." He nods, but I can see the apprehension written all over his face. The moment I'm out of his sight, I let the panic settle inside me.

It's not just Sunday. It's late Sunday morning. I should be at my mother's. I should have had her house cleaned. I should have had breakfast cooked. My brother should have already given me several warnings, and my mother should have already called me every motherfucker in the book.

*You don't need them, Delilah. You're not weak right now. Your beast is caged…or is he?*

He's not.

I've had more physical pain this week than I've had in years. Everything is going right. Bryce is teaching me to deal. He's helping me to cope. I don't need my brother's iron fist or my mother's emotional abuse. And yet I feel restless, that familiar need, the darkness, rearing its head up again out of custom, habit or simply masochism. It's there and it's crawling all over me.

"Delilah?" I turn to find Bryce standing in the bathroom door. "You okay?" Concern. Sweet concern about me—the girl who is obviously damaged beyond repair.

Anger sparks inside me. It's not directed at him, but I have no one to take my wrath out on—nothing to distract me. It's just him and me in this tiny house that's starting to shrink around me.

"Love," he says, patience and understanding laced in his words. "I know something is wrong."

"Well, look at you, Einstein. Nothing gets past that brain of yours, does it?" My outburst has me immediately feeling guilty, and my hand fists at the back of my hair.

"Cut the bitch act, babe. I—"

"It's not an act!" I snap. "It's not some ploy to get you to hit me." My arms swing around the room dramatically. "I'm not acting like some whiny brat just for you to punish me. I need…" I inhale deeply, then exhale to try to calm myself.

His head tilts to the side—silently appraising me with mild curiosity as if I'm some kind of science monkey. It pisses me off further.

I lower my voice, and explain. "It's like feeling like ants are crawling all over me. Like any moment I'm going to explode. For two years I've spent my Sunday mornings dealing with the shit in my life the best way I know how. Then you come along and fuck up my whole routine and I don't know…" I start pacing. "I think I need to leave. I think I need my routine again, go to my mother's." I cinch my robe tighter around me. Fidgety. Nervous. Confused.

I'm hyperventilating. And he's closing in on me. Then entire room is closing in on me. Caging me. I'm panicking. My skin is sweaty, and clammy.

Bryce approaches, watching me steadily. "Do you know what I do on Sundays?" he asks, in a tone so gentle I feel warmth spread through my belly and dull the itch there. I shake my head.

The corner of his lip turns up—his hand grasps mine. "Come on." He leads me to the bedroom—kissing the back of my head before giving me a gentle push inside. "Get dressed." I spin on my heels to face him, but he's already disappearing down the hall.

I don't really want to go anywhere with him. I want him to hurt me. I want to drive to Baton Rouge. I want my brother. I want my beast back in his cage. Then I want Bryce to hold me and let me cry in his chest as I recover. But I find myself slipping into the same clothes I wore yesterday. By the time I'm dressed, he's standing in the doorway.

He's wearing his cut—the sight of it making his appearance one of authority despite the tenderness in his eyes. It's warm enough out to not need a jacket, but he holds both of ours in his hand. A leather bag is slung over his shoulder.

"Where are we going?" I ask, hugging myself and pinching the very back of my arms. It feels good, and relieves a little bit of the tension coiled tight in my chest. If he notices, he doesn't say anything.

"Riding."

My eyes sweep across his body once more—taking in the weathered leather of his cut and dirty patches. "But your bike isn't here." I pinch myself again, and this time he steps forward and takes my hand—bringing it to his lips to kiss my palm.

"One of the guys brought it over last night while we were gone. It's in the shed." He tugs on my hand. "Come."

*Come.*

The way he says the word has heat flashing between my thighs. The moment is fleeting, but it was there. And it felt good —better than pain. But after it's passed, I become anxious with the confusion, and dig my nails into my palm.

I'm handed a helmet, which I manage to tighten all on my own. He checks it anyway before assisting me on the bike once he's sure it's secure. He lifts his leg and slides on the seat, the move fluid and graceful. I lean back against the sissy bar, and can't help but wonder if he'd put it on just for me.

Loud, rumbling pipes echo around us—vibrating the backs of my thighs and my ass. He leans the bike to lift the kickstand, and my arms fly instinctively around his waist. He smirks at me in the mirror. I'd rode before, but I was shit-faced drunk both times—not caring one way or another if I face planted the asphalt or not.

Fisting his cut in my hands, I press my chest against his back as he steers us down the driveway and onto the asphalt road. After a few minutes, my grip loosens and I relax. I tentatively slide back on the seat and straighten—allowing the sissy bar to support me.

I move with him—my body instinctively trusting him to handle the iron horse as he leans with every curve of the road. The wind feels good in my face. The air is clean, crisp with just a hint of exhaust fumes.

It's not enough to have me forgetting the incessant urges inside me, the swarm of bees buzzing around my head, or the feel of tiny insects crawling over my skin. But the silence is peaceful, and I find myself enjoying the ride as much as one can in my state.

I have no idea where we are. All I know is that we've crossed the highway, only to continue down another country road. The houses are miles apart—few and far between. Herds of cattle and rows of chicken houses are scattered sparsely throughout the rural community.

I hate I can't enjoy the full experience. But every time I feel myself slipping from my thoughts, and ignoring everything that isn't the view, reality comes barreling back.

*It's Sunday.*

And for the first time in two years, I'm not where I'm supposed to be. As much as I want to hate my mother, I can't. It's not in me to hate. Just like it's not in me to love. But a love for a mother is different. I care about her ... worry about her wellbeing.

If I'm not there to give her money, how will she pay her bills? How will she buy groceries? What if she's sick, or hurt? They don't even know how to contact me. And if they have a phone, I'm not aware of it. There was no need for them to call and ask me anything. They knew I'd be there on Sunday—just as I always had...just like I thought I always would.

My hands tighten on my thighs. The tips of my fingers curling into my jeans and punishing the flesh. It's not enough. I need more. I'd pull my hair, but it's trapped beneath my helmet. Looking down at the rough, gray asphalt as it passes in a blur, I consider what it would feel like to drag my skin across it at our current speed.

A hand on my leg makes me jump, and my eyes shoot to the mirror to find Bryce staring back at me. His full face helmet shields everything but his eyes from view. The sincere gaze locks on mine as his hand rubs up and down my leg—not squeezing or pinching, but slow soft strokes I find comforting, when it should feel irritating.

His hand leaves me as the bike slows, before turning down a small right-away that's been cleared of timber. Woods line both sides of the path—thick cutover surrounded by a web of trees. I notice several of the trees are marked with orange tape intended for loggers.

I look over Bryce's shoulder to find a clearing ahead. It's deep and wide, stretching for thirty or forty yards before another thicket of trees and underbrush continue. As we near, I realize the clearing is a ravine. At the bottom is the river, scattered with huge logs and stones that create several tiny waterfalls.

The moment Bryce cuts the engine, the peaceful sound of flowing water fills my ears. The tranquility alone is powerful enough to drown out the buzz I've been hearing all day.

I walk next to him down a narrow, uneven path through the thick woods. It's a bit of an incline. The movement tames my breathing, but the pressure of everything else still weighs heavy on my chest.

We come to a clearing that overlooks the river. It's serene, the landscape a portrait of massive trees, flowing water and sandy banks. Bryce climbs over a pile of rocks and takes a seat on a flat, smooth stone that rests at the top. His legs dangle over the sides just above the water. Patting the surface beside him, he motions for me.

"Sit."

I climb up, stumbling over the jagged rocks, but he grabs my elbow to steady me until I'm seated. Our thighs touch, and the connection burns me through my clothes. I'm so aware of his presence. It makes me uneasy.

"Here." Smoke swirls around me as he passes me a cigarette. I take it, greedily pulling a drag—inhaling the smoke deep into my lungs, delighting in the slow burn. *Damn, I wish I had some weed.*

I finish my smoke in silence. No sooner is the butt floating down the river than he's passing me another one.

"My mama lives in Baton Rouge," I say, speaking without thought. "Her and my brother. I did have a shitty home life. I was a nuisance to them...a waste of space and nothing more than another mouth to feed in their eyes. And neither ever let me forget it.

"When I was ten, my school contacted child services when I repeatedly showed up covered in bruises. I lied, of course. Even at a young age, I knew what story to tell. But they came anyway. Asked a bunch of questions, scribbled some words in a notebook and left. The next day, my dad left too. My mama blamed me."

Bryce fingers a lock of my hair, but stays silent. My eyes fixate on the slow-moving current of the river as the memories resurface—bringing with them the same feelings of inadequacy they always do.

"They made me believe it was my fault. Not a day passed that I wasn't reminded of why we were poor. Why my mama couldn't have nice things. Why my brother had to play on the neighbor's swing set. I was abused and it was my fault, because I got caught. "

Pulling the last drag from the cigarette, I let it singe the tip of my fingers before thumping in the water. Another is lit, waiting for me, and I accept it. Chain smoking is not something I practice, but in this moment, it feels right—much like spilling my dark secrets.

I blow out a puff of smoke and look out over the land. In my peripherals I can see Bryce watching me. "Sometimes I would go weeks without speaking. The darkness was my friend. It was my escape. Then, as always, I'd fuck up and do something stupid. My brother would beat the shit outta me, and I was back to reality."

I let out a breath of laughter that holds no humor. "So that's what I do on Sundays. That's how I cope. I got to Baton Rouge, and provoke my brother until he gets angry enough to hit me. Whether I need it or not, it's a constant trigger." I finally turn to face him. His eyes are guarded, giving nothing away. "Now do you see the level of fucked up you're dealing with? I can't be fixed, Bryce. This is who I am."

His finger lingers in my hair as he appraises me silently. His expression unchanging—the monotony of his soft stare calming me.

"I know exactly what I'm dealing with, Love. And like I said before, I know what you need." His admission makes my body quake. I need a distraction. I need to focus on something other than the way his eyes on me make me feel.

"Whose land is this?" I ask, running my fingers through my hair—unable to resist giving it a slight pull.

"Luke's." I look up and find his brow furrowed as he watches me a moment before he turns to face the water. "His company owns it. We'll be cutting the timber here in the spring."

"We?"

He nods, his hands clasped in his lap as he keeps his attention on the water below us. "I transferred to Hattiesburg. Took a job with Carmical Construction."

"Why?" I ask, my hands worrying the bottom of my shirt.

He faces me then--a deep, pained look flashes in his eyes, but he quickly conceals it. "I needed a fresh start." I start to ask "Why" once again, but he cuts me off. "You look beautiful today."

Wow. Well, that's one way to change the subject. "Thank you." I drop my gaze, feeling shy and antsy all at the same time.

"Do you know what I love about this place?" My head pops up at his change in tone—dark and...*dominating.* I shiver in response as I meet his fierce, powerful green eyes. He points to something, but I can't look away from him. "That tree."

He stands, helping me up before leading us down the pile of rocks and away from the water. I stop a few feet behind him, looking up at the tree that looms big in front of me—my head tilting completely back until I finally see the top.

The trunk seems too narrow for such a tall tree. Winter has stripped it from its leaves, but it's just as magnificent—maybe even better—as it is now. The web of roots surrounding it protrudes from the ground making it appear alive.

"Ever since I laid eyes on this, all I could think about is how sexy you would look tied to it." He closes the distance between us —his stride predatory and wanting. I swallow. His hand lifts, dragging a finger over the curve of my jaw. "Naked...wet... begging..."

My thighs clench. The movement causes my brows to draw in confusion. My body is at war with my mind—battling the wave of emotions his voice and my thoughts both bring.

"Take off your clothes, Love." His demand leaves no room for argument or question. But my bewilderment won't let me comply. I can't make sense of what's happening. He leans in, his face so close to mine our noses nearly touch. "Now," he growls, the sound coming from deep in his chest.

I nod, my lips parting as I pull in a ragged breath. Trembling fingers move to the button on my jeans. It takes a few tries, but I manage to unbutton and unzip them. He doesn't rush me, he just stands merely inches away and watches—his eyes promising dangerous wrath if I don't obey.

I'm so shook up, I don't realize I'm still wearing the knee length boots until my jeans are at my hips. I look around nervously for something to hold onto. Then they land on his outstretched hand. I chance a look in his eyes. They're still brooding.

I grip his forearm, and look away—using him for balance as I pull off first one boot, then the other. My shirt is next, and I lift it over my head—my entire body quivering with need. I'm just not sure what that need is. The thought once again has me feeling wary and unstable.

"All of it."

My hands fist at his command. Not from anger, but to feel the bite of my nails. When I feel the sting, it's enough to give me the courage I need to reach behind me and unclasp my bra. I feel modest out here in the open. My bared flesh in the natural lighting seems forbidden and dirty.

Bending, I wiggle my panties over my hips and step out of them. When I straighten, one arm covers my breasts while my hand splays over my sex. The air is cool, but my skin breaks out in a sheen of sweat.

"Why are you hiding from me, Love?" Bryce asks, more gently this time, but with firmness that demands an answer.

"This seems...too erotic." I flush at my admission, but my eyes cast up to his. He's completely vague, giving nothing away.

"I've seen every inch of your body. Why are you ashamed now?" Mild curiosity sparks in his thick accent.

I look away, shifting from one foot to the other. "I don't know," I answer honestly. "I don't understand this." I hiccup a small sob, as tears prick the back of my eyes. I'm always aware of what I need—my mind and body working in perfect sync together. Never have I felt horny and afflicted at the same time.

The blurring of the line is enough to send me into a crazed, carnal frenzy.

"Something's not right," I say, shaking my head vigorously. "This isn't right." My breathing becomes harsh—my heart beating heavier in my chest. The flow of the river becomes a dulling, distant sound—replaced with the constant buzzing of my mind.

"Shhh..." Bryce soothes, cupping my cheek in his hand. "Calm down, Love. I'm right here."

*He's right here.*

*He's right here.*

I repeat the mantra over and over as I nod, noticing his voice silenced the annoying hum of my mind. He kisses my lips, parting them with his tongue before invading my mouth—sweeping it once before pulling away. My lips tingle from the touch.

"Do you trust me, Love?"

"Yes," I breathe, my answer instant. Earning me a smile.

"Good girl. Stand with your back against the tree, Love. Hands at your sides." I take a deep breath, facing the river as my hands fall from my body—exposing me to him. I'm aware of him watching me, and chance a look. He swallows hard, drinking in the sight of me naked in nature—my back pressed tightly to the rough bark of the tree. I bend my knees and rub against it.

His eyes narrow. "I've been watching you hurt yourself all day, Love. I'm tempted to spank you for it." My eyes widen in desperation at his words. "Stay right there. Don't move." I nod, his voice enough to scare me into submission.

I watch as he removes his cut as he walks back to the large rock where we were sitting. Retrieving the leather bag he'd brought, he opens it and places his cut inside—pulling out a length of rope as he does. Turning back to face me, he glides casually, confidently toward me, uncoiling the rope as he pierces me with his glare. For a moment, I think he might hit me with it. My shoulders sag in relief at the thought.

I stand in awe of the way his muscles flex against his shirt as he tosses the rope around the tree. He moves in front of me, his stance wide—boxing me in. I close my eyes and inhale his manly scent. It's even more delicious and palpable in the clean air.

The rope feels wrong on my skin. I was looking forward to the scratchy burn of the thick fibers, but this rope is coated making it smooth to touch. I grumble.

Quirking an eyebrow, he pauses and looks up at me from beneath his lashes. "Problem, Love?" I wiggle against the restraints and he gives me a wolfish grin. "You didn't think I'd let you off that easy, did you?"

My anger spikes, as it often does in anxious times like this. But right now, I'm thankful for it. Anger is better than not knowing what the hell it is I'm feeling. There's no denying it. Like a vise, it grips you—forcing you to surrender to its hold. It might possibly be the greatest emotion of all.

When he steps back, his grin fades and his lips part. I follow his hooded gaze, finding my body very snuggly strapped to the tree—the rope crisscrossing over my stomach, thighs, legs and shoulders. I strain against it to test its strength. It doesn't give in the least.

"Perfect," he mumbles, reaching out to drag a finger across my collar bone. My anger dissipates. My sex floods with desire. My mind worries with uncertainty.

I want to enjoy this. I want to feel the full, sexual impact of being tied to this tree, teased, fucked and completely ravaged by him. But I can't concentrate. I need something else too. I need pain...sweltering, blistering, beast-caging pain.

"Please," I whimper, wiggling my hands—the only part of my body other than my head that's free.

"Please what, Love?" His innocent question makes me want to kick him in the groin and send him tumbling down the ravine and into the frigid water.

"I need..." *What?*

He raises his eyebrows expectantly. I rest my head against the tree, turning it so I'm facing away from him. "I need you to spank me."

Gripping my chin in his fingers, he forces my eyes to his, then drops his hand. "There'll be no pain today, Love. Just pleasure."

"But I need the pain," I argue, knowing once I feel it and it's over, I can enjoy this experience in its entirety.

"Do you?" He sounds amused. "Because these," he tweaks my nipples with his fingers, "aren't hard because it's cold." He's right, and as if I need to assist in proving his point, sweat beads across my forehead.

"I'm cold," I blurt, unsure of what else to say to deter him.

His mouth comes to my ear, nibbling my earlobe before whispering, "Then maybe I should warm you up." My comeback catches in my throat when his head dips, and his mouth closes over my nipple.

Blissful sensations ripple down my belly and to my pussy, fully awakening the lingering desire. I try to buck my hips, but the rope prevents the movement. I let out a cry of frustration—the demons of my mind protesting against the onslaught of his mouth as he continues to knead and suck my breasts.

"Stop!" I scream, my voice carrying across the wide river—bouncing off the trees and echoing around us. His mouth retreats. "Just stop...I can't handle it." I'm breathless, wanting and needing the pleasure of his mouth and the pain of his hand... his belt...one of the logs floating in the river.

"Tell me what you need, Love." He's so calm and controlled, while I'm falling to pieces—the only thing holding me together is the rope that binds me.

"I...I need you to spank me, Bryce. Please!" I add, in a desperate attempt to persuade him.

"I think you need something else." His hand trails up my thigh. "Look at me, Love." I do. I don't want to, but dammit, I do. Those *eyes*... Those *motherfucking* eyes. They shine with the same hunger I feel in my groin.

Thick, calloused fingers spread the lips of my pussy. His eyes darken at the feel of my slick folds. I whimper, aroused by his touch and confused by it all the same. "You tell me to stop, but your pussy is wet for me." He trails kisses up my jaw to my ear. "Soaking. Fucking. *Wet*." His accent is strong. His words pronounced. His hand unrelenting as he continues to tease me—making my body convulse when his fingers brush my swollen clit.

"Stop," I breathe, but it's weak...so weak. I feel my beast weakening too. Bryce's hands on me wearing him down. My head hurts with the pressure of what to do. I'm teetering on the edge of shark-infested waters—knowing if I fall I'll either be swallowed up whole, or ripped to pieces. Lose, lose. One outcome as dangerous as the other.

"I hate this." A tear rolls down my cheek. I can't stop it. My discombobulated state pushing me toward disaster. Pleasure... Pain... Do I even know the difference at this point?

"Think of me, Love. Relax your mind, and think of only me," he whispers, pulling his hand from between my legs to catch my tears. I can smell my arousal on his fingers. "Think of me kissing you." He presses his lips softly to mine. "Licking you." His tongue dips into the hollow at my throat. "Fucking you." His hips press against mine. I can feel his stiff length on my belly—throbbing in need even through his jeans.

"I can't—"

"Shhh..." His finger covers my lips. "Don't talk. Just feel." And I do. His mouth is everywhere—trailing kisses along my collar bone. My shoulder...my chest...my nipple—nipping at the sensitive flesh, before moving lower. His hands slide down my hips as he licks and nibbles his way down my belly—to my exposed sex. His tongue dips between my folds, teasing my clit with one...two...three...feather-light strokes before he pulls away.

"Eyes on me." I raise my heavy lids to him, but they drop to his waist when he reaches to unbutton his pants. I watch as he releases his stiff cock from the confines of his jeans. The long, thick length is large, swollen and appearing just as big in his massive hand as it does in my small one.

"I'm going to give you a choice, Love." He's so close I can feel his heat, but he doesn't touch me. "I can spank you." My eyes move to his. He's serious. "I can hurt you. Make you cry. Watch you crumble. And when it's over, I'll be here to hold you. I'll take care of you. Just like I always have."

The war in my head rages once again—charging toward the arousal with guns blazing. *Why does he have to be so confusing?*

He pumps his hand harder, the motion making me avert my eyes to cock. A bead of pre-cum leaks from the tip. I run my tongue across my bottom lip. "Or I can fuck you. I can make you feel good. Make you scream. You'll still crumble, but it will be from pleasure so powerful, it'll make pain seem dull in comparison."

He steps closer, rubbing the head of his length against my pussy—smearing his pre-cum over the smooth surface. "And when it's over, I'll still hold you and take care of you, Love. Let me take care of you." Dipping his head, he brings his eyes level with mine.

"Nothing feels as good as you," he whispers. "Tastes as sweet as you...smells as divine as you..." Something shifts inside me. The dirty admission along with the deep tenor of his voice has want surging through me.

No.

Not want.

*Need.*

"So what's it gonna be, Love?

The war between my emotions is over. The victor has been announced. And the glory goes to this man—this deliciously, sexy, awe-inspiring man who ultimately owns me.

My whole world is centered on him.

I smell only him.

Taste only him.

Breathe only him.

Want…need…crave…only him.

"I want you to fuck me."

His nostrils flare at my decision. The vein in his neck thickens with the rush of blood. Reverence and pride ignites in his eyes—the emerald greens luminous even in the bright light of the clear afternoon.

The heat of his mouth consumes me as he crashes it to mine. His tongue dances with fervor, desperately caressing mine in an erotic kiss filled with a passion he's never shown before. His hands work feverishly to untie my bonds, never breaking our connection. The moment I feel the rope fall away, my hands are on him.

Clawing his skin…

Marking him…

Staking my claim…

I need to be closer to him. On him. Inside him. No more Bryce. No more Delilah. Us as one—feeding off each other's hunger.

I push his shirt up his body, desperate to feel the heat of his skin. He breaks the kiss long enough to rid his shirt in one swift movement, then his hands are cupping my face again—claiming my mouth.

My hands lock behind his neck, gripping him tight as I climb his body. One arm slips around my back, holding me to him while the other lines up the head of his cock with my pussy that throbs in anticipation of him.

Gripping my ass in his hands, he pulls me to him as he thrusts his hips—burying himself completely.

It's savage.

Raw.

Brutal.

*Fucking perfect.*

I cry out, he roars, our voices primal and filled with animalistic rage. He fucks me hard, ruthless in his drives. The viciousness of his impalement barbaric and merciless.

*Beastly.*

My womb quivers. My walls contract. My pussy spasms with every jerk of his hips. I feel it…building and building inside me—threatening to desecrate me entirely when it erupts.

"Give it to me, Love." Bryce's voice rumbles through me—rattling my insides. "Come for me."

His demand sets off the bomb inside me. I detonate around him. The explosion is devastating—rendering me speechless. I don't breathe. My heart doesn't beat. All I see is green, and all I feel is him.

He is my rapture.

I'm weightless. I leave this world and soar on the wings of euphoria to that Elysium he promised me. The release is not only sexual, but mental.

I scream with pleasure that pain can't compare to. The surge of white-hot bliss coursing through my body is only a fraction of the reprieve I feel in my mind. Then I'm crumbling. He's watching. I fall apart and he puts me back together—one shattered piece at a time.

Just like he always has.

Just like I knew he would.

Just like he promised.


Moments pass slowly. One minute blends into the next, while he holds me to him. My body and mind are both liquefied. Neither of us speak. I'm not sure of his reason, but mine is simple—I don't think I can. I'm exhausted.

My eyes close. My breath deepens. I'm so close to sleep, curled comfortably in his arms. When he speaks it's so startling, I jump. He, in turn, laughs.

"Not funny," I murmur, nuzzling further in his chest when he starts to pull away.

"We need to get back, babe." *Babe.* The word alone is enough to snap me back to reality.

But my reality is actually pretty damn perfect. After today, we'll return to the clubhouse. There I'll have everything I've ever wanted. My independence...my job... I'll still be free to do who and what I want—all the while knowing that Bryce will be there to catch me if I fall.

Thirty minutes ago, I was "Love." In this moment, I'm "babe." Tomorrow, I'll be "Delilah." I'm nothing more. Nothing less. And I'm good with that—better than good.

But him? He will always be who he's always been.

Devil's Renegades SA Bryce, *Hattiesburg, Mississippi.*

And I'm good with that too.

# CHAPTER 24

The ride back to the house was better than the first, but not as exciting as I'd hoped. I wanted speed, wind and adrenaline. It's hard to get that at thirty-five miles an hour.

"You promised me a ride, you know," I say, clambering off the bike and stifling a yawn. I point to my mouth. "See? That's how boring it was. Like riding a golf cart."

He smirks. "Why don't you take a nap? I've got some shit I need to handle." I'm too tired to argue, not that I would've anyway. A little distance might be a good thing. I need to start preparing myself for when we go back to the clubhouse. I can spend the alone time processing everything that happened.

But when the bed comes into view, I don't even bother undressing. I fall face first on the mattress and close my eyes. Within moments, I'm asleep.

It's dark when I wake up—quiet. Too quiet. I'm still in my shirt, but my boots and jeans lay in a pile beside the bed. I smile. Warmth spreads through my belly as I stretch. *Always taking care of me...even when I'm sleeping.*

I know Bryce is near. I can feel his presence even when I can't see him. Besides, he wouldn't leave me alone without telling me. After a hot bath, I dry my hair, and slip on my robe. It's then that I start missing him, and worrying just a little.

It all fades—worry, longing and the need for distance when I see him leaning against the counter in the kitchen. He's wearing leather from head to toe. His cut pulled over a black hoodie, his chaps covering his denim legs. Chains hang down his sides and stretch across his stomach. A thin black riding cap sits snug and low on his head.

*Son of a bitch, he's sexy.*

"Feel better?" he asks, smirking at the way I gape at him.

I lick my lips. "Much." The word is released on a breath. His smirk widens to a grin.

"I put some clothes on the bed for you. Get dressed. We're going out."

"Out? Out where?"

He winks at me. "I believe I owe you a ride."

Once again, I find a pile of my own clothes on the bed. Fashionably sexy, but warm. *Who the hell is choosing these outfits?* I make a mental note to ask as I layer myself in leggings and a snug-fitting turtleneck before pulling on my jeans and a thick sweater. All black—just like Bryce.

The weather in south Mississippi makes no sense at all. One day you're in flip flops, the next a parka. Tonight it's cold, even though today it was warm and sunny. Craziest shit ever.

I zip my boots up my legs, and grab my leather jacket before going to meet him back in the kitchen. He rakes his eyes up and down my body before finally speaking. "You look good." Not beautiful. Not sexy. Just good. But the thickness in his voice and darkness in his eyes says he likes the way I look very, very much.

"These are for you." He tosses me a pair of leather gloves. They're new, stylish and even have the little pads on the index fingers so you can operate your phone while wearing them.

"A gift?" I tease, fanning myself with them. "How thoughtful of you Mr...." I frown. "What's your last name?"

"Parker. And don't ever call me that." His tone is playful, but I know he's serious.

*Bryce Parker... I like it.*

"Mine's Scott, by the way."

"I know." Of course he does.

"So," he says, pushing away from the counter. "You ready?" The wickedness is back, and nervous thrill ripples through me.

"Always."

"I thought you said this was going to be fun!" I yell, leaning up so my mouth is next to the vent on his helmet. Once again, we're slowly making our way down the curvy back road toward the highway. But just as I say the words, we near the intersection and I'm blinded with the flood of lights coming from several bikes parked in the median.

Bryce had removed the sissy bar, forcing me to cling tight to him or fall off. My grip had been loose the entire ride, but it tightens when he wracks the pipes—notifying his brothers of our arrival. Pulling back on the throttle, he falls in line with the pack.

Two by two, we ride hard and fast down the highway. Bryce and I are on the outside next to Scratch as we barrel through the night riding so close, I can reach out and touch the handlebars next to me. I'm finally getting that ride I was promised. It's fucking exhilarating. The wind in my hair, shallow breathing, heavy beating heart, rush of adrenaline and feel of Bryce between my thighs is the most thrilling thing I've ever experienced.

The fun part is when we break from the highway and hit the busy streets of downtown. Traffic is heavier here, but we flow at a steady pace—sometimes breaking away from the pack to split cars or pass in the turning lane. Even through my leather jacket and layers of clothing, I can feel the bite of the cold air. It just makes it that more intense.

By the time we arrive at the small building with a wooden sign labeled "Last Call," I'm shaking. And I have no idea if it's from the cold or the adventure of it all. But whatever the reason, it takes me a moment and a little help from Bryce to climb off the bike. My shaky fingers struggle with the strap on my helmet, but he makes quick work of it before removing his own—replacing it with a plain black cap he wears backwards on his head. *So sexy.*

"What'd you think?" he asks, smirking down at me.

"I t-think I w-want to go again," I stammer—following up my admission with a laugh.

Taking my hand, he leads me inside. I'm surprised to find Dallas, Red and Maddie already seated at a table. Although they're not at all surprised to see me. I stay behind Bryce as he makes his way toward the bar—stopping several times to shake hands with some men, hug others and even a few women.

"Two buttery nipples and two double Jack's." He orders our drinks, then slides down the bar a little and tips his chin to the space beside him. I'm stepping forward, but am forced to stop when a brunette sidles up next to him.

Jealousy crashes through me. I hate this woman—this... *Lady Riders Hattiesburg, MS...whatever in the hell* that *means.*

Bryce turns sideways, so that he's leaning against the bar—his body facing her. But he looks at me—his eye closing on a wink while a smile tugs at his lips. The woman notices, and spins slowly around.

She smiles as she leans back on her elbows, and drags her eyes lazily down my body. Through the dim lighting and smoky haze of the room, I notice her face is quite pretty—prettier than mine.

"Well, hello, Pocahontas." Remember when I thought that was a compliment? Yeah... I'm not so sure about that now.

But I smile anyway. "It's Delilah."

She holds her hand out. "Lady Riders Bic, Hattiesburg. Nice to meet you, Delilah." *She's so pretty...and nice...and something else I can't quite put my finger on.*

"Bic is the president of our one and only female support club," Bryce says, motioning to the bartender to add another round to our order. Bic nods in agreement, but continues to smile at me.

Then it hits me. She's a lesbian. A very sexy lesbian, that seems quite interested in having me for dinner. I'm game if her and Bryce are down for a threesome. But something tells me she's not into men—at all. *Bummer.*

Bryce passes me a shot, then hands one to her. He wordlessly offers it up, and we drink. The thick, sweet liquid warms me instantly. I lick my lips—partly from the deliciousness, but mostly because I know Bic is watching. Her eyes widen when they drop to my tongue. It's good to know I still got it.

She sets down her empty glass and straightens to full height. She's just as tall as me, but her stance holds a little more authority than mine. Good thing I've gotten used to the submissive role, or else I might be intimidated.

She leans toward me, and I inhale the citrus scent of her hair as she presses her lips dangerously close to my ear. "See you around, *Delilah*," she whispers, tucking something inside my hand before walking away. I shove the piece of paper I'm sure contains her number in my back pocket and meet Bryce's eyes.

He's smiling back at me, amusement evident in his stare as he shakes his head. "What?" I ask on a shrug.

"Nothing." He holds his hands up in defense, passing me my drink. The crowd gathers around us. I give my attention to the men, hugging them all—laughing and joking with them. They act as if I haven't been gone for three days, and I wonder if any of them are aware of where I've been.

I start to ask Bryce, but he speaks first. "Go hang with the women. I'll catch up with you later." He turns—joining his brothers as they disappear out the back door. I really don't want to hang with the ol' ladies. Even before I look, I know their eyes are on me.

I take a sip of my drink, thankful for the liquid encouragement. Spinning on my heel, I find exactly what I'd expected. All of them looking at me with curious stares. I smile as I stride to the table in the center of the room they're all seated around.

"Okay," Red starts, before I can take a seat. "Is it weird that I missed you? Because I have."

"Did you miss me, or the pot?" I quip, crossing my legs under the table and leaning back in my chair.

She shakes her head. "No, we got the pot. We broke in your room and found it. Nice lingerie collection, by the way."

I roll my eyes. I should've known they'd be snooping while I was away. Come to think of it, the shirt Red's wearing looks familiar...

"So? Did y'all finish?" My brows draw in confusion at Dallas' question. She dismisses the look with a wave of her hand. "Luke said you went to Lake Charles to pack up Bryce's house. I always wondered what he lived in. Wait." She straightens in her seat. "I bet it was like a medieval cave, wasn't it?"

"Ooh!" I turn to Red. "I bet he has a Rottweiler. Or a Doberman. A junkyard dog that he feeds the souls of small children to."

I laugh--mostly in relief at their ignorance, but also at their absurd perspective of who Bryce really is. "Actually, he lives in an older house that is surprisingly charming and very remote." I inwardly sigh at the memory of all that he'd done to me in that house. How he'd fucked me...spanked me...held me...how I fell in love with him.

"You suck at this," Dallas murmurs, the disappointment evident on her pretty face. "Nobody wants him to be normal, Delilah. The bad stuff is easier to believe, even if it's not true."

"Well," I start, leaning forward, not wanting to be a buzzkill. All three lean in with me—hungry for information about the infamous Bryce. Even Maddie who'd been silent the entire time. "There was this one room that had these chains in the ceiling. He claimed it was for punching bags, but who needs two punching bags?" Their eyes widen at my story.

"I knew it," Maddie whispers, shaking her head. "I told y'all that motherfucker kills people." She makes sure only we can hear her, but I look around anyway to see if anyone is listening. They're not.

"Maddie, I've killed a guy. Doesn't mean shit." I'd heard of Dallas killing a man, but to hear it from her own lips puts a whole new perspective on the information.

"No," Maddie argues, her tone so hushed our heads nearly touch as we lean in to hear. "I mean, he's killed *lots* of people. He's like a hit man or some shit."

"The club don't have hit men!" Dallas snaps, her whisper laced in annoyance.

"They did."

"No, they didn't."

"Well, they could have."

"Well, they don't."

"Whatever."

"Whatever yourself."

I feel like I have whiplash by the time their argument is finished.

"I think he's a dominant," I say, just to see if they already knew that. They're silent for a moment, tossing the idea around in their heads. After a minute, Dallas shrugs.

"Wouldn't surprise me. All these guys have a dominant nature. You know," she says, turning to me, her whisper dropping even lower. "Luke's a dominant."

"What? No!" I guess my fake surprise worked, because she's nodding her head to reassure me.

"He is. I mean, he doesn't like make me do submissive stuff or nothing, but he has spanked me before." Now she has my attention.

"Really?"

"Yeah. One time we"—she motions with her finger at the three of them—"flew to Texas on this mob guy's plane to his house. Somehow, Luke found out and drove six hours one way, walked in my office, took his belt off and whipped my ass."

My nipples harden at the vision of Dallas getting spanked by Luke. Then my cheeks flush at the reminder of my own "belt whipping" encounters. I shake the thought from my head. "Damn. That's a little extreme, ain't it?"

"Not really. In this lifestyle, it's not unusual for men to enforce their women's behavior. I'm lucky my man punished me in a way that was deserving, but kinda arousing too. If Luke were any less of a man, I wouldn't have all my teeth." She beams at me and I smirk.

"Luke's a really great guy. You're lucky to have him, but he's a lucky man too." My admission is genuine. Dallas is a great person. Luke is a great man. Despite the demons of their past, they make it work. I'm glad they have each other.

"You know," Dallas drawls, her eyes slowly dropping to my chest. "I've always wanted to do it with a girl."

Her admission startles me. And turns me on. I quickly stand, nearly tripping over my own feet. "So!" I announce on a nervous smile. "Who's ready for another drink?" Sex with Dallas will *never* happen. I couldn't fuck an ol' lady. No way...

My thighs tingle as I make my way to the bar—Dallas' words playing on a loop in my head. Bic's number simultaneously burning a hole in the back pocket of my jeans. But the desire I feel isn't really for either of these women. Green eyes, strong hands and a thunderous cock are what fuel my hunger. And they belong to the man who just walked through the back door.

His lips quirk and his brow furrows in curiosity. He looks happy. Sexy. Tasty. I'm hungry...fucking starving for his hands on me. I want him right now. In this bar. He can take me on the pool table...against the wall...in the bathroom...

His mouth widens into a full-on smile. He tilts his head toward the door, and I nod. The bartender calls to me—asking me what I want. I ignore her. My feet move on their own accord—drawn to the promising look in Bryce's eyes.

I follow him out. The back patio of the bar is swarming with people. The thick scent of marijuana hangs in the air. I breathe deep, trying to absorb the calming power of its aroma. But my body is too amped to feel its effect.

A streetlamp illuminates the back of the building except for one small section that's shaded by the shadow of the dumpster sitting several feet away. Bryce steps into the darkness, pulling me with him. He presses my back against the cold bricks, and boxes me in—his body looming large in front of mine.

Anyone with an imagination could squint through the darkness, and make out our forms. But the chatter doesn't die and no one seems to notice us.

Placing a finger over my lip, he whispers, "If you're not quiet, my brothers are going to know we're here. And they're going to watch me fuck you." I whimper, and he presses his finger harder against my lips. "This ain't the clubhouse, Love. My brothers aren't the only people out here."

My eyes roam the crowd, noticing the unfamiliar faces and lack of cuts on the majority of the people for the first time. I shrink back—searching for more darkness, but there isn't any. I'm not modest in front of the club or their affiliates. But just like at the river, there's something dirty about this--fucking in front of complete strangers, most of which are average citizens out to have a good time.

I look up at Bryce who seems to delight in my uneasiness. A twinkle of mischief sparkles in his eyes and that wolfish grin bares his pretty teeth to me—making them appear even whiter and more perfect in the darkness.

"When I start, I'm not going to stop until I'm ready. I don't give a fuck who's watching."

You know what? Come to think of it, I don't really give a fuck who watches either. I want this. I want him. My carnal craving is worth the slight tinge of humiliation that's quickly dissolving.

"Fuck me," I pant, and the air between us shifts at my words. His mouth covers mine—our tongues meeting in the most erotic dance. My fingers move to his waist, unbuckling his chaps and then his belt. Seconds later, he springs free—his cock hot and hard in my hand. The flesh sears my fingers as I slide them along the soft skin—gliding over the bulging veins that swell further at my touch.

His hands are on my hips, tightening and relaxing in time with his groans that I silence with my mouth. He breaks the kiss and spins me around. My hands slap hard against the brick. The cold impact stinging my palms. Quick fingers unzip my jeans and push them down my thighs—taking my leggings and panties with them.

Cold air tickles across my naked ass, and I bite my knuckles to suppress a moan. He pulls my hips back to him, one hand pressing on the center of my back urging me lower.

"This is going to be quick, Love," he whispers in the darkness. His hand smoothes across the soft flesh of my ass before dipping between my folds—finding me wet and ready for him. He lets out a low growl and presses the head of his cock inside me before stilling.

Wrapping my hair around his fist, he gently tugs. My chin lifts and my head falls back. His lips come to my ear—the movement forcing his cock to slide a few inches deeper inside me. "Don't come until I do." It's his last words before he jerks his hips. The impalement makes me cry out, but his hand in my hair tugs, cutting off the sound.

He stills again. "Shhh...quiet, Love. I don't like an audience." My mind drifts back to the first time he fucked me. He'd stolen me from the group of men and kept me all to himself. *"Your room. Where is it?"* were his exact words.

The slick sound of my arousal mixed with our harsh breathing fills the air. My pussy is tender from the brutal sex we had earlier, but the feeling is delicious—making me even more aware of having him inside me. His pace quickens, and I bite my knuckle hard enough to break the skin in an attempt to contain my whimper of pleasure.

Our perverse act in front of a crowd, whose unawareness could change any moment, has my walls clenching tighter around him. I fight against the orgasm that threatens, centering my mind on how much greater it will feel when we come together. I'm afraid I won't last much longer. To add to the pressure of trying to hold back, his hand moves to my clit—his finger rubbing circles on the swollen bundle of nerves.

"Bryce..." I hiss, knowing he's well aware of what he's doing to me.

"You ready to come for me, Love?" I mewl. "Let it go. I want to feel that sweet pussy come around my cock." I release at the same moment he pulses inside me—flooding me with his heat. His hand slips from my hair, and covers my mouth—stifling the screams I'm incapable of holding back.

White light flashes behind my lids as I give myself over to the sensations. Every beat of my heart sends another jolt of pleasure surging through me. It feels so good. Too good. I don't care that my pants are at my knees, or that I'm pressed against a building and stuffed with cock. It doesn't matter that people stand merely feet from us while we're hidden in the shadows of a dumpster.

That's Bryce's way—stripping me away from reality and escaping with me to a little place I can only describe as nirvana. This man will be the death of me. And my raw, swollen pussy dampens further at just the feel of him sliding out of me—already begging for him to take me again.

He pats my ass to get my attention. "Come on, Love. Get dressed."

"Ugh," I grunt. He must've anticipated my slow return from paradise, because he's already assisting in pulling my panties up my legs. I'm being lazy and I know it, but I stand with my cheek pressed against the bricks while he clothes me, one layer at a time.

Spinning me to face him, he cups my face in his hands. "You look just fucked."

"And you look cocky," I tease, giving him a lazy smile.

"Shouldn't I be?"

I flip my hand in the air and wrinkle my nose. "Eh."

He starts to say something, but a noise on my left draws both our attention. It doesn't take me long to put names with the three bodies silently watching from the side of the building.

I smile. "You girls enjoy the show?" I call out. They freeze, knowing they'd just been caught. I half expect them to run, but instead, I'm forced to eat my words as Bryce laughs in my face at Red's admission.

"Eh..."

# CHAPTER 25

I couldn't help but cringe the entire ride to the clubhouse. Bryce rode behind Regg, who rode beside Luke, giving me a full view of the ol' ladies who rode bitch—proudly sporting their property patches on their backs. *Ugh.* I prayed like hell no one I knew saw me as we sped through traffic. I damn sure didn't want anyone to get the idea that *I* was an ol' lady. *And they think clubwhores are beneath them. Whatever.*

Bryce kept shooting me curious stares in the mirror during the ride. When we're back at the clubhouse and everyone else has already walked inside, he grabs my elbow and pulls me back.

"What's up?" he asks, narrowing his gaze on me. "You don't think people suspect I'm your"—I swallow the bile that threatens—"*ol' lady*, do you?"

He laughs at that. Shaking his head, he tucks a wild strand of hair behind my ear. "I don't do ol' ladies, babe. Not my thing. Everyone knows that." A lesser woman might be offended. But I breathe a sigh of relief.

"Good." I shiver, and Bryce mistakes the move as me being cold and ushers me through the door.

As much of a welcome escape as the little house was, there's nothing like coming home. The smell of leather, wood, smoke, booze and sex lingers in the air. I stop and inhale. *Ahhh...*

I don't get to enjoy it long before I'm being pulled down the hall and into my room. It looks just like I left it. If anyone visited it while I was away, they made sure not to leave any evidence of their stay.

The mental note I'd made earlier surfaces. "Who packed clothes for me?"

"Luke," Bryce answers, taking a seat on the bed to unzip the legs of his chaps.

"Really?" It shouldn't be surprising, but I'd assumed it was Linda or one of the other girls who worked here.

"Yep. Apparently, he's into women's fashion." He smirks at his own joke. "I'm going out of town tomorrow."

"Why?" I ask, unable to hide my disappointment.

"Got some loose ends to tie up in Lake Charles. I'll be back in a couple days." I don't think about what it will be like when he's away. Instead, I focus on the fact that he's here now. In my room. Undressing. And he told me he was leaving when really he had no reason to tell me at all.

"Well, be careful." What else can I say? I rummage through my drawers, searching for nothing in particular. I said I wasn't going to think about him leaving, but I can't help it.

"Hey." His breath is on my neck as he comes up behind me, dragging his hands up my arms. "Shower with me."

He doesn't wait for my answer. He just steers me in the direction of my bathroom. While he starts the water, I strip, noticing he's already naked. I trail my eyes down his neck, his back, to his ass that's toned, smooth and tinted perfectly—a result of his olive complexion.

"Stop lookin' at my ass, babe."

The tension in my shoulders lifts. "Well, I can't help it. It's such a cute little ass."

He faces me, shielding his *cute little ass* from my sight. "There's nothing little about me." I laugh. "You don't agree?" he asks, pulling me flush against him. His cock presses against my belly. "What about this?" He swivels his hips. "Is this little?"

I feign a look of innocence—widening my eyes and opening my mouth on a small O. "No..." I shake my head. "That thing's a monster." He rolls his eyes, fighting a smile as I continue to tease him. "It's sooo big."

"Really?" He shoots me an incredulous look. I bite my cheek to keep from laughing. This is just too much fun.

"Do the other bikers pick on you?" I turn my lips down on a frown. "Is that why you need me to reassure you?"

"You're an asshole. You know that?" He's trying to appear wounded, but it's hard to keep up the façade when a smile is stretched across his face.

"You like this asshole." As I say the words, his eyes darken and the smile fades. His hold on my hips loosens, sliding around to cup the cheeks of my ass.

"Yes, I do." I have a feeling his admission doesn't necessarily pertain to me, but the forbidden part of my body he once said he wanted to fuck.

"We should shower," I pant. Forcing my mouth closed, I swallow hard.

He smirks down at me--desire and pleasure flashing in his green eyes at the turn of the conversation. "Waiting on you, Love."

After our shower, I was sure his dirty talk that stirred my sex, added with the thrill of soapy hands roaming my body, would be enough to prime me to take him once again. But he had a different idea in mind.

Wrapping his naked body around mine, he kissed me sweetly and tucked my head into his chest—keeping his hand on the back of my head to hold me there. My sexual cravings reduced from a rolling boil to a light simmer as I relaxed against him. He knew what I needed. And it wasn't his cock. It was the intimacy.

The embrace is a promise that even though he was leaving, he'd be back. That what we had wasn't just about sex, but two people who found comfort and solace in each other. He hadn't admitted it, or even let on that he found that those same reassurances in me, but deep down I knew it.

I felt it. I wasn't in this alone. I needed Bryce. He'd become such a vital part of my life. And there's no doubt in my mind that a part of him needs me too.

Bryce is gone when I wake up. I know he won't be there, but I walk down the hall to the front room in hopes he'll be sitting at the bar waiting for me. He isn't.

I grumble to myself as I start my morning coffee. Reaching under the counter, I close my eyes and send up a silent prayer that my cigarettes are still here. My hand closes around the box and I smile. Pulling it out, there's a small note attached to the pack.

*Thought you might need these—Bryce*

"What you so happy about?" Linda asks, sidling up on the barstool and motioning me to pass her the smokes. I remove the note, and hand them to her. "Uh-uh." She shakes her head. "Let me see."

"It's nothing." I shrug. "Just the receipt. What you been up to?"

The note is forgotten, and she starts to ramble on about shit she's been doing since I've been gone. I find out that like the ol' ladies, Linda is under the impression I've been in Lake Charles helping Bryce pack up his house.

The story is actually a pretty solid one. If it were true, it wouldn't be the first time the club hired me to work outside the clubhouse. I've never helped someone move, but I have entertained at other clubs' parties, and made house calls.

"So," Linda says, standing and looking around. "What's on the agenda today?"

"Cleaning. This place is a wreck." I wrinkle my nose, noticing the scattered bottles, overflowing ashtrays and muddy floors, and I dread whatever state the bathroom is in. "Did y'all do anything besides party while I was gone?"

Linda shakes her head, completely unashamed. "Nope. And ain't gonna do it today. Some of the other girls will be by shortly." She grabs her purse, and shoots me a wink. "Put them to work."

Yeah. Like that was gonna happen.

I'm a bit of a neat freak. I can't help it. It bothers me. But staying busy has always kept my mind occupied. Today I use my work as a distraction from Bryce. There's no room for thoughts of anything else. He consumes them all.

When the place is clean, it's well into the evening. Several patches are here drinking beer, playing pool and just hanging out. I never really understood why they hung around so much. But my best guess is that they're lonely. Most of the regulars don't have children or wives. And the ones that do don't like them very much, I suppose.

"Hey, doll. Remember me?" I look up from my phone to find Eagles' Prospect Drake staring back at me. No. Not Prospect. Drake is now a full patch. If it wasn't stitched on his cut, it can be seen on his face. The club has definitely stripped him of his innocence and humility. Now he's as cocky as the rest of them.

"Of course I remember you!" I beam, flashing him my best smile. "Congratulations." I gesture to his patch, noticing his chest swell with pride. "How is everything going?" I put my phone under the counter, giving him my undivided attention.

"It's good. Different." He bites his lip, dropping his gaze to my exposed cleavage. Obviously, he's not in the mood for small talk. "So you wanna fool around?"

I bite my cheek to keep from laughing. *Fool around?* That's almost as bad as "taking a roll in the hay." *Ugh.* I'd heard that one before.

"Don't think you wanna do that, Drake." We both look toward the direction of the voice coming from across the room. Crash doesn't look up as he chalks his pool stick before lining up his next shot. "I don't think our SA would like that very much."

SA?

"My bad," Drake says, getting up from his seat. "See you around, Delilah." I manage a smile, but it doesn't reach my eyes.

I'm not confused. I know this "SA" Crash speaks of. He's talking about Bryce. And as much as it pleases me that he wants me all to himself, it pisses me off just the same. I'm not his property. This is my job. He has no right telling me who I can and can't fuck.

It's not that I wanted to have sex with Drake. Actually, the thought of having sex with anyone other than Bryce leaves a bad taste in my mouth. Why buy a glass of milk when you can have the whole cow? *Is that how the saying goes?*

Doesn't matter. What matters is that he opened his big mouth, staked some weird claim on me and not once thought to ask me how I felt. *Just like a man...*

"Babe?" Crash twirls his empty beer bottle in his hand. "Can I get another?" I snatch it from his fingers. He smirks—enjoying this. "By the way, Bryce didn't say anything. I just noticed y'all been spending a lot of time together." *That dirty little shit...*

I can barely contain my relief, though. Grabbing a beer from the cooler, I pop the top and slide it across the bar to him. "Well, I think that's for me to decide, Crash."

He shrugs. "I could give two shits what you do. But I don't want Bryce rippin' off my head because I didn't try. Now I can say I did."

"Well, thank you."

"For what?"

"For not giving two shits. I take my independence and my job very seriously."

"I do what I can." He winks at me and takes a pull from his beer. He glances over his shoulder before turning back to me. "So," he says, leaning in close. "You wanna fool around?"

I smack him with my dish towel. He laughs and walks away, holding the beer above his head. "Thanks, babe. It always tastes better when you get it." *Sure it does.*

Sleeping sucks without Bryce. Having him next to me three nights in a row has spoiled my body. Now I'm too cold. Feel too light. Smell too much like me and not enough like him.

I somehow manage to make it through Monday night without him. Granted, I only got about two hours of sleep, but it's Tuesday morning, and the knowledge that he's coming back tomorrow lifts my spirits.

The day is long and monotonous. Everyone but me seems to have shit to do. I notice that both Crash and Scratch, who live at the clubhouse, have taken up company with two of the other girls here—Reese and Katy. In witnessing this, I can't keep Crash's words out of my head.

*I don't think our SA would like that very much.*

When they look at me, I see a softness in their eyes. Almost as if they're happy I'm no longer available to them. I am, but apparently they don't see it that way. They're loyal to Bryce. And even though Crash claimed Bryce hadn't said anything to him, the club was respectful enough to keep their distance until they were sure.

Once again, I go to bed alone and missing him. I hadn't realized his absence would have this kind of effect on me. I long for him to return. Ache for him deep in my chest. But it's nothing like the anxiety I used to feel. This is different...sorrowful.

I'm lying in my too-big bed when my phone buzzes with a notification. I nearly break my neck to get it—knowing it's Bryce. I'd wanted so badly to contact him, but didn't want to bother him. *Or seem desperate...*

Bryce: *Hello, Love.*

Me: *Hello, yourself.*

My cheeks hurt and I realize it's from the wide smile on my face. Good grief. How lame am I? All he said was hello. *Love.*

Bryce: *Am I interrupting anything?*

Me: *Kinda. I'm giving head...to my PILLOW!*

I laugh at my own joke. I wanted to wait for his reply before I added the punch line, but I chickened out. Besides, I'm no fool. I'm well aware that he knew damn well I wasn't doing anything. He just wanted to hear me say it.

Bryce: *You're funny. How was your day?*

Me: *Boring. Yours?*

Bryce: *Shitty.*

My smile drops. I feel my chest tighten. I don't know why it hurts me that he had a shitty day, but it does.

Me: *I'm sorry. If I were there, I'd make it better.*

Damn how I want to be there with him. I'm calculating how long it would take me to drive to Lake Charles. Then I remember I don't have a car. I'm contemplating stealing one when he texts back.

Bryce: *You already have. Goodnight, Love.*

I don't text back, because what do you say to that? Nothing. So I curl under the covers and try to process these feelings in my chest—feelings he once said weren't real...only an idea.

Now I'm not so sure.

I'm up early awaiting his return. I put on full makeup, curl my hair and even wear the uncomfortable, hip-hugging jeans that fit so snug across my ass.

The minutes turn to hours, and I begin to regret my decision to wake up so early. Unable to stomach one more second without knowing, I ask Crash what time "the guys" will be back. He gives me a knowing smirk, but doesn't call me out.

"Late. They have church today." He pinches my chin. "We got shit to do too, so relax. You got the place to yourself until tonight."

I pout all the way to my room. It's a little after noon when I lie down to take a quick nap. I set my alarm for thirty minutes, and drift peacefully with the knowledge that I won't be seeing him anytime soon.

It's a damn good thing I got that nap. The clubhouse might have been dead today, but it's packed tonight. Myself along with the other girls are either behind the bar or serving beer on the floor. When the place is this crowded, there's too much going right now for the men to request any private company.

It's unusually busy for a Tuesday, and when I ask what in the hell is going on, all I'm told is someone's getting a patch. There are too many chapters, too many different clubs and way too many patches for me to keep up with who's in line to get what. It could be a full patch given to a Prospect, a new officer patch, a special patch for those that do special things, a territory patch...

*Could it be?*

It is. This is Bryce's patch party. Tonight, they're celebrating his transfer. He'll get his Mississippi bottom rocker. I've been awaiting his arrival since early this morning. Every time the door opens I look to see if it's him who walks through it.

And he just did.

He's dirty and tired. His leather looks worn and weathered. But the moment he sees me, a fire ignites in his eyes. I feel the same scorching flames licking at the inside of my thighs.

"Hello, stranger," I greet, somehow managing to control my urge to fist pump the air at the sight of him. Giving him a wicked smile, I slide a shot of Jack across the bar to him.

"Hello, yourself." He shoots me a wink and throws back the shot. Signaling me for another, I pour it as he turns to greet the men who've formed a line behind him.

"Ain't he the sexiest thing ever?" Reese, another clubwhore, says as she rapes him with her eyes. Throwing back the shot I poured for him, I give her a possessive glare.

"He's unavailable." There's a warning in my voice—a warning I have no right to give.

She huffs out a breath and rolls her eyes. "Says who? His wife? Unlike you, Delilah, I have no problem fucking married men."

"I didn't say he was married. I said he's unavailable." I must have growled or something, because this time I got her attention.

"Ohhhh." *Um...yeah, bitch. Move the fuck along.*

"How tired are you?" I ask Bryce, once he's facing me and the line along with Reese has dispersed.

He quirks an eyebrow at me. "I guess that depends."
"On?"
"On what you're really asking."

Returning the bottle of whiskey to its rightful place, I let my lips part and the hunger in my eyes tell him exactly what it is I want.

He doesn't acknowledge the gathering crowd ready to toast his transfer. He doesn't care that this is his party, and people have come from miles away just to congratulate him. It doesn't bother him to abandon his brothers or club affiliates, because right now, he wants the same thing I do.

Throwing back one last shot, he jerks his head toward the hall. "Waiting on you, Love."


"Motherfucker!" I scream. I forgot how good it felt to be ravaged by this man. OMG.

"You missed this cock, didn't you?" I moan at his question that's said just above a whisper, yet makes me shake harder than if he'd have yelled it.

I did miss him. Damn, I missed him. Not just the sex but him—all of him. His whiskey-scented breath, massive cock, dirty mouth and big hands that seem to hold me tenderly and roughly all at the same time.

I'm on my knees, my face pressed into the mattress and my ass high in the air. The taste of him still lingers on my lips. The scent of him invades my senses. The feel of him can be felt in places deep within my belly as he drives into me over and over. It's too much and not enough, and only he can make my body feel this good.

We come together—one big explosion of orgasm powerful enough to keep us both sated and satisfied for years to come. I hope it's always like this. I hope we never become a stalemate with each other. I want every time to be as intense as this time.

"I missed you," I admit, when I'm curled to his chest. His breathing is even, letting me know he's near sleep. Part of me hopes he didn't hear my admission, but of course he did.

"I missed you too. A fuck of a lot more than I should." I try to sit up so I can look at him, but he holds me in place. "Go to sleep."

"But I'm not tired," I pout, wanting him inside me again.

"It wasn't an option, babe." His voice is a little thicker, and I know he's tired. So I give in. Not because I'm sleepy, but because he is. And he missed me...

*A fuck of a lot more than he should...*

# CHAPTER 26

Every night for the rest of the week, I'm aware of his eyes always on me as I work—watching me, following my every move. None of the men approach me—warned off by his deadly gaze. He doesn't verbally announce that I'm spoken for, but the silence of his stare speaks volumes. So I spend my evenings behind the bar serving drinks, or in the kitchen making pizzas and crockpot dinners for our guests.

I don't miss the attention of the men. Bryce more than makes up for my lack of companions. He's spent every night in my bed. Sometimes he fucks me. Other times, he just holds me. I'm not sure if he realizes what he's doing to me—which is making my biggest fear become reality.

I'm in love with him.

Not just the idea of it.

Real love.

The kind of love that makes my stomach flip and my heart stop when he walks through the door after he's been at work all day. The kind of love that makes my world right whenever he's in it, and lonely and meaningless when he's not. My life is filled with distractions, but they're never enough to give my mind a moment's rest from him. He consumes me.

"What you thinkin' oo hard about?"

I smile and turn my head to where he's sitting across the room. It's late—nearly three in the morning. He has to be up in a few hours, and I wonder why he hasn't forced me to abandon my bartending duties and come with him to bed like he has several nights this week.

"About us." My honest answer wasn't one I'd anticipated. But due to my sleepy state, it's not a big surprise either.

"Us?" He smirks, pulling his big body from the couch and walking toward me. "What about us?"

I watch him until he's leaning on his elbows on the bar, motioning for me to hand him a beer. When my back is to him, I ask the question that's been weighing heavy on my heart. "What are we doing, Bryce?"

When I don't get a response, I know he's waiting for me to face him. After a deep breath of encouragement, I do. He regards me cautiously—narrowing his eyes as if it might help him read deeper into my mind and the reason behind my question.

"I feel like this is something. Is it?" I take a pull from his beer, then pass it to him as I reach for my cigarettes. Instead of answering, he grabs the smoke from between my lips and puts it in his mouth—lighting it and taking a deep drag.

"Hey, gorgeous, can I get a drink?" Crash asks, slicing through the thick tension with his sweet charm and playfulness. His smile is infectious, and I offer one in return.

"Of course."

"You get the message from Luke?" Crash's voice is low behind me as he speaks to Bryce. I know I shouldn't, but I eavesdrop on the conversation—taking my time making his drink.

"Didn't know there was a message," Bryce mutters, and out of the corner of my eye, I see him reach inside his cut for his phone. They speak again, but I can't make out the words. When I hand Crash his drink, Bryce is talking, but his eyes are on me.

Crash nods, then takes his drink. "Thanks, babe." He takes a sip. "Ahh," he says on a wink, and I know his signature line will soon follow. "Always tastes better when you fix it." With one final glance in Bryce's direction, he turns and walks back to the pool table surrounded by half naked women. They'd been playing strip eight ball—a game I'm a master at, but wasn't invited to participate in.

"Did you tell them not to touch me?" I ask Bryce, watching Reese shake her fake tits in Crash's face.

"When I'm here, you're mine," he answers simply, following my gaze to the ridiculous game happening on the other side of the room. "I never did know how to share." He's attempting a joke, but this is serious to me.

"So you told them that?"

"I didn't have to."

I look at him then. His expression is guarded. "What does that mean, Bryce? If you've staked some claim on me, don't I have a right to know?"

"I haven't staked any claim on you, babe. But when I'm here, I like to have you to myself. My club respects that."

"And when you're not here?"

His eyes darken, and his jaw ticks. Either he hasn't thought about this, or he assumes I'll stay monogamous even in his absence. And I will. But this is my job. So if that's what he expects of me, then I, in turn, expect to hear him say it—that way, there's no question that my body is off limits. And job or not, I want to hear him say it. I long for him to tell me I belong only to him.

Silence stretches on, and I'm reading between the lines. My gut tells me as bad as he wants to say it, he can't. Not without it feeling like some kind of commitment. I'm not asking for a ring, or a patch, I just want honesty. And maybe for him to confess that deep down, he has feelings for me too.

The door swings open, and I jump as it collides with a loud boom against the wall. "Church. Now," Luke snaps, scanning the clubhouse and the several members who are still awake. His eyes roam over me and he nods. "Delilah."

I swallow hard at the fierce look on his face. Whatever is going on must be pretty damn serious. The men disappear behind the door of the chapel. Over the next half hour, more arrive. Despite the late hour, none of them look tired. They all wear that same fierce look as Luke.

"We're going to bed, Delilah," Reese tells me, her and another girl already heading in the direction of Crash's room. She stops at the door and turns to face me. "You staying up?"

I nod. "For a little while. Good night." My head swims with thoughts as I busy myself around the room. *What's going on? Is something wrong? Will Bryce finally admit he doesn't want me with other men no matter if he's here or not? How will I feel if he tells me he doesn't care what I do?*

"Um, Ma'am?" I roll my eyes at Cook, Prospect for the Devil's Renegades.

"Why do you call me ma'am? I sucked your dick, Cook. I think you can skip the gentleman routine." He glances nervously over his shoulder and I follow his gaze to where Bryce is staring at us from inside the open door of the chapel.

His body is tight with tension. The look on his face mean and hard. I'm not sure if his reaction is because he heard what I said, or if it's from the conversation happening around the table. I hope like hell it's the latter. But a part of me rejoices in the thought of him getting angry over images of me being with someone that isn't him.

I turn my attention back to Cook. "What you need, honey?" I ask, feeling guilty for his embarrassment. Prospecting is hard enough. He didn't need the added drama of me and Bryce.

"Coffee."

"You make the coffee, Prospect." Bryce's voice booms across the room. "Delilah, go to bed."

I frown at his demand. "But I can—"

"I said, go to bed," he snaps, leaving no room for argument. But this is my job. I want to help. That's what the club pays me for.

"Really, I don't mind."

"Now, Delilah!" This time, it's Luke's voice I hear from inside the room. Feeling much like the Prospect, I hang my head in humiliation, and quickly disappear down the hall.

In an attempt to relax, I run a hot bath—dumping nearly an entire bottle of soothing lavender bubble bath in the water. *Why didn't I think to grab a bottle of wine on my way out?* It's possibly the only thing that could make this better.

No.

There is one thing that's better.

In the very back corner of my closet is Red and Dallas' stash of weed. I open the baggie containing several tightly rolled blunts, and pull one out. *Hell, they won't miss it.* I grab my iPod, lock my bedroom door and escape into my bathroom—locking that door as well.

I light the candles around my tub, cut out the lights and sink beneath the water. Leaning back, I select a random playlist and fire up the blunt. The smoke is instantly calming, and I feel my muscles relaxing further with every drag.

My mind still worries with thoughts of me and Bryce, but they're less intense. It's easy to process them, come up with a reasonable solution and be confident in my conclusions without the added stress of "what if I'm wrong?" I decide from here on out, I'll face all my issues while under the influence of Willie Hux's finest weed.

Somo's "Ride" fills the room, and I sing along—resting my head against the pillow as I close my eyes. My hand slips beneath the water, stroking my pussy. The flesh is soft, satiny and a delicious, warm sensation spreads through me.

I'm rolling my hips in time with the beat of the song. A soft moan escapes me, but it's overpowered by the sound of a door shutting. My eyes fly open and my pulse quickens as I scan the room. I'm alone, but the doorknob to the bathroom is wiggling. Seconds later, I hear a click and Bryce appears through the smoky haze.

The candlelight illuminates him, and his shadow dances on the walls. He doesn't look angry anymore, only curious as he takes in the sight of me smoking and my body buried beneath a mountain of bubbles—hiding my hand that lays motionless between my thighs.

Taking the blunt from my fingers, he pulls it to his lips. I watch as he inhales deeply, holds it in a moment, then releases on a slow breath. His eyes shine even brighter in the dim lighting —hungry and pleased at what he sees.

"I have to leave," he says, his voice thick and filled with regret.

"I figured as much."

He looks sad a moment, then his eyes rake down my body and his lips twitch. "You look guilty. Like you got caught with your hand in the cookie jar." I'd laugh at his joke if I didn't want him so bad.

"Come here," I breathe, already feeling the saliva build in my mouth at the thought of what he might taste like.

"You givin' out demands now?" He quirks an eyebrow, but I know he wants it as bad as I do.

"Would it help if I said please?" He doesn't answer—just silently appraises me. After a few moments, he slowly closes the few feet of distance. By the time he's next to me, I'm on my knees.

Looking up at him through my lashes, I slide my hands up his thick thighs. I unbutton his jeans, then lower them until his cock hangs heavy in front of me. I take a moment to appreciate its magnificence before fisting my hand around his shaft.

"You like that, babe?" he asks, and I feel a tinge of disappointment.

"Call me Love," I whisper. His eyes darken and his jaw tightens.

"No hands, Love." His command instantly has me releasing him and gripping the side of the tub. "Open up for me." My insides clench as he fists his cock and I make a small O with my mouth.

"You're gonna have to do better than that." I part my lips further, relaxing my jaw and my throat in preparation for him. He grows harder at the sight of me on my knees, mouth open, matching his fiery stare.

His hand wraps around my neck, lingering there a moment while he softly strokes my cheek with his thumb. Then he slides it around the back of my head—fisting my hair as he pulls me closer to him.

Slowly he pushes inside my mouth. With only the head in, he pauses a minute and closes his eyes as my tongue caresses him. His lips part, and his eyes slowly open. He pushes deeper inside my mouth, not stopping until he touches the back of my throat. I force myself to relax further, urging him deeper until my eyes fill with water and I've nearly swallowed him. He pulls out and I take a deep breath, before he pushes back inside.

The sound alone is a turn-on for me as he fucks my face—quickening his thrusts as his fist tightens in my hair. When he pushes deep, I hold my breath until he pulls back—allowing me to breathe once again. The slight torture has me nearly dry humping the side of the tub. As bad as I want to slip my hand back between my thighs, I want to hold out even more. I know if I wait, it'll be that much better when he does it. His fingers are much more magical than mine.

I feel him tense, and know he's near. I continue to take him deep, and am sure to massage the bottom of his shaft with my tongue on every thrust. "Deep breath, Love," he says, his voice still completely controlled even when the rest of him is not. I pull in a breath just before he drives to the very back of my throat—almost triggering a gag reflex I didn't know I had.

His hot, salty come slides down my throat with ease. The sight of him in his weakest moment, the feel of his hand fisted in my hair and the guttural sound that rips through his chest is almost enough to have me climaxing with him.

The moment his cock stops pulsing, he withdraws it from my mouth—as if he feared I'd held my breath for too long. Hell, I could've lasted a lifetime. Just looking at him would be worth turning blue in the face.

"You have a pretty impressive head game," he teases, but the shock and awe at what we'd just done is evident in his voice. His hand loosens in my hair, tenderly massaging my scalp as he smiles down at me.

I lick my lips and return his smile—pleased that he's happy. To me, it's as satisfying as if I were the one getting head, not the other way around.

"Did sucking my cock make you wet?" His dirty, erotic voice causes my sex to clench in need.

"Yes..." I hiss, dragging the word out as my hips buck against the side of the tub.

"Do you want me to fuck you?" Instead of answering his question that is obviously rhetorical, I give him a pleading look and grind my thighs together—sloshing water over the side of the tub.

Wrapping his hands around my arms, he pulls me to my feet. "Step out, Love." He holds me steady as I do, my legs too shaky with excitement to function on their own accord. Spinning me so I'm facing the mirror, he grinds his hips into my ass. "I want you to watch while I fuck you from behind."

I groan as I watch him in the mirror. His eyes are focused on his fisted cock as his other hand rests on my shoulder and urges me lower. My breasts hang heavy, my nipples grazing along the edge of the cold porcelain sink.

"So wet," he murmurs, dampening the head of his cock before sliding it further up to the forbidden hole that has me tensing. "I can't wait to fuck this sweet little ass." *Yeah...that's never gonna happen.* But even as I think it, I can't control my body as it pushes back against him.

My eyes flutter closed as he sinks inside my dripping pussy. My walls quickly stretch to accommodate his massive girth. "Open your eyes," he growls, fisting a hand in my hair and tugging my head back. I meet his gaze in the mirror, struggling to find the green pools that are hidden beneath his hooded lids.

I love when he takes me like this. Stripping me of all my power. Hands fisting in my hair to hold me in place. Powerful thighs slamming into me on every drive. "Don't come, Love." But his demand is too late.

A jagged scream rips through me as I come around him. He bites out a string of obscenities at my defiance, but quickens his pace—prolonging my orgasm. His touch, his talk, his thrusts are vigorous and brutal. They compel me to respond almost immediately.

His hand in my hair loosens as he stills inside me—flooding me again with his release. The thick warmth coating me brings on a whole new sensation. His body pressed against mine while he's seated completely inside me makes me feel whole...infinite.

He pulls out of me, but the feeling doesn't fade. Even though I ache at his loss, there's something in just his presence that instantly replenishes it. I turn to face him, delighting in his warm embrace. Leaning down, his lips brush mine in a soft, chaste kiss.

"Never let a man treat you like you're anything less than perfect. Because you're not."

Releasing me, he turns and walks out—leaving me staggered by his words. Like everything else he's ever said to me, it registers with not just my brain, but my heart. It's terrifying—knowing I love him and unsure if he feels the same. Yet oddly, it doesn't matter. He'd just told me I was perfect. And even "I love you" can't top that.

# CHAPTER 27

Bryce wasn't the only one to leave that night. Several of the men went with him on his quest to wherever. Luke was not one of them. He'd spent all of Saturday at the clubhouse, and somehow I felt like he'd taken Bryce's place in watching my every move.

Midnight has come and gone, and now that we're in the early hours of Sunday morning, I can't help but think of my mother. Without any need for pain, I could give two shits about the bastard of a brother I have, but my mom weighs heavy on my mind and my heart. *Is she okay? Does she miss me?*

I know going to see her is a huge risk, but it's one I'm willing to take. I plan to use my weekly pay to buy her a phone so I can keep in contact with her. At least that way, I'll know she's all right. And it will make this trip to Baton Rouge my last one, unless she needs me.

After asking Linda if I could borrow her car, I go to my room and start the process of removing my makeup. When my face is clean, I slip into my sweats and grab my small stash of cash from my closet. Just as I'm raising my window, I hear a knock at the door.

I start to ignore it, but decide there's really no reason to. I'm pretty sure it's Linda, and can't hide my surprise when I discover it's Luke. Bad thoughts consume me, and I immediately worry something might have happened to Bryce—who I haven't heard from since he left.

"Everything all right?" I ask, shoving my hands in my pockets to hide my nervousness.

He looks over my shoulder to my window that's still open. His jaw tightens, and his eyes harden. "I need you to work today."

I frown up at him. "But it's Sunday. It's my day off."

He shrugs. "Well, I need you to work." His behavior confuses me. Even though he tries to remain detached, I can see he's battling with something. It's almost as if he's pissed he even has to ask.

"Can someone else not handle it? I have some things I need to do today."

"Nope. I need you."

I let out a breath, torn between telling him no and giving in. He senses my struggle, and relaxes slightly. "I've never asked you for anything, Delilah. I'm asking you for this." I meet his eyes—as blue as the ocean. Earnest. Almost desperate. Too desperate.

I narrow my gaze. "Did Bryce put you up to this?" His silence is a dead giveaway. "He did, didn't he?"

"There's an out-of-state support charter that'll be here shortly. I need you up front by noon." With that, he turns on his heel and leaves.

I slam my door with both hands. When that doesn't help suppress my rising anger, I slam my window. Pacing the room, I dial Bryce's number, but it goes to voicemail after the second ring.

"You have no right asking Luke to force me to stay here," I yell into the phone. "It's not fair and you fucking know it." I end the call, and wait for him to call me back. An hour later, I've stomped holes in the carpet and he's yet to return my call.

Finally, I'm exhausted enough to sleep. But when I close my eyes, it's not Bryce I ache for. It's my mom.

"Damn, you're sexy."

I smile up at our out-of-town guests' road captain. He's a good-looking guy—younger and free of the stress lines that are often found on a biker who's been in this lifestyle for years.

"So are you, baby."

My voice sounds nervous and unsure—exactly how I feel. I really don't want to fuck this man. I only want one man in my bed—in my room. But he's not here. And although he made sure to tell Luke I wasn't to leave the clubhouse, he didn't bother telling him I was off limits to other men. If he had, then I wouldn't be having this conversation.

"Strip for me. I want to see that pretty little pussy I've been hearing about."

His words make me sick. If Bryce has said them, I would moan and become wet and ready at the dirty talk. But this isn't Bryce. And for the first time since I've been employed by the Devil's Renegades, I feel ashamed. *Like a whore...*

"Hey..." The road captain's voice drops with concern. "You okay?"

I shake my head, fighting back my tears as I hug myself. "I'm sorry."

He gives me an understanding nod. "It's fine, gorgeous. No pressure here." I'm thankful for his warm words. It'd be better if he were an asshole about this. Maybe then I wouldn't feel so guilty for disappointing him. "You look like you need a hug." He smiles down at me.

"That would be nice."

He steps forward, wrapping his arms around me. I shiver in his embrace, not feeling the protection or reassurance I feel in Bryce's arms. I can't even pretend that this man is him. He's too small...his scent is off...his hold too polite.

A loud boom makes me jump, and the man's arms tighten protectively around me as he looks over his shoulder. I peek around his arm to find Bryce's big body looming in the doorway —dangerous and deadly.

"Get the fuck out," he growls, and the man immediately releases me. Bryce takes me in with one sweep of his eyes— finding me still fully clothed and hugging myself. Another shiver wracks through me and my eyes well with tears. He mistakes my look for that of terror, and his cold, lethal glare centers on the road captain.

Before my mind can process what's happening, his hand is around the man's throat and lifting him off his feet. I scream for him to stop, but there's a distance in his eyes as if he doesn't realize I'm even in the room.

Seconds later, my room is filled with patches as they look to Bryce who has a gun trained at the man's head. His finger is on the trigger, ready to kill the gentle man who had done nothing wrong. Luke appears then, and I beg for him to make Bryce stop —telling him that the road captain had done nothing wrong.

Resting a hand on Bryce's shoulder, he mumbles something in his ear. I see Luke mouth my name, and the steely look in Bryce's eyes softens when they land on me. I'm still screaming, crying, begging him to stop. He releases the man and drops his gun, forgetting him completely as he turns to me.

I don't run to him, but I don't run away either. I'm not scared of Bryce. Even in my state, I know he only did what he did to protect me. But again, he misjudges my reaction for fear, and lifts his hands in the air as he cautiously approaches me.

"Calm down, Love. I'm not going to hurt you."

If I could manage my sobs, I'd tell him I know that. But I can't. So I just stand here and continue to slowly break down until he's close enough to touch me. The moment I'm in his arms, I shatter. And like always, he catches the crumbling pieces.

"Shh... I'm sorry. I overreacted."

"H-he didn't hurt me." I cry into his chest.

"I know that now."

"Bryce?" Luke asks, and I've never been more thankful for Bryce's big body that shields me from the crowd still lingering in my room.

"I got it," Bryce says, but Luke isn't convinced.

"You sure, brother?"

"I said, I got it." This time, the tone in his voice is enough to have Luke nodding, and leaving us alone.

Bryce cradles my head in his hand, raining kisses across my hair. "I'm not angry at you, Love. I never was. Please don't think that." His words are enough to break through the moment, and remind me of why the current events transpired in the first place.

"Well, I'm angry at you," I say, pulling out of his hold. I walk to the bathroom, my legs rubbery but managing to hold me up.

"Why are you mad at me?"

I splash my face with cold water. My tears have stopped, but my chest heaves every now and then as I fight to control my breathing.

"I know y-you told Luke not to let me leave the c-clubhouse." I hate myself for sounding weak. I wanted to be strong— confident when I told him how wrong it was of him to try to control me. My words don't seem as threatening when I'm stuttering.

"That was for your own good." I meet his eyes, finding them not the least bit apologetic.

"Well, that's not for you to decide, is it?" He seems wounded by my words. *Good.* So why do I feel guilty?

"Are you really pissed at me for stopping you from going to your mother's? After what you told me about your family, do you just expect me to let you go?"

"What I expect is for you to trust me to make my own decisions." I shake my head at my own words, closing my eyes and taking a moment to find what it is I'm really trying to say.

"How can I trust you when you continue to put yourself in danger? If you hadn't tried to go, then I wouldn't have had to stop you in the first place." *Well, that did it.* At his admission, my eyes are open and glaring at him.

"What do you really want from me, Bryce? Do you expect me to stay here under your command, do only as you say and be okay with not getting anything in return? What about me? What about what I want?"

He gives me a disbelieving look, like he can't believe I have the audacity to stand here and question him. "This is about you. *Everything* is about you, Delilah." Pain and confusion flashes in his eyes, but he doesn't elaborate. Well, fuck that. He's gotten off easy long enough.

"I love you, Bryce." He stills at my confession—sliding the mask over his face to hide his emotions. "I am in love with you. And it's real, so don't even try to tell me it's not. You may be able to control me physically, but you have no say over my heart."

I take a step closer to him. He looks like he might want to back away, but he stands his ground. "I love you," I repeat, the words flowing effortlessly from my mouth. "And you don't have to love me back. But you do have to accept my feelings for you. So if you want me to be only yours, then say it. Because if you don't, then you have no right to interfere in my job or my personal life."

Time passes as he stares back at me unblinking. I can't read him. He's completely guarded. I know I'm nearing my fate. Either he'll commit, or he won't. There is no other option here. The longer he stands unspeaking, the more anxious I become. I need an answer. I've given him an ultimatum, and he needs to tell me his decision.

Then he blinks. His eyes narrow slightly and his face hardens. "You're wrong, Love." I stare back at him confused. "I have every right to interfere." He stalks toward the door, and I follow. I'm bewildered, angry and unsure of what in the hell just happened. I'd told him I loved him, and he hadn't even addressed it.

"Bryce!" I call, quickening my pace to meet his long strides. He doesn't slow as he walks confidently down the hall and into the main room. "Bryce!" He ignores me, but my yell draws the attention of everyone in the clubhouse.

"Delilah is off limits," he announces, his voice just loud enough to carry across the room. "If you touch her, I'll put you in a fuckin' coma." The chilling tone in his threat has every head in the room nodding, even mine.

He pauses at the door, pointing to a Prospect, but turning his steely, green eyes on me. "She never leaves your sight. If something happens to her, something happens to you. Understood?"

"Got it, SA."

He narrows his gaze on me—daring me to defy him ... promising me wrath if I do. I will, and he knows it. The knowledge hardens his voice and his menacing glare.

He growls one final order—warning evident in his demand. "Watch her." Then he's gone.

I turn my back on the curious stares, and disappear to my room—well aware of the Prospect hot on my heels. I slam the door in his face, and lock it behind me. Seconds later, he's managed to pick the lock, and strides in just as I'm climbing out the window.

I'm surprised when he doesn't follow me through it. Instead, he emerges from the side of the building moments later just as I'm on my fifth push-up—trying to burn off some of this nervous energy. I hate it's Cook, who has nearly a year of prospecting under his belt. It'd be a lot easier to shake a rookie than it would be one who's skilled in following orders.

Cook is every bit of six foot, cut and very handsome. But he holds no comparison to Bryce in my eyes. I sneer at the thought. I don't want to find him attractive anymore. Especially now when all I want is to hate him—hate him for walking out ... for not acknowledging I love him ... for not telling me back ... for forcing me to comply when he has no fucking right.

"Why do you listen to him?" I ask, glancing over at Cook who leans against the side of the building.

"Because that's my job."

"No...your job is at The Country Tavern," I correct. "Where you work Tuesday through Saturday. He's not your daddy, you know." I'm trying to push his buttons, but he's unaffected.

"You're right. He's not my daddy. He's the sergeant at arms for the Devil's Renegades...a club I very much want to be a part of."

"Why would you want to be a part of any club that *he's* in?"

"Probably the same reason you do." I narrow my eyes on him. He just smiles.

"Bryce is a dick," I grumble.

"That's your opinion."

"You're a dick."

"That, too, is your opinion."

The inability to get a rise out of him pisses me off further. So I focus my energy on continuing the exercise regimen that already has my body screaming in protest. I push through it, rolling to my back on the cold ground when my arms start to give out.

A hundred sit-ups later, I'm gasping for air. *Where did Bryce go? What is he doing? When will he be back?* The unanswered questions have me furious. *Where the fuck is my beast when I need him?* But that's a question I do have the answer to. He's sleeping—tucked tightly away in his cage where Bryce left him.

I wonder how many days it'll take for either Bryce or my beast to return. Without sexual release, I'll need pain. And no Bryce means no release. I chance another look at Cook who's doing just as he was told—never taking his eyes off me. I decide then if my beast shows back up before Bryce, I'll make sure it's Cook I provoke to beat the hell out of me.

*Slimy bastard...*

"What time is it?" I ask, looking up at the darkening sky.

"A quarter after five."

*Damn... Would today ever end?*

"Take five, Prospect." *Luke...great.* "How you doin', Delilah?"

"What do you think?" I mutter, wishing like Bryce, Luke would disappear. *I wonder if I can outrun him...*

"I think you're upset, and you don't want us to know it, so you're acting pissed."

I turn my head to look at him. He smirks down at me, hands in his pockets as he towers above me. From this angle, he looks so much bigger. "I *am* pissed. Very pissed."

I sit up and he offers me his hand. I ignore it and stagger to my feet, brushing the dirt and grass from my clothes. "So you love him," he says. It's not a question.

"So you eavesdropped."

He shrugs. "Maybe."

"You can't let him do this to me, Luke." He regards me a moment, then shrugs again.

"Then quit."

I startle at his suggestion. The thought hadn't even occurred to me. Now that I'm aware of it, I'm faced with a new dilemma. If I quit, I'll be free of his hold. But with that, I forfeit any possibility of ever seeing him again. Could I do that? Did I want to? In this moment...absolutely.

"Fine. I quit."

When he shrugs again, I want to punch him. "You can't."

"Why the fuck not?"

"Because I need you." At one time, his words would be endearing to me. Now, not so much.

"For what?" I ask, throwing my hands up. "It's not like I can do anything. Your guard dog threatened to put anyone who touched me in a coma. You have plenty of women here to cook, clean and serve beer—"

"True," he says, cutting me off. "But none of them do it as well as you." He winks and leans in, dropping his voice to a whisper. "Don't tell them I said that."

"I'm serious, Luke. I'm done. I gave him my heart and he pissed it away."

Luke lets out a breath, the humor gone from his face. "Be patient with him, Delilah. He's...damaged."

"And I'm not?" I snort, finding it ridiculous that Luke chose me of all people to pull the damaged card on.

"Fair enough." He fights a smile, and despite my efforts to suppress it, I feel my own tugging at my lips. "Give him a couple days. He'll come around."

"And what in the hell am I supposed to do until then?"

He grins down at me. "Drive Cook crazy. He's had it easy the past eleven months. I want him to earn his patch."

"Fine," I say on a breath. "But Luke..." I level him with a look, letting him know I mean what I say. "I can't do this forever. I won't. What he did was wrong. He hurt me. And I'm tired of being hurt."

He nods, his blue eyes sincere and full of empathy. Pulling me in, he hugs me tight. I welcome his embrace. Much like Bryce's, it has the power to make me feel protected and wanted. "I know, babe. It'll all work out. I'm sure of it."

*Well...at least someone is.*

\*\*\*\*

"Get out of my room!" I scream, hurling a shoe at Cook. He dodges it easily, cocking one eyebrow in amusement. I throw another and he sidesteps it again—seeming bored at my endless attempts to get him to leave.

Last night, he slept on my floor. This morning, he followed me to the front room, and watched me while I drank coffee and smoked. The only time I haven't seen him is when he asked someone to relieve him long enough to use the bathroom. Then he was right back in my sights.

When I ate, he ate. When I slept, he slept. When I worked, he watched. I was going fucking crazy—and he didn't care. Actually, he seemed to rather enjoy it. But when he refused to let me shower with the door closed, I lost it. That's where we are now.

"I will *not* let you stand there and watch while I shower. I mean it, Cook. You're overstepping your boundaries."

"I have no intention of watching you, Delilah. But the door stays open." His cool, calm demeanor pisses me off more than him being my shadow.

"Call Bryce. Right now. Get him on the phone."

He shakes his head. "Bryce is busy."

"I'm getting Luke."

"Luke's gone. Won't be back till tomorrow."

I grind my teeth, wishing I had a gun and imagining how good it would feel to blow his kneecaps out. "If you don't call him this instant, I'm going to ram my head into the wall, knock myself unconscious and force you to call. Then you'll have to tell him I'm hurt. In turn, he'll hurt you."

He shoots me an amused look. "You'd do that?"

"Damn right I would."

"Why don't you just call him yourself?"

"Because I don't want to speak to the bastard. I want you to call him, and deliver my message."

He shakes his head. "Nope."

"Fine." I shrug. "Have it your way." Snatching his beer bottle from the dresser, I slam it against the corner—shattering the end. Glass shards and beer fall to the carpet. He moves quickly, but stops when I put the jagged end of the bottle to my arm.

"Delilah," he warns, putting his hand out. "Give me the bottle."

"Call him," I deadpan. "You have two seconds." Something in my eyes has him pulling his phone from his pocket. I don't dwell on the thought of if I'd have actually done it or not—I'm too afraid of the answer.

I can't hear Bryce's voice, but know the moment he answers. Dread fills Cook's eyes. It makes me smile. "She wants me to tell you she refuses to shower with the door open." Silence a moment, then he speaks again. "She's pissed. *Really* pissed." His brows draw in confusion at Bryce's reply. "No. none of that."

It hits me then that Bryce is asking about my behavior— using the knowledge to determine whether or not I'm slipping into the darkness. My heart flips at his concern, then hardens when I remember what an asshole he is.

"Tell that motherfucker I said he'll know when I've reached my limit, because it'll be too late."

Cook swallows hard and extends the phone to me. "He wants to talk to you." He almost looks apologetic. Well, he can go to hell.

"I'm not talking to him." My defiance earns me a pleading look from Cook. I give him an evil smile. *Now he knows how it feels.*

He puts the phone back to his hear. "You hear that?" Turning the phone in his hand, I'm thinking he's ending the call. But Bryce's voice echoes through the speaker phone.

"The door stays open, Delilah. That's final."

The sound of his voice makes my knees go weak. I don't want to fight with him. I want to cry. I want to tell him I love him, and to please come back. That whatever demons he carries are my demons too. That I'll help him overcome his fears, just like he helped me. After all, knowing he's damaged is the only reason I haven't left this world behind, and started my own life. The club can't force me to stay here. I'm here on my own free will, and I'll stay as long as I think Bryce and I have a chance. He didn't give up on me, and I refuse to give up on him. I can't. I love him too much.

"Do I make myself clear, Delilah?" My sadness starts to lift at his ridiculous demand. Only he has the power to put my emotions in such a frenzy. If he'd given me just the slightest sign of the Bryce I know, then I could play this out differently—make him feel guilty for putting me through this. But this isn't *my* Bryce. This is *SA* Bryce. And he's an asshole.

"How about I strip naked and shower *with* Cook? How would you like that?"

Cook's eyes widen, and he shakes his head in disbelief at me —giving me the finger.

"That's not gonna happen, babe." *Babe...hmph.* "Get in the shower then go to bed. All you're doing is making this harder on yourself."

My anger skyrockets. "You're a fucking coward, Bryce! You're too big of a pussy to face me yourself, so you sic your lapdog on me. Well, fuck you!" I'm yelling, spitting, shaking with fury. *I hate myself for loving him.*

"You finished yet?" He seems bored by my outburst, making me that much more angry.

"I hate you."

"No, you don't."

"No, really. I do."

"Take a shower. Leave the door open. Then go to bed."

"Or what?" I taunt. "You gonna *punish* me? Well." I let out a breath of laughter. "I know *that's* not gonna happen. You'd have to ask your little bitch boy here—"

"Enough!" My lips immediately snap shut at his tone. I know better than to treat any man with a patch with disrespect. It's one thing to give a Prospect hell, and throw shit—as extreme as it may sound. But degrading him as if he's beneath me is another.

I mouth "sorry" to Cook, but he dismisses it with a wave of his hand. I feel better knowing he doesn't hold it against me—despite the anger and disappointment in Bryce's voice. What the hell does it matter what he thinks anyway? It's not like he's here.

"Do as you're told, Delilah. And watch your mouth with *my* Prospect. Or it'll be you that's degraded, humiliated and *punished* in front of the entire club."

"You wouldn't," I hiss, fear prickling my skin at just the thought.

"Oh, I would. One more disrespectful word to him, and I'll tear your ass up while everyone watches." I swallow hard, and notice even Cook seems uncomfortable at the threat.

"I'm done," I whisper, avoiding Cook's eyes. I drop the bottle from my hand, and take a step. The instant I do, I realize it was a mistake. "*Shit!*" My hand flies over my mouth just as Cook takes Bryce off speakerphone.

"Nothing," I hear him say, shooting me a pleading look. I nod, motioning for him to wrap it up while I balance on one foot. "She's still pissed... Got it."

He ends the call and shoves the phone in his pocket, taking a step toward me. "Let's agree to never discuss whatever in the hell it was going on between y'all during that phone call," he says, sweeping me up in his arms and carrying me to the bathroom.

"Agreed. My foot hurts."

"Yeah, no shit. You got a shard of glass in it," he mutters, setting me on the counter and taking my foot in his hand. "Where are your tweezers?" I reach in the drawer next to me, then hand them to him. "Be still."

From my position, I could easily kick him in the face and bolt. But guilt still weighs heavy in my chest from earlier. "Look," I start, fidgeting with my shirt. "I didn't mean what I said. I don't think you're a lapdog or a bitch boy."

"If anyone else would've said it, I might've been offended. But I know you didn't mean it, Delilah. And for what it's worth, I hate this for you. Whatever in the hell this is," he adds on a mumble.

I smile. "Thanks." He pulls the glass from my foot, and helps me down from the counter. "It doesn't hurt anymore," I say, when his brow furrows with concern. After watching me walk on it a moment, he's convinced.

"I'll clean this up. You go ahead." He starts out, then turns and narrows his eyes on me. "Door open."

I force a frown, drop my eyes and nod. "I know," I whisper. I pull my shirt over my head which prompts him to leave. As I step in the shower, I'm smiling. Playing the weak, wounded role was going to be easier than I'd thought. It wouldn't take long before I had Cook eating out of the palm of my hand. And maybe, once I earn his pity, he'll let down his guard—giving me that small window of opportunity to escape.

\*\*\*\*

Tonight makes the third night Cook has slept on my floor. I've been laying the guilt on heavy—giving him the full effect of an uneasy, depressed Delilah. And since it's the weekend, the sadness and anxiety I've been showing hasn't really been much of a front at all.

I've been listening to Cook snore for the past thirty minutes. Slipping out of bed, already wearing my sweats, I pull on my shoes and start my well-planned escape.

"It's locked, Delilah." Cook's voice has my heart nearly jumping out of my chest. He doesn't even sound sleepy, even though he was snoring only moments ago. "Actually, it's nailed shut. But you're welcome to try if it makes you feel better."

I give my window one last look, before dropping my shoulders in defeat. "It's been three days," I whine, falling back into bed. "How much longer are you going to do this?"

"How much longer are you going to do this?" His question throws me off. *How long indeed?*

"You know what?" I ask, getting out of bed again. "I'm not. I'm done." I start down the hall, and hear him running behind me. "I quit. I'm through. I've held out for as long as I can."

"Delilah, wait. I can't let you leave. Please don't make me force you."

The thought of him hitting me to make me stay halts me in my tracks. He nearly collides into me. "Oh no," I whisper, feeling panic starting to swim slowly through me. I don't even realize my hand is pulling at my hair until Cook takes it gently in his.

I shake my head, looking up at him with wide eyes. "It's happening." He has no clue what I'm talking about. The confusion on his face is mixed with fear. He's not sure if this is some ploy, or if what's happening is real.

But it is real. Very real. I feel it. My beast is awake. My mind burns with need for pain. My body aches for sexual release. I'm a whirlwind of conflicted emotions. I thought for sure yesterday I was only imagining my anxiety. But now it's clear. And it scares the hell out of me.

I *want* Cook to hit me. Just the thought that it might be a possibility awakens the need inside me. I have to have it. How had I gone so long without it? Had the memory of Bryce been enough?

Bryce.

Fear engulfs me, bringing me nearly to my knees. The heartache is a devastating blow to my harsh reality--Bryce doesn't love me. He knew I would break, but still he refused to release me just as he refused to be here with me. I was a fool. I'd believed the power of my love was strong enough to bring him back to me. I'd told him I loved him—told him it was okay to not love me back. And what did he do? He left. Without explanation —only orders, and only to Cook.

*Watch her...*

Bryce worried I might have reached my limit when I got angry the other day. He knows that anger is my last felt emotion. Still, it wasn't enough. He'd deserted me. Left me at the mercy of a man who was not only unaware of my condition, but under strict instruction to not touch me.

"What the fuck are you doin'?" Cook whisper-shouts, looking around for something—anything—to help him. "Delilah, talk to me."

"No...no, no, no, no..." I push his hands away from me, digging my nails into my skin, and whimpering at the tiny sliver of release. "I'm so stupid!" I cry, stinging tears falling down my cheeks. The hate I feel toward myself is the same I'd felt all those years ago when my mother insisted my father's leaving was my fault.

I'd finally understood it was...just like now.

This...me falling apart over a man who doesn't love me...this is my fault. I can't blame Bryce for not loving me. How can he? I'm not worthy of love.

"Delilah!" Cook grabs my shoulders, shaking me hard. The feeling is delightful.

"More," I whisper. I feel him tense. Then I'm thrown over his shoulder and he's walking down the hall, back to my room. He sets me on the bed, keeping one hand on my arm while he presses buttons on his phone.

"Don't call him," I say, knowing he's wasting his time. But I'm too late, and can hear the ringing through his cell.

"Something's wrong," he snaps, anger flooding his voice. "What the fuck is goin' on, SA?" His voice becomes more and more distant, as if he's speaking far away. "I can't—" His words are cut off, and I wonder if Bryce interrupted him, or if I'm slipping further into the darkness, quicker than I'd imagined.

Pain spreads deliciously through my arm, and my vision clears. I look down at Cook's hand to see his grip has tightened. "Delilah!" He snaps, holding the phone out to me. "Talk. Now." He pushes the phone next to my ear.

"Love?" I whimper. "Can you hear me?" I nod, dropping my head and letting my tears pool in my lap. "An answer, Love."

"I hear you," I whisper. "Why did you do this to me, Bryce?"

"I...I needed some space to think. I shouldn't have left so long. But I'm coming, Love. I'm on my way. I'll be there in the morning."

I shake my head. "No. I don't want you. I won't let you hurt me anymore."

"Delilah, please." His voice is pained, but it's too late. He doesn't get to love me because he feels guilty. It's not fair.

"Stay away, Bryce. I'm done."

"Listen to me, Love." His voice hardens, and I listen because he still yields that kind of power over me. "Calm down, and try to sleep. Cook won't leave your side. I'll be there before you wake up."

"I get it, you know," I say, completely resigned. "My mother, my brother, Mario...you. There's one common denominator with all of you. And it's me."

"Delilah..."

"It's not your fault, Bryce. I'm not mad at you. I just wish you'd told me sooner. But again the blame falls on me. I should've known when I told you I loved you, and you left, that what I've always believed was still true. I'm undeserving."

"That's not—"

"Good-bye, Bryce." Pulling the phone from my ear, I hang up and power it off. I'm aware of Cook's eyes on me, and his hand still on my arm. "Cook," I say, meeting his gaze. Pity is there—shining bright in his dark brown eyes. "I understand you have a certain duty to your club. But I'm tired." Tears pool in my eyes again. "I just want to go home." I crumble inside at the word. *Home.* It has no meaning to me, because it's something I don't possess.

"Please," I beg. "Don't make me stay here."

He stares at me a long moment, then pulls a set of keys from his pocket before laying them on the dresser. With a small, sad smile, he wordlessly turns and walks into the bathroom—shutting the door behind him.

I grab the keys along with the stash of cash from my drawer. I don't bother to look back as I walk through the clubhouse for the last time.

I'm behind the wheel of Cook's vehicle, miles from Hattiesburg, when I realize where I'm going is the one place I don't want to be. But I continue on. After all...

It's Sunday.

But through the thick haze in my mind, I can hear a voice telling me this isn't what I want. This is not who I am anymore. I'm stronger than this. So I fight against the urge to give in to my weakness as I drive.

My mind drifts back to the last time my beast surrendered. I'm at the river, tied to the tree. Bryce's soothing voice is coaching me—telling me to choose. Promising me the pleasure outweighs the pain. But I can't focus. There are too many distractions. Headlights on the highway...speeding cars as they pass in a blur.

I feel myself slipping into the darkness, and I tighten my grip on the steering wheel. "No!" I shout, searching for that river, that tree and Bryce's face once again. I need to find it. I need to be there. I need to revisit that place that, and live in that mindset where I fought my beast and I won.

I squeeze my eyes shut for a second and it's there—I'm there. I can hear the water. Smell the scent of Bryce's skin. Feel his hands on me. But when I open my eyes, it fades.

Relaxing, I check my mirrors to see no one is around. I'll rest my eyes for just a moment...just long enough to find the strength to fight...

Just for one second...

That's all the time I need.

# CHAPTER 28

I open my eyes and a bright white light stares back at me. For a moment, I think I'm dead. The thought is paralyzing, and as my other senses slowly wake to the sound of a steady beep, and the scent of iodoform, I realize I'm not dead at all. I'm in a hospital room.

Something tightens on my arm, and I drop my gaze to the blood pressure cuff surrounding it. It begins to hum as it inflates —the Velcro crackling loudly in the large, open area where I lie alone. I lift my hand and find something similar to a clothes pin clamped on the tip of my finger.

I start to take inventory of my limbs. Two legs, two arms, I can wiggle all my toes and fingers. I can see out of both eyes, breathe on my own, and there's not a tube down my throat. In a nutshell, I think I'm going to survive. Nothing even hurts.

There's some kind of contraption attached to a cord with a button on the end of it, laying next to me. Out of pure curiosity, I press it. The IV bag next to my bed hooked into my arm makes a whooshing noise. Moments later, I feel myself getting drowsy. Ahh...a morphine button. I'd heard about those...

"You're awake!" *I am now.* The annoyingly cheerful voice belongs to a middle-aged woman who wears pink scrubs and has a short, stylish haircut that frames a face that's quite pretty. *I wonder if she...*

"How do you feel?"

"Where am I?"

She frowns at my question. "I should get the doctor. One moment." She disappears and I close my eyes. Sleep begins to take me almost instantly.

"Well, hello!" *Are you fucking kidding me?* This time, the annoyingly cheerful voice belongs to a much older woman in a white coat with a stethoscope dangling from her neck.

"I'm really sleepy," I admit, hoping she'll disappear and let me rest.

"I know, but let's take a look at you first." *Shit.* "Do you remember how you got here?"

I shake my head. "No."

She presses the end of the stethoscope to my chest and listens a moment before speaking—just as I'm starting to drift. "Well, you had a wreck, and you're at Slidell Regional Medical Facility. They airlifted you around five thirty yesterday morning."

"Yesterday?" I croak, taking another quick inventory to make sure I didn't miss something that would require me to be out for over a day.

"Yes. You crashed into a bluff just off of interstate fifty-nine. You're lucky to be alive."

"So, what's wrong with me?" I hold out my arms that feel heavy, noticing my hospital bracelet. "And why does my name say Jane Doe?"

"Well, you didn't have any identification on you, and the truck you were driving was registered to a deceased man." *Cook's father...he'd died several months back.* "The police haven't been able to get in contact with the next of kin, but promise to keep us informed. As for the other, you had some internal bleeding and brain swelling. But we ran another catscan this morning and the swelling has decreased. We managed to stop the bleeding with a minor surgery. You should be fine in a couple weeks."

"Was anyone else in the wreck?" I ask, trying to force myself to stay awake. But my efforts are slipping.

"No. Just you."

I close my eyes and breathe a sigh of relief. She asks my real name then, but I'm too far gone to answer.

Pain wakes me this time. My entire body throbs with every beat of my heart. I search frantically for the button, but it's not here. Pressing the intercom on my bed, I page the nurses—not stopping until someone replies.

"I'm dying," I say, figuring that should about sum it up. A few seconds later, the same nurse and doctor from earlier reappear.

"What's hurting on you, honey?" the doctor asks.

"Everything. Everywhere."

"Your stomach?"

"Yes!" I yell in frustration. "My fucking hair hurts. And my throat is so dry..."

"We'll get you some ice chips for now."

"Can I get my button back?" As I say it, I feel the nurse slide it into my hand.

"It fell off the bed. Can we get your name, miss? A next of kin to call?"

"Carmical," I breathe, feeling my body as it starts to numb from the morphine. "Luke Carmical. Hattiesburg..." Then I'm gone again.

My throat feels like I've swallowed barbed wire, as movement wakes me. I'm being rolled down a hall—fluorescent white lights passing above me just like in the movies. I lick my dried lips, but it does no good. My tongue is like sandpaper.

"Where are you taking me?" I whisper. When I don't get an answer, I lift my hand and my nurse's face appears.

"Hello, sunshine!" She's way too freaking happy. "We're taking you down for another catscan."

"Water."

She nods. "I promise the moment we're finished, I'll get you some water." Her face flushes and her voice drops. "You have some good-lookin' company waiting for you." No doubt she's talking about Luke. I can tell by the faraway look in her eyes that she's fell victim to his charm.

I'm not in any pain, so I know I'm pumped full of drugs, but I guess my body has slept long enough. I'm awake for the entire catscan. When it's finished, I'm wheeled back to my room. I was hoping we'd pass by the waiting area and I could see Luke.

*Liar...*

Truth is, a part of me hopes *he's* here too. Only so I can tell him to his face that I hate him. But that's a lie too. I don't hate him. I love him too much. Who gives a shit if he don't love me? I'd give up my morphine pump just to feel him hold me one more time. And that's saying something. *This morphine is the shit.*

I watch the nurse shuffle around the room, wrinkling my nose when she empties the blood bag. *Blood bag?* "Is that?"

"Yes, you have a catheter."

"Why is it—"

"It's common with your injuries."

"But isn't that really ba—"

"I assure you, it's fine."

"Can I finish a fuckin' sentence?" I snap, then squeeze my eyes shut. "I'm sorry."

"Don't be." She beams at me. "I think what you need is to see your brother."

"And some water," I add, tempted to get up and get it myself if she doesn't deliver in the next three seconds.

"Already got it, honey." She adjusts my bed so I'm sitting up. I feel pressure in my lower abdomen, but still no pain. Handing me the cup, she pats my hand. "Is your brother—"

"Married?" I ask, cutting her off and giving her a dose of her own medicine. "Yes. He is."

She rolls her eyes. "I'll send him in." I nearly smile at the regret in her voice.

When Luke strides through the door a few minutes later, my eyes well with tears at the sight of him. He's definitely giving the nurses the full LLC show—wearing leather and looking as devilishly, dangerously sexy as ever. In their eyes anyway. My tastes are... bigger.

"Hey, babe," he smirks, brushing my hair off my forehead and leaning to kiss me there. "How ya feelin'?"

"Good. Better now." He swipes a tear with his thumb.

"Good. That's real good, babe."

"I totaled out Cook's truck," I admit, although I'm pretty sure he knows that by now.

"I'll take care of it."

I shake my head. "It's not your place."

"Yeah...it is."

I don't argue, my mind is too busy trying to talk myself out of my next question. I give in though, unable to wait any longer. "Have you talked to him?" I ask, noticing the flash of sadness in his clear, blue eyes.

"Of course."

"How is he?"

The corner of his mouth tips. "Worried about you."

"I'm worried about him," I admit, figuring after our last conversation, he feels partially responsible for this.

"He's good, babe. You focus on getting you better." He gives me a wink, catching another stray tear. "He'll come, you know. All you have to do is tell me he can, and he'll be here."

"The Bryce I know wouldn't ask."

He laughs at that. "You're right. And he may or may not be waiting in the lobby, surrounded by Slidell's finest boys in blue. He doesn't take well to being told no."

"They wouldn't let him in?" I ask, knowing if my body wasn't numb, I'd feel heat pooling in my belly at the knowledge that he's here.

"Only me. Said you told them I was your next of kin."

"I did say that."

"I'm glad." Pain registers on his face. "You scared me, Delilah."

"I didn't mean—"

"You're very precious to me, and the last twenty-four hours have been hell. Please don't ever put me through that again."

I nod. "I won't. I promise." He smiles then, reaching down to place a lingering kiss in my hair. "Luke?"

"Yeah?"

"Will you get him for me?"

He smirks, tipping his chin toward the door. "He's already here."

# CHAPTER 29

How I hadn't felt his presence, I'll never know. Or maybe I did, and it was him that warmed my heart, and not Luke's words. His stance is relaxed, his hands hanging loosely at his sides as his green eyes take me in—absorbing me completely. He doesn't look sad or pained, only thoughtful. I'm aware that we're alone only when I hear the click of the door when Luke closes it behind him.

"Hello, Love," he says. The sound carries across the room—blanketing me.

"Hello, yourself."

He smiles then, grabbing a chair as he comes to sit next to my bed. He takes my hand in his—careful to not pull any of the tubes hanging out of me. Dipping his head, he plants a sweet, lingering kiss on the back of my hand.

"I don't know what to say here, Bryce."

He lifts his eyes to me, shaking his head. "You don't have to say anything." He kisses my hand again before cradling it between both of his. "It's time I did some talking."

The sincerity in his voice makes my mouth even drier, and I lift the small Styrofoam cup to my lips before taking a generous pull. *Best damn hospital water ever.*

"That college roommate I told you about? She wasn't just my roommate... she was my fiancé." I still at his admission. "I loved her." Hurt registers in his green eyes and I feel it in my heart. "She was a pain addict. I tried to help her, but she was too far gone...damaged beyond repair. I thought my love would be enough, but it wasn't."

His eyes center on me. I can see the wound is no longer fresh, but still affects him. "She took her own life the day after I proposed. She left me a note, apologizing to me and telling me I was the only real thing she'd ever had. That she would never be enough and I deserved so much more."

As I listen, I realize all of a sudden why Bryce knew so much about my affliction, my need for pain, and it makes me admire and love him all the more. So much that my heart hurts more than any other part of my banged-up body.

"For years I lived with the guilt. I thought maybe if I hadn't met her, or if she hadn't loved me then she'd still be here." He pauses a moment, and I squeeze his hand. In turn, he kisses my fingers again. Then takes a deep, staggering breath.

"The club helped. I found peace in it. Then I met you." He smiles then—a genuine smile that replaces the sadness in his eyes with happiness. "I didn't want to fall for you...damn, I didn't. But I couldn't help it. At first I felt like maybe if I helped you through this, then somehow it would give meaning to her death."

He shakes his head, some memory resurfacing in his mind and softening his face. "But you captivated me, Delilah. She became nothing more than a distant memory..." He drops his eyes. "When you told me you loved me, it brought it all back...the pain...the guilt...it was worse than I remembered."

He clears his throat—fighting against his emotions. When he meets my gaze again, I'm a blubbering mess and he's completely in control. "I was wrong to walk out on you, Love. I let the best thing in my life suffer because of my own tainted soul. And I should've told you that night how I really felt."

His hand comes to cradle my face, his thumb brushing across my cheek and smearing the heavy flow of my tears. "I do love you, Delilah." My heart flips at the words. "I've loved you since the first time you gave me your trust. You make everything right. And there is nothing better in this world than you."

The sincerity in his gaze and conviction in his voice brings on another flood of tears. But I'm tired of crying. He never had to tell me he loved me, I've known it all along. And although his words play on a loop in my head, I want to do something to lighten the mood.

*There is nothing better than you.* I sigh.

"Nothing?" I ask, smiling up at him.

He shakes his head. "Nothing."

"Not even Harleys?"

"Don't get cocky, babe," he smirks. I start to feel drowsy suddenly, and find he holds my pain button in his hand. "Sleep, Love."

"Will you be here when I wake up?" I ask, letting my eyes flutter closed. I give up my fight and surrender to sleep at his promise.

*"Always."*

If I were to lay in the middle of the road, have hot tar dumped on my body and let a fleet of Mack trucks roll over me, I'm pretty sure it wouldn't come close to the pain I feel in this moment. The only part of my body I move when I wake is my eyes, and even that hurts.

Bryce is sitting next to my bed, sleeping soundly. Even his presence and the reminder of his confession aren't enough to dull the pain. Pressing the intercom button on my bed again, there's a low beep before the nurse's voice crackles through the speaker. Bryce's eyes spring open at the sound.

"Can I help you?"

"I'm dying again," I whimper, and when a small sob pulls at my chest, I have to fight the urge to scream in pain.

"The doctor is on her way," the nurse responds.

"Love? You okay?" Bryce stands, and moves to touch my hair.

"Please don't touch me." He pulls back his hand, worry creasing his brow. "If they're not here in the next five seconds, rip this motherfucker to pieces."

He fights a smile. "Gladly."

"How you feeling, Miss Scott?" I roll my eyes at the doctor's ridiculous question.

"Why does everyone keep asking that? I feel like shit. Fix me."

"Well, I do have some good news." She flips through a chart —stealing a glance at Bryce who stands at the head of my bed. "Your catscan results are clear. No more swelling and no more bleeding. We'll start some therapy tomorrow, get you up and moving and you'll be back to normal before you know it."

"Yeah, that's great and all, but what about now? Where's my button?"

She gives me a tight smile. "We'll be administering your pain medication orally from now on. It's been three days. It's time to take the next step toward recovery."

"Three days?" I screech, then wince when something tightens around my abdomen. I push back the covers and lift my gown to find a large bandage that stretches the length of my stomach. "What the hell is this?"

"We had to make a rather large incision to go in and stop the bleeding. We were able to cauterize the blood vessels and stop the bleeding. It wasn't as major as we'd thought."

"Are you fucking kidding me?" I feel Bryce's hand on my shoulder, but I ignore it. "Not major? This," I point to the gauzed taped to my belly, "this is major. Huge."

The doctor isn't the least bit fazed by my outburst. "You're alive, Miss Scott." She pats my foot and gives me an understanding look. "Be thankful you're here. When you first arrived, I didn't think you'd pull through. You're a very lucky young woman."

What is it about people saying nice things that make me feel like shit? She's right. I am so very lucky. Not only am I alive, but there is a very, very sexy man, wearing leather, looking down at me as if I'm the most beautiful sight that's ever graced his presence.

"Has it really been three days?" I ask, allowing him to feed me the pill the nurse had left.

"Yes." He looks so tired. How had I not noticed before?

"I'd tell you to go home and get some sleep, but I'm not. I want you here. If I have to suffer, you suffer."

He laughs at that, the tone rich and warming—making me feel better instantly. "Sounds like a plan."

I stayed in that godforsaken hospital for nearly two weeks. I thought it was a little extreme considering after day five I could get around on my own. But they were worried about me developing blood clots, and insisted I stay until I was healed. So I did. As did Bryce.

He never left my side.

The club took care of both of us. We didn't have to eat not one shitty meal the entire time we were there. They fed us, clothed Bryce and even sent flowers when I complained to Scratch that the room smelt funny. Every day I had a fresh bouquet.

The day has finally arrived for me to go home. Bryce insists they wheel me down in a chair to the front. I roll my eyes, but don't argue. Besides, I'm kinda getting used to this overshow of affection. I've never had it before.

Everyone is here—waving at me from a distance. Either I smell funny or Bryce's death glare warns them off. He's been so worried someone would hurt me if they hugged me too hard. Something tells me I won't be getting fucked hard anytime soon.

I'm lifted inside a truck I don't recognize. Bryce comes around to the driver's side and I sigh when I see him in the natural light wearing a T-shirt and jeans. Colorful tattoos swirl up his thick arms. He'd look dangerous if I hadn't been dealing with the big teddy bear he really is for the past couple of weeks.

"Put this bitch in the wind," I say, propping my legs up on the dash. "I'm so ready to be home."

"Speaking of home." Bryce glances over at me as he pulls into traffic—following behind the pack of bikes that drove here just to escort me to Hattiesburg. "I thought about buying the little house from the club."

I raise my brows at him. "Really?" *It's where we fell in love.*

"Yeah." He shrugs, seeming a little nervous. It makes me smile. He's never nervous. "I thought it'd be nice to have a place of our own."

"Our?" I gasp and smack his arm. "Are you asking me to move in with you?"

"Well, I wasn't going to, but if I say no now, it'll be a dick move." I narrow my eyes and he laughs. "Yes, Delilah. I'm asking you to move in with me. Get our own place. Live our own lives."

"And my job? What about that?"

"You can still bartend if you want. Or maybe you can focus on becoming what you've always wanted."

I frown. "What?"

"A trampoline gymnast."

I shake my head at him...this man I love more than life...this man who loves me back...who says I'm better than everything...

Except Harleys.

\*\*\*\*


Its day four and I've settled comfortably back into life at the clubhouse. It's as if I never left. My duties are still the same—minus me having sex with other people. I told Bryce I wasn't quite ready to leave yet, and he told me to take my time—he wasn't going anywhere. And he hasn't.

The ugly scar that runs from the center of my stomach to well below my navel is a daily reminder of how close I came to losing my life and everyone in it. It's jagged and uneven—a result of the emergency surgery. I guess when someone's lying on your operating table bleeding from the inside, vanity takes a back seat to survival. I can't complain, but I am slightly self-conscious—especially since Bryce has yet to make love to me.

I've tried like hell, but he yields his calming control over me, and I give in to his embrace instead of my desire. Him holding me is nearly as rewarding as him fucking me senseless. Not quite as good, but almost. But I don't feel like there's an absence in my life without the sex. And I guess the pain of the wreck was enough to last me a lifetime. I've found that all I need is him, and it's just enough.

I feel like a new person. It's as if my life before Bryce never even existed. Only one memory still haunts me, and it only rears its ugly head on Sundays—which just so happens to be today. The constant trigger immediately took me back to that dark place deep in my mind the moment I woke.

I can't help but worry about my mother. The troubles of my mind have kept me distant all day and Bryce has noticed. The looks he kept throwing at me were a dead giveaway. He acted as if any minute I might snap and do something stupid. I haven't and I don't plan to. I just needed some time and space to think—which is what I've been doing for the past two hours.

My phone is ringing. What if it's my mother? The thought is fleeting and I roll my eyes at my ridiculous assumption. Swiping it from my dresser, I find Bryce's name flashing across the screen.

"Yes?"

"You finished feeling sorry for yourself yet?" *Insensitive prick...no wonder I love him so much.*

"Only if you have something better for me to do at," I pull my phone from my ear to check the time, "three in the afternoon."

"I might." I can hear the smile in his voice. I'm smiling too.

"Fine. But don't disappoint me."

Opening the door, I find him on the other side. His face is scruffy with a two-day beard. His eyes are sparkling and his lips are smirking—making me want to stand on my toes and kiss them. I wish I could say my reaction to his appearance doesn't affect me like it once did. I can't. He still makes my belly flip and my toes curl.

"Look out your window." I stare at him in confusion, but do as he said. Raising the blinds, my breath catches in my throat at what I see merely feet from my room.

A trampoline.

I'm still staring in shock at the most thoughtful gift anyone has ever given me, when I feel him standing behind me.

A trampoline.

For me—the aspiring trampoline gymnast.

Beaming, I turn to face him and cup his cheeks in my hand. "You got me a trampoline!" I squeal. Pulling his lips down to meet mine, I place a sloppy, wet kiss in the center of them. "Thank you!"

Okay, enough of that shit. My hands shake as I struggle with the window. I hear him laugh as it takes me a few tries before I finally get it. Crawling through, I motion with my hand for him to follow and he rolls his eyes—he can't fit.

"I'll use the door." Yeah, yeah, yeah.

"Bring me some socks!" I yell at his back. I'm too damn excited to wait, so I climb on barefooted. I'm mid-flip when I see him approach, carrying in his hand a pair of my socks.

"I'm guessing you like it," he smirks, tossing them at me.

"Like it? I fucking love it!" I bounce on my ass a few times before coming to a seated position. "I haven't jumped on one since I was a kid. My childhood best friend had one. We lived on the damn thing. It's like riding a bike. I still got it."

Pulling my socks over my feet, I stare up at him as he stands there smiling—looking as happy as I feel. "This is awesome," I say, then burst out in a fit of laughter for no apparent reason. I can't remember being this excited over anything. "I've missed you today, by the way."

"Yeah, I can tell." He's joking and it's a damn good thing. I doubt I'll do anything else for the rest of the evening but jump. "Don't overdo it."

"Watch this," I say, ignoring him. My incision is healed and I'm too excited to feel any pain in this moment anyway. Getting to my feet, I find my balance before I start jumping—higher and higher until I've built up enough momentum to perform my air back handspring.

"Impressive."

"I know," I say, flipping again.

"You're gonna do this all day, ain't you?"

"Yep."

"Then take this." He pulls his hoodie over his head. Beneath it he wears a muscle shirt, and my breathing becomes more erratic at the sight. *Maybe jumping isn't all I want to do...*

Tossing me the hoodie, I catch it in midst of a toe touch. "Did you see that?"

"Seen enough, babe. Have fun." He throws his hand up as he walks away. I pull the hoodie over my head, never slowing my jump.

Without really realizing what I'm doing, I manage a double-flip half-twist thingy, before landing perfectly on my feet.

*Olympics...here I come.*

# CHAPTER 30

The sun has disappeared behind the trees—leaving a line of red and orange clouds in its wake. I'm taking a small break, lying flat on my back and staring up at the colorful sky. The change is so swift, I want to make sure I don't miss it. Well, that and I can no longer feel my legs.

"Heads up." I look up to see Bryce approaching just as he tosses a bottle of water at my feet. I greedily suck down the cool liquid I hadn't realized I was craving until now.

The trampoline dips with the weight of Bryce's body as he rolls next to me—stretching the net taunt and forcing me into his side. He must have anticipated the move, because my head rolls perfectly to his shoulder as his arm comes around my back.

"If you break my trampoline, I'm kicking your ass," I tease, although a part of me is very, very serious. He ignores my comment as he rolls to his side, leaning on his elbow smiling down at me.

"You look happy." He tucks a strand of my hair behind my ear.

"That's because I am." *So very happy...* "Why did you get this for me?"

He shrugs. "Because I like to see you smile." My heart does that pitter-pattering thing in my chest. "I have something else for you too." He hands me an envelope.

Opening it, my smile falters slightly when I see the name at the top—*Priscilla Scott*—my mother. Below it is an account number and a recent deposit of one thousand dollars.

"I know you worry about your mother," Bryce starts, sweeping my hair back from my face. "So I pulled some strings and got her bank account information. I wired the money, and mailed her a phone." He points to the phone number at the bottom of the page.

"Call her, Love." He tips my chin so I meet his gaze. "And no matter what happens, remember that I'm here. That I love you. And you're never alone." Pressing his lips to mine, he gives me a soft kiss before rolling off the trampoline and walking away.

I pull my cell phone from my pocket. It takes a few tries for me to get the number right, and even then, I struggle with what to do. Bryce had made it possible to contact the one person missing in my life. Not only that, but he'd made sure to ease my worry and guilt by sending her money to ensure she had a way to pay her bills. And he did all that because he loved me.

I don't want to taint our love with ghosts of my pasts. I want to lock them up along with my beast and throw away the key. But I need closure. I need to end my relationship with my mother, or take the first steps toward building a new one. With a deep breath, I hit send.

"Hello?"

"Mama?" I choke on the word, silently waiting for her reply.

"Delilah?"

"Yeah, Mama. It's me. How are you?" The background noise is silenced, and I assume she muted the TV.

"I've been better. Where are you, girl?"

"I'm at a friend's," I lie smoothly, still not ready to tell her where I live.

"What? You too damn good to visit your own mother? I bet your little fast ass is in trouble, huh? I don't know how you got this number, but you ain't got no right calling me and askin' me to bail you out." I close my eyes, resigned by her words.

"I'm not in trouble, Mama. I just called to say hello."

"Well, it's a fine time after I ain't heard from you in weeks. If you ain't got the audacity to come see me face to face, then don't bother callin'." For a moment, I'm sure she's hung up. But then I hear her heavy breathing.

"I won't be calling again, Mama. But you have my number if you need me. Take care of yourself."

"Uh-huh. You'll be back. You always come crawlin' back."

I bite my lip, shaking my head hard even though she can't see it. "Not this time. Not anymore." I hang up—staring at the first sign of stars as the sky darkens further. I don't cry. I don't give in to the crushing pain in my chest. I hold tight to it—cage it just as I'd planned.

What could've been hours later, I feel Bryce gather me in his arms—wordlessly carrying me through the clubhouse and to my room...our room.

He handles my body much like he handles my heart—ridding it completely of anything that can separate us. My body isn't the only thing naked as he curls around me beneath the covers. My soul is bared to him—raw, exposed and open...

Climbing over me, he's sure to keep his weight off my body as he kisses my eyes...my cheeks...my lips. "My Love," he breathes, and the word adds a brick to the gaping hole my mother left in my chest. "So sweet..." His mouth trails down my throat, and between my breasts, hovering just above the start of my nasty scar.

"So beautiful." When he plants a tender kiss on the raised flesh, I'm sure he healed it completely. "Everything about you is precious, Love...perfect." Another brick is laid, and the hole becomes smaller and smaller.

"I'm going to make love to you—slow, sweet love."

I let out a moan, my hands finding his muscled arms and raking down the heated, tattooed skin. "I'm going to worship your body... I'm going to take care of you, Love." His head dips between my thighs and in one sweeping move, his tongue glides between my folds—stroking and caressing the burning, quivering, neglected flesh. My back bows. My hips buck against his face. His mouth covers me—drinking me in as if my arousal is vital to his existence.

I come hard, suddenly. Pleasure flows lazily through me—touching every part of my body until I can feel my orgasm in the smallest of places...behind my knees...between my toes...in my ears.

I'm coming down, and he's climbing on—pushing my knees apart gently and taking his place between my thighs where I welcome him with a moaning, wanting invitation. He presses inside me—slowly filling me. He stretches me, kisses me and pulls back to look at me beneath him—surrendering my body and my heart to only him.

"Give it all to me, Love," he whispers, his thick cock stroking my walls at a deep, measured pace. "Give me your fears...your burdens...your guilt..." His lips trail up my neck, and to my ear. "Let me have it, Love. If you do, I promise for the rest of your life, all you'll have to do is let me love you."

Everything lifts. I feel weightless as I release it all. He asks, I give. That's all there is. There is no patch. There's no title for me to hold. I am not his property. He is simply a man—a biker...the sergeant at arms for the Devil's Renegades.

I am simply a woman—a damaged, scarred woman...a clubwhore who fell in love with a dark Prince Charming.

As I lay in his arms, spent, sated and breathless, I reflect on this thing called love I never felt worthy of. I know there'll be times when I doubt it. Times when I question what we have. Times when I feel like good just won't be good enough.

Then green eyes will find me. They'll burn bright with reassurance, promise and that hint of darkness I crave. He'll come to me, offer his hand, and I'll take it—fueled by desire and curiosity. One layer at a time, he'll expose me. I'll submit. And he'll ravage me...claim me...remind me that I belong only to him. Because I do.

My name is Delilah Scott, and I was a clubwhore.

That was my job.

That part of me will always be...in my past.

But Bryce? He is my future.

And I thought it was my story I was telling. Turns out it was ours.

BOOM.
DONE.
FINISHED.
THE END.

# About the Author

Kim Jones is a writer with big dreams. Inspired by her personal experience inside the MC world, she's chosen to write biker romance stories that are authentic—expressing the true meaning of brotherhood and the lifestyle of motorcycle clubs.

In 2013, Kim began her self-publishing journey. *Saving Dallas*, her first MC series, is based on the life of an influential president who juggles the pressures of the *Devil's Renegades Motorcycle Club,* and the search for true love.

Taking the club life and her career a step further, Berkley will be releasing *Sinner's Creed*, her second MC series, in March of 2016—an inside look into the life of a 1%er and his sacrifice for what he believes in.

Kim plans to continue to self-publish off her *Saving Dallas* series, and has signed a two book deal with Penguin-Random House for *Sinner's Creed.* She resides in south Mississippi with her husband, Reggie, two dogs, a cat and a donkey.

You can stalk Kim here:

http://www.kimjonesbooks.com/
http://www.facebook.com/kimjonesbooks
http://www.twitter.com/authorkimjones
Instagram: @kimjones204

# Sinner's Creed

## Prologue

I knew the man in front of me was doomed.

This was a test. I had to prove my loyalty. The club had my pride, now they wanted my innocence.

The knife I held in my hand would be kept as proof that I was guilty of murder. It wouldn't help my case that the man was begging for his life, on his knees in front of me. We were the only two on the video. It was everything they needed. My fingerprints, my weapon, and my face. The club would use it against me if I ever turned on them.

I wasn't scared to take this man's life. I knew he deserved everything he got and so much more. What scared me was knowing that if I did this, there would be no saving me from the depths of hell, from the fiery roads of eternity or the haunting sounds of this man's screams, which I was sure would give me nightmares for the rest of my days.

But, this club is all I know. I'm out of options. Either I prove myself now, or I walk away and never look back. I look up at my grandfather, who gives me a nod of encouragement. His black eyes are full of hate. They have the same effect on me now as they did when I was seven. He is the only man I fear, and the only man I don't want to disappoint.

The club means something to me because it means something to him. He is all I have. He has molded me into the monster I've become. If I knew for sure that not becoming a killer would ensure me a spot in the afterlife away from him, I would take my life right now. But, I know there is no place for me but hell. With him. For eternity.

I can only hear the man's screams, but I see my grandfather mouth "pussy." He is growing impatient. I have to make a decision. So, I ask myself, *Is killing this man worth pacifying the demon-possessed grandfather who raised me? Is taking a life really worth seeing the small, temporary sparkle of pride in his eyes that I've never seen in my twenty-one years? Is it worth the small mustard seed of hope that this will make him love me?* You're fuckin' right it is.

I kill the man with the brutality that the club expects, stabbing him multiple times until his face is unrecognizable. I let the faith I have in my grandfather's love fuel me. I let images of him smiling and telling me he loves me fill my head, and block the sight of the face I am butchering.

When I am finished, I search for him in the crowd, but he isn't there. When I finally notice the men around me, the body is buried and the evidence has been collected. They all wear a look of pity on their faces. Their eyes apologize for what my grandfather is, and what I have become. They can keep their guilt. They can save their sorrow. My cold, dead heart is at the point of no return.

The hell I once feared is now a desire. Satan isn't there anyway. He is here. His eyes are black as night, his heart is cold as ice, and the words *Sinner's Creed* are tattooed on his back. The same poisonous blood that runs through his veins runs through mine.

Hell is my home and Satan is this man, the only father I know. And if evil is he, then evil am I. I don't need his pride. I don't need his love. He wanted a monster; he got one.

I am the spawn of Satan.

I am the son of Lucifer.

I am Sinner's Creed.

Made in the USA
Lexington, KY
12 June 2016